FAMILY
PORTRAIT

Family Portrait

BY SAM HENSLEY, JR.

FRANKLIN WATTS   1988
NEW YORK   LONDON   TORONTO   SYDNEY

Library of Congress Cataloging-in-Publication Data

Hensley, Sam.
Family portrait.
Summary: A college football player relates the life
he has lived with an alcoholic uncle, and describes his
relationship with his girlfriend's family, something
that has given him a semblance of the family life he
has missed.
I. Title.
PZ7.H3984Fam 1988   [Fic]   88-17120
ISBN 0-531-10611-X

To my mother and father,
whose unwavering love and support
helped their son achieve a dream

All streams run to the sea,
  but the sea is not full;
to the place where the streams flow,
  there they flow again.
  Rejoice, O young man, in your
youth, and let your heart cheer you
in the days of your youth; walk in
the ways of your heart and the sight
of your eyes. But know that for all
these things God will bring you into
judgment.
  Remove vexation from your mind,
and put away pain from your body; for
youth and the dawn of life are vanity.

Ecclesiastes
1:7, 11:9 & 10

In my earlier years it was often a source of great trouble for me that I missed my parents so much. Whenever the loud banter of the elementary schoolyard brought mention of family, I fell silent, scalp bristling, heart surging, until I thought my vision would blacken, blood burning under cheeks and forehead as though pitching up a barrier between me and anyone else. The circle's attention would shift, innocently, inquisitively, toward me, bringing the first tentative intrusion into my sphere of private yearning. A young girl's image remains clear: slender frame draped in a blue dress, white socks, saddle loafers, arms swinging at her sides in the unceasing energy expenditure of children. "It must be strange without parents," she offered. Her manner was not threatening but sympathetic, and for a moment I felt the pressure ease, the blood drain.

Then a boy stepped up, the tallow-faced son of one of the backwater families that lived at the outskirts of town, families whose source of income was elusive and whose children would emerge from the pine-ridged, red-clay hills each day to attend school with children of more prosperous backgrounds; his hair unwashed but raked with a wet comb, T-shirt a pale gray from cheap detergent, dark blotches beneath rough fingernails.

Half-curious, half-mocking, he said, "Who kilt yore momma an' daddy, anyway?"

Steam popped a valve, my knuckles sailed into his face, and so such altercations went until my persecutor had been reduced to a bewildered, whimpering heap of dust-smeared boy, or until he had done the same to me, for I attacked regardless of size, grade level, or reputation in fistfights.

The profane eloquence of children matured, and when someone first referred to me as a son-of-a-bitch the result was the same, for they had implicated my mother, who had left me for a day in the care of friends when I was two and with my father climbed aboard his single-engine airplane for a tour of the coastline, where the plane spun in and was lost. The admonishments of teachers, counselors, and principals regarding my behavior served only to strengthen the notion that, because I had no parents, something was wrong with me.

At my entry into high school these incidents had ended, as had murmurs I overheard concerning psychologists (suggestions Forrest summarily dismissed when haled into conferences with school officials— "He's only putting up for himself"), but the bitterness did not diminish. Instead it turned inward, to reside deep within me, cold and black, the way I imagine a shell fragment might lodge in a wounded soldier, at first too inconsequential to merit surgery, remaining for many years in the tissue of an aging veteran, usually forgotten but always there, until shifting perilously close to a vital organ or nerve. In a similar condition I lived until the summer Forrest almost got me killed.

The wake of any human lifetime is ever-lengthening and strewn with events and faces—some remaining clear and unmistakable, some bobbing more distant and indistinct, and others slipping, perhaps mercifully, beneath the swirling and murky surface of memory. Always, though, we are left to watch only our wakes and what has been and therefore to understand only part of what we encounter; the future cannot be observed and pondered as it approaches but merely experienced when it comes upon us—often unexpectedly and sometimes violently—as the present and reflected on as the receding past.

Thus, at the time, I did not understand much of what happened during my stay in Forrest's home. But after ten years looking back on the past, I realize that while this impassioned defense of my missing parents caused me difficulty it also shielded me from pain I might have otherwise endured. Since Forrest—an uncle and only surviving relative—was all I had in their stead, I defended him as well. And mostly from myself . . .

Change was always a fearful thing for me, and on this morning of great change I had known I would continue to lie awake in bed. So I had risen before dawn and laced on running shoes, soles worn thin from a full summer of preparation. Leaving through the back door, I had noticed Forrest's bedroom was empty; but rounding the house, I saw his pickup truck parked in front. I had decided not to search for him until I returned.

Now I was far out along the main highway. When I had begun, fog had filled the valley, cloaking fields that spread from the roadsides and lapped the slopes of hills, a short band of asphalt emerging from gray always a few strides before me. I heard nothing but my own respiration and the steady slap of shoes, which did not bound back to me off the fog but fell dead on the earth; a silence so dense that when a car passed—appearing from behind, loaded with dour, scrubbed faces heading into town for breakfast and Sunday school—I was startled by its sudden presence and hiss of tires on the damp highway, until the car slowly crept by and vanished.

But as I neared home again the fog began to dissipate, revealing lowlands as though an organic, primordial cloud had begun to collect under the force of its own gravity to form solid masses—houses, fences, utility poles. I passed the sign that read: Assembly Shoals City Limits; and in a long, gradual curve stood the Owenses' two-story, white frame house. The railroad passed a hundred yards behind the house (during nights I spent there as a young boy, when a train would rumble through the valley, that house would shiver from foundation to peak—not a frightening event but regular and comforting, the world in its familiar pattern); beyond the tracks the Cahala River cut a wandering course through the fields.

Here the highway, avoiding a wide bend in the river, brushed the edge of the valley floor; I ran left across the highway, away from the Owenses' house, and ascended the half-mile, rutted, clay-and-gravel road that wound steeply to Forrest's pale yellow house on the hillside. Legs burning, lungs contracted, I struggled to Forrest's pickup truck in the drive and collapsed against it.

The air above the valley lightened clear and cool but was disturbed by a humid, heavy current that bore another hot day. The sun had climbed higher behind the hills to the east, and light knifed the trees along the crest, searing fire creeping up the opposite slope, poised to spill blindingly over the peak. A distant call of a rooster carried faintly from the valley, where the fog faded almost as I watched.

When my breath returned, I pushed open the

kitchen door. Inside, I filled a glass with orange juice and dropped two slices of bread into the toaster, then noticed Forrest asleep in his living room recliner. I went in and stood over him. The room was chilled; he'd left the window open during the night. Yet even in the fresh waft from outside, the sharp, sour smell of liquor clung to him, hung over him. The first swallows of orange juice settled into an acidic pool in my stomach. I folded his arms across his chest— he stirred, breathing deeply once, turning his head against the chair back—and covered him with a blanket from the linen closet, leaving him to sleep. I knew it would be useless to wake him.

In the short hallway that led from the living room to our bedrooms I picked up the phone and dialed.

"Hello?" came the answer.

"Mr. Owens. This is Jeff."

He paused. "Oh, *Jeff*. Are you at home? I thought you had to be at the bus station."

"I do. That's why I'm calling. I need—if you don't mind—I could use a ride. Forrest is asleep and, well, I don't think I can—I don't want to wake him."

"I'll be happy to give you a ride."

"Thanks. I appreciate it. Can you wait thirty minutes?"

"Whenever you're ready."

"Thirty minutes will be fine. Thanks again."

I returned to the kitchen, where slices of blackened toast sat half-sprung from the toaster. I felt no hunger now that I had been forced to ask this favor of Mr. Owens. He knew of Forrest's drinking; he had understood on the phone. Why did I still feel the need to cover the truth? The toast crumbled down my throat like ash.

When I stepped from the shower, full daylight glowed through the curtains over my bedroom windows.

The room was virtually filled with the bed and a dresser and nightstand and was entirely cramped by the open trunk on the floor. Before closing the trunk I considered taking along one more thing, the portrait photograph resting on the dresser.

In the picture stood my father, Michael Alton Waters, once a military man, posture efficient and square-shouldered. In fact his entire figure was a composite of straight lines, from the cut of his suit through a narrow neck to an angular face. A single incongruity in his features occurred at his nose, where the cartilage was offset due to a break suffered, according to Mr. Owens, in a football game. My father's hand rested on the shoulder of my mother, Jennifer Dawson Waters, Forrest's sister and only sibling, seated in the picture, smiling in the unrestrained fashion of motherhood that contrasted almost shockingly with the closed-lip line of my father's mouth. Long, auburn hair cascaded over her shoulders, and in her arms she cradled me, Jeffrey Alan Waters, as an infant. In an abrupt assertion of independence I decided to leave the photograph behind.

I dressed and again passed through the rear door to the backyard. Dew beaded on grass in the shade of the house and trees. Our yard was a small encroachment on the wooded slope and lay uncluttered but for folding lawn chairs and an old tire I'd hung from a pine branch. The tire was suspended six feet from the ground in front of a net tacked up between two tree trunks. I had spent many hours throwing a football at that target.

My success as a high school quarterback had always seemed an anomaly to me, since I had never been particularly big or fast and had not even developed an interest in football until the eighth grade, when Forrest suggested I try out. Anxious to please him, I agreed, and eventually a strong throwing arm began landing my name each autumn Saturday on the sports page of the Assembly Shoals *Appalachian Herald* and even brought along a few college scholarship offers to continue the endeavor in return for my education. The state university was only two hours away, accessible to the Owenses and to Forrest (who had even taken me to a game when I was younger) and I never seriously considered another school. Today I was leaving to begin preseason practice.

I strode into clear light, past the old net and tire, up a short rise at the rear of the yard to the paddock. Beast had heard the screen door slam and waited at the fence. Forrest had unexpectedly presented him to me when I was twelve, though I didn't know then how he could afford such a gift, and the only time I'd ever broken a bone was falling off that horse. (After a spill Forrest would call to me, "Climb back on the beast," and we had the name.) I rarely rode anymore, the enthusiasms of boyhood now drawn elsewhere, yet my affection for him remained. I walked along the fence to the sagging, bow-walled barn, and Beast followed. I tossed grain and hay into his feeding trough and changed his water; then car tires crunched gravel in front of the house, a horn sounding twice.

Inside, I stopped once more where Forrest slept in his chair. Leaving him now and knowing I wouldn't return until Christmas, I suddenly could recall only the times I'd enjoyed this life under his guardianship. Strangely, it seemed there had been many—fishing, ball games, sometimes even just talking.

In the driveway I hefted my trunk into the backseat of the car and climbed in front with Mr. Owens, and we began our descent along the scarred, clay road that wove an erratic path from the pale yellow house down to the main highway.

"Thanks for the ride," I said. "Sorry for the inconvenience."

"No trouble," he answered. "Mrs. Owens would've come along too, but she wasn't feeling well this morning. She's got that arthritis, you know—cool mornings are the worst. So I'll just drop you at the station and stay in town for church."

He was dressed for Sunday: gray suit, pocket watch and fob, a hat pushed down over thinning white hair and an age-blemished scalp. A blue haze from his pipe wisped about his head. Before I was born, my parents had lived in Assembly Shoals; the Owenses had known them and had regarded me as their grandchild from the day I'd arrived with Forrest. They had been especially watchful when I was younger, making sure I had meals when Forrest would not reappear until the darkness of early morning.

Under Mr. Owens's two-fisted control, his sedan—a longtime servant, rusting undercarriage, thin tread—jounced on a slow and cautious course. "They really should fix this road," he said around the stem of the pipe that was clenched firmly in his teeth. This comment accompanied each trip Mr. Owens made to Forrest's house.

"Every winter when it gets so muddy, Forrest asks them to pave it," I said. "But the city won't put in the money when we're the only ones living up here."

The road ended at the main highway. To the left it was three miles into the heart of Assembly Shoals. Out here the valley lay wide and quiet—grazing meadows, apple orchards, the Owenses' house across the road. Mr.

Owens edged the car onto the sun-bleached asphalt slab, and we started into town.

The thought of Forrest's indifference to this occasion—he had not even kept himself in condition to say good-bye, leaving me once more to depend not on him but to find another way—this thought settled on me now like a hill of sand. "I think I'm going to get my own car soon," I said, seizing this idea as the method of final emancipation from him. "Maybe next summer. I should have enough money then."

Mr. Owens drew a puff—a dry smack of lips—then freed one hand from the wheel to take the pipe from his mouth. "I'd just worry about schooling and football. You can take care of other things when their time comes."

I did not rebuke him but turned to the window, clinging to this great resolve.

Assembly Shoals was a large town, with its own school system, separate from the county, and a modest hospital and its name printed in the third-largest-size type on the state map. We came first to the poultry barns and after that the chemical plant, familiar in its forbidding massiveness. Since it was Sunday, no smoke spiraled from the huge smokestack, and no throat-coating smell hung over the road; yet this jumbled monument of technology—networks of pipe, holding tanks, aeration ponds—always seemed to harbor some ominous secret of chemical mutation.

Closer in we came to the carpet mills, where most people in Assembly Shoals earned their paychecks, the parking lots empty today. We passed Assembly Shoals High School, home of the Fighting Stallions, an ample, wandering, red-brick building spread over a wide plateau atop a low hill, with only one wing visible from the highway. From a glance at that building, summer was evident: grass grew untrimmed along the base of the walls, blinds were lowered, a gutter dangled.

The railroad parted from the highway, crossing the Cahala on a wooden trestle to run through town on the opposite bank of the river. Then we were downtown—Main Street to the locals. On one side stood a long row of trim, corniced two- and three-story establishments fronted by a wide sidewalk. On the other side lay the river; at that point the Cahala flowed through the middle of the valley and jaggedly rent the city of Assembly Shoals in half, the halves connected with low-slung bridges. Everything along Main Street was closed except for diners that served early breakfast, plate glass doors open in vibrant morning air; later the doorstops would be kicked out and air conditioners and ceiling fans switched on, after the sun gained altitude over the mountains.

Staring at the street, which I had seldom seen at this hour on this day of the week—quiet, vacant, but content—I suddenly realized Mr. Owens had spoken to me. Blankly, I turned to him.

"I asked if you've eaten," he repeated.

"Oh, yes sir. But thanks anyway."

"I saw you running this morning. You must be hungry."

"I'm fine, really. Besides I can't be late."

When we arrived at the station, the bus was already taking on baggage. I bought my ticket and a football magazine from the newsstand while Mr. Owens waited at the curb and puffed his pipe. Seeing it was time for me to board, he said, "Well, good-bye, Jeff. Good luck and enjoy yourself. We'll be in the stands come the first game."

We shook hands; his grip felt cool and dry, not as firm as it had been when I was younger.

"I will," I told him.

I turned from him and climbed aboard the bus, dropping into a window seat.

We never went on anything like a vacation, Forrest and I. We could not afford it and never felt a need for it. There had been occasional fishing trips when I was in high school: we would load the gear in the back of Forrest's pickup and leave for the weekend late on a Friday night, if it wasn't football season. Normally, though, we fished at places close to home. Holidays such as Christmas were spent with the Owenses; summers I worked, usually at the lumberyard, to earn the only money I ever saw (often to pitch in for groceries). Most of Forrest's time was spent trying to find or hold a job.

I'd skimmed the magazine when I looked up and noticed the sun gleaming on dry summer fields and the highway—a liquid asphalt stream pouring from the shimmer ahead—and the hills sinking into gentler piedmont, as though some hand had smoothed the wrinkles in a huge bedspread; and only then I was not merely conscious of what was transpiring but was also heavily filled with a deeper awareness that for the first time since the age of two I was leaving Forrest and Assembly Shoals behind.

Stuart met me there. "Ice Waters!"

In the sunlight like a fractured heliograph—dazzling pinwheels glaring from windshields, chrome bumpers, metal awnings—I turned to the voice and saw him sunk in his sports convertible, the top lowered, his hands and long forearms embracing the steering wheel.

He heaved himself out and ambled toward me. "You're late," he said. His gait was casual, flippant, but did not mask the fluid athletic assurance of motion, every gesture in easy coordination with the rest of his body.

"I'll bet ten dollars you were still in bed fifteen minutes ago," I told him.

"Careful. I'll lie and take your money."

We stood behind the loose knot of passengers assembled beside the bus and waited for my trunk to appear. Though I had seen little of Stuart Hall since the beginning of summer, we didn't shake hands or extend greetings other than innocuous sarcasm. We were friends; any gesture or word of recognition of this fact would have been unnecessary and uncomfortable, a breach of our silent code.

Stuart loomed above everyone else on the sidewalk. We were the same age, but equal age had long before ceased to guarantee even roughly equal size. He stood six feet, four inches tall, two hundred ten pounds, and in our senior year at Assembly Shoals High School he had been the newspapers' choice as All-Region tight end. Jammed down over his aimless shock of blond hair was a tan beret that resembled a bloated pancake, an accoutrement he deemed as essential to his sports car as wheels. He wore a T-shirt, shorts, tennis shoes, and white socks that strained and almost gleamed against the dark muscles of his calves, and on the peeling bridge of his sun-blistered nose perched a pair of sunglasses. His unshaven jaw blithely worked a wad of gum.

We had been friends since fifth grade, when he had accused me of stealing his brown-bag lunch. I told him he was crazy, a costly accusation, but after pummeling me he felt sorry about it and apologized. He never found out who took his lunch. I'd made sure no one saw me eat it.

In high school he had christened me Ice Waters, partly because I performed with an appearance of nonchalance during football games, mostly because I rarely did anything he considered the least bit exciting. It came to him during a scrimmage, after I pitched a touchdown pass to him over the fingertips of two defensive linemen as they engulfed me under their lunge. Stuart tugged off his helmet and trotted back to the huddle, ball tucked under his arm, his face flushed with spontaneous enthusiasm. He blurted a shout like a scientist stumbling upon a monumental discovery after long research. "He's Ice Waters! That's what he is!"

It had stuck.

We stood now in the heat, sweat tracing cool tracks down my back under a knit shirt.

"How was summer school?" I asked.

He nodded. "Good. I think I'm in good shape."

"You'd better be. I see you've had no trouble finding time for a tan."

"I study better outdoors. In fact I read somewhere that extended exposure to ultraviolet light stimulates memory gain."

Stuart would admit that his grades in high school had placed him in no danger whatsoever of honor roll infamy, but his endless and preposterous excuses belied a whimsical mind. He had resided at the university most of the summer, attending remedial classes for incoming freshman athletes whom the deans suspected might encounter academic difficulties and thus jeopardize their eligibility for varsity sports. My trunk was deposited on the sidewalk, and we hoisted it into the car. Stuart raced the engine, flipped on the radio, and we lurched away from the curb and down the street.

There were many accesses to the university, but most gave little indication that you had entered the confines of higher learning. It was an old institution that had swelled and absorbed adjacent properties for over a hundred years, spilling far beyond its original boundaries. Some grounds remained walled, but at other points along the perimeter, buildings once exterior to the university had been purchased, annexed, and put to use, so that the wide, quiet streets now fed into the university proper in a subtle and almost servile transition. I had been in this town before, when I was younger, to see a football game with Forrest and more recently while being recruited to play there myself. Hence, it was a familiar place, yet now every building and street corner and stately, overhanging tree seemed to stamp a clear and distinct impression on my mind, for here a great and significant portion of my life was to be spent.

Stuart had wanted to play football at the university for as long as I'd known him. I had made up my mind the night the head coach visited my house: through parted curtains I had watched the headlights swing down the long road. Immediately I turned to Forrest, who stood in the center of the living room, studying a thumbnail.

"Well?" I said. "What did you think?"

He looked up at me. "About what?"

"About *him*. About what he said."

He rubbed his face and started for the kitchen. "He didn't have much to say."

I felt my enthusiasm begin a familiar, slow descent into my stomach. "He didn't *talk* a long time," I called after him, "but I thought he *said* a lot." I sprang from the couch and followed him.

Forrest was rummaging through the refrigerator; he pulled out the milk bottle and took a long drink from it.

"You had to think something about him," I said.

Forrest held the milk in his mouth as though tasting it for the first time, then swallowed and exhaled. "He's not a smooth talker," he said, closing the refrigerator door. "He didn't try any of that smooth talk."

My hopes climbed again. I shoved the toaster aside and sat on the counter. "Then you liked him?"

"You're the one that has to like him."

I frowned but remained far from disappointed. Pronouncing someone void of an unsavory trait was as close to a compliment as Forrest ever got. In this way I had found his approval.

Stuart whipped through avenues of fraternity houses and slatternly student apartments within walking distance of the campus; then we arrived at the heart of the university. Here the newer, functional, prefabricated concrete library and classroom buildings stood in architectural imbalance among older, more distinguished structures with Doric columns and curving staircases garnished with iron railings—all built in various decades of growth on the best available land, oblivious to any unifying scheme. We hummed past the football stadium, empty, one end yawning. It caught Stuart's attention, and he reached for the radio dial to lower the volume.

"You can start for this team, you know," he said, wind snatching his words and the hair that bushed from beneath his cap.

"What? C'mon with that—"

"You can start for this team," he repeated indignantly, anticipating a rebuttal, "if you just don't wait for someone else to make the decision for you."

I opened my mouth to speak again, but Stuart would not be hauled up short.

"I'm telling you, I've seen those rag-arm pantywaists they call quarterbacks out here this summer. Remember high school? When you got into your first game, you were so nervous you almost ran to the wrong huddle. That was before you earned your nickname. Don't let that happen again. Don't worry about proving yourself. I swear, you always seem to think there's this big ordeal you're required to go through before you can enter the damn Temple of Fulfillment. You're on the outside waiting to be invited in. I don't know where it comes from." He turned up the radio again. "Oh man, this is my *song*!"

He enjoyed this song no more than any other, except that it served now to drown any debate. "You are such a *jerk*," I shouted into the wind and the throbbing rhythm from the radio—a pathetic counterattack to Stuart's deep, soul-exposing slice. Retaliation was useless and actually unfair, for Stuart's blunt observations were not malicious but were instead the product of his absolute intolerance for the circuitous manner in which most people ever achieve anything. He honestly could not imagine that anyone might hesitate to reach for something they wanted.

At our request Stuart and I had been assigned as roommates. He had resided in the athletic dormitory during summer school; all that was left was to move in my things. Afterward we descended a damp stairwell to the cavernous, plumbing-laced storage room under the stadium bleachers, where the manager issued our football equipment. Following dinner, a noisy first gathering of the freshman recruits, we strolled outside the dining hall. To the west the sun still glowed amid an escarpment of distant cumulus clouds, glazing darkened windows and marble columns with orange light, and I knew the storefronts along Main Street in Assembly Shoals would be tinged with the same color in early evening. Now, though, I imagined Assembly Shoals resting somewhere on the opposite side of the earth.

"Let's take a walk around campus," Stuart suggested.

Instantly I prickled with suspicion of him, well

aware he had scouted the whole place long before. But I followed, realizing the futility of resistance. As I expected, Stuart turned our walk into a beeline for one of the solemn, oppressive, red-brick dormitories in the center of campus.

"I met some people here during summer school," he said. "They're taking this session, too."

He never went out of his way to visit "people"—only girls. He was quite serious about his girlfriend, who had another year of high school remaining. In her presence, in fact, Stuart underwent a remarkable personality change: he behaved like a normal human being. Yet Stuart's disposition to seek the company of females came as naturally as breathing. I'd never been interested in a steady girlfriend, and he'd made it his mission in life to find one for me.

So, as though on a leash, I trailed him up the stairs to the third floor and down a dim hallway. I could not turn back, the only action more humiliating than going along. Most of the rooms were closed and quiet and wouldn't be occupied until the start of fall term. In the hallway, empty paint cans and scraps of fresh lumber sat in small heaps, the residue of summer renovations. One door stood open a few inches.

"If you're up to something—" I warned. Stuart ignored me and knocked.

"Come in," a female voice responded. "*Stu*-art!"

"Hello, ladies," Stuart said. "I brought a friend I want you to meet. This is Jeff Waters. Jeff, this is Anne Thomas and Stacy Cottrell."

Anne, the source of the squeal, studied at one desk; Stacy sat cross-legged on her bed, surrounded by a low battlement of books. The room was a testament to an intense and resourceful college existence. Every space along the walls was stacked high: a miniature refrigerator, an elaborate stereo system assembled atop overturned milk crates crammed with battered music albums, bookshelves created from wooden planks and cinder blocks. The closets opened on fashion disarray, and on the floor large baskets overflowed laundry. The descending sun gleamed on the white trim of a single window and cast bright, distorted rectangles against the wall above Anne's desk.

"Have a seat," Stacy said, motioning to the foot of the bed.

"I hate to interrupt," I told her, lowering myself to the edge of the mattress. "You look busy."

She drew a heavy breath, shifting her position, books sliding from their piles into the indentation under her weight. "Summer school finals. I took three courses this term. Trying to get ahead on some credit hours, but it's crazy sometimes."

"You're a—what year?"

"Rising sophomore."

"Ice Water's playing quarterback here," Stuart announced over his shoulder. He had taken the chair from Stacy's desk and pushed it close to Anne, who giggled protests at his rummage through her desktop clutter.

"I know," Stacy said to me. "I saw you play in high school. I'm from Assembly Shoals."

"No—really?" I said, intrigued. "But I don't remember you. I knew most of the people in the class above—"

"Actually, I'm not *from* Assembly Shoals. We live out in the county. I went to Summit County High School."

I had to admit, in the secure recesses of my own knowledge, that Stacy Cottrell commanded my sincere he lunged forward. The ball fell to earth beyond his outstretched hands and skittered to a stop on the grass.

I'd run into Stacy on a few brief occasions about the campus yet remained at a loss as to how I would engage her long enough to inquire about a date. The easy conversation at our first meeting had begun to seem like an aberration, an exhibition on her part of simple courtesy rather than of genuine interest. At last I decided that when the water is cold, it's best to dive right in.

When I mentioned my decision to Stuart one evening in the dorm room after dinner, his eyebrows soared on his forehead. "You're joking," he accused. "You're serious?"

"I'm serious," I said. "I'm going to call her."

He slammed shut his textbook and tossed it on his desk with a disconcerting thump, with the same effect as a poker player seeing the last raise, suspecting a bluff. "Do it now."

I felt suddenly caged under his stare. Staring down at an open economics book, which had become an illegible alphabetic scramble, I said, "I haven't thought what to ask her."

Stuart flung himself to his feet as though catapulted from the chair. "Oh, no you don't! You're not getting out of it now, no sir! Her number's in the student directory. You find it and call her."

Snatching his beret, planting it on his head, and switching off his desk lamp, he moved toward the door. "I'll leave you alone. You want something to eat?"

"We just had dinner, for crying out loud."

"You're going to call her?"

"If you'll get out of here."

attention. From a year's experience she recited methods to avoid the crush of the common student herd at any university function, from course registration to meals in the dining hall. When I spoke, of sports and other mundane facets of our rival high schools, her thin lips pursed attentively, her dark forehead creasing above clear green eyes and a nose so smoothly unobtrusive that only in profile did it seem to project away from her face. She laughed easily, full teeth in a broad exposure, reddening flat cheeks and pressing them up under her eyes. Smiling beneath waves of cinnamon hair pulled toward clasps at the back of her head, slender legs and arms angled from shorts and summer blouse as she hunched in the center of her studies, Stacy presented such an affable and unguarded image that I was startled by a notion that I had known her for a long time. Our conversation left me as oblivious to Anne Thomas and Stuart as I was to the chipped, parchment-colored plaster on the walls. When Stuart abruptly rose and said, "Time to go," my head snapped to face him, and I blurted, "Now?"

"Yes, now. Team meeting? Nine o'clock? Remember?"

Only a wall clock convinced me that an hour had indeed passed. I noticed that since our arrival the rectangles of late sunlight on the wall had faded. We excused ourselves and left the building. Outside, day had finally ended, and lights now glowed: streetlights, lights above doorways and in scattered windows.

When we had walked a short distance, Stuart said, "Well?"

I looked up from watching my feet saunter along the dark sidewalk, which radiated warmth from a day-long bake. "They're nice," I shrugged.

"You held quite a consultation with Stacy. How about it?"

"She's from home," I conceded, cautiously.

"I know," he said. "She likes you."

"She's—pretty."

"Pretty? What's pretty?" He laughed and struck his hands together like thickly fleshed cymbals. "But I *knew* you'd like her."

"I didn't say I like her. How can I say if I like her when I just met her? I just said she was nice-looking."

"She likes you."

"How do you know *that*?"

"See, you do like her. You wouldn't want to know how I know she likes you unless you liked her."

"This is absurd."

"She likes you. I can tell."

I turned away, shaking my head.

"I knew you'd like her," Stuart said. "I *knew* it."

He deftly wove his web, spewing insults and contradictions, awaiting a flinch or stumbling step, when in the confusion truth would be snared. Sensing the sticky cords closing around me, I finished our walk in the darkness without saying another word.

Stuart was right about Stacy Cottrell, and he was rig about football. By midseason, with the offense grindin down, seizing at the hands of upperclass quarterback like an engine burned dry of oil, finally expiring shor of points on almost every series of plays, I became el-evated to first string. This sudden high status for a freshman provoked first a dare and later a regular con-test among the players during practices: each receiver would take a turn running straight down the field; I'd allow them thirty yards, then hurl the ball as far as possible. None of them could catch up to it.

Our fastest receiver tried it, and when he'd raced thirty yards I lofted the ball into a long, spiraling arc. Watching the flight over his shoulder, the receiver glided another ten yards with his smooth blur of legs, then perceptibly changed pace, sprinting harder; the glide became a gallop and finally a flailing of heels as

When he was gone, the room seemed like a well-lighted mausoleum. There was no sound anywhere—a rare circumstance in the athletic dorm—not in the darkness outside the window, not in the hallway. Silence washed in my ears until it became a sound itself, the surging of blood that constantly whispers on the inside of eardrums. I found Stacy's number and procrastinated by copying it on a slip of paper, then rehearsed three or four openings, and finally dialed, pitching myself into that great unknown in which the continued rotation of the earth on its axis seems dependent on one girl's caprice. An unfamiliar female voice answered.

"Is Stacy there, please," I asked.

"Hold on a minute."

Music, conversation, laughter carried over the line, then a hand clamping over the mouthpiece. It was a roller coaster finishing its slow haul up the first hill, at that eternal moment before it is released to plummet down the tracks, leaving heart and stomach in the seat behind.

"Hi, this is Stacy."

My breath escaped, too hard and too fast. "Stacy? This is Jeff. Jeff Waters. How are you?"

"I'm fine," she said. "Haven't seen you in a while." Her tone was pleasant but not exuberant.

"I know. Um, sounds like a party."

"Oh, it's nothing," she insisted. "Just a few friends."

I gripped a mass of coiled telephone cord in my free hand. Though the room was not hot, sweat had dotted my forehead. "Well, I won't keep you away," I said. "I wondered if you'd like to go out Saturday. We could have dinner after the game." The invitation had been too abrupt. There followed a silence in which I decided it might be best to disappear into the black and electric void of the telephone line, like water down a bathtub drain; I could dial myself to another country.

Apparently she had stepped into the hallway with the receiver, for I could no longer hear the music and other voices. "S-ure," she said at last, slowly. "That sounds fine. I'd love to."

I felt released from a smothering clench. "Great. We can go after the game, after I shower and change. You can meet me outside the locker room."

"Okay. I'll see you then."

We exchanged good-byes, and I listened for the click at the other end, then the dial tone, welcoming that sound like a delectable drink. I flopped onto the bed, turning over on my back, hands behind my head. The conversation replayed through my brain; I winced when I remembered not asking her what kind of food she liked. The time for reflection was short, however, since Stuart would soon return. I went to my desk and opened a book under the lamp. I had foolishly assumed that asking Stacy out would be the most difficult task. The hard part, of course, would be telling Stuart that she had agreed.

Fifteen minutes later he came in; I leaned over the book, boring my eyes into the page. The door closed; a paper bag crumpled. From the corner of one eye I saw the tan beret sail across the room and land on his desk; his hand appeared over my shoulder and deposited a large milkshake within the circle of my arms around the book.

"Here," Stuart said. "I brought you this anyway. You could use the calories."

"Thanks," I said, still feigning study. I sensed his vision like a noon sun on my shoulders.

"Well?" he asked finally.

"Thanks for the milkshake," I said.

"You know if you didn't call her I'm going to break your arm. Your throwing arm."

I glanced at him, twisting my face in annoyance. "I called her. Satisfied?"

"And?"

"No earth-shattering event. She said she'd like to go out after the game Saturday."

Stuart bellowed to raise the dead, and the muscles in my face contracted involuntarily into a smile. When I did not look up again, he nudged me in the head with an elbow. "Congratulations."

"You can stop that anytime," I told him.

He went to his desk with a hamburger and french fries and a milkshake of his own, dropping into his chair and leaning back in it. He poked a few fries into his mouth.

I stirred the milkshake in the cup, then drew on the straw. "You *are* going to let me use your car Saturday, aren't you?" I asked.

"Fine," he said in comic contemplation, waving the paper cup in the air, "but let's see to it that this little tryst doesn't become inconvenient, forcing me out anytime you need the room for your animalistic gratifications—"

"I think I'm going to throw up. You have got to be the most disgusting miscreation God ever— Look at yourself! You shove food into that bloated face like there's no tomorrow—"

"—not that I can't be accommodating now and then—"

I smoldered in a frustrated attempt to muster any real indignation toward him, like trying to light a campfire in a monsoon. "Why don't you just shut up?" I said, stabbing a ludicrous, scolding finger at him. "You talk too much, you know that?"

"—unless you want me to watch."

To reverse this tide I could do only one thing: I sprang and punched him in the chest. He tumbled over backward in the chair, face flickering circles of true surprise, and crashed to the floor in a hail of french fries. I pounced—the only way I could maintain even a momentary edge on him in a fight was never to let him regain his feet—and we lurched against one bed, thudding it against the wall. I drove my fists into his stomach. "You gonna shut up now? You gonna stop talking about her like that?"

He laughed and locked his arms around my head, hot breath spiced with mustard burning in my face, squeezing until colored spots swam in my eyes. "Stop it!" I shouted into his shirt, clawing and kicking. "You're crushing my skull!"

He released me, and I rolled away; Stuart stood, tugging off his shoes, and leapt onto the bed, springs groaning beneath his bulk. He raised his arms above his head, glaring down at me like the Angel of Death, and shouted, "Prepare to die, mortal!" He sailed from the bed and crashed on top of me with such force I thought the floor might collapse, and I was smothered under him again until the door flew open. We untangled and whirled to see standing before us, face hewn in dark stone, the assistant coach who had drawn monitoring duty that night. Our laughter melted; my heart slid into my stomach. Before me unfolded the endless miles of extra laps we would be running after practice. Stuart rose to his knees, his chest heaving deeply as he breathed, hands on his thighs.

The coach surveyed the wreck, hand still on the doorknob; finally his gaze returned to us, and he said quietly, as though commenting on the weather, "I'll shoot my dog if we didn't tell you guys no foolishness in the dormitory."

I turned away but noticed Stuart staring at him, the gleam returning to his eyes, the corners of his mouth beginning the upturn into an almost imperceptible smile. Panic crawled over me; I shook my head and almost spoke aloud for Stuart not to say anything. We were in enough trouble already. But before I dared to utter a word, he brushed a hand across his mouth and burst out like a rifle report. "Ice Water has a date!"

He crumbled again to the floor in a seizure of laughter. The coach's expression remained grave but had relaxed that minute degree that told you he was completely disarmed. He averted his eyes from Stuart, pretending to survey the room again, but I knew if he'd watched Stuart another moment the agonizing control under which his face strained would have been shattered with a grin, and all vestiges of his authority—like the pretense of my anger—would have been lost in the sweep of Stuart's irresistible audacity. I sat on the floor, my back against the bed, scalp burning and ears throbbing where Stuart had gripped me in the headlock, and I watched him laugh. The coach simply left, closing the door behind him.

"I saw you play in high school only once, but that game was plenty," Stacy said at our table in the claustrophobic pizzeria several blocks from campus, where they pounded and rolled fresh dough and shoved it on paddles into ovens that breathed on the room. Every year Assembly Shoals High School played Summit, the county school, in the last football game of the season, and the rivalry approached hysteria. For a week the custodians at each school scrubbed paint from brick exteriors or replaced smashed windows as vandals traded forays at night.

On the day of the game a parade marched through Assembly Shoals, and afterward in the stadium parking lot fistfights would break out between county and city factions.

"You don't care much for football, I take it."

"Not like some of those people back home," she said. "I'm sorry, but it's simply not that important."

I felt not the least offended by her frankness, instead was even more curious about her. I wanted to hear everything, not all at once but in a slow peeling back of the layers of this other person's lifetime, until I knew her and knew what it was like to be her. That this person was also female and sent my spine quivering like gelatin made me wonder later whether my curiosity was simply a product of deep arousal. Perhaps arousal intensified the curiosity. At that moment my only clear desire was to listen to her speak far into the night. Her closeness was intoxicating.

The waitress brought our soft drinks in thick plastic cups. Dry-mouthed, I took a long gulp and with it a lump of crushed ice to chew out of habit.

"Ice for Mr. Ice Waters?" Stacy grinned. "Why does Stuart call you that?"

"It's from football," I said around the shrinking mouthful. Then, cheeks numbing, "Actually, he thinks I'm—cold. *Reserved* I guess is a better word." I was uncertain of this talk, whether the fascination for inner thought was mutual.

Stacy did not stay with the current. "Stuart put you up to this?"

"No!" I said. "I put myself up to it."

"Girl back home?"

"Me? No."

She seemed satisfied, but I was flustered that she could not see the chaotic swirl inside me, the intense attraction. I felt as though a huge stone had been plopped into a boiling kettle, abruptly cooling the water to a simmer.

When the pizza had been set before us, and we lifted slices trailing threads of cheese to our plates, I said, "Your name, your last name—it sounds familiar."

Stacy thought that over for a moment. "My dad's sheriff," she offered.

I told her that was it: Sheriff Cottrell of Summit County. My closest contact with him had been the day after the bomb scare at school. A couple of football players had decided to create a stir, so they collected three or four railroad flares—convincing imitations of dynamite. They attached an alarm-clock face to the flares and wrapped the bundle in copper wire, stowing it in the gymnasium boiler room. The fire alarm sounded, and the building was cleared before discovery of the fake. The pranksters had intended to stay home from school and phone in an anonymous threat, but an elderly janitor with a heart condition came across it first and was never again much use with a mop and pail.

The school board hadn't seen the joke, and when the perpetrators were found out, they landed in juvenile court. The next day Sheriff Cottrell appeared to address the football team. He arrived in his own car and wore jeans and a windbreaker—no uniform. Few of us would be involved in such a thing, he realized, but any similar incidents would be treated as serious matters. He thanked us for listening, wished us luck in our game that week, and left the field.

Stacy's face pinched into a frown. "I can't understand why anybody would want to do something like that," she said.

"People just do stupid things sometimes."

She fell silent, pondering her fork as she twisted it slowly in the topping of a half-eaten pizza slice. Her hair was not tied back but still swept away from her face. She wore a cream blouse that seemed to darken her complexion and the pensive furrows across her brow. "Yeah, I suppose," she said finally.

"What do you think about your dad being sheriff?" I asked.

"Well," she began, setting the fork aside, "he seems to enjoy it. He's been at it for five years. But he does woodworking, you know? He has this woodshop in the back, and sometimes I think he'd just like to lock himself in there and carve and hammer all day. He's up for reelection next fall. Been reelected twice already. But he says this race will be tough."

"I'm old enough to vote now," I said.

"He claims he'll need all he can get."

"What about you?" I asked. "What do you want to do?"

Stacy inhaled, hitching up her shoulders in a shrug, then allowing them to stoop with a sigh. "I keep telling myself I want to be a lawyer."

I nodded silently, eagerly sensing the emergence of something from behind a scrim of thin cordiality.

"I'm always sure until I have to say why," she continued, as though I'd pressed her about it. "One part of me wants to be a prosecutor, because if my father brings someone in, I know he's already given them the benefit of the doubt, and they deserve whatever they get—"

"You sound like an only child," I told her, surprised myself by the interruption.

She stared so piercingly at me I was afraid I had offended her. A morsel of pizza hardened in my throat. "Why do you say a thing like that?" she said.

"You mention your parents a lot," I said, "your father, anyway. You're—you seem—protective—about him. Am I right?"

"No. I have a brother. But he doesn't live at home anymore." She waved a hand in the air the way she would brush away a fly. "But what I meant was there's this other part of me that knows people just do stupid things, like you said. They don't intend any harm— they're confused or afraid, maybe searching for something—" Her voice lost its force, dying quickly as a summer squall on a lake. "Who knows why people do things? There're a million reasons. But this is boring and I'm not making the least bit of sense."

"No, please—"

"I'd like to hear about you. Not football. Your family or something."

A knot tightened in my stomach, wrenched by this sudden shift of focus, but in this confiding atmosphere slowly relaxed again. "Um, my parents are dead."

Stacy sat back in her chair. "Jeff, I'm so sorry—"

"No, it's okay. It's been a long time. That's why I moved to Assembly Shoals, to live with my uncle. I was two then."

"Only child?"

"It's just me and my uncle."

"What happened to your parents? You don't have to say—"

"They went up in my father's plane off the coast. They got caught in a storm and went down somewhere in the water. Searchers never found the wreckage. I don't remember anything about it."

"Can I ask you something?" she said, after a pause.

"Sure."

"I'd really like to know."

"What?"

"Do you get along with your uncle?"

"Yes" was my reflex response. Then, "Well, we have to stay out of each other's way sometimes. When he drinks too much, I don't like being around him."

"He never *hit* you, did he?"

"No, nothing like that at all. He just turns off to everything. When I think about it, it seems very out of character that Forrest would ever raise children or even get married. He certainly didn't take me in because he especially wanted me. I guess he did it for my mother—his sister. He said it was the only place I could go. It's as though"—and I struggled here, never having been able to firmly grasp this notion of Forrest—"he did it to spite the world—told me it was an unfair world that let my parents die that way. He thought he could take my parents' place."

My explanation seemed to have been lost on Stacy, but I couldn't blame her, for it also failed to fill a dark emptiness inside me.

"But you do things together?" she asked.

"We fish together. And he likes sports. We'd go out and pitch a ball when I was younger."

"No, I mean things now," Stacy said.

"Mostly fishing now. We get along well enough."

She stared at the checkered tablecloth as though it were a chessboard that she was studying for her next move. I thought she said, "It's not the same thing, anyway," under her breath, but I let it go.

4

The season extended to a long string of Saturday afternoons, when the clean symmetry of a scrimmage line would dissolve and swarm into a heaving mass that surged to the ground under its own weight. If I had to cover the ball and turn it upfield myself, the suffocating pile of tacklers would pick itself apart above me to reveal the glaring, cobalt-blue sky, or a leaden canopy of cloud sodden with pneumonic autumn rain; and always the bands swelling in brassy caterwauling and the thunderous partisans festooned with color in the open-ended bowl; until the crowds thinned as the air grew biting, and it became apparent we would not win as many games as we lost; leaving finally a wind-browned field and silent bleachers fluttering with wrappers and soda-smeared programs.

When examinations for the fall term were finished, Stuart and I loaded his car like a pack animal and left on a gray December morning that crouched over the deserted university like sleep and left the campus seemingly lapsed into hibernation. Along the wide highway the sun glimmered meekly behind the gauze of clouds, and on our arrival in Assembly Shoals the Cahala River flowed like a calm passage to death, dark skeletons of trees lining crystalline, magnifying water that tumbled over shelves of smooth stone. I noticed the subtler changes in town, apart from the shift of seasons: new paint on lamp posts, an added traffic signal, a vacated store on Main Street.

Stuart dropped me at my house; the pickup was gone. Inside, the kitchen was silent except for the electric hum of the refrigerator, and the rooms had acquired the stale, cloistered smell that came with winter. I went out to the barn and found Beast looking well fed. I led him to the paddock—his breath twin jets of mist, his head bowed—and shoveled out the stall. It was midafternoon. With nothing more to do, I unpacked the trunk, then lay on my bed and, instantly familiar again with its contour, soon sank into sleep.

When I awoke, alert, already buoyed above a black pool, the clock read five-thirty, and daylight had begun to fade into the oppressive murk of an early winter evening. I went into the kitchen for water, not turning on any lights, content to adjust first to the pallid wash from outside. As I set the empty glass in the sink, the door kicked loose suddenly from its jamb. My throat went dry despite the drink. A silhouette lurked beyond thin curtains that covered the panes in the top half of the door. I heard a jangle of keys, then the opening grew wide, and Forrest entered the dimness. He shouldered the door tight against the cold outside and flipped the light switch. Wresting himself from his overcoat, he flinched at the sight of me, dark eyes flaring for a moment, like still-warm coals uncovered in a mound of ash; then his hands dangled at his sides, broad frame stooping, and the flare in his eyes faded as quickly as a flash of heat lightning. I stood at the sink, blinking at him in the sudden flood from the ceiling light, running my tongue over my lips.

At last he raised one hand and rubbed his nose. "You liked to scared the hell out of me," he said.

"Sorry," I said. "I told you I was coming today."

"Yeah, well, I just wasn't thinking about it right then. What're you doing in here with all the lights off?"

"I fell asleep. I didn't even hear you drive up."

He nodded, shuffling his boots on the mat inside the door. With his thick hand he reached into his coat pocket and plucked from it a tattered paper bag that had carried his lunch.

"How's work?" I asked. "You still working at the mill?"

"Hmm. It's money." Forrest absently searched his pockets again as though for something else to say. "Hungry?" he asked.

"Starving. Haven't had anything since breakfast."

"Want to eat in town?"

"Sure. Sounds fine."

The diner was a long rectangular room, faintly green under naked fluorescent tubes, with a counter and floor-mounted stools on one side and a row of booths along the opposite wall. A certificate from the County Health Department hung behind the counter with a rating of Sanitation Grade A. That required a stretch of the imagination. We slid into a booth, and the waitress took our orders.

"Tough luck this season," Forrest said. He sat with

his back to the wall, legs stretched out across the seat, one arm resting on the table. He put his head wearily against the wall, eyes half closing. "Too bad I didn't see more games."

"You had to work. We could have done better. Four and seven. We'll be better next year. We aren't losing hardly anybody to graduation."

Forrest's head snapped forward again as the waitress returned with coffee. He dropped his feet to the floor and twisted around in the seat to get at the cup. "They should have played you more," he said, looking down. "You were the best they had."

"I did all right. I started half the games. Stuart didn't play much at all, only on kickoff teams."

"They should have let you throw more. They run the ball too much."

"We've got a good backfield."

"You've got the arm. They should let you throw more."

I didn't argue with him, for his seething tone indicated he had made up his mind about something and would pursue the argument to any end a challenger wished to carry it. He gazed into a mirror of black coffee before reaching for cream. The coffee swirled muddily, then Forrest tapped the spoon on the ceramic rim, a sound oddly similar to an aluminum baseball bat striking a ball, and I was jolted by that sound and lost in a vision from the previous spring: the dirt-patched diamond at Assembly Shoals High School, our centerfielder relaying the sweetly stroked single to the infield, the ball flipped again to me on the mound.

When the next batter stepped up, I tried to nip the corners of the plate, but the umpire screeched "Ball!"

on two pitches that looked like strikes to the home crowd, and the heckling began. I stalked behind the mound, letting the insults from the bleachers scorch that umpire's ears for a while, and Forrest's voice rang the loudest. Then I marched up the mound and delivered one the batter had been waiting for, and he hooked a liner to left, a strong throw holding the lead runner at third and leaving the bases loaded.

"Damn if he ain't making those boys throw it right down the middle," a voice shouted.

"Check the per-scription in them glasses, ump!" said another.

"God Almighty, ump, call the game the way it's supposed to be!" Forrest roared.

These voices began to strain my concentration, and I pitched three straight out of the strike zone to the next hitter. In the dugout our coached glared at me, jabbing a finger at his temple. "Don't walk that runner home, son!" he warned.

I spun in a curve at the hitter's knees, but the umpire shook his head. "Low! Ball four." The crowd erupted, apoplectic, springing to its feet and stamping the ramshackle bleachers, bellowing as the runner trotted to the plate from third. Our coach stormed from the dugout, neck veins popping, screaming that the umpire was the worst ever to disgrace the game.

Then Forrest was spotted, already over the fence, walking a deliberate line toward the infield. Had he been running he would not have been intercepted. But the coaches and other umpires converged on him, and he pushed his open hands into faces as they approached, wading forward until the tangled knot halted his progress.

"Just treat him fair!" Forrest shouted. "That's all! Just give him the fair calls! I ain't asking for anything else!"

Two police officers took him under the arms and guided him toward the gate as the home plate umpire, a dough-faced stump squeezed into chest protector and shin guards, tugged off his mask and wiped his forehead with a handkerchief. I stood away from the commotion, praying for a miraculous change of identity, or at least a chance to slip unseen into the crowd, as scattered caps were collected from the ground.

The officers had threatened to haul Forrest in for public intoxication and assault but finally ejected him from the grounds with a warning. Everyone had agreed the umpire was terrible; I only wished that Forrest had stood up for me in some other way.

He took a long slurp from the coffee cup, looking at me for the first time since we'd been seated. "Grades okay?"

"Yeah."

"Good. Keep those grades up." He sipped again. "Tell me about this girl." One corner of his mouth curled upward almost imperceptibly.

I felt my blood accelerate. "It's like I told you in my letters. Stuart introduced us, and we've been seeing each other for a couple of months. She's already home. She finished exams early and caught a ride back."

"Steady girl?"

"I guess so. But the funny thing was, like I told you, she lives in Assembly Shoals. Actually out in the county. And I'd never seen her. Her father is Sheriff Cottrell."

Forrest had raised his coffee cup halfway to his mouth but held it there, eyeing me. "Really?"

"He really is."

He smiled and sipped, laughing once deep in his chest as he lowered the cup.

"What? What's so funny?"

He waved a hand and said, "Nothing."

"I want you to meet her," I said. "This is serious."

"Sure, sure. Is she pretty?"

I widened my eyes and nodded. "I'm supposed to have dinner at her house tomorrow," I said. "It'll be the first time I've met her parents. I don't know, should I take them something, to thank them for the dinner, you think?"

Forrest shook his head. "Not unless you just want to."

"Will you let me use the truck tomorrow?"

"Soon's I get home from work."

The plate glass windows of the diner quivered in their frames as a train rumbled along the other side of the river. The headlight swept in an ever-tightening circle until the dark, thundering form of the engine appeared. When we had finished eating, Forrest pushed his plate back with his thumb and yawned.

"How's the mill?" I said.

"You asked that already. It's fine."

At home we built a fire; the temperature outside had fallen sharply. Forrest reclined in his chair. There wasn't anything on television, so we sat watching the flames.

"The horse looks like you've been taking good care of him," I said.

Forrest turned his head on the chair back to look at me. "Yeah, he's a good old horse."

"You've been feeding him too much, though. He's fat."

He said nothing after that, and soon his breathing

deepened, and I watched him from my seat on the floor, my arms around bent knees. He seemed to waver at the verge of sleep; then his body flinched suddenly, and he raised his head. "I'm going to bed," he said. He pushed himself heavily from the chair, took one uncertain step, then straightened, rubbing his face.

"Okay," I said. "See you in the morning."

"'Night."

I wasn't tired myself, having slept that afternoon. No light other than the fire graced the room, and I studied the logs as they burned and tumbled in on themselves, the embers showering sparks up the chimney, then glowing silently red in the bed of ash. I just felt like sitting, thinking.

5

As I steered into their driveway, the pickup headlights swept thistled brush, dormant trees, and a split-rail fence that lined the top of the river bank. It seemed a large house for a family of four—actually three now, I recalled, since Stacy's brother no longer lived at home. The two-story, white clapboard structure—austere, no trace of Victorian ornamentation—opened to a long porch on two sides of the first floor and projected dormers upstairs. Yellow light seeped warmly along the edges of blinds drawn in the windows.

Stacy met me at the front door and led me through the foyer into the living room. "I'll get Mom," she said.

The living room impressed me as hospitable, with high ceilings and deep sofas, along with chairs, a braided rug, and a brick fireplace where logs burned low. In several spaces—on the end table, on the mantel, on one of the built-in shelves by the fireplace—sat photographs of Stacy's family: her parents at the ocean, Stacy in a softball uniform and in a high school graduation gown, a recent sitting of the three together. I studied those pictures for a moment, troubled by some indefinite incompleteness about them; finally I decided it was nothing.

"Mom, this is Jeff Waters," Stacy said, ushering her mother in from the kitchen.

"Hello, Jeff," Mrs. Cottrell said, drying her hands on a terry-cloth apron tied at her waist. "We've heard a lot about you."

Mrs. Cottrell held the same slight stature as Stacy, with the same green, iridescent eyes that would flash like sun on a lake when happy and brood darkly when angry or upset. Long, chestnut hair—finer, less wavy than Stacy's—lay clasped behind her head, and at her temples and along her hairline the skin flushed pink under a thin sheen of perspiration, face washed in stove-top heat. "I know you two are glad to be home for your vacation," she said. "I'll have dinner ready in a few minutes. Please, make yourself comfortable. I hope you like roast beef."

"Yes ma'am. That's fine."

Her floral print dress flicked at her knees as she stepped purposefully to her work. Toward the rear of the house a door closed.

"That's Dad," Stacy said.

I remained standing as he entered the room with an armload of firewood. "Hello," he said to me, cordially, as though passing a stranger on the street. "Stacy, would you get the screen, honey?"

Stacy removed the fireplace screen, and Mr. Cottrell spilled the wood in a clattering heap, then pulled off his gloves finger by finger and dusted them over the hearth. "You must be Jeff," he said, extending a hand.

"Nice to meet you, sir. Need any help with that?"

"No, thanks," he said, crouching again by the fire and tossing split oak on the embers. "I think this will hold us for now. I'm Stacy's father by the way, in case you're wondering." He rose and started for the kitchen. "Momma," he called, "let's get food on the table; we've got three starving young people out here."

Mr. Cottrell's charcoal hair clung to his head in tight curls. He was tall, full-boned but not brusquely muscular in a blue flannel shirt. His mouth seemed nothing more than a straight line, much the same as my father's mouth in the photograph on my dresser.

The dining room was a dim cubicle tucked between the kitchen and living room and fitted precisely with an oval cherrywood table and four sturdy chairs. Stacy and Mr. Cottrell migrated to adjoining seats, apparently their regular places; I hesitated, until Stacy pointed, "Jeff, you sit across from me." Mrs. Cottrell surveyed the spread—thick roast, china bowls of green beans and steamed squash, woven basket of dinner rolls—in the fretful manner of a hostess never quite satisfied with her table. Mr. Cottrell coaxed, "Sit down, Momma. It's all here." At last she untied her apron and drew herself up in the chair opposite her husband.

As Mr. Cottrell carved slabs from the roast, the thought struck me that the place I occupied belonged to Stacy's brother, and I grew restless imagining his unexpected appearance: the abrupt, shuddering gust from outside, luggage dropped wearily inside the door, a rush of embraces and backslaps and laughter, all hands tugging to free him from a heavy coat. "You've timed it perfectly for supper," his mother would say, and he would advance to his familiar seat, only to halt before this outsider standing awkwardly there. After apologetic introductions his smile would return and he'd pump my hand, and the shifting of chairs and the setting of one more place would occur, my presence a disruption of the uniform and long-standing arrangement of this family's table.

I found myself seriously attempting to calculate the possibility and time of such an arrival but recalled that Stacy had never told me what he did or where he lived or even his name. On the verge of inquiring about it all, I held the question when Mr. Cottrell set the greased carving knife on the edge of the platter and lowered his head. "Our Father," he said, "we thank you for this food, for this family, and for our friends, and ask your blessing on us all. Amen."

During the meal, conversation consisted mostly of football and school and how Mrs. Cottrell managed to freeze so many vegetables for the winter months. Afterward Stacy and Mrs. Cottrell began clearing the table for dessert.

"That was quite a meal, Angela," Mr. Cottrell said.

At ease now, warmed by the pleasant pressure of a full stomach, I took this opportunity and turned to him. "Stacy said she has a brother. Is he coming home for Christmas?"

Immediately I sensed I'd brought on disaster. Leaning over the table as she reached for our plates, her face taut, Mrs. Cottrell glanced first at her husband then at Stacy before vanishing into the kitchen. Stacy drifted to the kitchen door. I silently appealed to her for an indication of what I'd said wrong, but she looked only at her father, awaiting something.

Strangely, though, in this atmosphere of sudden tension, Mr. Cottrell showed no sign that I had been ill-mannered. He traced patterns in the tablecloth with his finger, almost as if he had not heard my question, the only sound the popping fire in the living room. Mr. Cottrell brought the napkin from his lap and wiped his mouth with it, folding it on the table and passing tongue over front teeth. "Unfortunately, Bobby doesn't get home too much now that he's on his own," he said, looking at me at last. "So I don't imagine he's going to make it this time, though we certainly hope he will."

"I see," I breathed, barely aloud.

Mrs. Cottrell reappeared with desserts in either hand, her face plastered with an effusive smile. "How does apple pie sound?" she said.

"You'd better like this stuff," Mr. Cottrell said, "since my own blood went for the cause slicing those apples."

He told the truth; a bandage bound his left thumb. I watched those hands, unable to look at anything else. The right fingers inspected the bandage, then moved away and lifted a fork, bringing its edge down, severing the tip of pie wedge and a dollop of vanilla ice cream, lifting the bite to his mouth. Mr. Cottrell raised his head, chewing slowly, and looked across the table into space, finally glancing at me and catching my stare long enough only to wink, hardly more than a bat of his eye. Somehow, it seemed that the damage had been repaired.

"Stacy, why don't you show Jeff your father's wood-shop when you're through?" Mrs. Cottrell suggested.

"Mom, he may not be interested in all that."

"Stacy says you work at McPherson's Lumber Yard in the summers," Mr. Cottrell said.

"Yes sir," I said. "I remember loading some orders for you."

"Hmm," he said around a mouthful of pie. "Take out a good bit of lumber from McPherson's."

"Grant did this table and chairs," Mrs. Cottrell said, taking her seat again. "You don't think you'd want to show Jeff the woodshop, Stacy?"

"I'd like to see it," I said. "You do very good work, Mr. Cottrell."

"Thank you, Jeff. It's just a hobby, really."

Stacy frowned, but after finishing dessert we excused ourselves, and she led me through the kitchen to the back door and out into the raw wind.

"Mom thinks everybody is just *dying* to see Dad's workshop," Stacy said as we descended the concrete steps.

Near the back door a pole-mounted light illuminated a circle of yard; the sheriff's patrol car was parked under the light. Beyond a few tall pines stood a squat, gray-wood building with a tin roof and empty, black windows. A cord of firewood lay piled against an outer wall. Between the gusts of wind I heard the river flowing behind the woodshop.

Inside, Stacy found the light switch beside the door, and a single overhead bulb blazed on. "This is it." She shrugged.

A long workbench lined one wall, tools scattered over it and suspended on nails on a swatch of bare plywood paneling below shelves filled with cans of lacquer and enamel paint. On the opposite wall hung four unvarnished, high-back chairs, similar to those in the Cottrell dining room. In the center of the floor a dusty canvas tarpaulin covered a piece of machinery, and lumber perched in low stacks in the litter of wood shavings.

"This is his lathe under here," Stacy said, lifting an edge of the canvas cover. She brushed her hands together and moved to the workbench to lift a smooth, rounded section of bone-white wood—the rough of a chair leg. "This is what he's working on now. He's making a set of chairs for somebody."

"Stacy," I said, but from my tone she knew what I had to ask, and she did not look up, turning the wood in her hands. "I hope I didn't—I mean, about your brother—"

"It's okay. It's nothing. They had an argument." She tossed the wood onto the workbench. "You want to see a movie?" It was not an offer but a plea. She felt hemmed in, by me and this room.

"Anything you like."

We closed the workshop and cut across the yard again to the house. Mr. and Mrs. Cottrell sat in the living room, she in a chair with a paperback book, he on the end of one couch perusing the evening edition of the Assembly Shoals *Appalachian Herald*.

"Jeff and I are going to a movie," Stacy announced, then turning to me, "I'll get my jacket."

Mrs. Cottrell lowered the book to her lap. "You know, it's hard for us to plan an evening out sometimes," she said. "If there's an emergency call, Grant usually has to help take care of it."

Mr. Cottrell didn't look up. Opening the book again, Mrs. Cottrell fell silent. I took a chair, waiting for Stacy; overhead the heavy floor of the house creaked as she moved about upstairs. And waiting in the chair, I started as though slapped when I realized what was wrong in that living room.

Among all those pictures of the family, there was not a single photograph of Bobby Cottrell.

I thanked them for dinner, and we rode into town in Forrest's pickup. Stacy sat dispassionately in the undulating light of the theater, laughing softly on a few occasions when comic relief entered the lives and times of the improbable characters on the screen, tolerant of my arm around her but not settling as she normally did in the crook beneath my shoulder. On the way home she remained sullen. I peered at her next to me in the pale glow of dashboard instruments that cast weak shadows of her features toward her forehead, hair tucked under a stocking cap. The truck tires whined, almost a plaintive wail, on cold pavement. "It's like this—" she began. Then she stopped and drew a heavy breath.

From the projection of her voice I knew she looked down as she spoke. I did not take my eyes from the road now, afraid that any sign from me of anticipation would wither the resolve she had summoned. My mind was swirling, as if I stood at the edge of knowledge I had to learn yet did not want to face. The headlights channeled into moonless night as though into some pitchy, viscous substance; thin cracks in the asphalt snaking into the bright swath to disappear under the truck; hills and floodplain farmland and river lined with tree sentinels floating from utter blackness like indiscernible images of a dark dream; distant house lights beckoning feebly, almost without hope, across a chasm deep as time.

"What happened," she continued, "was that Bobby and Dad had an argument. Bobby was out of high school, he had a job, but he ran with a bunch of wild guys, and they kept getting into trouble—vandalism and things. So three years ago Bobby and a couple of others were caught breaking into a house. Dad brought him before the judge, but the owners of the house agreed to drop the complaint if the boys paid him for the damage. The judge gave Bobby a warning and let Dad promise to see to him, since he was the sheriff. Bobby had been in trouble before so Dad laid down the law. But Bobby couldn't handle the restrictions, and he was gone within a week. He was legal age and could go off on his own if he wanted. Dad said this was a choice Bobby'd have to make himself, that he could always come back if he agreed to stay out of trouble. It was the hardest thing I've ever seen Dad do, not to go after Bobby."

Stacy's shoulder rose and fell against mine in a shrug. She had spoken in a careful voice, not tremulous but measured, and I knew she would not discuss this subject at length. Curiosity goaded me.

"Where is he now?" I asked.

"We don't know. He wrote once at the beginning to say he was all right. Now we don't hear from him at all." These words rang with a strained tenor of accusation. She shifted on the seat, then silence cloaked her. I turned and found her gaze focused on knitted fingers on her lap.

"Dad never mentions it," she said, tone lowered again. "Neither does Mom, for that matter. It was a strange thing with Mom, though. They talked about getting counseling for Bobby—"

My ears tingled at this revelation, but I did not interrupt her.

"—but she said that would make him feel something was wrong with him, that we should work it out within the family. Then the week after he left, I went into the living room, and she was standing there holding the pictures, the ones of Bobby, and she stared at me as though I'd caught her at something. She stood there with those pictures, and I remember so clearly, she smoothed her dress with her free hand, like she was

[63]

concerned about her appearance, of all things; then she raised that hand and just lightly touched the frames of the pictures and said, 'I can't look at them now. Not with him gone.' I remember it exactly. It didn't seem like she was speaking to me—more to herself. And I didn't say a *word*. I can't believe I stood by and didn't say a word."

When we reached the house, I accompanied her to the porch, where we stood apart beneath dark eaves. She hunched her shoulders against the cold, a gesture at once vulnerable and heroic, submerging hands into coat pockets.

"Stacy, you shouldn't have worried about telling me," I said, attempting consolation and also grateful that she had revealed this secret.

"I know, I know," she answered, shaking her head in frustration. "And I'm sorry about tonight. It's not because I'm ashamed of what he did or was so hurt when he left that I don't face it. I miss him, and I admit that. It's just that Mom and Dad—we don't talk about it. I'm not *used* to talking about it."

"Go inside. You're freezing out here."

"You want to go to church with us tomorrow?" she asked. "We're Methodist, if that matters."

"Sure, I'll go."

I stepped forward and kissed her, though dutifully, without that suffusion of excited contentment and vague desire, for my attention had been lured from the threshold of that generous and warmly inviting house, far out into the abysmal, unrelenting night where there wandered an inexplicable young man who had abandoned security to attain some freedom, some knowledge I could not comprehend. Yet despite this bafflement I was disturbed by a greater sense that, though we'd never met, I knew him well. As I returned home, I found myself again attempting to conjure an image of his face, and as I mechanically brushed my teeth before the bathroom mirror, I was hauntingly visited by the thought that it was not Bobby Cottrell at all wandering in the night alone. Rather, it was me.

6

Church attendance had never been a high priority in Forrest's household. Mr. and Mrs. Owens were lifelong members of Assembly Shoals First Baptist, and as a young boy I had accompanied them, sometimes at the expense of a bribe and other times, when Forrest left me with them overnight, because I had no choice. I received my immersion there, at the behest of the Reverend Clayton Cobb, at the age of ten.

Reverend Cobb was a gangling, slat-footed elderly gentleman who smiled broadly in casual company. But when he perched on Sunday mornings before his flock, and truth and the Spirit began coursing through his veins, he thumped an open Bible with the flat of his fist and strode from side to side, sweat trailing down hollowed cheeks, one hand always gripping the lectern the way he might steady himself in a gale, the other hand reaching down from the pulpit as if to snatch the uncleansed from their wallow in the sinful mire. He rarely yelled but assailed with the force of desperate conviction. His tirades were seasonal, and while he breathed hot damnation in summer, I knew that today over in the Baptist church he would be sadly shaking his head, lamenting the ways of a godless world, winter seeping into the sanctuary as an ancient furnace coughed futilely in the basement.

The Baptist choir provided lilting accompaniment for Reverend Cobb; they sang so well it made your flesh creep. They also fielded the best church league softball team. By contrast, in accompanying the Cottrells I discovered the Methodists were remarkably more docile, always let out on time, and had more reliable heating.

Following the service that Sunday, we descended the stone steps of the somber brown Methodist structure, Mr. Cottrell clasping many of the gloved hands in the crowd. He paused at the corner. "Jeff," he said, searching his trouser pockets, then handing me his keys, "would you please escort the ladies to the car and warm it up for me? I need to see someone."

The Baptist and Methodist churches stood on opposite sides of a large yard by the river. Apart from several wrought-iron benches the yard was occupied only by spacious shade trees. In summer, when services concluded, the two congregations spilled onto the communal grounds to mingle. In winter, however, the trees fell bare and the grass curled brown, swept clean by the wind, and everyone hurried to their cars after church. We watched Mr. Cottrell make this unusual winter crossing as we walked to the parking lot. From the outpouring down the Baptist church steps a lone figure detached itself to meet him. I started the car and turned on the heater; when Mr. Cottrell returned, I climbed in back with Stacy.

"Sorry about the wait," he said. His cheeks pulsed amber from the cold. "That was one of my deputies. He phoned this morning and said he needed to speak with me."

"*That's* who that was," Mrs. Cottrell said, then, voice bracing, "You don't have to go somewhere——"

"No, no. He just wanted to tell me about a call they handled last night. Broke up a pretty good fight at the Hang-Out. Something about a gambling debt."

My stomach soured, and nausea reeled toward my head. The Hang-Out Saloon was a block-walled dive, standing with windows black behind neon beer logos along the steep, clay-shouldered highway north of Assembly Shoals. I faced away from Stacy, certain my own vision would betray what it had seen that morning: Forrest gulping down water over aspirin, ice in a towel on a blackened eye and swollen lip.

"Hit my face on the side of that tallboy of your mother's," he had said. "I swear we got too much furniture in here. Came in last night in the dark and tripped over the rug there. Could've given myself a concussion."

I had no evidence to disprove his story, but long years of experience would not allow me to concede Forrest the benefit of the doubt.

Stacy met him for the first time that afternoon; the exchange was courteous, the best I could've hoped for. Then I led her through the house to the back yard, where the December sun dazzled but from such an oblique angle it provided little warmth.

"It's a beautiful view here," Stacy said.

"I think you'd find more houses on this road if it

weren't so hard to reach. Along the ridge there," and I indicated the wooded slope that rose behind the shelf of our house and lawn, cresting a hundred yards above us, "you can really see, even beyond the valley. We'll go up there sometime."

"What's that for?" She pointed to the net and tire.

"I put that there in high school. A target for a football."

We walked to the barn and found Beast in his stall. I dug a scoop into the barrel where his grain was stored. "This is Beast. Forrest gave him to me when I was twelve."

"That's the worst name for a horse I've ever heard," Stacy said. "Let me feed him."

A disk of ice had formed on the surface in Beast's water bucket; I fished it out, tossing it to the ground with a splintering crack, and refilled the bucket.

Stacy ran her hand along Beast's muzzle as he ground the oats between yellow teeth like grist under a millstone. "You should trim his whiskers."

For a moment we silently watched the horse.

"Your uncle looked rough."

"He said he fell," I told her, taking no comfort that I had not lied. "Stacy, he's hard to get to know—"

"There's nothing to explain. I thought he was very polite."

On Christmas Day, Forrest and I ate dinner at the Owenses' house—a traditional yet uneventful occasion, since Mr. and Mrs. Owens had always acknowledged Forrest with little more than quiet disregard. That evening I stuffed down another large meal with the Cottrells, and when we had finished and cleared the table, Stacy and I settled into the living room in our individual encampments near the edge of sleep, amid the wreckage of gift boxes and tattered wrapping paper.

From the kitchen came the clap of dishware as Mr. and Mrs. Cottrell, having refused our help, scrubbed and stacked dinner plates, until Mrs. Cottrell returned to announce, "It's snowing outside."

Christmas snow, even in the foothills of the southern Appalachians, was such an infrequent occurrence that we roused ourselves to peer through the windows. Tiny flakes drifted downward in concentration so thin that each flake could be distinguished, flaring like particles of hot ash as they fluttered into the glow from the porchlight, expiring as droplets of moisture upon the ground.

We dropped again into our chairs, Mr. Cottrell now joining us with a newspaper, but we weren't there long before the telephone jangled. Stacy demonstrated a startling surge of energy, springing from the hearth where, with her back to the fire, she had been sitting so quietly her mother had asked if she felt ill from eating too much. Stacy had said she guessed that was it. Mrs. Cottrell summoned her to the hall phone, but Stacy took it upstairs, staying on the line for half an hour.

"Looks like you've got some competition," Mr. Cottrell said from behind the newsprint.

"Oh, you are just terrible," Mrs. Cottrell huffed. "Jeff, don't even listen to him."

Mr. Cottrell lowered his paper and studied his wife over the half-lenses of his reading glasses. "Was it male or female when you answered the phone?"

"Well, it was a boy, but of course that doesn't mean anything."

"Sounds to me like competition," he said, raising the paper again, not once looking at me.

And though his comments were a gibe, my mind stirred in uneasy motion; the observation too neatly fit the circumstances. Stacy returned, suddenly cured of her gastric ailment, and snared me by one arm, leading me to the basement to play Ping-Pong on the new table her father had constructed in the woodshop. I asked about the call, but she brushed the subject aside, and when I persisted, she became annoyed.

"It was nothing," she said. "A friend from high school."

Her protests seemed too adamant, and I stewed within myself for three days. But nothing else occurred to strengthen my suspicions, and soon this incident lay buried in my memory, in the way that a crust of new snow fell in subsequent weeks like a shroud over the earth.

The university lay untouched by snow that winter and escaped all but a few days of piercing, skin-wrinkling rain, left instead to shut itself tight against bright air throbbing with cold, clamped under a hard freeze. The hourly bustle of students transpired with a self-imposed economy—direct, purposeful, tightly wrapped surges between porticos, breath steaming from raw faces as if from engines shuttling on predetermined tracks. Loitering conversations were conducted not outside but in the warmth of reverberating, marble-tiled foyers of libraries or dormitories.

In early March the first warm disturbances from the southwest brushed the flesh, sun slowly assuming higher arcs, regaining strength, until spring showers were borne in on steady breezes, dripping from eaves and draining in gutters like melting ice. Stacy and I saw each other regularly during these months but for extended periods only on weekends, when we would saunter into town for a movie or a meal away from the bland, volume business of the dining halls, or when we'd spin Stuart's sports convertible out into the surrounding countryside, top down and wind whipping. Since our transportation was always borrowed, trips home to Assembly Shoals were infrequent.

Spring football practice—three weeks of off-season drills designed to maintain the players' conditioning—was orchestrated in April in the mud of an unseeded practice field. May heralded the final and complete throwing open of the campus, with students returning to their natural environment: lounge chairs on roofs and patios of fraternity houses, or grassy quadrangles between now uninviting classroom buildings. The fresh scent of blossoming earth rose in the air, and Stacy herself became more alluring, tan and bare-shouldered in cotton sundresses.

With the arrival of summer and school dismissed for the year, we found what I wanted at Inez and Pete Morgan's Top-Quality Used Cars, a dusty gravel lot on the main highway north of Assembly Shoals, not far from the Hang-Out Saloon; in fact it was Forrest who first suggested the place. When Mr. Cottrell drove us out one sultry night, the prices were soaped in bold numerals on windshields gleaming under rows of red, white, and blue pennants and bare light bulbs populated with moths. The Morgans' inventory included a 1967 Mustang, and though a few dents had been hammered out of the body, the motor idled smoothly and held some power back. With the bill of sale in my pocket, I found Stacy in the driver's seat, twisting the steering wheel side to side, making a noise in her throat like car tires squealing.

"Let me drive it home," she said.

I told her she was crazy and to move over.

Forrest said I'd struck a fair bargain but noticed the accumulation of mileage. "So watch out for little things," he warned.

Our first outing in the Mustang came the following Saturday, when Stuart invited us to go water skiing.

Stuart was accompanied by his girlfriend Drena, a wide-shouldered diver on the Assembly Shoals High School swim team with hazel eyes and blonde hair cropped short for diving, the attractive, lithesome girl Stuart might be expected to have on his arm; yet what he found enthralling about her—and not the other minions who flocked and flirted for his attention—was her disregard for him. She handled Stuart expertly, like a patient trainer with a brash colt. She curtly uttered her disapproval when Stuart wandered afield, and if he persisted, she simply gave him enough rein to tire himself out, and he always came trotting home.

Canton Lake was a reservoir ten miles above Assembly Shoals. The Cahala had been dammed, an unnatural interruption of its inexorable course, slowly submerging the valley behind, with serpentine inlets and coves creeping into the hills. As a consequence of this method of formation, the lake ended where the forest began, thick growth flourishing to the water's edge, except where granite bluffs vaulted skyward and where the shore had been bulldozed for beaches. Mr. McPherson, who owned the lumberyard where Stuart and I worked during the summers, agreed to let us use his cabin on the lake for the day. Stuart and Drena brought up the Halls' powerboat behind his father's truck; Stacy and I followed in my car.

We arrived at noon, ate lunch, and changed into

our swimsuits in the cabin, then skied most of the afternoon, until the wind blustered and gray, grim clouds
advanced over the trees across the lake, blotting out the
sun. The water turned the color of tarnished brass. The
air cooled, chills tingling on our reddened skin, and the
western sky heaved as an unbroken bank of clouds, dark
and solid as a slab of slate; and above the whine of the
outboard we heard storm rumblings. Stuart, a tireless
and effortless skier, trailed the boat, knifing the wake,
oblivious to the weather, but I signaled to him we were
going in, pointing to the sky. Turning to look, he nodded. He gave a low whistle as we loaded the boat onto
the trailer. "Looks like it's coming up a good one," he
said.

A charge of lightning crashed to the lake's opposite
shore, solid slate now filling half the sky, treetops bow-
ing in the gusts, then flinging upright again. Thunder
popped—a succession of cannon fire, fading to the east.
The canvas boat cover fought our grip, wind snatching
leaves from tree limbs and swirling red dust in our faces.

"That'll hold," Stuart said. "Let's go!"

"We're right behind you."

Stuart and Drena scrambled into the truck and
pulled away, the boat jouncing on the trailer behind
them, taillights glaring as they disappeared into the
forest on the curving dirt road. Stacy and I ducked into
my car. A turn of the key in the ignition produced only
a click of the starter. "Oh, perfect," I muttered.

"Try it again."

The first raindrops spattered the windshield. Wind
rocked the car, stripping more leaves and whole twigs
from lashing boughs, and through the trees the opposite
shore had vanished behind a brown screen of rain. An

eerie and abnormal darkness had gathered so thickly I could barely see Stacy's face. I turned the ignition again—still nothing—and swallowed, a tightness in my stomach settling like a stone into an oozing lake bed.

"Won't it start?" Stacy asked, her voice honed of any casual intonation.

"No," I snapped. "It's the battery or maybe the connections. There's no way to fix that here."

"What about Stuart and Drena?"

We peered into the murky air at the empty road that entered the forest, alive in the wind. "No," I said. "No, it's too late to catch them. They'll come back when they see we aren't behind them."

I pumped the accelerator and listened once more to the dead click of the starter. Lightning ripped the sky once again, flooding the forest and the interior of the car with a blue-white shock like a bomb, and thunder exploded in the same instant; I flinched and saw Stacy shrink in her seat next to me.

"Oh Lord, Jeff, I don't like it," she said. The drops thumped faster now, merging into the larger, singular sound of torrential rain. "I really don't. It could be a tornado. I can't see anything."

"Okay, I know. No, it's not a tornado. It's just a thunderstorm."

"It's bad."

"It just blows and thunders a lot at the first. I've got the key—you want to go back inside the cabin?"

"Yes."

We flung open the car doors. "Bring your clothes!" I shouted.

We dashed for the cabin but were drenched before mounting the porch steps. I wrestled open the kitchen door, rain billowing in cold mists under the porch eaves and against our backs. A flip of a light switch by the door left the kitchen in darkness.

"Wind must've taken down a power line somewhere," I said.

Stacy touched my arm. "How are we going to see?"

"We'll find something."

"Listen to it come down." The words seemed to stick in her mouth.

The rain plunged over the roof, not in broken waves but with an incessant roar, the way I imagined it might sound if the cabin were on fire, swallowed in flames. Running my hand along the gritty counter, then the cold edge of the porcelain sink, we passed through a doorway into the living room. A glare of lightning illuminated a fireplace, a deer's head mounted on the poplar-paneled wall, a sagging sofa, a writing table against the far wall, and stairs to the loft. The room smelled of dry must and yellowed newspapers. "I remember seeing a kerosene lantern somewhere, near the fireplace," I said.

We groped to the fireplace and found a lantern on the mantel. Fishing my hand into a drawer of the writing table, I discovered a matchbook; as I lit the wick, my nose stung with the sudden sharp odor of burning kerosene.

"Won't it smell up the room?" she said.

"I'll put it in front of the fireplace, and the smoke will draw out."

In steady light that now tinged the room I saw the chilled, prickled skin of slender legs that emerged from a one-piece swimsuit riding high on the paler flesh of her thighs. "Why don't you change?" I suggested. "You can use the bedroom."

Sunken in thought, she stared at the lantern light, not at me. "Okay," she muttered, and padded across threadbare carpet toward the bedroom.

"Wait," I said, "we can look again—"

I burrowed my hand into the writing table drawer jammed with refuse and uncovered a short candle stump; the orphaned lid of a mason jar served as a base.

With her loose bundle of clothing pinned under one arm and the jar lid and candle poised in the other palm, Stacy stepped into the bedroom under the muted rush of rain, pushing the door behind her but not all the way, leaving it open perhaps a foot. I sat on the couch, which faced away from the bedroom and toward the fireplace and French doors that opened onto the front porch and the lake, but I kept watching that opening and through it the back wall of the bedroom. I could not see her, only a dim, dancing yellow glow of the candle she carried, light not quite filling the room, leaving darkness up against the ceiling in the one corner I could see; then her shadow, blurred, quivering, moved onto the wall, and the light steadied—she had set the candle down. Her shadow lingered, larger than herself but not monstrous, still fuzzy in the flicker. Unaware that the candle cast her image onto the wall and thus into the mesmerized line of my sight from the couch, she raised her hands and slipped the straps of the swim-suit from her shoulders, peeling the suit downward, bending, stepping from it, straightening again; and for an instant the light seemed to suspend in perfect projection, the shadow a clear outline, a profile of the length of her unclothed figure, and the only sound I heard was the battering rain.

I felt the warming, then the constricted pulse; my throat tightened and my heart strained to work the blood. But in another moment Stacy had moved, and the shadow passed from the wall, only the indistinct flicker remaining. I turned away, watching the lightning flare through panes of the French doors. Finally, the bedroom door creaked softly, and Stacy returned to the couch in shorts and a T-shirt. Her hair was mussed from a towel she carried. Sitting on the edge of the couch, she dropped her canvas shoes to the floor.

"Better?" I asked hoarsely. "If you're still cold, I can find a jacket or a blanket—"

"I'm all right. I was just shivering in that wet bathing suit."

I nodded and became aware of my own trunks uncomfortably damp on my skin. "I think I'll change, too." In the bedroom Stacy had left the candle on a chipped pressboard dresser, melted wax droplets skimming down hardened spines on the candle into the overturned mason jar lid. Water, milky in that weak light, streamed outside panes of a single window, and wind tapped a pruned hedge branch against the glass. Pushing the candle to one side on the dresser, I checked that my shadow did not also hover on the back wall (she had not closed the door, and neither did I—an opening of trust, almost). I pulled off my swimming trunks, toweled the dampness, and slid into underwear and tennis shorts and knit shirt. I picked up the candle, flame fluttering and dwindling in the stir of air, and entered the tiny bathroom enclosure, where her swimsuit hung inside out over the curtain rod in a rust-stained shower stall. Draping my trunks there, I found that I carefully avoided touching her swimsuit, though not from shame. Instead, it seemed this intimate piece of fabric held some great revelation that, once acquired through a long caress between fingertips or even a casual brush of a hand, would consume the savor of anticipation as its price. I feared the churning of vital emotion inside me would become tangible and therefore diminished.

Filled now with another, singular thought that had to be told, I blew out the candle and returned to the living room, where Stacy had not moved, still sitting on the couch with her back slightly curved, elbows on knees, watching the rain through the windows.

"Well," I sighed, "there's no phone, so that's no help. We'd have to walk to the other side of the cove to reach the next house, and we'd drown before we got there. Anyway, I'm sure the lines are down all around. But Stuart should really be coming back soon. He'd have to know we weren't behind him."

"They'll notice us missing, eventually."

I moved to the couch and sat beside her, leaving a foot of space. The cushion sank low beneath me, and I sat as she did, elbows on knees, hands clasped. "I'm sorry about the car," I said. "It's an old battery."

"There's nothing you could do about it."

Outside, the rain overflowed the gutters and streamed off the porch roof like a waterfall. The rain fell so hard that when lightning seared the air the ground remained hidden beneath a mist of cascading water.

"Sorry I shouted," she muttered, looking down.

"When?"

"About the car not starting."

"Don't worry about it."

Sitting on the couch, the words I had to say welling in my throat and on my tongue but clinging there like sorghum, I felt distanced from her. I lowered myself to the floor. "You seem—pensive," I said, facing the windows.

"I was thinking about Bobby," she said, her tone more familiar. "Actually, my parents. Since Bobby left they've had this dread that something might happen to *me*. Not that they suffocate me, watching all the time. But there's one child missing, and they're not sure why, and inside they worry about the one that's left. I hurt for them when they worry like that. Jeff, they'll start to wonder and come out in this to look for us. Won't Stuart come back?"

"As soon as he notices we're not following them."

"They're home by now."

"We should just stay where we are," I said, looking at her. "When the rain lets up, I'll go out and try to start the car."

After a long moment Stacy slid down beside me, stretching her legs out, crossing her ankles, leaning her head against my shoulder, our backs to the couch. I put my arm around her and could feel where the sun had burned down all afternoon, her shoulders warm through the cool T-shirt.

"Bobby used to bring me skiing," she said.

My tongue felt swollen in my mouth. "You didn't tell me that," I said stupidly. "You looked good out there."

"He taught me how. He was—is—a great skier. When I was younger, he'd let me go with him, and it took me forever to learn, but he never got upset. He'd ski behind the boat with me, right beside me yelling, 'C'mon! You've got it!' Whenever I fell, he'd let go, too, and swim over to ask if I was all right, if I wanted to try again." Her voice trailed, and she turned on her side, head under my chin, hair smelling dry from the afternoon sun.

Within minutes the wind had slackened and so had

the thunder, which occurred now as a low and occasional rumble. Pale lightning revealed finer rain; the sound of it beating the roof was fainter, a soothing whisper. The woods and lake had fallen dark under evening as well as rain, window panes black and empty behind the silver reflection of lantern light.

Stacy yawned widely, and I felt the movement of her jaw against my shoulder. I sensed she might fall asleep now, too soon, and I began to tremble. I tensed every muscle to control it; my stomach contracted into a mass of cold rubber.

Stacy lifted her head. "What's the matter?"

I shrugged. "Nothing."

Slowly, she lowered her head, then looked at me once more, her face gathered in perplexity. "Jeff, you're shivering. Are you still cold?"

"No, no—" I searched for a piece of lint on my shorts, her stare hot on the side of my face. I could no longer even glance at her. Like a man attempting to speak in desperate thirst, I breathed the words, "I love you." I had never said that to anyone. At last the cords in my neck relaxed a degree for me to turn to her.

Her mouth opened slightly as if to speak, her eyes searching mine, but remained silent; she blinked and rested her head again on my shoulder. My breathing shortened with this rejection, and the darkness beyond the windows seemed to close on me. I feared and yet almost hoped that the lantern would spend its fuel and fade, that the lightning would cease, and that Stacy and the couch and the cabin and earth itself would fall away into black infinity, leaving me in numbing nothingness.

But Stacy returned her stare to me. "I love you," she repeated, as though she too were testing the words. My body ceased trembling, calm against her. I kissed her, a light graze of dry lips, then deeply, unlike the cool, accommodating, decorous kisses outside her dormitory room or on the porch of her parents' house; and when I felt the first warm pass of her tongue, the long months and this night seemed to hurtle together to a point of intense focus. We surfaced finally—as though from water, easily, with full lungs, not kicking but merely floating upward—and she tucked her head under my chin. Her breathing deepened as the rain continued. I could not have cared less if rescue never arrived.

Stacy was awakened by the sound—sloshing, splashing—before I moved; she pulled away from me, crouching and rubbing her face. Beyond the silver reflection in the black windows a pair of conical headlight beams glinted on falling rain in front of the cabin, gleaming on my car and shrinking as though toward the narrow ends of megaphones until their source appeared. Tires spattered through the froth and halted with a tight squeal of brakes.

"That must be someone," Stacy said, struggling to her feet.

At the French doors we pressed our faces to the glass. A broad figure climbed out of the driver's side of a pickup, crossed through the headlights to peer into my car, then turned and looked at the cabin, finally jogging toward us.

"It's Stuart," I said, and as I yanked open the door,

he bounded up the steps, then stopped short, tossing his hands in a gesture of consternation and relief. He wore trousers and waterproof hiking boots, plastered to the ankles in fresh mud, and a raincoat with the hood over his head, water dripping in front of his face from the crest. "Here you are!" he groaned. "What happened? Stacy, your mother is about to pop an artery."

Stacy pressed back her hair with her hand. "I know. Let's just get out of here."

"Battery went dead," I explained.

Stuart nodded; we extinguished the lantern inside, gathered our shoes, and ran to the truck, which no longer towed boat and trailer. We bounced and sprayed along the road foaming with mud, wiper blades slinging water; and leaning over the steering wheel, Stuart said, "I thought you were behind us. I swear I did. We got out to the main road, and it was coming down like the end of the world, and there were headlights behind us all the way. I thought it was you."

"It just went dead," I said, "and by the time we realized it, you were gone."

"I took Drena to her house," he continued, "and then I went home. Your mother called, Stacy, wanting to know where we were. I told her you should have been home a long time ago. I came back this way to look, and Mr. Cottrell drove uptown to see if you'd gone there."

"The battery was fine this morning," I said.

"We'll come back tomorrow and jump it," Stuart said.

Inside the Cottrell house, ablaze with light in the rain, someone heard us drive up; the front door swung open, and Mrs. Cottrell paced onto the porch as we climbed the steps. She seemed to uncoil like a tightly wound spring. "You found them. Thank the Lord in Heaven. What in the world happened, honey?" Her eyes perused us head to bare filthy feet.

"The car wouldn't start," Stacy said, not stopping but wiping her feet and entering the house, "and it was storming, so we had to wait till somebody came back for us. I'm going to shower and change."

Mrs. Cottrell turned again to me, palms resting flat on her hips.

"I'm awfully sorry," I said. "The battery went dead, and I thought it would be better to wait in the cabin."

"Oh, I understand. I'm just so glad there wasn't, you know—an accident."

"Yes ma'am. Well, I should go on home now. It's getting late."

"You most absolutely will not!" Mrs. Cottrell commanded. "You're wet and muddy, and you don't have a stitch of proper clothes on. You come in and we'll fix you up. You can shower in the other room. Won't you come in too, Stuart?" She gripped my elbow gently but insistently and guided me toward the door.

"No thanks," Stuart said, the hood of his raincoat down now. "I need to get home."

"Suit yourself. But please drive carefully. We certainly don't want any more emergencies tonight."

"I will. I'll call you in the morning, Ice Waters."

"Yeah," I said. "Thanks."

Mrs. Cottrell closed the front door and led me up wide, uncarpeted stairs to the second floor, a part of the house I'd never seen. "Mr. Cottrell went into town thinking you might have gone there," she said. "But he'll just be glad to know you're back safely."

The dim second floor hallway was furnished with a settee and long throw rug; at the far end the waxed wood flooring glowed under a closed door—Stacy's room, I figured. To the left stood another door, and Mrs. Cottrell entered it and switched on an overhead light. I followed, still holding my shoes, and watched her open a chest of drawers. "Here," she said, "are a pair of old jeans, and some socks, and there're a few shirts hanging in the closet. I hope they'll fit well enough." She stepped into the bathroom, and I heard the rustle of a shower curtain, the banging of a cabinet door. She came out again. "There's soap and a towel, so you go right ahead and get washed up and come down whenever you get finished." She closed the door, and I heard the stairs creak lightly in the hallway as she descended them.

Rainwater drained in murmurs above, muffled by secure roofing and solid rafters. I stood at the foot of a double bed, clutching my shoes in front of me, fingering the laces. The bed was made, the room well-kept and smelling of polish—no dust on a desk or chair or on the dresser and mirror. The edges of a photograph of Stacy curled in a frame on the dresser. I looked again at the clothes in the open drawers and realized with a cold creep along my spine that this "other" room and these clothes belonged to Bobby Cottrell. I wondered at his mother: she had entered the room and moved about it impassively, as if it were nothing more than guest quarters, certainly not a reminder of her missing son. As though he had never lived here at all.

I showered and slipped on a pair of his bleached-out jeans, a close fit. From the closet I chose a shirt—a garish print of tumbling, multicolored ocean waves—and pulled it over my head. Finding myself in front of the mirror, I felt the same dizzying fascination of looming above a black and bottomless well. We had never met; I didn't even know what he looked like. Yet in these clothes in this room I sensed some deeper knowledge about him. For an instant—a span of time like the name or the face that flickers across the mind, too elusive to be remembered—I shuddered with a fear that I might be sent careening, wildly, disastrously, into the night. Even as I sneered at this thought when it had passed, I tried to imagine what things he'd done while wearing these clothes.

Stacy sat in the living room when I came down. She had put on long pants and a thin blouse with sleeves rolled to the elbows. Looking up from a magazine, she unfurled to a straight-back posture, blinking once, face hardening like concrete. "She gave you Bobby's clothes," she said, voice laced with incredulity and accusation.

I nodded, chafing under her inspection.

Her shoulders at last stooped a degree. "I used to hate that shirt," she said, mildly now. "He would wear it just to irritate me. But it threw me seeing you there with it on. I thought—" She lowered her gaze to the magazine. "Mom knew you'd be hungry. She's fixing you something."

"You eating?"

She looked up, again as if momentarily untracked by my appearance, then said. "No," and rose, leading me into the kitchen.

After this reception by Stacy, I entered the kitchen apprehensive about the reaction her mother might experience upon seeing me in these clothes. But when Mrs. Cottrell looked up from the sandwiches she'd assembled on the counter, she smiled brightly and said, "Feel better?" No hint of recognition or remembrance. Apparently she had been entirely successful in blocking her own son from her mind.

"Sit down and I'll have you something to eat in a minute," she continued. "You must be starving. Mr. Cottrell called from the coffee shop in town, so he should be here shortly. Do you like tuna salad?"

"Yes ma'am."

Stacy took a chair beside me. Mrs. Cottrell set a sandwich and milk on the kitchen table as the sound of a car in the drive cut through the rain. Headlights swung in the backyard and blinked out; a car door slammed. My appetite abruptly retreated: I felt responsible for the events of the evening.

The back door to the kitchen opened, and Mr. Cottrell entered with the fresh smell of rain. He stamped his boots on the footmat and tugged off his broad-brimmed hat and slicker. "I see the waterbugs have returned."

"They made it, thank goodness," Mrs. Cottrell said. "Some sort of car trouble."

"The battery went dead after Stuart and Drena left," I told him. "Then this storm popped."

"It's been a real gully-washer," he said. "They've had flash flooding in the lower end of the valley. Momma, I sure could use one of those sandwiches."

Mrs. Cottrell had already put one on a plate for him. He drew a glass of water for himself at the faucet.

"I'm sorry about all the trouble," I said. "I really feel bad about it."

Mr. Cottrell pulled back his chair across from me and sat. Resting his forearms on the edge of the table, he studied his plate for a moment with his head down, and I almost bowed mine, thinking he was about to say a blessing. Instead, he looked up at me. "Jeff," he said, "there are some things, no matter how much we cuss and spit, that we simply can do nothing about, and blaming ourselves or someone else for them is only more wasted energy. That kind of worry will absolutely drain you, wring you out like the dish rag in the sink. You're all right, and that's what counts."

"Yes sir," I mumbled, looking straight at him.

He bit off one corner of the sandwich and shifted it to his cheek, reaching over and patting Stacy on the arm. "Well, champ, how was the skiing? Mmm, you got some of that sun today, my little french fry."

"It was fun," she said. "But I'm out of practice."

Forrest wasn't there when Mr. Cottrell dropped me at my house, and he hadn't shown up by morning. Even so, I was eager to tell him he'd been right about that car.

Stuart's call woke me late in the morning. At Mr. McPherson's cabin, the air hung rinsed of haze, sun glinting on the top of my car parked in the clearing amid puddles the color of creamed coffee. The lake shimmered calmly again, yet along the edge, where broad, overhanging branches shielded the glare, the water churned red-brown from last night's torrent and the Cahala River's muddy effluence, soaking high into the oily, clay-smelling mat of pine needles beneath the trees. Though it was Sunday morning, a few powerboats already chopped the water, and sailboats etched bright triangles against the opposite shore. Stuart pulled up his convertible next to the Mustang. I remembered the swimsuits Stacy and I had left behind and went inside to retrieve them.

"Damn," he muttered, shaking his head when I returned. Then again, "Damn. Why was I in such a hurry to leave? You really had it figured out, though, didn't you?"

"What are you *talking* about?"

He had raised both hoods to connect the jumper cables. "It was perfect," he said. "Secluded cabin. Good rainstorm to keep anyone from bothering you. Just wait until I drive away, then tell her the battery's dead."

"Is that what you think?"

"I wish I'd thought of it yesterday."

"If you think I made up the dead battery, why are you jumping it?"

He brushed his forehead with the back of a grease-smeared hand. "You two were here—alone—and nothing happened?"

"No."

" 'No' as in 'yes, something happened?' "

" 'No' as in *'no*, nothing happened.' "

"No other articles of clothing tossed aside in the tussle?"

"I already told you—"

"Did you check carefully? Should I go in and have a look myself?"

"You can tear out the floorboards for all I care; there's nothing to find because nothing happened, and even if it did, do you honestly believe I'd tell you?"

Tilting his head, he studied me with one eye, then ducked under the hood of my car and announced, "I don't believe you."

"Why don't you just shut up?"

"Sure, sure."

"I mean it; I don't think it's funny."

"I said okay."

Though I knew how his mind worked, Stuart's insinuation shocked me, more so because such a thought had not once entered my mind last night. I remembered her kiss and before that the lantern-lit shadow, which arose before me now as if I were seeing it again that moment. But I had not considered rising from the couch and moving to the partly open door, pushing it back slowly until it revealed her clutching the towel against herself in surreal candle glow, damp swimsuit limp at her feet, water streaming ouside the window panes behind her. She would have stared, not angrily but motionless with surprise and uncertainty, pressing the towel with one hand flat to her breast and the other against her abdomen, bare, untanned flesh of her hips visible at the edges of the towel, and I would have waited in the doorway, watching only her eyes and silently asking this of her.

Instead, I had remained on the couch. We were not merely unprepared, but such an episode would have been a tense and fumbling embarrassment, threatening and perhaps destroying a bond—delicate but stronger than physical contact—I sensed we had formed.

Yet I had easily imagined a greater intimacy, and I became disturbed that the events at the cabin might have appeared to others as they had appeared to Stuart. This fear fed on uncertainty all afternoon until finally it had grown so troublesome I found myself that evening at the Cottrells'. Avoiding the house, I went directly to the back, and crossing the yard I heard a steady whine of machinery from the woodshop. I hesitated at the door, then opened it and entered, swinging it slowly shut behind me. Inside, a single light bulb burned overhead, and Mr. Cottrell leaned over the lathe, eyes unblinking behind goggles, his hands directing the blade smoothly over the spinning length of wood. Shavings flew in an arching stream from the lathe, specks settling on the curls of Mr. Cottrell's head and the dark hair of his forearms. A huge fan spun in one corner, pushing warm air around the room. I approached and waited for him to notice me. In the windows the evening light faded.

He straightened, rubbing his neck, the tail of the stream of shavings falling to the floor. "Hello, Jeff," he said above the noise of the lathe. "What can I do for you?"

I buried my hands in my pockets. "I didn't want to disturb you," I said, almost shouting. "I needed to talk to you—to tell you something—when you have the time."

"Now is fine." He stooped again, and the blade made contact with the spinning wood and created a new stream of shavings. He glanced up at me and nodded.

I drew a breath of heavy air. "It's about yesterday."

Again he nodded, not looking up this time.

"Well—I—," and I stopped, unable to shout it, the sound of the lathe boring into my brain. Dots of sweat formed above my lip.

Mr. Cottrell raised himself to his full height. His hand found a switch and flicked off the power to the lathe. Instantly the whine began a steady journey down the decibel scale, becoming a low hum, slowing until I could see the grain of the wood turning, noise and motion finally ceasing altogether. The fan continued to spin quietly, but the silence of the lathe was sudden, absolute, and miserable. "Jeff," he said, "is something the matter?"

"No sir, that's not it at all. It's just about yesterday. I've been thinking about it. I didn't want you to wonder— We were up there a long time—" I looked at my shoes and would have given anything never to have gone in there. Shame nauseated me; would I only be casting suspicion on myself by asserting innocence? I waited for him to say something, but he remained silent. "We were up there a long time," I went on, "but nothing happened."

"Nothing—happened?"

"That's right, sir."

Mr. Cottrell frowned at me, his face an expression of complete and perfect bafflement, one of the few times I ever saw him show any expression whatsoever; at last he tilted his head back slowly, mouth forming a tight circle and eyebrows lifting as understanding dawned and spread over his face. For just an instant, I thought I had seen a smile creep to his mouth as he turned to drop the blade on the workbench. But that vision quickly vanished, so quickly I wasn't sure I had seen it at all; and when he turned to me again, lowering himself to the wooden stool by the workbench, his face had resumed a familiar solemnity.

"I really wouldn't—" I continued, slower.

He raised his hand in acknowledgment, nodded, and hooked the heels of his boots over the bottom rung of the stool. He pulled off the goggles, revealing red circles around his eyes, and brushed shavings from his hair. "Jeff, you're a fine young man, and I'm glad you and Stacy have taken an interest in each other. And I know you wouldn't take advantage of her in any way. Your coming in here to talk to me just reaffirms that. But more than any of that, I must tell you I trust my daughter's judgment. I trust her to do what she knows is right in whatever situation she finds herself."

"Yes sir," I said.

"And Jeff?"

"Sir?"

Here he groped for words—another rarity, for he never spoke without reflection. His face gathered, pensive, almost urgent. "Don't be afraid—if there's something on your mind, bothering you—to tell me. You should talk it out with those close to you. It's the best way."

"I will."

He ran his fingers over the wood in the lathe. "Get your car fixed?"

"It's running fine now that I got it charged. I'm going to get a new battery tomorrow."

We listened to the hum of the fan for a moment.

"Well, thank you, Mr. Cottrell," I said.

"That's all right."

I left the woodshop feeling as though I had scrambled from under a boulder. Before I reached the back steps of the house in the twilight, the whine of the lathe had drifted once more across the yard.

"It will be my only chance to get away before the election," Mr. Cottrell said at the dining room table. "We could use another strong back to help carry the gear, Jeff, if you'd like to come with us." Thus he suggested to the family a short vacation camping along the coast.

I agreed, never having seen the ocean, and that weekend we loaded the Cottrells' green-gold, rattling, chrome-dangling station wagon and headed south, mid-July pooled over Assembly Shoals like hot bathwater.

We drove out of the hills, through the piedmont—pecan orchards, forests of lodgepole pines, acrid sulfur odor of pulp mills—and finally onto the coastal plain, where marshes spread away from narrow shoulders of the road and Spanish moss bearded the trees. By evening we had reached the inland channel and parked the car there, staggering under the hoist of packs to our backs and catching the last ferry across to the barrier island, a natural preserve populated by deer and wild horses roaming through dense tracts of palm and the twisting trunks of live oaks. From the pier we hiked along the only access to vehicular traffic—a sand-rutted, tree-canopied fire road that cut through the center of the island, parallel to the beach, which rested somewhere beyond the cloak of the forest.

As we moved north in gathering darkness, black tree boughs etched hard against paler sky above, I strained for a glimpse of the ocean, closer to it now than I had ever been. Dusk and high dunes obscured the view. I listened for its sound beneath the low hum of insects on the weak breeze that stirred thick air. It seemed to roar and yet lie silent at the same time, as though its sound were something deeper, almost an emotion, and I began to wonder if this sound I surely heard came instead from within me.

"Will we be able to see the water before dark?" I asked eagerly, near pleading for permission to shuck my pack and scramble through the trees to witness this phenomenon that covered most of the earth, that so many others had already seen.

"You may have to wait until morning," Mr. Cottrell answered. "We still have to set up the tents, and once night comes it's easy to get lost out here."

The road at last brought us to the campsite, where we kindled a fire in a shallow pit in the sand. We pitched both tents, one for Stacy and her mother, another for me and Mr. Cottrell, then cooked foil-wrapped potatoes on the embers and warmed canned beans in a blackened skillet. After supper we sat outside the tents, letting the fire cool to a red pulse beneath charred wood, darkness pushing in now, closer than the forest, almost absorbing us. Above the trees a few stars glimmered through ocean haze, diffused, like drops of oil coming apart on the surface of water.

The campaign for reelection, or at least his desire to escape it for a time, had brought Sheriff Cottrell here, and knowing only what Stacy had told me, I asked him what he thought.

"Several candidates want the job," he said. "First come the party primaries in August. Then the general election in November. Emory Patrick should win the other primary. He's a very wealthy man. Owns the chemical company and an interest in the mills. Whoever faces him in the general election will have a tough fight."

"I've seen his signs along some of the roads," I said. "He's even taken out billboards."

Mr. Cottrell only nodded, staring into the fire.

Something about this matter bothered me, but I wasn't sure how to approach it and continued to circle. "I've seen the others with signs, too. Handing out bumper stickers and flyers."

"It should be a close race," he asserted, distantly, as though answering some thought of his own.

I cleared my throat. "Are you holding back for something?"

He raised his face to me then, features varnished a weak orange from the fire, his figure pressed forward in relief from the blackness that seemed on the verge of pouring around from behind and consuming him. He raised one eyebrow, a single muscle contraction that twisted his expression into one of plaintive amusement, and I recoiled, afraid that I had insulted him. But he said, "You'd make an astute politician. Those others are shaking every tree and turning every stone looking for the votes, and I haven't so much as tacked up a sign or poster. And here I sit three hundred miles from Assembly Shoals, the primaries less than a month away."

"You needed time to yourself." Mrs. Cottrell spoke in a low, maternal tone, as though her husband had been groping for justification, reassurance.

"That's part of it," he replied. Then to me, "And part of it is I can't match someone like Emory Patrick dollar for dollar in a political campaign. It was a long time before I paid off the debt that piled up the first time I ran. Now, as an incumbent I get a few small contributions from friends, but you can't expect more in a town the size of Assembly Shoals, and the money that does come in isn't much to work with. So I have to wait, and spend what I can a few weeks before the election.

"But maybe waiting is the best thing. Usually, one of two things can happen to someone who's held public office for several years. People can get suspicious, or feel that you've grown haughty in the job, and they'll want you out. Or they get used to you and won't vote against you because it's unpleasant, like firing someone. I'm not sure yet which is happening. You see, Jeff, my past performance has become an issue in this election. Not that I mind, and people have a right to make a change if they don't like what they've seen. But I'm left in a position of watching the other candidates storm the fort, and when folks have heard the noise, they'll turn to me and ask, 'What have you got to say to that?' Then I'll answer for it best I can."

"It just boils my blood," Mrs. Cottrell said, voice kinetic like a taut, plucked string. "They don't realize how hard he's worked and the good things he's done. And mind you, it isn't the voters and your next-door neighbors and the everyday people on the sidewalk that started thinking they needed a new sheriff. It's these others in the race, fighting like a pack of starved dogs over the soup bone. There's nothing there, but they'll gnaw on it anyway because it's all they've got."

"In politics," Mr. Cottrell said, "it doesn't matter how a thing gets started, a rumor or an accusation, because you can't stop it once it's going. You either hang on and hope it passes or let it roll over you, and sometimes it rolls over you anyway. So all that matters is that people are thinking maybe someone else could do better."

Stacy's voice snapped next to me. "How can they think something like that? How can they believe it?"

"It's the nature of the job, honey. You don't even have to perform poorly at it. If people don't see significant changes, if things look the same as always, they start listening to someone who promises to go in and uncover the manure and shovel it out. Everyone loves a show."

Stacy sighed, then clipped the breath, muttering, "Well, they're all bastards—"

Across the low fire, a flashlight flicked on in Mr. Cottrell's hand. The beam searched for an instant, then found Stacy's face and came to rest there. "Stacy, I won't have that—"

She squinted in the white glare, tilting her head where she sat cross-legged on the ground. She raised a hand in front of her face, palm outward. "That hurts my eyes."

The light disappeared. A gust off the ocean whirled lightly again through the trees, not a sleepy, pine-softened whisper that at night often brushed the ridge and Forrest's house, but a drier, unfamiliar breeze that rus-

tled palm and clattered leaves of magnolia and seemed
to carry something greater than sleep behind it.

"Sometimes," Mr. Cottrell said, "people want to
hear great promises and believe them."

I woke, the canvas tent walls soaked with milky light;
Mr. Cottrell slept, not snoring but rasping each breath
through his nose. My ears strained for occasional notes
of birds in the trees, the only sounds beyond the tent.
Wriggling from the sleeping bag and collecting shoes
and socks, I unzipped the tent flap and ducked outside.

Early morning had gathered gray, warm, and wind-
less. The tent where Stacy and Mrs. Cottrell slept stood
quiet. The fire had gone cold, a single tendril of smoke
curling from the pit of blackened ash. I pulled on my
shoes and started through the trees, picking a path over
the inner sand dunes, thirty feet high, the color of salt;
then through a narrow strip of meadow that separated
the inner dunes from the lower, outer dunes, spined
with sea oats. Stepping over this final obstacle, shoes
slipping deep into clean, fine sand, I stood at last at its
edge, and even here, away from forest cover, there
stirred not a trace of wind on my face—the reason no
sound tumbled from surf. The ocean lay absolutely still.

Above, a ceiling of low clouds hung dense, leaden,
pressing down air until I could almost feel its weight
on my shoulders. Far over the water these clouds broke
before a sky of pale cream, brightening before sunrise.
The ocean reflected this shifting collage, and along the
horizon sky and sea blended together and made it difficult to discern where one ended and the other began.
Above the water sloped a yawning stretch of smooth,
hard-packed beach, desert brown, littered with an irregular band of crushed shells and kelp where the ocean

had reached high tide and then receded during the night.

Stumbling from the low dunes onto firm beach, I walked toward the ocean. With this broad, empty expanse before me, I grew impatient and began to run; and arriving at the water's edge, I turned up the beach and continued running, invigorated by discovery and solitude and the enormity that could be perceived in a single glance.

I saw waves now but nothing more than ripples that crested and slapped like water tossed from a bucket. I stripped off my shirt, and sweat soon clung to me, coating my skin in the humidity. Ahead, a twisted, spindling form rested on the barren sand, and, calves and thighs tightening like fists, heart pounding against ribs, I vowed to reach it before stopping. The object loomed finally as a great shape of driftwood—bathed in brine, salt-cured, the smoothed skeleton of a tall tree. A thick trunk was suspended on its side at my waist level by limbs sunken into sand where the tide had left it to the air and sun. I collapsed against the tree, and when my lungs had drawn full again, I sat to pull off my shoes for a swim.

Looking over the ocean and still breathing heavily, I felt wrenched suddenly by sickening curiosity. Could my parents have died off this same shore? Seething blood constricted my throat, swelling the skin of my face, and I was shocked by a surge of shame I hadn't felt in many years. My fascination shamed me, and the smell of the ocean soured my stomach, and I could not believe immersion in that water was anything other than cold, black, horrible.

But to defeat tears that pressed around my eyes I waded hip deep, then plunged, surfacing again and tossing aside dripping forelocks with a jerk of my head. Sand and sweat dissolved from my skin. The warm water felt heavy somehow, not buoyant, as though it held no life, not like churning surf that hisses white, foaming with air. I swam out, fifty yards or more, draining my mind with physical exertion, until another, more pleasant thought came to me that I might be swimming in water that had flowed here from the Cahala, that every river and stream, though feeding maybe into some larger migration, eventually, irresistibly finds a way to the ocean. This thought elated me; I dove to touch the gritty sea floor, then pushed myself up again, until, tiring from treading water, I stroked for shore, finally clambering in sodden shorts onto the beach, clean, salty-wet, exhausted.

The sky had become pink above parting clouds and seared white at the ocean's horizon, where the sun bubbled like a molten drop gathering on the rim of earth and slowly falling upward. Retrieving my shirt and drying with it, I noticed a distant figure approaching me the way I had come on the gradual, sweeping curve of the beach. Stacy neared, barefoot at the edge of the water.

"I followed your footprints," she called from twenty feet. "I heard you get up. Thought I'd never catch up to you." A frown lined her brow when she stopped in front of me. "You went swimming."

I nodded and passed the damp shirt over my face again.

"It's no good now," she said. "There's almost no waves. There aren't *any* waves."

"It was all right. I'd been running. How'd you sleep?"

"Like a rug. I was finished after all that traveling

yesterday. The mosquitoes got fat on me, though. This tree is huge."

She had scrambled into the driftwood tree, gripping bare limbs as she balanced herself on the trunk.

"I wonder how it got here," I said. "I mean, if it could've come from the mountains, from home. A storm could've washed it into the river."

"No, that's too far."

"But what if it did? It could be the same tree you climbed in somewhere else."

"I don't think so."

Her rejection of my theory disappointed me, but she did not understand.

"You want to go farther up the beach or head back?" I asked.

Mr. Cottrell had stoked the fire to prepare breakfast, she told me, so we started for camp. It was not light-hearted happiness I felt now but the contentment of new-found knowledge, not the sense that existence was untroubled but that somehow it occurred within a proper and orderly scheme. As we walked along the beach, the patient tide beginning another advance, I became overwhelmed by the conviction that I belonged, to Stacy and to everything. "How do you think it would be," I blurted to her, "if you knew everyone, and knew what they did, and could walk up to anyone on any street in the world and just start talking to them?"

Stacy stared at me for a moment, then shrugged, looking past me to water that glared with low sun. "I guess that sounds nice. But it isn't possible."

"Think about it, though. I went swimming right here, and someone else thousands of miles away could be swimming in the same ocean at this same moment."

"What makes you think of something like that?"

"I don't know. It's just that even if you're by yourself, it seems hard to feel alone here."

We camped at the island for three days before returning to Assembly Shoals. I helped Mr. Cottrell post campaign signs in willing store windows and friendly yards; he won the August primary by a narrow margin, with Emory Patrick winning the other primary as expected. In all, the rest of the summer would have been unremarkable if not for the day Forrest and I went fishing.

A quarry near town had been abandoned for many years, left to flood with deep, apple-green rainwater that mirrored limestone bluffs, and the state had later stocked the lake with bass and bream. We prowled the rocks along the water until dark and caught twenty fish between us; when we arrived home in the pickup, I piled together a sandwich for supper and went to bed early, since sweltering work at the lumberyard loomed for me the next morning.

In my throat and stomach fluttered vague dread, and I lay suddenly awake without knowing why, as though disturbed by a dream I couldn't remember. I stared at the ceiling without seeing it, listening for any sound above the hum of crickets that carried through windows gaping in hot air. I wore nothing but undershorts, having squirmed from beneath the covers during sleep, and the damp sheet chafed my shoulder blades. I lifted my head slowly, afraid that even hair brushing the pillow would obscure a revealing noise. Over the window directly beyond my feet the curtains rustled, glowing faintly yellow from the light over the back door. I raised myself to the edge of the bed; the clock read nearly two. Standing, I paused in the middle of the room, then crept to the other window that opened onto one side of the house. My mouth tasted just like dust.

On the trees outside, an inexplicable blue light swept repeatedly from an unknown source. I stared dumbly, then every muscle wrenched as a pounding on the kitchen door burst through the hallway and seemed to shatter the house. The dread inside me flashed through my body and numbed my skin; with heart roaring in mouth and ears I dashed from the bedroom, into the hallway, through the living room, all in darkness. In the kitchen I saw the blue light again, sweeping into the windows from the driveway, and a brighter beam streaming in, sliced by blinds into separate flat rays. I raced to the door and swung it open.

Only later did I wonder what might have happened had someone else been at the door, had it been Stacy, for instance, and me appearing in nothing but under-shorts; though I'd not thought to turn on the kitchen light, I stood dazzled and exposed by a pair of headlights that flooded the doorway. In other circumstances it might have been humorous. But a uniformed figure stood before me, the screen door propped open against his body; behind him a patrol car idled, blue lights spinning insistently on top. His head lowered as he glanced at my state of dress; then he looked directly at me, rubbing his nose. "Are you the only one at home, sir?" he asked. His voice was unenergetic, though level and official.

I could not see his face against the lights from out-side. "No," I answered. "I mean, my uncle's here."

"I see. What about your parents? Are they at home?"

"I don't have any parents. They're dead."

He stood silent and motionless for a moment before leaning forward in the doorway, studying me. "You're Jeff Waters?"

"Yes."

"I saw you play football in high school," he said in a tone that indicated an apology. "I have to ask that you and your uncle bring the barest essentials you need to leave the house and follow me to the highway."

My mind swam through this request. I stared past him to the patrol car, then again at his shadowed features outlined in the light at his back. "Leave the house?"

At that moment the light in the kitchen blazed on, and I wheeled, still squinting from the headlights. Forrest lowered his hand from the wall switch and entered the kitchen from the living room. He wore a stiff-legged pair of blue jeans, the fabric of his pajamas poking out at the waist. A flannel shirt hung unbuttoned across his broad chest, and he had rolled the sleeves to his elbows. His calloused feet were bare. Forrest's hands found his hips. "What's going on?" he muttered deeply.

The young man took one step forward, standing just inside the door, letting the screen close softly against his hand. Moving away from him, I saw the insignia of a sheriff's deputy on his sleeve, the shirt heavily stained under the arms. His face was clear now but unfamiliar, oddly reddened but pasty-white underneath, as though he'd been standing too close to a fire. Darkened eyelids drooped, and I wondered if he might fall asleep standing. His voice, however, did not waver. "You're going to have to move out. We're going to have to evacuate you folks, and I wish I could say for how long but I just don't know."

"Evacuate?" said Forrest. "Why?"

"The chemical plant went up, sir," the deputy answered. "I'm afraid they're losing it."

10

"We'll be along," Forrest said.

"No," answered the deputy. "I have to make sure everyone leaves."

"Get some clothes," Forrest ordered quietly after a pause.

When I realized he was speaking to me, I obeyed. Passing from the kitchen into the still-darkened living room, I heard the deputy say, "If there's no one outside of town you can stay with, we'll be setting up a shelter in the Summit High School gym. Food and cots."

"We have friends," Forrest said.

I dressed hurriedly and stuffed clothes and a toothbrush into a duffel bag. Forrest came down the hall, rubbing his face with his hands, no more disturbed than if he'd been wakened by an urge for a late-night sandwich. "Stick some things in there for me," he said. "We'll go to Flea's."

In a few minutes we had gathered the barest essentials and followed the deputy outside. "How do I know somebody ain't going to break into my house while I'm not here?" Forrest said.

"Nope, we're moving everyone out," the deputy told us.

Forrest grunted at that.

"Ya'll the only ones up on this ridge, aren't you?"

We told him we were. "How long since this happened?" I asked, senses slowly returning.

"Couple of hours ago. Went up like a torch. Without some wind those fumes might just squat in the valley. You go on ahead; I'll be down after." The patrol car shifted its idle, as though it was impatient for our departure.

"Let's take both cars," I said to Forrest. "I want to stop at the Cottrells', then I'll come on to Flea's later." I faced the deputy again. "You haven't evacuated all the way to the sheriff's house, have you?"

The deputy propped one arm on the car roof, the other on the open door as he waited. He spat into the dust. "No, just to the town limits, for now."

Forrest climbed into the pickup, and I drove the Mustang, Forrest leading and the deputy following me, and our procession wound its way down the dirt road to the main highway. Before we reached the valley floor I could see a yellow radiance above the trees. We stopped where the dirt road ended at the slab of highway; to the left, three miles north, I saw the fire. Flames rocketed into the air, glowing against the black undersides of smoke billows that rolled skyward and swallowed stars. An engine company hurtled past us on the highway, sirens piercing deep night with a knifing, marrow-chilling shrill. The trucks became blots against the yellow and orange flames, then shrank from view, almost as though they had driven into the heart of the fire and been consumed. I touched my tongue to dry lips.

Forrest turned right on the main highway ahead of me, and I followed; in my rearview mirror the deputy cut his blue lights and pulled out of dust settling over our road. Then he too sped toward town to disappear into the conflagration. We passed the Owenses' house, dark and empty, its occupants vacationing for the week. A few miles beyond I turned off the highway for the Cottrell house. Out here lights illuminated many windows; two or three people stood atop front steps or out on lawns, rubbing their eyes, watching distant, glowing smoke rise above the valley. When I reached the Cottrell house by the river, every light burned. "Oh, it's you, Jeff," Mrs. Cottrell said at the door. "I thought maybe—" Her voice drifted away, muted by unutterable possibilities, her stare lingering beyond my shoulders into the night.

"They made us leave," I said. "It doesn't look like there's too much to worry about here. Fire's a long way off."

She composed herself again. "Come on in." It was an order, not an invitation; she ushered me inside with a stiff sweep of her arm.

Stacy sat on the couch beneath the front windows, poised uneasily on the edge of the cushion, cradling a cup of coffee with both hands. She wore a nightgown and robe, her bare ankles crossed in front of her. Looking at me blearily, she released her right hand from the cup, fingers massaging the corner of one eye.

"Hi," I said. "Thought you hated coffee."

"I do." Her words were almost slurred. "I can't stand it, but I had to have something."

I sat next to her and put an arm around her shoulders. "You okay?"

She closed her eyes, then looked at me and nodded. "Mom just woke me up a few minutes ago. I can't believe she was letting me sleep."

"They won't get close if it's too dangerous," I offered.

"I wish there was something we could do."

"I can stay, if you need me to."

Mrs. Cottrell had entered from the porch and stood now before the couch. "You're so nice to offer. But you don't have to stay unless you want to. You know you're welcome." Then her face became alarmed. "Oh Lord, Jeff, do you even *have* a place to stay? I wasn't even thinking. Of course you can stay here—"

"Forrest has a friend who'll put us up," I said.

"Are you sure?"

"Yes, ma'am. But I don't want to leave if you need somebody in the house."

"We'll be all right," Stacy said.

"We can call, I suppose," Mrs. Cottrell said, "if we need you."

"This guy doesn't have a phone. But I'll come back as soon as it's daylight."

I often believed Flea Sturkey belonged in an asylum. The rest of the time I supposed he was as sane as anyone else and simply enjoyed making people think he was crazy. The power lines and red-clay, overgrown road eventually found his house in the southern hills of the county; it was a split-log cabin, actually, squatting in what purported to be a clearing. Rusted shells of cars rested on concrete blocks, weeds pushing up through broken-out windshields. The grass grew waist-high all around the cabin, and Flea never cut it, simply hacking out a path with a scythe where he thought he might have left something he needed. This was a dangerous business, since snakes traversed freely through his yard.

Flea had played halfback on the Assembly Shoals High School football team with Forrest—miniature but could scamper, Forrest told me. He often went fishing with us, but he was the worst fisherman I'd ever seen. I never knew how he made a living. When I was a young boy, he had convinced me that he ate snake meat as a staple food. He had pan-fried a garden snake for proof.

Dim lights laced the windows when I pulled up beside Forrest's pickup, and as I climbed from my car, a voice ripped loose in the cabin. "Who the *hell* is it now?"

"It's me," I told him, banging on the screen door. It rattled in the jamb.

"Go away! Just get the *hell* away from here! What's with you people barging in and waking me up in the middle of the night? I ought to blow your head off with my twelve-gauge!"

I peered through the rust-blackened screen that bulged outward in its frame, then opened the door and entered the low-ceilinged cabin. Flea didn't even own a shotgun. He sprang to his feet and grabbed me by the shirt, pulling me across the room. His hair fell to his shoulders as usual, the number of black and gray strands about equal now. His beard was long and unbarbered, and a meadow of swirling hair covered his chest and arms and even his back. He wore a dusty pair of fatigue trousers and battered basketball shoes. The top of his head didn't reach my eye level.

Forrest sat passively in the remains of an uphol-stered chair that oozed stuffing from half a dozen lacerations. The fingers of one hand loosely surrounded the sweating dark glass of an open beer bottle on the chair arm.

"Look at this runt," Flea said, bringing me forth for inspection. "When's he going to grow? I want to know when's he going to grow? You play football, you say?" He pointed at Forrest. "You remember when we played football? By God, we could show these young loggerheads something about playing football. Weren't those the days?"

Forrest chuckled once, more at Flea than at anything Flea said. Then Forrest's eyes deepened, only a trace of smile remaining. "Yeah, those were some days."

A dulling sensation of lack of sleep, when blood turns to syrup, had overtaken me. "Let go, wild man," I said. "Is it okay if we stay the night?" I went to the hammock he'd strung up in one corner of the room, climbing in, swaying gently.

"I want to know when's he going to put some meat on?" Flea said. "He ought to drink beer. I drink beer."

"And it's done wonders for your growth," I said.

He rubbed his lean belly and grinned. "Made me hairy."

"Can I sleep up here?" I asked.

"You can sleep there," Forrest said.

I lay on my back and weighted lids slipped over my eyes.

"So the whole damn place went *whoosh*?" I heard Flea whisper, dramatically, as though trying to draw out every detail from Forrest. That was all I remembered.

Nothing seemed familiar when I woke. I heard a sizzling, and sharp light outside stabbed my eyes, dilated with sleep. At last I recognized the scene beyond the window of Flea's cabin, with sun glaring straight down on the leaves, and I spilled out of the hammock onto the floor, landing on my side.

"Watch it, stick," Flea said. "That's a genuine wood floor you're beatin' your body against. Don't suppose such a light blow would do it no harm, though." He stood at his electric stove, cackling to himself, scraping a spatula along the bottom of a deep frying pan that spattered grease and spewed wisps of smoke toward the ceiling.

I yanked myself to my feet, head heavy, face swollen from too much sleep. "What time is it?"

" 'Bout twelve-thirty," he said.

"Damn," I breathed. "In the *afternoon?*"

"Don't know. Could be midnight, but I wasn't ever too good at telling time by the sun."

Forrest emerged from the tiny bathroom, plumbing whining as water escaped down the toilet. He looked at me, pressing back his hair with his hand.

"Forrest, I've got to leave," I said. "I told Stacy I'd be back by morning."

"Hey!" Flea called. "What about breakfast? How're you going to grow without eatin' breakfast?"

"I really can't. What is that *smell*, anyway?"

"Beer omelet."

When I reached the Cottrells', however, I discovered the time for alarm had passed. In the front hallway Mrs. Cottrell pulled a plastic cleaner's bag over the mud- and greased-splotched sheriff's uniform on a hanger. "Two or three firemen were sent to the hospital," she explained. "Smoke and fume inhalation, you know. The plant was a total loss. And there were more explosions, Grant said, and the phone ringing all night and, Lord, just everything." She draped the uniform over one arm and sighed, her face weary. "I'm just relieved no one was seriously hurt. He's asleep now. He didn't get home until an hour ago. Let me go up and tell Stacy you're here. I don't want to shout for her; I might wake her father."

So it turned out that the broiling, billowing cloud of chemical fumes didn't become trapped in the valley, instead rising straight into the atmosphere above Assembly Shoals to dissipate harmlessly over the mountains. For days afterward the curious could be seen venturing along the outside of a high chain-link fence, gazing at mounds of charred rubble and heat-deformed steel. Mr. Cottrell remained silent about the fire, repeating official department statements even to the family, particularly when the Assembly Shoals *Appalachian Herald* reported that the sheriff's office suspected arson, and we knew better than to ask him about it. There were articles in which the plant's owner, Emory Patrick, charged that local authorities, headed by a county sheriff who had "trouble keeping his own kids in tow," were conducting an unproductive investigation.

He visited the Cottrell home two nights before Stuart and I were to return to the university for the start of football practice. Stacy and I were seated before the television when he appeared at the door; from the rear of the house Mr. Cottrell had seen him arrive and approached from behind us as we answered the knock. Emory Patrick was a bulbous, disproportioned man, the trousers of a seersucker suit swelling around his thick girth, then bagging over spindly legs, skin showing pale and blue-veined as his strides up the front steps tugged high-cropped hems above the tops of his socks. A white shirt hung damply on his body, sleeves rolled above varicose elbows, coat slung over one arm, loose tie dangling from a neck that merged with his jawline somewhere within the folds of a double chin. Stubble darkened a hot, red face, his chin and forehead glistening with perspiration. Plastered against his scalp lay thin, slick strands of black hair, and he clutched a sweat-stained hat by the brim. He seemed no friend to a humid summer. "Need to speak with you, Sheriff," he said in the doorway.

"Fine, Emory," Mr. Cottrell said. "Why don't we sit on the porch? Angela's fixing lemonade, if you'd like some."

We then understood the gravity of this meeting. Mr. Cottrell used the front porch only for sheer relaxation or the most serious consultations. He eased the screen door shut, and we heard their feet tread across the wooden porch floor outside, saw their figures shuffling past sheer curtains over the living room windows.

"C'mon," Stacy urged. She turned down the television and led me to the couch beneath the windows.

"Stacy," I whispered, "he's going to know."

We dropped to the couch, her stare fixed to the television screen across the room, but her face intent on every word uttered outside. I put my arm around Stacy's shoulders and risked a glance through the window. Behind us, obscured but visible through thin fabric, Mr. Cottrell sat in the porch swing, his boots planted squarely on the floor, hands resting on thighs. He slowly, almost imperceptibly rocked the swing, so gently that the chains suspending it from the ceiling didn't creak. The light above him glared harshly, drawing moths that flicked manically against the bulb. Mr. Cottrell never seemed to notice us, instead staring at Emory Patrick, whom I could not see directly behind me on the other side of the window. I heard wicker fibers straining as he shifted his weight in a porch chair. Their conversation could not have been clearer had they been sharing the couch with us.

"—and it's been two weeks now," Mr. Patrick said, "and none of your people can tell me anything. You claim someone burned my plant to the ground, but you have no idea who it was. This is a devastating loss—not just for me but for the whole community. People suddenly out of work, clients losing production time looking for new suppliers. Just devastating."

Mrs. Cottrell appeared from the kitchen with a pair of drinking glasses on a serving tray. She went out onto the porch and said, "Excuse me, but would you gentlemen care for some lemonade? It's been so hot out lately."

"Thank you, ma'am," Mr. Patrick said. " 'Preciate it."

"Thank you, honey," said Mr. Cottrell.

A pause followed, filled only by ice clinking as the men turned up their glasses and lowered them again. Mrs. Cottrell came back inside, face tense until she noticed me and Stacy; she stared at us quizzically, then pointed to the empty tray in her hand. "You two want some lemonade?"

We shook our heads.

"Sound on the TV's awfully low."

"We can hear it fine, Mom," Stacy said in a barely audible tone.

"I mixed plenty of lemonade, if you want it." She glanced fretfully out at the porch and left the room for the kitchen.

Ice clinked again, more clearly, as when no liquid

is left in a glass. "That was good lemonade," Mr. Patrick said. "You tell Mrs. Cottrell she makes good lemonade."

Stacy's face burned, and she silently, acidly mimicked the words "That was good lemonade."

I peered again through the window. Mr. Cottrell held the same posture, slowly rocking the swing, holding his glass in his lap with both hands. "Yes, she does. I'll tell her."

Behind us I heard Emory Patrick place his glass on the porch floor, wicker straining with the movement. When he spoke again, his voice was lower, secretive, as though afraid Mrs. Cottrell might still be within earshot of unsuitable words. Apparently he never suspected our presence inside the window. "Now, Sheriff," he said, "I want to speak not only as a constituent and a citizen but also as a candidate for the office which you hold. I feel this is exactly the type of inefficiency that has been allowed to creep into the sheriff's office in this county. It's simply a shame—tragedy, really—when a man is faced with the direct effects of the worst calamity this town has seen in many, many years and cannot expect the law enforcement agencies responsible for his security to concentrate their most intensive efforts toward bringing proper retribution for the act and insuring that such a thing will not happen again."

He stopped, and I pictured a saliva-jowled hound panting in summer shade under a porch after beating out a long run in the heat. I strained my eyes in their sockets until they ached, trying to glimpse Mr. Patrick behind me without betraying my intent. Stacy continued to stare at the muted television screen, her ears so red I would not have been surprised had they been hot to the touch. The wicker chair groaned once more, and after a moment we learned that Mr. Patrick had retrieved a handkerchief from his pocket; he blew his nose loudly. Turning again to the television, I heard him lean forward to replace the handkerchief.

Mr. Cottrell remained silent so long I wondered if he'd left the porch. Finally he cleared his throat, having waited, it seemed, for Emory Patrick to vent his steam. "I can assure you," Mr. Cottrell said, "we are doing everything we can to find out who was responsible for that fire and to protect other businesses from the same tragedy. The evidence collected seems to indicate arson. I must say I share your concern and that we're doing our best."

Mr. Patrick said, "I just hope the results of your efforts prove out your assurances."

The chains of the porch swing jangled, and the wicker chair squeaked with the relief of pressure in the seat; both men had risen to their feet.

"I would wish good luck to you," Mr. Patrick said, "but that's being a little two-faced in an election. So I'll just say I hope the winner of this race will be the man most capable of serving as sheriff of Summit County. Don't you think that's a fair thing to say?"

"Yes, I do," Mr. Cottrell said. "I think that's perfectly fair."

Heavy footsteps descended the porch steps. "I'll be in touch," Mr. Patrick called, not cordially and almost as a warning, his voice more distant now, coming from the yard.

Stacy tugged at my shirtsleeve, and we hurried to the other couch where we had originally been seated in front of the television. She had turned up the volume again and fallen against my arm when Mr. Cottrell entered from the porch. We didn't turn to look at him.

As he passed behind the couch, his hand came to rest on Stacy's shoulder. "Stick to law. I'm afraid you'd starve as a private detective."

Stacy slumped in the seat, arms crossed defiantly, her brow furrowed with dark lines, blood pooled beneath her face. At last she snapped her head around in the direction her father had been moving. "Dad, he's a—"

But Mr. Cottrell had already retreated into the kitchen. The screen door to the back steps bumped softly shut.

When I left that night, I saw behind the house a light still burning in the woodshop windows, and the drone of the lathe carried far out over the river and the valley.

11

On campus, summer held a tenacious grip as we lugged ourselves around the practice field before the start of my sophomore season. Sessions were conducted in early morning, grass heavy with cool dew, and again in late afternoon after the sun had begun a torturously slow descent to relieve us with shadows. The trainer handed out water bottles and kept hoses ready to douse the poorly conditioned who fell out of drills in serious danger of heat prostration. After several days of this labor the coaches named me first-string quarterback for another year.

The swelter continued into September and through the first two games, finally breaking at month's end. Leaves withered and fell without any fanfare of color, collecting in gutters as a late hurricane spun off the Gulf of Mexico and dumped rain across the Southeast, even as far north as the university, soaking a plaster of decay until groundskeepers could scrape it away. Autumn progressed rapidly after that and finally that first outward plunge from dormitory foyers each morning brought breaths of mist; and the slice of warmth each afternoon narrowed and faded in shrinking days, until cold settled into the air and under skin for the duration of winter.

The cold had already crept into the masonry of our dorm room when the phone jangled before dawn one November Wednesday. Across the room Stuart lifted his tousled head, squinting at a frosted window and gray new light beyond, then groaned and twisted his bulk on the bed to face the wall, coiling himself in blankets, leaving me to answer. I had studied American history the night before, and the names and events had dissolved in the murk of dark sleep, so my brain sloshed now like a sodden sponge in a skullful of alphabet soup. I felt oddly detached from the tingle of floor beneath bare feet. "Hello?" I said, baritone from relaxed vocal cords.

"It's me," Stacy said. "Mom called from home a minute ago."

Slowly, like the float to the surface of a pool after a deep dive, I remembered the date and why she would be calling.

"He won," she laughed. "Dad is still sheriff of Summit County."

I smiled, rubbing my eyes, clutching my arms across the thin T-shirt covering my chest. "I knew he would, Stacy. I was sure of it."

The final count had been close, and later when I found an opportunity to ask Mr. Cottrell about it, he said, "People will surprise you, Jeff. Emory Patrick attacked me so often, hoping I guess to blow smoke where there wasn't much fire, that some people thought it was unfair. Anyway, that's what I hear from most folks that come around and talk to me about it. This town's small enough still that it can feel like a family sometimes. And if one member of the family accuses another unfairly, the family will usually react against the dissension. A lot of people believed what Emory Patrick said. But there were enough that thought I should stay."

It became an autumn of vindication, not only for Sheriff Cottrell but also for our football team, which surprised the conference by winning seven and losing only four. The record earned us an invitation to a postseason bowl game, and in December they all made the trip to Atlanta—the Cottrells, the Owenses, and Forrest, who appeared the night before the contest at the hotel where the team had been put up. Following dinner the players had drifted into the polished-marble lobby, browsing the newsstand or dumping themselves into thick sofas and lounge chairs arranged under chandeliers. I saw Forrest standing against a wall across the room, a newspaper in one hand; he motioned for me. He opened the paper and flipped through it, not reading, instead glancing over the top of the page at people milling about the lobby. He wore charcoal-colored trousers, a dark blue blazer, and a red knit pullover shirt. The collar of the shirt stood upturned on one side of his neck; he seemed to chafe in these unfamiliar clothes. He was clean-shaven, a heavy scent of aftershave lingering on him. When I approached, he closed the newspaper, folding it along the crease, then folding it again and tucking it under his arm. His hands opened the jacket, found the front pockets of his trousers, and buried themselves there.

 "When did you make it in?" I asked. "I didn't expect

to see you until after the game. Some hotel, don't you think?"

"They're doing you right," he said, eyes darting glances around the room again. "I've been visiting some people."

"The Cottrells are looking for you. They'd like you to sit with them."

"I've got my seat. So how do you feel?"

Immediately I grew defensive: Forrest never solicited information about my health. "What do you mean?"

"The game. Are you ready?"

"Yeah, I hope. Is your stomach upset or something?"

"No—"

"Fix your collar."

His knotty fingers absently fumbled with the collar but never managed to tuck it under his lapel.

"You want an antacid?" I asked.

"No, I'm fine. We have a good team, you know. You're going to win it. The papers here have you picked as the favorites."

"I don't know, Forrest. It's going to be tough. Why are you so nervous?"

"You'll win. You've got to feel good about winning it."

I shrugged. "I suppose." For some reason I fought his suggestion of confidence.

"What kind of attitude is that—"

"The coaches tell us a thousand times a day not to underestimate any opponent."

"But you *can* win it?"

"If we play well—"

Forrest nodded and wiped a palm across his mouth. "Listen," he said, "how much do you think you're going to win it by?"

My chest tightened with a spasm, and I reeled, suddenly afraid of him. "I don't know," I said, voice reverberating in a darkening tunnel, Forrest blocking any escape. "How would I know that? What difference does it make anyway?"

He shifted his newspaper to the other arm, surveying the room once more; we were alone on that side of the lobby. "It makes a difference," he said, "if there's money on the game."

Dinner hardened like cement in my stomach, skin chilling in a sudden draft of cold despair. "Forrest, that's not funny. Don't even talk like that."

"It makes a difference," he repeated, his tone becoming explanatory, as if the reason for my disbelief might be ignorance of a point spread.

"No kidding it makes a difference!" I blurted, my voice bounding an octave. I imagined every pair of eyes in the lobby staring at us, and I turned to see. No one appeared even mildly interested. "Forrest, don't talk like that." I pleaded with him now in hissing whispers. "Do you know how much trouble we could get into by your saying something like that?"

"I'm not asking you to lose the game."

"*Forrest—*"

"You're not going to throw the game," he said, voice calm. "You're going to win, aren't you? What does it matter to you by how much? If you can win by less than ten—"

"Stop it!" I told him. I was certain he wasn't drunk, but I wanted to grab his arm, shove him into an empty room and barricade the door so no one would hear. "Shut up, I'm telling you," I said, rambling now. "This is crazy. Who put you up to this? Just shut up, okay?"

"I could do real well with this," he said.

Anger bled through the fear. "How could you even ask me to do something like that?" I snapped. "You just forget it. I can't believe you." I began to back away from him, shame sickening me, and Forrest suddenly became the image of a stranger, someone I'd never known before.

"Win by nine," he said.

I pivoted on my heel and staggered away, head quivering in disbelief and denial. Forrest had for the first time violated the family bond; he had used our common blood as justification to ask my collusion in something of which I could not possibly be a part. Abruptly I noticed Stuart standing before me.

"Hey," he said, "Forrest was over there a second ago."

I heard myself say, "He had to leave."

Stuart eyed me gravely for a moment. "You look pale. You aren't getting sick, are you?"

"No," I lied.

I turned anger and shame outward, sprinting onto the field that next day with a single and consuming purpose of putting every possible point on the board. I threw for two touchdowns, and when the receivers were covered, I pinned the ball under my arm and slashed the line myself—"Never seen you move your feet like that," Mr. Owens told me afterward—clenching my teeth into the mouthguard and ducking into tacklers the way one of our bull-shouldered halfbacks would have done, taking the helmet-ringing jolt head-on. No doubt would be left—not to anyone watching or, most important, to me—that I had played with everything. We won it, twenty-eight to ten, and when it was over I sank to the floor in front of my locker, unclasping shoulder pad straps, the last ounce of steamed blood cooled and spent. After I showered and dressed, Forrest was nowhere to be found.

I did not see him again until I returned home for Christmas vacation a week later, on an oily-dark late Friday night, when I found him in the kitchen brewing coffee. His breath streamed sharp from a mass of cinnamon gum—a flavor he often chewed to cover the smell of liquor. Foil wrappers littered the kitchen table; he'd heard me drive up. Glancing at me as I dropped my bags to the floor, he rubbed his face and poured a cup of coffee from the percolator. He sipped and swallowed around the gum, leaning against the counter. "You home for a while now?" he asked.

I only nodded at first, fearful of this conversation, my hatred of him quelled now, my only desire to forget the whole incident. I didn't even want him to apologize. "It's Christmas, Forrest."

He sipped again, delicately, as though concerned that his own hand might spill coffee down his chin. "How's the car?"

"It's fine."

"Don't go anywhere tonight," he babbled.

"I'm not. I just got back."

"It's late. You don't need to be out this late. You should go to bed. I'm going to bed."

"You go on to bed. I'll lock up."

"Good night." He set the cup on the counter, turned, and walked an admirably straight path from the kitchen.

Coffee before bed meant he'd been drinking, all

right; still, a melt of relief passed through me. By tacit mutual agreement I knew that the subject of his betting the bowl game would not arise between us.

I saw little of him during vacation. He even missed Christmas dinner with the Owenses; at one o'clock, with the turkey growing cold, we started without him and spoke only in subdued pleasantries as we ate. My food descended to my stomach in thick lumps.

After dinner I suppose Mr. and Mrs. Owens thought the table had been cleared, that I was sitting in the living room; but one more dish remained, and as I carried it down the short hallway to the kitchen, I heard their whispers and halted, out of sight beyond the doorway.

"I don't know if I can take this kind of thing anymore," Mrs. Owens said, voice quavering. "I really don't think I can. I just wish you'd talk to him."

"Ella," Mr. Owens reflected in measured, thoughtful, unhurried syllables, "what would I say to him?"

Dishes clattered in the sink. "Look at the example he has set for that boy! If Jeff didn't have a—a sense of common decency, there's no telling what he might be like. And for all these years we've stood by and said nothing—"

"Jeff's in college now. He's an adult. I don't see that any good will come out of making a fuss over it now. You'll only push him away."

"We should have taken him from the very beginning. We should have insisted that Forrest Dawson let us have him. 'It's what I owe my sister,' he said. If Jenny Waters had known how bad it would get with her brother, she'd have wanted Jeff with us. I know that in my heart."

I heard a squeak of plumbing, and the kitchen faucet

trickled, then sprayed, water drumming so forcefully into the sink that it almost washed out their guarded voices.

"He tried to give Jeff a home," Mr. Owens said, "a home with what was left of his own family. Jeff's old enough to know right from wrong, and he has never seemed to be any worse for having lived with his uncle. Now it's Christmas Day. Let's not spoil it."

"Yes, it's Christmas, and it's already spoiled."

I'd never known the Owenses had wanted to adopt me, and suddenly I hated two people who had never shown me anything but kindness. I hated them because they had dared suggest that one who shared my blood was unworthy. At that moment I saw Forrest only as an extension of myself, not as who he really was. Guilt thrust me from the dim hallway into the well-lighted kitchen to end this conversation. Mr. Owens turned to me, pipe in hand. His voice now came too pleasantly. "Jeff, thought you were in the living room."

Mrs. Owens shuddered at the sink, a momentary quake through a tiny figure (too slender to have borne children, Mr. Owens had told me years ago), a figure that I remembered lifting from the floor as a younger boy to prove my strength. She did not turn to face me, instead drying her hands and pinching between two fingers a tissue from her apron pocket, dabbing nose and cheeks beneath eyeglasses, slipping the tissue again to the pocket, holding her arms close to her body as though afraid I might see the motion.

"There was another dish, sir," I said.

The day soured further after supper at the Cottrells' house, when Stacy became engaged in a long telephone conversation.

"Who was that?" I asked when she came down from her room, where she had taken the call.

"Nobody."

"Nobody? You don't usually talk for half an hour to nobody."

"A friend from high school. Okay?"

"Who?"

"You don't know him."

"Him?"

Stacy faced me, her deep-green eyes flaring, then darkening until utterly cold and hostile. In that instant I became a stranger to her and this house.

"*Him*?" I repeated.

"You know," she said, "this is the kind of thing where you either trust me or you don't."

"I just asked a simple question. You'd tell me unless there's something to hide."

"I told you already it was nothing." She spoke as if snipping off each word with scissors. "So let's just not talk about it anymore."

But a boil of pride already rolled inside me; my dignity, assailed by the insults I'd overheard at the Owenses', swelled to meet this new threat. By God, I did not need deceit from her."This isn't the first time this has happened. Why don't you just come out and admit you're seeing someone else?"

She set her palms flat against her hips and fought to steady a trembling chin. "I can't believe you said that."

"You'd better tell me who you're seeing." Sweat burned at my temples.

"I can have a phone conversation without telling *you* every detail."

"Well, you can sure as hell not expect me to sit

around reading the magazines while you conduct your social life."

"It was *nobody*—" her teeth clamped her lip, eyes gleaming with a film of moisture. "I've been thinking, maybe—maybe we're a little tired of each other."

I would tolerate no more. Without a word to Mr. or Mrs. Cottrell I stalked from the house and into the frigid, cloudy night. Reaching the yard, I balked, zipping my jacket, watching strands of Christmas tree lights beckon from the front window, summoning an excuse to drop the subject and march back up the porch steps. But my body, propelled by a fuel of self-righteousness, strode to the car, and once I had started the engine and pulled away from the driveway, I decided my body had been right.

I could not understand Stacy's refusal to answer my accusations, unless, I concluded, my suspicions were correct. I resolved not to make any first effort at reconciliation, though I often had to remove myself from the presence of a phone.

Christmas vacation passed; I did not even offer her a ride back to the university. School reconvened with only a few awkward, infrequent, and accidental meetings between us. It became a contest between stubborn wills; and the longer I waited before seeking her out again, the more I believed the one who spoke first stood to lose. Stuart kept watch on her; more important to him even than finding me a girlfriend was aiding his gender in wars of nerves with capricious females. I didn't recruit him as a spy, but I didn't refuse the information either.

"There's usually some guy with her," he reported, "but not the same one for long. Don't you give any ground, pal. Just let her play her game."

I approached other girls that winter, some through Stuart's introduction and others who had previously attracted my interest even when I had been dating Stacy. In fact, I plotted for Stacy to see me with them, escorting them to her familiar haunts—the main library, the dining hall, and on weekends the pizzeria in town. But Stacy remained dispassionate, quickly stifling a momentary spark of surprise whenever she caught sight of me, looking away again as though she had glimpsed merely another unknown face in the bustle. I would retreat, sullen and frustrated by my own vindictive tactics.

By the time mild winter had merged into spring in a blur of warm rain I had grown accustomed to the separation and even enjoyed the freedom, left now to see whom I pleased and, at the coaches' blunt insistence, to rescue a few sliding grades. I had not spoken to Stacy for a month when the time arrived for spring football practice. It was my custom to stay a few minutes after each practice to take extra throws, and one clear afternoon following two days of rain I was again the last to leave the field. The grounds outside the locker room were deserted; dropping my helmet and the duffel bag of footballs beside me, I flopped onto the wooden bench near the door to unlace mud-encrusted cleats. Sounds of showers, raucous male voices, banging lockers rang from the high ceiling inside.

Movement flickered in one eye, and I turned and saw that a figure had appeared at the corner of the building. I would have paid no attention to him had he not simply stared at me behind mirrored sunglasses. He then grew indecisive about something, peering around the building, rubbing his hands, finally returning his gaze to me.

I tugged off my shoes and struck them together to loosen the mud. My neck prickled as I sensed this stranger's observation, until slow, purposeful footsteps approached me across wet sod. I did not raise my head again until he halted before the bench; I saw only a pair of new, freshly soiled tennis shoes, toes pointing toward me. My eyes followed the length of his body. He wore jeans, a denim jacket, and above the sunglasses a blue baseball cap. His brown hair bristled from his scalp in a crew cut, and the line of a scar fell from beneath the left lens of the sunglasses, ending just below the corner of his mouth like a path of a tear. Instead of his eyes, I was confronted with twin images of myself.

The sunglasses came away in his fingers; the scar ran to the corner of his left eye, and his pupils were a remarkable and hypnotic golden-green, like sunlight lancing the surface of a clear lake. He stood with arms slightly cocked at his sides, hands poised as though ready to encircle my throat. For a moment I thought he would challenge me to a fight. Then the reason he looked so familiar sent a shiver through me.

If Stacy had been a boy, that would have been Stacy standing before me.

"Hello," he said, his voice edged with uncertainty.

"Hi," I answered. My head spun. I could not swallow.

"You're Jeff Waters?"

I nodded.

"I'd like to speak to you for a minute if that's all right."

My throat seemed packed with cotton. "I don't think I know who you are," I said thickly, not knowing why I denied the image. Perhaps I just wanted to hear him say it.

"I think you do," he told me. "I'm Bobby Cottrell."

"Oh Lord," I whispered. Still sitting, I stared at him in a whirl of bewilderment and fascination, and in that instant I was flooded with an awareness that I had eagerly hoped to meet him.

He watched me, arms at his sides, and the repose of his hands seemed forced and unnatural, as though they were tethered to his body. "I want to talk to you," he repeated finally.

I shook myself from my stare and stammered, "Sure, of course—" I rose slowly, frowning at him. "Bobby, does Stacy know you're here?"

Alarm flashed on his face, hands contracted into fists, and he glanced at his surroundings again before his eyes arrested me as surely as if he'd snatched me by the collar. "No," he said. "She can't know I'm here. If you're going to tell her, I'll have to leave."

Suddenly I feared he might turn and run. "I won't tell her, I swear it."

The locker room door burst open, and two of our massive, muscle-girded linemen plunged through, laughing and feigning punches at each other. I tensed.

"Better get ready for dinner, Ice Waters," they said, passing the bench. They acknowledged Bobby only with nods and moved on.

Bobby eyed them suspiciously, then relaxed in careful degrees.

"She won't be around," I assured him. "I want us to talk."

He nodded. "Okay."

"Wait right here," I said, lifting the duffel bag of footballs from the bench. "Don't go anywhere." Then I remembered Stuart, that he might appear through the door at any moment and start asking questions. "Tell you what's even better," I said. "Go around to the other side of the building and wait there. I'll be back in ten minutes."

He nodded again and moved around the corner.

My heart was pumping frantically. I hauled the footballs inside, showered in scant seconds, and managed to avoid Stuart altogether. Running a comb through dripping hair, I found Bobby outside leaning against the brick wall, hands now in his pockets. "We can go over to the stadium," I said, grateful for this flash of foresight. "Nobody'll be there."

He agreed, and we crossed the street and then the huge parking lot, populated by a few scattered cars this late in the day, through the gate and into the lower level of bleachers. Almost all of the seats had fallen into shadow now, except for the top rows in the upper deck that blazed metallically in oblique sunlight. The sky was dissolving from a hard, cloud-tufted blue to dusky, creamy gray. The turf in the bottom of the bowl had not fully recovered from dead winter—a rectangle of weak green water-color. I sat forward on one of the long backless benches, propping my feet on the bench below, elbows planted on thighs. With one seat between us, Bobby sat straight-shouldered, hands in his lap. A tingling breeze fanned us at the threshold of a cool night.

We remained silent at least a minute. My heart had calmed, but I hesitated to speak first, not wishing to distract him from his purpose in seeking me out. Bobby seemed enthralled by the empty field, his gaze running from goalpost to goalpost.

"I bet you like it here, don't you?" he said finally, his tone coarse with scorn.

I followed his stare. "What do you mean?"

"Well, I don't know much about sports, but everything is so easy here. Everybody plays by the same rules, and if they don't, some guy in authority runs over with a whistle and penalizes the offending player. The goal is simple—just score more points than the other team. There's no doubt about success or failure; you either move the ball across the line or you don't."

"It's only a game," I said, somehow pushed to the defensive. "It's a way for me to pay for an education."

Bobby turned to face me, leaning toward me the way he might scold a child. "Only a game. But thousands and thousands of people come here to watch it, because it's easy and simple, and they can pull for one team or the other and then *their* lives become easy and simple." He raised himself up again, tilting his head toward the open end of the stadium. "It's not like that out there, away from this—this concrete monument to simplicity."

[139]

"I guess so," I said idiotically, thrown by the implication of his reasoning and his sneer of contempt. At last I recovered, given over to curiosity. "Can I ask you something? How did you even know about me?"

He laughed—actually a nervous hiss through clenched teeth. "Stacy told me."

"But you said—"

"I haven't seen her in four years, but I call on her birthday and every Christmas."

"No!" I said.

Bobby tilted his head like a dog hearing a strange noise.

The accusations I had made to Stacy roared back to me so furiously my head pounded and eyes swam, and a burst of denial almost brought me to my feet. "I don't believe you. She would have told me."

"No, she wouldn't because I asked her not to. I told her not to tell anybody. Dad would find out."

"Bobby, I thought she'd been seeing someone else—"

He lowered his head, then looked at me again and said, as though trying to explain something much deeper than my understanding, "I've been her brother a lot longer than you've been her boyfriend."

I scowled at him, then at the long rows of empty bleachers below us, and my senses slowly regained their equilibrium, truth settling on my shoulders like the chilling, gathering dusk. "All the time it was you," I said. "We had a party on her birthday, and Stacy went upstairs and shut the door and talked for half an hour. Your mother was fuming. And all the time it was you."

Beside me he became speechless, motionless, like a sculpture. I turned to study his expression, which was fixed on space. "Mom would have been more upset had she known who it was," he said at last, distantly.

I could think only about the photographs missing from the Cottrells' living room. Together we watched light evacuate the stadium for a while.

"But if you called," I said, ending the pause, "wouldn't your parents have known it was you if they'd answered the phone?"

"No, I have different friends at the base make the call and ask for Stacy, then I get on the line—" His voice faded, and he eyed me, wondering if I'd caught the slip.

I had. "You joined the service," I said.

"Look, you can't tell anyone what I say to you. You can't even tell them I was here. Not Stacy or anybody."

"But if someone asks—"

"They won't ask. They'll never even suspect that I came to see you. They don't even know where I am. Give me your word you won't tell them."

"Bobby, if you only knew how badly they want to see you—"

"Your word."

I swallowed a long breath. "My word," I said.

He blinked at me for a moment, then the tension abandoned his darkening figure, and he seemed satisfied. "Good. I think I can trust you."

As he told me where he was stationed and of the road that had led him to the military, I thought how this explained Bobby's posture: once careening, he had allowed himself to be harnessed, but it was a false complacency, and he reminded me of the unbroken mares I'd seen on horse farms outside Assembly Shoals, horses steadied by their handlers but quivering as the saddle was slipped on, poised to flare into a whirl of high hooves and bowed neck. Something unsettling worked beneath a taut discipline of his body.

"I'm in the military police," he said. "I like totin' a weapon." A smirk spread across his face. "Totin' a gun just like Dad. I guess I'm more like him than he realizes."

I slid the sole of my tennis shoe across the gritty concrete beneath the seat. "They say you were a wild kid," I prompted.

"Who's they?" he asked, smiling. "Everybody?" He made fists of his hands and tapped knuckles together in his lap. "I did some crazy things, all right. I can't believe I did some of them now."

"Some people think you got off that burglary charge because you were the sheriff's son. Emory Patrick tried to make it an issue in the election."

"No, I didn't get off—wasn't going to, anyway, until I left. Dad set a curfew for me and was going to make me get a regular job, plus volunteer work on weekends for Mr. Thompson—the guy whose house we broke into. Everyone agreed, so it was perfectly all right. But it was too much, I couldn't handle it. All I could think of was that I had to leave—" His voice had become frenetic, almost desperate, then fell away, his face growing darkly creased as another brooding thought surfaced in the last glimmer of dusk. "And Emory Patrick can go straight to hell—"

"You must know about him."

"I didn't know about him until Stacy told me the things he said. He upset her like I've never seen. I wasn't sorry to hear that his plant burned down."

"That," I advised him, "almost cost your father the election. They never caught whoever did it."

"Well, I almost wish it had been me. I wouldn't have really done anything like that. Oh, but I did some crazy things. Dad had a new car, and I opened her up on the main highway one night, spun it off a curve and piled it around a tree." He pointed to the long scar on his face. "Nearly lost an eye."

"Can I ask you something else?" I said, enthralled by the vision of his past he'd begun to reveal.

"Sure."

"Those things you did when you were younger. Why'd you do them?"

"Why?" he repeated, as though asking the question of himself.

"What made you do them?"

"God, I don't know," he said, voice rasping now as though he were about to cry, and I felt repulsed by his sudden weakness. He continued tapping his knuckles together, head shaking as he stared across the shrouded field. "I was suffocating. You've got to understand, Mom and Dad and even Stacy are all alike. They want things that are familiar, a close family and a town where they know everyone and sitting in the same pew at church every Sunday. I swear to God they could live in that same house up in the hills and be happy forever. Anything beyond their own world just doesn't matter much. But I couldn't stand not knowing about things outside of that stagnant little mill town. Every birthday and Christmas that came along I was supposed to be having a great time, but it was just the same people celebrating the same occasions over and over again. They were strangling me and didn't even know it."

"If you were so concerned about your freedom, why did you join the military? They don't exactly encourage individual expression."

"I roamed around for a while, but I had to make a living. I've traveled in the service."

"So you want to see the world," I offered.

He turned to face me squarely. "You don't get it at all, do you? You don't understand worth a damn. Not just see the world. There's so much else out there—"

"People are pretty much the same wherever you go," I said, impressed with my own wisdom.

"Yes, they are, but at the same time they're different. I'm not sure what holds it all together. You know, I had these strange thoughts when I was a kid—if I went to another part of the world, would the sky be the same color, or would I be able to breathe the air. People that far away seemed so different I wondered if the world itself would be different where they lived. But if you don't understand already, I can't explain it."

"I think I do understand," I said, partly because I was afraid Bobby's opinion of me would diminish but also because of a deep, faint recognition that stirred inside me, somehow like the recognition I had experienced the previous summer, when I had gone swimming in the ocean for the first time.

"You can have your own family," Bobby said, "or hometown, a religion or a government, too, I guess, but there's always something—bigger. I can't explain it. I want to know where I fit in. I can't be at peace with my own family until I figure out where I fit in with the damned human race."

He shifted on the seat, leaning closer to me. Even so near I could barely distinguish his features; no lights burned in the stadium except at the open end above the main gate. The darkness that closed around us seemed to fill his eyes. I became aware of my open mouth—a cool wind stirred over parted lips—yet I could not think to order it closed. I felt drawn to those eyes, almost absorbed by them, and drawn to the knowledge that lay beyond them.

"Listen," he said, "you've never had a family—" and blood rose in my face, swelling veins in my neck, and I felt a repulsion again, not at him but at myself, a self-hatred more intense than I had ever experienced. I hated myself for not having grown up as he did, surrounded by true family.

"—you've never had a family," Bobby said, "and that's what you really want. That's what you've wanted your whole life. And you're finding it at my house. I can just see Mom and Dad bringing you in and pulling up your chair to the dining room table and making you feel welcome. I know them that way. And you love that part as much as anything else about Stacy, because you've never had it."

"What makes you so sure about all that?" I snapped, but the question hung in the air between us as an admission, not a retort.

"From the things Stacy told me, from meeting you now. I don't know, I can just see things like that." His tone was not boastful but full of sincere belief. He paused, as if waiting to see whether I accepted this explanation. "But me," he continued, "I've always had that. Maybe if I hadn't I'd be just like you. But I know what it is to have a close family, and it is important to me, though I know it doesn't seem like it after I ran from them. I'm glad I have it, only I can't help wanting to know more. The world's a much bigger place than just one family."

Though I was shocked by his frankness, he had spoken so casually and knowingly about my best-hidden thoughts that I actually felt relieved that he understood, that he voiced what I knew but would have never said aloud myself. This relief became a comfort, a realization so strong it seemed to have grown within me rather than having been spoken by someone else, a realization as great as seeing the ocean and comprehending its enormity.

"I want to see the world," I said, almost childishly, still vaguely fearful that he thought of me as inferior. "I want to know more about people."

"Sure," he said, "but a big part of you will always stay with your family, wherever you find your family. You'll always want to depend on the same people." He exhaled a deep breath as though he had just accomplished some momentous task. "That's why I came here, though."

I searched his face. "Why *did* you come here?"

"I'm checking on you."

"You're checking on me," I repeated, allowing indignation to crest in my voice. "You're checking on *me*."

"That's right. When I called Stacy Christmas before last, she said she was very interested in someone. Not like other guys she'd talk about. I hadn't heard of you—like I said, I'm not interested in football—but she told me you were a hot-shot quarterback that lived in Assembly Shoals. I couldn't take leave in the summer to find you there. Someone might have recognized me. So I came here."

"Making sure your sister isn't dating an ex-con or something?" The sarcasm soured in my mouth, and I was afraid he had taken it as a barb.

Apparently the barb had not found flesh. "Well, I did want to see for myself. But I do trust her judgment."

And I wondered at that moment if he knew just how much he truly had become like his father.

"Family is very important to Stacy, just as it is to you. She has to find somebody like that. She wouldn't make it with somebody like me. She'll always be close to her home and family. Maybe you two won't stay together, but I wanted to meet you. I want to know how you feel about her."

"That's personal—"

"I came a long way."

I shrugged. "We haven't seen each other much lately," I said.

"Do you love her?"

"Well, yeah, sure I do. Look—"

"Have you slept with her?"

"Don't ask me that," I said, bristling at this inquisition, but his expression remained one of pure curiosity, as though his question had not been the least inappropriate, and I told him the truth. "No."

"Are you going to marry her?"

"Bobby, I don't know! How could I know a thing like that? We aren't even out of school yet."

"I have to make sure whoever she's with will take care of her."

"Stacy doesn't need a lot of taking care of. It's been a long time since you've seen her, you know."

"Hmm—" he said and abruptly sank into deep reflection.

I watched the outline of his figure for a moment. "Stacy's here. You could go to her dormitory right now and see her."

"I'm not ready yet. Not now." He turned to me. "And don't tell her I was here. It'll only hurt her."

"I won't. But you should see her."

He shook his head and looked away.

Across the field the long parallel rows of bleachers

had vanished behind a flood of night that had poured into the stadium.

Bobby seemed to notice the late hour at the same time. He stood. "I'd better go."

"I have to get to the training table," I said, standing with him. "I've probably missed dinner already. But we could talk later."

We started down the bleachers toward the field.

"No," he said. "I should leave."

"You could stay. You can sleep in our dorm room. We could talk some more."

"I can't."

"Will you come back?"

He looked at me. "I don't know. I might."

"Where are you parked?" I asked him. "Do you have a car?"

"It's beyond the practice field."

We passed through the main gate and stopped at the edge of the parking lot, where buzzing, vaporous streetlights had winked on.

"You weren't what I expected," I told him.

"You knew more about me than you thought," he responded. "You knew I couldn't have easily left that family."

"Know what else I think?"

"What?"

"I think you want to go back."

"I will. But it'll have to be in my good time. I just cause them grief when I'm there. And Mom—" He shook his head slowly. "Oh yes, Stacy told me about Mom, how she won't even mention my name. Stacy wouldn't have told me that, but I pressed her about it because I already knew the answer. It's Mom's natural reaction—

she feels betrayed, feels like I've betrayed the family. I don't really blame her for it."

"If you're waiting to change," I said, bracing myself for a rebuff, "it may never happen. If you're looking for some great meaning to everything, you could be looking for the rest of your life. You may just have to come to terms with your family the way things are now."

He merely stared at me, nothing more, for several long, expectant seconds, then turned his head, shoving hands into pockets, shoulders stooping—a very unmilitary slouch. And for the only time that evening it seemed that our roles had been reversed: I had told him something he had not realized or perhaps had simply refused to admit.

Finally, I spoke again, "Did I pass inspection, sir?"

"Yes," he said, looking at me again without smiling. "I guess you did. Don't forget your promise. Don't tell her I was here or where I'm stationed. I don't even tell her that over the phone, because she'd do something stupid like try to find me."

"I won't forget."

He extended his hand and clamped it around mine. "I'll see you again, someday," he said. He pivoted and crossed the parking lot, tossing a wave over his shoulder.

I watched him cross the expanse of empty parking lot, passing through glimmering, aureolic cones thrown down by streetlights, and this passage through light and dark made him seem ghostly, an apparition that finally vanished from view. I could not escape the thought that I had just met someone who knew me better than I knew myself. It was like watching a close friend leave on a long journey. And I realized I had never felt closer to anyone else.

13

I made amends with Stacy, not apologizing but simply asking if she wanted to spend time together again; she curled her lip under front teeth, nodding finally but keeping her eyes from me, apparently still convinced I had wronged her, which indeed I unwittingly had. As spring warmed into summer, whenever I watched her eyes—green and clear like Bobby's—my stomach snatched into a knot of remorse that I could not tell her what I knew. But I never felt tempted to break my vow: the conversation in the football bleachers had been such an unexpected and startling event that I'd grown almost certain it had occurred in some dim other life-time, if at all.

In the first week of June my sophomore year drew to an end, and the university at last disgorged its restless student population upon beaches and home and summer employment. I had been in Assembly Shoals for two days when Forrest, like a somnolent bear rousing from winter's sleep, began to take notice of my interest in Stacy. "Why don't you bring your girl over this weekend?" he asked over dinner at our kitchen table.

"Stacy?"

"You're still seeing her, ain't you?"

"Uh-huh."

"Bring her over and we'll cook steaks or something. You ain't even let me meet her."

"I most certainly have. You're just never around to see her."

"Well, bring her over. Few years and you'll be off on your own and I won't even know what kind of girl you like. I'll spring for some steaks."

I watched him pop the cap on a Coke bottle. Occasionally in the past he had experienced fits of parental responsibility such as this, making me do homework (before high school), watching me at sports, setting limits on television viewing, making me eat vegetables. The thought flicked through my mind—what Mrs. Owens had said at Christmas—about Forrest owing my mother something.

"Okay," I agreed. What I felt like saying was "Don't try to make anything up to me."

I brought Stacy up on a Saturday evening. While I pitched a football at my tire and net, Forrest set the charcoal to flame. Only half of our backyard was cut, the mower parked in the grass, greasy pieces of the engine scattered on stained sheets of newspaper where I had disassembled it after it choked in a blue cloud of smoking oil. So we had set up lawn chairs and a grill on the mowed half of the yard, close to the house, and Stacy sat on the edge of one chair, ankles crossed beneath her and hands folded in her lap, watching Forrest slab meat onto the grill. Her posture and her apparel (too formal—dress slacks and ruffled blouse) reflected her discomfort in Forrest's presence; she had met him only a few times and, like most people who ever knew him, had failed to find an avenue of approach.

Yet as the steaks began to sizzle and drip, and smoke curled across the yard and through the trees on a light wind, Forrest asked her about college and sports and everything else he could think of, and she gracefully fielded every question and seemed to enjoy talking to him after a while. When I followed him into the kitchen to bring out iced tea, Forrest remarked, "She's a good girl."

I flushed with pride when he said that, though I was never sure what he considered a good girl since I rarely saw the women he pursued. Long before, I had asked him why he hadn't married.

"Couldn't never find a woman I could tolerate long enough to ask," he told me.

As I drove Stacy home that evening, I remained adrift with those thoughts, until she said, "Should I be taking this personally?" And I realized we had already stepped onto the Cottrells' front porch.

"Sorry," I said. "My mind was somewhere else."

Her parents occupied the living room when we entered, windows raised to invite cool dusk after one of this early summer's warmest days. They had not been home when I came to pick up Stacy, and now arrived the first moment I had seen them since my visit from Bobby. Suddenly I feared they might suspect that encounter simply by looking at my face. Yet at the same time I felt more comfortable, more self-assured than I ever had in that house, for now it seemed I understood something about their own family that they could not.

"Hello, Jeff," Mr. Cottrell said from the couch by the windows. "Flunked out of school yet?"

"No sir," I laughed. "They said they'd keep me at least one more year."

"How was supper?" Mrs. Cottrell asked, looking up from the sewing in her lap.

"Great," Stacy said. "Jeff's uncle is really a nice man. I ate too much, though—one of those big steaks from the butcher."

"Come here," Mr. Cottrell said to Stacy, voice abruptly serious and commanding.

"What?"

He folded his copy of the Assembly Shoals *Appalachian Herald* and handed it to Stacy, one finger tapping an article on the front page. "You should read this before you hear it anywhere else," he said.

"I still cannot believe it," his wife remarked, eyes intent on a needle as she stitched a dress shirt button. "He's a terrible man, I knew that. But this—" And she shook her head.

"Oh, no way," Stacy blustered, glancing at the paper, then shoving it at me, eyes wide for my reaction.

The headline announced that Emory Patrick had been indicted for burning down his own chemical plant. Reeling, I lowered myself to an empty chair. Stacy perched beside me on the arm. The article told of a miscreant from a neighboring county who had been seen near the plant the night of the fire. Later arrested and charged with the crime, he had claimed that Emory Patrick had hired him for the arson. Authorities had been unsuccessful in locating Patrick.

"Are you sure?" I said.

"We had enough to convince the grand jury," Mr.

Cottrell responded. "I think the fact that Mr. Patrick has slipped from view tells us a great deal."

"But why would he do that?" Stacy asked.

"Burn the plant? Well, he'd suffered some heavy financial losses, and there were problems with waste dumping into the river there. I suppose he timed the fire to make a campaign issue out of it. Had he won the election, he probably could've buried the whole investigation inside the sheriff's department."

"That guy turned Emory Patrick in to save his own skin," Stacy ventured.

"Certainly. A drowning man will grab for anything close. It took us almost a year to find that guy, but he only confirmed what I already suspected."

"You mean you *knew*," Stacy and I said, almost in unison.

"Not beyond all doubt. But he was the most likely culprit."

"You knew he had done it," I repeated, "and yet you let him say all those things about you."

"There was nothing else I could do. I had no proof— only speculation. Something they may not teach when you get to law school, Stacy, but it's often true that the guilty man makes the loudest accusations."

Mrs. Cottrell's head wagged slowly again in disbelief, eyes trained on her fingers steadily tugging needle and thread through fabric. We sat in silent reflection, crickets rasping beyond open windows. The whole episode settled as a sickening lump into my stomach. I hated Emory Patrick and felt betrayed by him, as if he had belonged to my own family. The force of my anger stunned me: it was the same I had experienced when Forrest asked me to shave points in the football game.

June ripened mild—good weather for fishing—and in the evenings Forrest would leave the mill after work, I would meet him from the lumberyard, and together we would drive to the limestone quarry. Those were golden evenings, brilliant late sun glinting on the lake surface, fish on the lines, laughter; and though he said little even then, Forrest listened, and I found myself opening to his familiar presence now that I had spent two years away at college. Home, though inadequate, seemed inviting after my long absence. I hoped for travel, I told him, and at least modest riches, and a family of my own ("With Stacy?" he asked, winking, and I shrugged but turned my face, reddening with a smile). Crazy Flea Sturkey joined us occasionally, cackling incessantly, hands gummy from baited worms, and after snagging his line on Forrest's shirt, he began calling, "Come, let me make ye fishers of men!" He repeated it again and again as he pranced around the lake, never catching anything, voice bounding against precipitous pink and white bluffs.

Following such an excursion one night late in the month Forrest and I arrived home with a catch of twenty-five bream.

"Looks like you'll be cleaning fish for a while," Forrest said, lifting rods and tackle boxes from the bed of the pickup.

"You know the rules. Doesn't matter who catches how many, it's an even split on cleaning."

"You do twenty and I'll do five," he said. He set down the gear and flipped through his keys in the light above the kitchen door.

"You do twelve and I'll do thirteen."

"Hmmph," Forrest grunted, which translated to

"We'll see about that." He had turned on the light inside the kitchen when he froze in the doorway.

Unable to squeeze around his frame, I waited behind, gripping the straining stringer of fish. "Forrest, come on," I said after a moment. "These things're getting heavy."

At first he didn't respond; then he rubbed his open palms on the backside of his trousers and took one step forward, allowing me to enter.

I moved inside with the fish and saw what had made Forrest balk. Blood drained to my feet. "Forrest, somebody's been here" was all I could think to say. I glanced at him, and he raised his hands to his hips; I looked again at the kitchen.

It had been wrecked. The refrigerator and cabinets stood open, counters and floor strewn with broken glassware and dishes, cans and ravaged boxes, eating utensils, the chairs from the kitchen table. The floor lay slick with water and splatters of milk and orange juice and the pulpy remains of food from the refrigerator.

Forrest stepped forward again, shattered glass and ceramic crunching beneath his boots. He stopped and lifted a hand. "Wait here." He avoided the debris and disappeared into the living room.

I heard him switching on lights throughout the house, returning finally to the living room, where he pulled open the front door. I went to the sink, picked out the broken glass, and set the fish in the basin, brushing my hands on my shirt.

The front door closed again, and Forrest came back into the kitchen. He righted a chair beside the table, dropping himself into it, sagging slightly, rubbing his face, then letting the hand fall to his knee. "No one's here," he said. "They went through the whole house. Punched out a window in the front door to get in. Just like before."

I glared at him like a carving knife slicing the Christmas turkey. "What do you mean *before*? You mean this has happened before?"

He looked at me, utterly without expression, then arched his eyebrows as though suddenly remembering an important message for me. "Two, three months ago. While you were at school. Come in just the same way."

"Forrest, did you call the police? What did they steal?"

He shook his head. "Nothing."

"And you didn't call the police? I can't believe it. I'm calling Mr. Cottrell right now."

I saw him glance at me as I started for the phone in the hallway, but he remained quiet.

Gravel spewed and popped the underside of a bumper fifteen minutes later: Mr. Cottrell in his patrol car but not in uniform, and Stacy came with him. Stacy gripped my arm, biting her lip, eyes alert with fascination and fear. Mr. Cottrell surveyed the kitchen; Forrest had risen and now leaned on one hand against the counter.

"Anything taken?" Mr. Cottrell asked.

"No sir," I said. "I checked everything that might be of value. Um—sir?"

He turned to me. "Yes?"

"Forrest said this isn't the first time."

Forrest eyed me for a moment, then shrugged at the sheriff. "Someone got in a while back," he said. "Opened the closets. Turned the furniture over. Nothing was stolen, so I let it go."

Mr. Cottrell nodded. "It's good to report things like that. May I look at the rest of the house?"

Forrest motioned him into the living room.

"Jeff, who would have done it?" Stacy whispered to me as we followed.

"I don't know."

Throughout the house, furniture was scattered, picture frames lay smashed on the floor, the closets spilled clothing. When Mr. Cottrell had seen it all, he stood in the living room and said, "It could have been just kids. I'm afraid there's not much that can be done. Since you're within the city limits, I'd notify the police."

So the Assembly Shoals police sent out a patrol, and Sheriff Cottrell spoke briefly with the two officers before they entered the house. Forrest led them in; I escorted Stacy to the sheriff's car.

"Jeff," Mr. Cottrell said, arms crossed as he sat against the hood, "is there anyone who—well, who might hold a grudge against your uncle for some reason? Someone maybe that he had argued with?"

I could barely make out his features in the glow from house lights. A breeze stirred over the ridge with a touch like cool linen, drawing patiently as soft taffy through the trees. My mind registered empty faces. "No sir. No one I can think of."

Then I looked away from him sharply, as though I'd been slapped, and felt my heart wither—a deflated balloon—temples hammered by the thought of Forrest's scheme at the football game, and his voice saying, "Win by nine."

"You're sure?" Mr. Cottrell prompted, eyeing me intently.

"Yes, sir," I breathed, two tiny, dry words that escaped around the mass like bread dough that had blocked my throat.

He fell quiet, then I saw the outline of his head nod slowly. "Probably just kids," he said. "There was nothing taken—?"

"I'll check everything again."

"There were things that could have been taken—television set, guns—but sometimes kids will break in without stealing. Don't want to be caught with the goods." He pushed himself up from the hood of the car. "Oh, I'm just thinking out loud. I'd always be sure everything's locked up when you're away, and leave some lights on, inside and out. There's not much you can do if people are determined to break in, unless you buy a dog or an alarm. It's pretty isolated out here."

"Yes sir."

He walked around to the driver's side and opened the door, the light inside blinking on; he studied the house again for a moment, then slid into the seat. I led Stacy to the passenger side.

"Are you hungry?" she asked. "They ruined all the food."

"We took sandwiches to the quarry with us," I said. "But thanks."

She slipped under my left arm, hugging me, one hand on my chest. "Your heart's pounding," she said.

"Well, hell, my house just got trashed," I snapped. Then, "I'll see you tomorrow, okay?"

"Yeah, okay."

She pulled away from me, face brooding now, more flustered at this hostility than worried about the night's events, and climbed in beside her father. I winced at my churlish behavior but felt better with her gone. Alone, I didn't have to lie.

Mr. Cottrell cranked the motor and swung around in the drive, and they descended along the dirt road, taillights blurred in swirls of dust. The Assembly Shoals police officers walked through the house and filled out a report, and after they left, Forrest and I cleaned the kitchen, sweeping and mopping until midnight, exchanging hardly a word. Before I went to bed, when I had recovered from the initial shuddering realization that someone had broken into our house, had invaded and tumbled it, I cleaned glass shards from the photograph of my parents and myself as a baby and replaced the frame on the dresser. I slept lightly that night, the walls of my room having lost their security. Every billow of the curtains seemed to veil an intruder creeping through the window.

But my greatest distress came with the image that inside this house itself resided a more insidious threat: Forrest.

A diagonal column of dawn sunlight chased this fear like a child's nightmare. And the next afternoon I had forgotten the incident almost completely when I remembered there was a promise to keep. In three days came Stacy's birthday.

14

The phone never rang. As evening lengthened and Stacy withdrew into herself, rising from her fog of thought to speak only when spoken to, I grew restless, the knowledge lurking in my mind, a curse that only Bobby could remove. When the guests—Stacy's old friends from high school, a few from the university—had gradually drifted to the yard and their cars, and the stereo in the Cottrells' basement gameroom had been shut off, and the remains of wrapping paper and birthday cake had been cleared, the house filled with silence that seemed to exert tremendous pressure on the ceiling, against the windows, against my eardrums. The clock on the mantel read half past midnight.

I couldn't pretend ignorance and ask her what was wrong. I couldn't even look at her. If they merely glanced at my face they would have to see that I was hiding something. I could only sit at the edge of a chair in the living room, waiting for the ring, certain that when it came it would be so sudden and shattering I would flinch as though with a convulsion.

But the phone never rang.

"This is certainly a spirited crew," said Mrs. Cottrell, entering the room. She cupped her hand beneath her daughter's chin. "You look tired, now that you're no longer a teenager. Twenty and tired. We can vacuum tomorrow; you should go to bed. Did you enjoy your party?"

Stacy didn't look at her, instead nodding once, almost falling into sleep it seemed; then she brushed aside her mother's touch, absently, not impatiently.

Mrs. Cottrell left the room for the kitchen again, untying the apron around her waist. Mr. Cottrell came in from the front porch, and some troubling notion simmered behind darkened eyes. His hands dropped like stones into his pockets. He stared at the clock on the mantel, as if having difficulty reading the time, then at Stacy.

The light flicked off in the kitchen. Mrs. Cottrell returned and slipped her hand through her husband's arm. "You ready to turn in?" she asked.

He seemed not to hear. At last Stacy realized she was being watched, and under her father's gaze—searching, not scolding—her posture slowly straightened, bafflement breaking through clouds over her face, as though she'd been accused of something she wasn't aware had happened.

"He hasn't called," Mr. Cottrell said, tone balanced between observation and question, "has he?"

His words spilled over me like ice water down my back. God, he knew! I swallowed a gasp and remained unnoticed, for Mr. Cottrell never took his attention from Stacy, never suspected what I could have told him.

"Who hasn't called?" Mrs. Cottrell asked offhandedly, still not comprehending. Her husband did not answer.

Stacy matched her father's stare, eyes wide, mouth slightly open, confused words welling up on her tongue. "What do you mean?" she whispered finally, almost inaudibly.

"I asked you if Bobby has called," Mr. Cottrell said.

Mrs. Cottrell pulled away from him then, expression advancing through several phases of shock, but she recovered after only a moment, glimpsing Stacy and me and speaking bittersweetly, "Grant, what are you *saying*," stretching the word and glazing it with a shallow laugh, the way she might cover an embarrassing remark dropped before a roomful of party guests.

Mr. Cottrell moved to the empty fireplace. He lifted one foot and set it on the rock hearth, hands still in his pockets. He twisted his shoe on the stones, and for a moment I thought he was crushing out a cigarette, a startling gesture for him since he never smoked. "Four years ago," he said, watching his foot, "on your birthday, you went upstairs to your room to take a phone call. I gave you that phone for your room just a couple of months after Bobby left, remember? I had a dish with a slice of cake and ice cream on it, and the ice cream had started to melt. It was yours."

He faced Stacy with an elaborate demonstration, one hand out, palm up, the other hand curved over it to represent a scoop of ice cream, as if it were essential to convince his daughter he had actually held this dish. "The ice cream was soaking into the cake, and I went up to tell you. The door was shut, but I heard your voice. I reached for the doorknob, and I heard you say, 'Bobby,' and I stopped. I held my hand right there on the doorknob but never turned it, and I listened, just for a minute, until I heard you laugh at something he said. Then I turned around and went back down the stairs." A broad smile came to his face, then slowly receded, like an ocean wave mounting the slow rise of a beach. "I remember when you were both in elementary school. You were in the second grade and he was in the sixth, and another kid in his class pushed you down in the hall. Bobby pounded the daylights out of him and got sent home."

Mrs. Cottrell had lowered herself to the couch, hand drifting to her mouth, then lightly clasping her throat, and she looked at her husband in desperation, head shaking, hardly more than a tremble, silently pleading for him to stop. When he did not acknowledge her, she turned away, eyes confused and bewildered.

Mr. Cottrell lifted his foot from the hearth and lowered it again to the floor. "You see," he said to Stacy, "I always thought he might try to talk to you. If he talks to anyone, he talks to you. But I wasn't listening in on you, I just heard. Every year on your birthday I've waited for you to get that call, and I can look at your face after you've been on the phone and at least know he's all right. Please don't be mad."

Stacy looked at the floor, but her father's speech had worn away any resistance, and she raised her head again, innocently, hopefully. "He calls on Christmas too, Dad, and I should have heard by now. He wouldn't miss calling."

Mr. Cottrell clutched his arms across his chest. "Do you know where he is?" he asked.

Stacy said no.

I was losing control of my breathing. If only that phone had rung; Stacy would have heard his voice and told him all the news and known that he was all right, and thus her father would have known, and my knowledge would have been unimportant, at least for another day. There would have been no need for me to tell them where he was. An emergency at home, a serious illness—that would have been different. In that event I could have called him myself, and he would have come, leaving my promise intact.

But why not call him now? I could tell him they'd waited for him to phone and had wondered if something had happened to him. That's what I would do: tomorrow I'd tell him to call. I had carried the promise this far; I would be damned if I'd break it here. Already the grip encircling my chest like a steel band began to ease.

Mr. Cottrell stood with arms crossed, shoulders sloped, head bowed to stare at his feet, his body a sculpture of indecision. Stacy remained on the couch, anxiously tugging her fingers, watching her father and waiting for some word or action from him. Beside her Mrs. Cottrell had not moved, hands folded tightly in her lap, eyes wide yet unseeing, the order of her world shaken for a second time. The first time had been when Bobby left and now again as she realized the break had not been clean, that a painful link survived, that Bobby had not simply disappeared from the family's sight and memory, as he had for her, to leave them in peace. Somehow I knew that reconciliation could come for Mrs. Cottrell only when her son again entered this house. I was certain the walls were pressing in on me, pushing me too close to them, my face inflamed as though sunburned, but in fact the family seemed to have forgotten my presence in the chair. I shut my eyes, but they were forced open again in a tremor that passed through me like nausea.

"I'm not sure there's much we can do," Mr. Cottrell muttered to his feet.

As I watched them, my secret tormenting me once more like a fever, a different image surfaced within me, beginning as a deep, incoherent awareness before slowly rising into conscious thought: I no longer existed as an outsider to this family. I had become an extension of Bobby himself.

And didn't that make sense? After all, I had been the last of us to see him. He had known almost everything about me, and I knew something about him. I knew that a part of him wanted to be here, wanted to return to his family and had never wanted to leave. Suddenly I became convinced I was that part of him. Later it was never clear to me whether this notion had bubbled up in my mind merely as an excuse for telling what I had sworn not to tell, or whether it evolved from something beyond my understanding, fathomless, like the crushing and absolutely black fluid at the ocean's foundation. But I had grasped this image for only a few moments when I heard a voice say, "I know where Bobby is." I was amazed to see their faces lift and turn toward me. At last I realized the voice had been my own. "And I know where to find him."

The valve had opened inside me, and it all spilled forth after that—Bobby's visit to the university, what he had said, where he was stationed—and though the words were formed in my throat they seemed to speak themselves, as if they weren't my own. My stomach and pulse quieted, and when the flow had been spent I was left with the empty but leaden sensation of perfect solitude, the catharsis that follows betrayal, only I couldn't decide if I'd commited this betrayal or been its victim. At least it was out of my hands now; I no longer stood in the middle. I'll tell him the next time we meet, I thought: they had been frantic and had to find you; had you been in my place you'd have done the same thing; anyway, you wanted to be found, or else why did you come to me? He would understand.

They were suspended in silence for several long moments. Stacy gaped at me as though the most wanted criminal had blundered into her living room, her face a blend of anger, fearful fascination, disbelief. Mr. Cottrell recovered first, blinking, and finally spoke, "A lot of things might have happened. He couldn't call if he was on duty— "

Stacy's head snapped around to him. "He'd have called. I've been here all afternoon. And Mom's been here. Mom, did anyone call for me today?"

Mrs. Cottrell's eyes focused on Stacy with alarm. "No," she said, hurling the word, bouncing abruptly from the couch. "It's so late, I've got to go to bed. It's too late—I can't think right now— You handle it—" She hurried from the room, tossing aside this command for anyone who would pick it up, staccato steps ascending bare wood stairs with a finality like clean-driven nails.

Mr. Cottrell watched his wife's departure, then turned to Stacy. "I could try to reach him," he said quietly. "I could make some calls."

He moved slowly from the room, arms still crossed in front of him; the light in the hallway flicked on, and I heard him settle into the cane-bottomed chair by the hall phone and lift the receiver. Stacy refused to look at me. I pushed myself from the chair and went out onto the porch. My head ached, and the air outside hung lighter, cooler, and although I found myself very thirsty, I could not go back into the house. I didn't know how long I stood at the edge of the porch, watching the night. Under a moon shades from full, a car rumbled on the dirt road, headlights advancing against darkness, gravel popping under the fender like hail on a tin roof; it clattered over the wooden bridge that spanned the Cahala River and continued across the valley, trailing a long, high, and slowly settling cloud of dust that gleamed ghostlike. When the car had passed, the sounds I'd been listening to returned: the low tone of Mr. Cottrell's voice, crickets, the lilting of the river.

Behind me the screen door swung open, and I turned in the half-light from the front windows to see Stacy, palms planted flat on the small of her back, elbows out, lip mashed between her teeth, eyes glistening and pooled above lower lashes. She drifted to the railing and peered up through blackened etchings of pine trees to the sky and stars.

"You—knew," she said haltingly, each word presented on a separate breath, "you knew how important it was for me to find him. Why didn't you tell me?"

"He made me promise not to."

As she turned to me, the tears gathered and fell, one from each eye, coursing over the cheeks, past her mouth, until they clung to the jaw on either side of her chin, quivering there and finally plummeting from her face. "That's how little you trust me?"

"Stacy, he didn't want you to come looking for him. He said he wasn't ready to come home."

She threw back her head, hands snatching into fists in the air as if grasping for something she could not see. "That's what he *told* you!" she said, voice pitched with anguish, new tears tumbling though she made no effort to brush them away. "He doesn't really mean that. What makes you think you know what's in his mind? Because he told you that? I'm his sister, and I know better than you how he is. He's afraid and a little mixed up is all. This is something this *family* has to work out, and you have no right stepping into it. You should have told me—"

I was afraid now, actually afraid that I had been right, that Bobby was more like me than I ever imagined and had wanted to return, that I should have spoken long before. "I gave him my word," I said, groping for the reason I had not told her. "Just like you gave him your word and didn't tell your parents he'd been calling you."

"That was in the family. And if you were so worried about keeping your word, why'd you tell us now? You didn't have to tell us—"

"I thought something was wrong." I hitched my thumbs in back pockets, lowering my guard and opening the truth to her even as it appeared to me. "I don't know. Maybe after seeing what your family was like, maybe I thought he really did want someone to bring him home. But I wasn't sure. Maybe that was just me, what I would have wanted for myself."

Inside the house Mr. Cottrell hung up the phone. Stacy rubbed her arms, though the air was warm, chin trembling in a long, indeterminate pause before the cane-bottomed chair scraped on the hallway floor.

"You should have told me," she repeated.

The spring on the screen door strained again, and Mr. Cottrell came out onto the porch. He watched Stacy's back, waiting for her to turn and face him, but she continued to stare out at the yard as she wiped tears with her fingertips. At last Mr. Cottrell shifted his gaze to me.

"No one can tell us anything tonight," he said. "They'll have to locate him and have him call tomorrow. That's all they could do."

Stacy shook her head, then spun and brushed past her father into the house.

"I know she's upset," Mr. Cottrell said when the screen door tapped shut. "She'll get over it. I'll talk to her."

"It's okay. Maybe I deserved it."

"No, you did what you thought was right. But I'm glad you told us. I think for now what we all need is sleep."

I nodded and said good night and followed the flagstone walk to the driveway and my car. The house was darkened, and Forrest had sprawled in his bed when I arrived home. Several times during the night I was jolted from sleep in heavy sweat by the thought that I had to be somewhere and could not reach the destination, or that someone was searching for me and I had not told them where I could be found. Eventually this distress exhausted me, and I dozed below the level of half-conscious imagination, until my name rang down to me, then again, drawing me up toward early light. I awoke, dry-mouthed and confused, before noticing Forrest at my door, a wooden stirring spoon in his hand.

"Jeff! I got up hungry, so I made breakfast. Eggs and grits and gravy. You want any?"

It was Saturday, the week's busiest day at the lumberyard, and following breakfast with Forrest I eagerly drove to work for the morning, a diversion easily justified: my employer, Mr. McPherson, needed a full crew, and the extra money was welcome. At one o'clock I picked up a hamburger for lunch downtown and returned to the house, where Forrest had tuned in a baseball game on television. I spent an hour throwing a football at the tire and net in the backyard, then showered, and at midafternoon decided I could no longer avoid a trip to the Cottrells' to find out what they had heard.

Stacy stood in the front yard when I arrived, pumping insecticide from a metal canister and spraying a row of fruit trees Mr. Cottrell had cultivated along one border of his property. As I approached across the yard, she shook her head, wiping her hands on the stained T-shirt she wore.

"Nothing," she said. "No one has called."

I was disappointed at this announcement yet heartened by her demeanor. This willingness to speak first was a concession, an offer of reconciliation that I glady accepted. I realized she would never apologize directly, or even feel that she should; and if I tried to discuss last night's argument, she would only retreat from compromise. Thus I merely said, "What have you been doing?"

She exhaled a sharp sigh. "I can't concentrate on anything. I was wandering around the house until Dad gave me this to keep me occupied. He called again this morning but couldn't find out any more. He's been in his woodshop for hours. Mom's been doing housework—I swear, *house*work—like nothing had happened. The bigger the problem that comes along, the harder she pretends that everything is normal."

"I think housework is for your mother what the woodshop is to your father."

"But Mom won't ad*mit* there's anything wrong."

I helped her finish spraying, and we put away the canister in a basement storage room, climbing the stairs to find Mrs. Cottrell folding laundry from a basket on the couch.

"So many things pile up during the week, Jeff, you just wouldn't believe." Her face was gaunt, as though her flesh had receded to leave skin drawn tight over bone. "Stacy, I need a few things from the store. Would you mind picking them up for me?"

Stacy assented without protest, clearly relieved to be out of her mother's presence, and we drove to the nearest grocery along the main highway. When we returned, Mr. Cottrell had come in from the woodshop, sitting in the living room with a newspaper, not in a relaxed reading posture but on the edge of a chair, elbows on knees, waiting to be summoned to his feet at any moment. In the dining room the table had been carefully set—china, crystal, napkin rings.

Stacy carried the groceries into the kitchen, then appeared before her father. "Dad, what is she doing?" she whispered. "She's in there fixing a huge meal. I don't feel like sitting through all that. I'm not even hungry."

"She's just handling things in her own way. Go along with it and don't criticize her."

But when her mother brought out serving dishes and proclaimed that dinner was ready, Stacy spewed an objection. "Mom, it's only five-thirty. We never eat at five-thirty. And we don't need all this food. This isn't the time for a lot of food."

Mr. Cottrell glowered at Stacy but said nothing. Smoothing her apron with open palms, Mrs. Cottrell surveyed the table and her daughter's face. "You have to eat, Stacy," she said. "You haven't eaten all day, and you need a good supper. Well, I may have cooked too much, but Jeff's here, and it's not often we all can sit down and eat together on Saturday—all of us off doing different things. I thought it would be nice to eat together. And you and Jeff will still have time to go out later—"

"Mom, we're not *go*ing anywhere tonight—"

"Let's eat," Mr. Cottrell said firmly.

Mrs. Cottrell looked at him, not with gratitude but with consternation that we might not appreciate the meal she had prepared. We pulled up our chairs and ate in heavy silence lifted only by Mr. Cottrell's blessing, in which he made no mention of Bobby though he often sought divine intervention in family matters, and later by a compliment to his wife on her cooking. The leftovers were ample, and when we had cleared them away to the kitchen, dusk had begun to close, dusk that even in the long days of late June came early each evening to this valley darkened by surrounding hills. As light diminished outside during the next hour, Stacy became animated with fretful motion, anxious to take some action to end the wait. Words at last seemed poised to burst from her, but before she could speak the phone rang.

Stacy bolted for the hallway, but her father's voice intercepted her. "No!" Then, more gently, he said, "Let me answer."

Stacy remained in the living room with me. Mrs. Cottrell lingered also, straightening pillows on the couch, collecting strewn newspapers, detached and hovering above a breathless pause into which her family had been pitched. But she was listening; when Mr. Cottrell's short, intermittent mumbles threaded from the hallway, her rustlings ceased.

I understood only his last words in the conversation, "I will come for him."

When the receiver was placed in the cradle—carefully, by the sound—Mrs. Cottrell turned, one hand lightly pressing her chest below the throat, abruptly resigned to face whatever new complications her husband would introduce. He entered the room staring at the floor, finally raising his head, and with extraordinary effort focused his attention on Stacy, then Mrs. Cottrell.

"He left the base last night," he said, tone strong but words disjointed. "With friends—they went out—into town—a bar. They don't know what happened. An argument—someone pulled a knife—" He was slipping again into his pool of grievous existence. "Tomorrow I'll make the arrangements." He released this sentence as if it were a rope he'd lost the strength to hold.

After several seconds I realized that the arrangements he would make would be for a funeral. This news did not shock me. I simply could not comprehend why he thought Bobby was dead. It was impossible. I waited for a blood rush of anger or sorrow. I didn't feel anything. Instead I was struck by a notion that I was nothing more than a machine, equipped for the intricate recording of sounds and images. I operated for the purpose of observing the reactions of this family in the wake of apparent tragedy.

"Dad!" Stacy pleaded, but he stared helplessly at his daughter, and a shriek gurgled in her throat but never came to her tongue. The flow of tears had already begun when she dashed from the room and up the stairs. Mrs. Cottrell's face descended into horror and froze there, so flushed of color it took on a dull gloss. Her fingers probed her cheeks, indenting the skin as if to determine whether it really had become waxen. Some automatic impulse led her to the kitchen.

And after more than a minute in my unclouded calculation of time, Mr. Cottrell moved toward the front door. He stopped when he came to me, eyes leveling with mine but absent of recognition, staring through me. He continued to the door, and heavy footfalls moved across the porch and down the steps.

I was perfectly alone in the room, as far removed from this family as its own dead son. I went out to the yard and to the side of the house, where my car was parked in the drive. I saw Mr. Cottrell in a faint gleam from houselights, standing at his fence that bordered the Cahala River, both hands gripping the top rail, head bowed below the line of his shoulders. He had not gone to the woodshop. It could offer him no refuge now.

So my body—the biological machine, a complicated arrangement of blood and muscle without a fiber of emotion—carried me to my car, started the motor, and drove me to the main highway. Independent of my awareness, a decision was made in the circuitry of my brain to drive past the dirt road leading to Forrest's house. I kept to the main highway, following it through Assembly Shoals and along the Cahala.

Ahead, a thundercloud had massed over the northern mountains, revealing itself towering in black atmosphere with startling electric charges of orange and white. As the grade of the highway steepened, I noticed that the river still held close to the roadbed, flowing past me in the opposite direction on a ceaseless course to Assembly Shoals and beyond, and for the first time since leaving the Cottrells' house, a feeling—simple and pure and consuming—began to stir within my physical shell. I wanted to find the place where the river began.

The interior of the car had grown stale, and rather than switch on artificial air I rolled down the window, wind buffeting my face over the sinking glass pane. I drove for an hour, into the next county and the next, and into the close, moist smell of impending storm. The river narrowed and gradually fell away from the level of the road and into the black void of deeper ravines, until headlights and lightning flashes illuminated only the road and a steeply sloping forest of lashing trees. Rain began to splotch the windshield, then pounded in a torrent, spraying through the open window and misting my face. After a moment it occurred to me that I was crying, fresh rain and salt tears blurring on my cheeks, crying freely like the rainfall itself. These tears seemed strange, for I couldn't decide if I was crying for Bobby or because I had lost the river.

Defeated and drained, I stopped the car in the middle of this road clinging to its shelf carved in the hillside, headlights barely penetrating, instead mirrored on a sheath of glassy droplets. Finally, I rolled up the window, turned, and headed south again. The river rejoined the highway as the valley broadened between lower hills, and north of Assembly Shoals the rain ceased, like the passage through a waterfall, leaving asphalt dry where the thunderstorms had not passed. Downtown lay empty under a sickening yellow pallor from streetlights, but outside the city a full moon hung brilliantly in abject darkness, in that fragment of night when the sun is positioned on the opposite side of the earth.

15

Not far from town, in a clearing on a wooded hillside, stood an abandoned frame church—doors boarded, windows blinded by shutters, paint faded and sun-blistered—and behind it, in a gently sloping cemetery, they buried Bobby.

Or so they told me, for even while I saw the casket resting beside an open grave I was not entirely convinced he was in it. I almost wanted to help lower it into the ground, to feel it lighter than anyone expected. It was true I had never seen Bobby with his family and thus had difficulty now seeing this family as incomplete. But it was more than that. I perceived no loss, not even in the vague manner I had experienced loss the night we learned of his death. Though I tried to dismiss my desire for more proof as mere morbid curiosity, inside me dwelt a belief that he was somewhere else, not in that casket.

When the eulogy had been given, Stacy lingered as the caretakers began removing the wreaths. I watched her from a few paces behind, my hands pocketed deep in slacks of a charcoal-gray suit. She stood stolidly in a wind that gusted across the hillside, dress snapping about her knees, hair tossing, her only movement a slow lifting of one hand, like dull reflex, to brush aside a strand of hair caught at the corner of her mouth. The sky glared a vibrant blue, adorned only with fleeting, vaporous tufts that resembled solitary billows from a steam engine; shadows cruised the ground as these clouds raced overhead on this unusual wind that hinted more of spring than summer.

At last she turned and stepped to my side, arms crossed over her breast, staring over the narrow vale, face draped with transparent resignation over a deeper expression of solemn despair, and crying now—silent tears, no sobs. She placed her head lightly against my shoulder, nothing more, and I raised an arm around her and led her away from the grave. Below us on the slope her parents had stopped to wait, Mrs. Cottrell's face composed but still waxen, shaded beneath a broad-brimmed hat, hands clasped low at her waist. Mr. Cottrell stood apart from her, arms fixed patiently at his sides. As Stacy and I passed between them, they turned, and together the four of us descended the hill to the car.

Mrs. Cottrell returned most easily to a normal life-style, since she had never really given it up. The familiar routine of home had shielded her from the pain of separation—outside the family's walls and its common extensions her son existed outside her consciousness as well—and it shielded her now from the pain of Bobby's death. But I sensed she also knew a greater peace after his death; if nothing else, at least each member of her family was accounted for. Her peace came with resolution, terrible but complete resolution.

She even spoke of Bobby after the funeral, the first time I ever heard her mention his name. Stacy and her father had disappeared after dinner one night, and Mrs. Cottrell beckoned me into the kitchen. A pan of brownies sat cooling on the stove; she began slicing squares with a long knife.

"Thought I'd give you first crack at these," she said. An oddly plaintive smile flickered across her face. "I haven't made them for a long time. They were Bobby's favorite. I just wanted to make them, I don't know why."

I thanked her and escaped to the living room with a glass of milk and the brownie on a saucer, confused by this commemoration, wondering how much significance I should bestow upon it, as if I'd just been granted the Holy Communion. I sat on one couch. A creak above the ceiling told me Stacy had retreated to her room upstairs; beyond the windows and front porch Mr. Cottrell trimmed hedges in early dusk. My attention was then suddenly snared by something else, as momentarily astonishing as a glimpse of your own face in an unexpected mirror along an unfamiliar wall. On the end tables, on the mantel, on the bookshelves, he was there; with a dog I had never seen; with a pair of water skis over his shoulder, smiling with surprise at the camera; with Stacy, knee-deep at the ocean as young children; a family portrait of the four of them together. The photographs of Bobby had been returned.

Mr. Cottrell righted himself more slowly from the tumult, remaining pensive at home and even when I saw him with his associates in town during the week, with an expression that seemed to reflect an unsettled stomach, until I became worried that the tragedy had affected his health. But two weeks later he called me aside, leading me to the split-rail fence from which he enjoyed contemplating the river and the valley, and said, "Jeff, I need your help now getting things back together. Especially with Stacy. She's been upset the most, but it's hard for me to help her sort it all out when I'm only now coming to accept what has happened myself. I know you were shaken, too. Bobby was your friend, from what I can tell, even though you knew him only for a short time. I know you and he shared a lot of things. But I think maybe it's a little easier for you to accept. Stacy needs something to lean on. It may be trite to say, but the living have to go on living. If you could get her interested in something, get her out of the house, get her mind back in the present, she'll be better off for it."

I told him I understood, and what he said about Stacy was true. At the beginning of the summer she had been looking for an introduction to the practice of law and had persuaded one of the attorneys in town to hire her as a clerical aide—filing documents in the disheveled office above a Main Street hardware store, carrying briefs over to the county courthouse. But following the funeral she avoided returning to work, complaining of fatigue. I had often wanted to show her the view from the ridge above Forrest's house, and finally one Saturday afternoon in mid-July I prodded her into agreement and packed a picnic supper. We saddled Beast and climbed on together.

A narrow switchback trail, chopped among the trees by some adventurer even before Forrest had moved into that house, led up the slope to a granite outcrop at the crest, a plateau bare but for moss and a few saplings that had worked roots into fissures. We tethered Beast to a tree at the edge of this expanse and spread a blanket on the other side of the ridge, where the outcrop fell away sharply to an unobstructed vista. Smaller green hills below us stood like swells on an ocean suspended in motion. No haze sullied the horizon, and the mountains to the north loomed almost within reach.

We unpacked supper onto sheets of wax paper—cold fried chicken, cornbread her mother had made, water from Mr. Cottrell's canteen. "You can see three states from here," I said, but I didn't push the conversation, and we ate in silence until she said, "I know you're trying to get my mind off Bobby, but bringing me up here isn't going to do it."

She had not spoken indignantly but in declaration. I thought it a good sign that she had offered to speak about Bobby at all. "Why?" I asked.

"Because you can see everything up here. Bobby would have loved it. He always wanted to see the whole world at once, like he was drinking his life and couldn't gulp fast enough." Then she shrugged in dismay. "I don't know, though. I hadn't seen him in four years. He might not have even been like that anymore."

"No, you knew him very well. But his home was important to him, too. I know I only met him once, but I could see that. He was going to come back."

"I have to tell you," she said, poking a slice of cornbread across the wax paper, "things come out in you sometimes, things like bringing me here, that remind me of Bobby."

This comment disturbed me. Vague visions of a future with her began to dissolve. "Is that going to be— a problem?"

She eyed me for the intent of my question, then said, "No. Actually, it's comforting sometimes."

"He and I were very different, too."

"I think it's just that a small part of him is a big part of you. Does that make any sense? I mean, he wanted to come home, like you said, but if you had been in his place you'd have never left. It was hard to see that in him, that he appreciated the family. It's strange, but listening to you sometimes makes me feel like I know Bobby better."

I would never have conceived that she saw my heart and thoughts so clearly. But I could not argue with her conclusions, because I had arrived at them myself long ago.

We watched the sun settle toward distant hills and finally slip behind them, leaving a yellow-white fan in the west that faded to orange and shrank like a dying lantern wick. The cloak of diffused light drew away from earth, deep space emerging gradually through an ethereal veneer. Beside a low moon the evening star appeared, and others would soon follow.

"We should go," I said, "or there won't be enough light to find our way back."

She agreed, and we gathered the blanket and picnic remnants and climbed on Beast, Stacy sitting in front of me on the saddle ("I want to drive," she said). The trail quickly grew dark, and the horse struck tentative hooves on stones and roots exposed in the path. After some twenty minutes we cleared the trees behind the barn. My eyes strained to discern shapes in thickening evening, buzzing with crickets. We rode past the barn and the paddock and into the backyard. "Let's see if Forrest is home," I said. "He'll have to turn on the barn light from inside."

A dim yellow bulb burned over the back door, but the windows were clamped against dense blackness inside. Then a shadow passed through the yellow glow.

"What was that?" Stacy whispered.

"Did you see that?" I said.

Stacy tugged the reins, and Beast balked, flipping his head and gnashing the bit, swinging hindquarters around so that finally he stood sideways to the house. He lowered his head and tore a mouthful of grass from the lawn.

Another shadow passed in the same direction through the light.

"Is that a deer?" Stacy said.

"I don't know. It's too dark to tell."

"It's deer," she said in muffled excitement. "I think there're two of them."

"Maybe. It didn't look like deer."

"Don't talk too loud, you'll spook them."

"Stacy, we can't wait here all night. Watch 'em charge for the woods when I yell."

Beast munched grass.

"Forrest!" I shouted.

Shadows whirled, and an air-splitting explosion flashed in our faces. Stacy exhaled a short, high squeal, and the earth fell away beneath us. I crumpled hard on my left shoulder, elbow ramming my side and spearing the breath from me. Something heavy pinned my left leg.

I writhed on the ground, lungs burning for air. With my free leg I kicked at the weight on me, panic closing like cold fingers around my throat.

"Jeff." Stacy's voice trembled a few feet from me, her figure feebly illuminated by the light over the door.

Finally the knot of my diaphragm relaxed to allow

a breath of speech. "Hey!" I gasped toward the house. "What the hell are you doing?"

"Jeff, my leg hurts."

An impossible calm took hold of me then. "Shh!" I ordered. "Be quiet a minute."

Voices rasped unintelligibly in the yard, then footsteps faded around the house. Reaching for Stacy, motionless on her back, I touched one shoulder, slid my hand down her sleeve, and gripped her forearm. "Be quiet a minute," I repeated.

On the other side of the house, car doors slammed, an engine cranked and raced, twin beams of headlights sliced the dark and swung around out of sight, the car careening down the dirt road in a flurry of pinging gravel. Night fell quiet again except for the crickets. I felt Stacy move.

"Jeff, my leg hurts."

"It's the horse," I said.

She sighed once, almost sleepily. "No," she said. "He didn't fall on me. Jeff, are they gone?"

"I think so. Just be still."

Every word spoken between us I heard resonantly and individually, like a spoon tapping crystal in the frozen air of winter. Certain that I'd become detached from my own body, I watched myself wriggle and twist my foot from beneath Beast and stand shakily, both legs throbbing. We were thirty feet from the house. I stepped toward Stacy and stumbled over a lump, the knapsack, and kicked it aside, dropping to my knees beside her. She sat up, drawing her left leg next to her body, right leg resting straight on the ground.

"I think they're gone," I said. Then, wrenched with rage and confusion, "Are you all right? They shot at us, Stacy. I can't believe it. They shot at us."

In the yellow light the line of her mouth was drawn tightly into a closed-lip grimace. She said, "My leg hurts."

"Which one? Here?" I was shocked at the clarity of these words. I touched her right knee, then the shin, and she inhaled sharply through her teeth. "Can you slide your pants leg up?" I said.

She gripped the denim delicately between her fingers and raised the hem a few inches. When I touched her ankle and calf, the skin was wet. "Oh Lord," I said. "Okay, you're going to be all right." Standing again, bones turning to water, I swore, wiping my mouth with the back of my hand. "I've got to take you to the hospital. You'll be okay."

I crouched to lift her, one arm behind her back and the other under her knees. Strength flowed into me again; she seemed weightless. I avoided the dark figure of Beast, perfectly still in the grass, and hurried without running around the house. At the front corner I stopped, peering in the direction of the road. In the light over the kitchen door nothing but my car occupied the drive.

"I think they're gone," I said.

I eased Stacy into the passenger seat of the car, then yanked my pockets inside out to find the keys. We jolted down the road into the valley and hit eighty into town, roaring down Main Street and cornering with a whine of tires onto the avenue that led away from the river toward the hospital. The entire interminable ride Stacy never spoke; she sat with head back and eyes closed, one hand on the edge of the seat, the other gripping her knee, face serene but whitened lower lip tucked under the even edge of her front teeth.

"Hold on," I said. The adrenaline was receding; I

could barely grasp the steering wheel. "We're almost there."

When the car skidded to a stop outside the emergency entrance, she opened her eyes and lifted her head. I vaulted to the passenger side and lifted her with rubber arms. Automatic doors swung open in front of me.

16

I woke in Bobby's room, in his bed. It was comfortable and somehow familiar, but I could not remember what had brought me here. My right leg ached, the flesh cramped and compressed, and I pulled back the sheet to uncover an elastic bandage wound around my calf, and the previous night beat back to me against a current of exhaustion and disbelief and pain-killing drug.

I had watched from the treatment room door as the doctor swung Stacy onto an examination table, her pants leg and tennis shoe splotched with dark stains, jeans frayed below the knee by small holes the width of a pencil. With a pair of surgical scissors he snipped the jeans from hem to knee and lifted fabric from the skin, delicately, as if peeling the membrane from a hard-boiled egg. Stacy's skin and slender calf were smeared with a greasy film of crimson blood.

"I'll have to cut your jeans all the way off," the

doctor had said. He turned to me. "I'll need to close the door." Then he glanced again, looking at my feet, signaling the attending nurse with a nod toward me.

Baffled, I had stared blankly at him for a moment, then at the nurse. Finally, I thought to look down. Below my right knee, on the outside of the shin, was a frayed tear in my jeans and a long dark stain beneath it. I had been fascinated, unsure this leg even belonged to me. But sensation had returned, like a long hypodermic needle pushed slowly into muscle.

My injury had been superficial, a deep gash. Stacy had been struck with four pieces of buckshot, but only two had penetrated the flesh, and only one lodged deep enough to cause real concern. The doctor removed the pellets and gave us pain pills, warning Stacy that her leg would likely remain sore for several days and to stay off her feet. Stacy's parents had rushed into the emergency room fifteen minutes after we arrived, and upon our release Mr. Cottrell insisted that I spend the night at their house. Then he left to investigate, and Stacy and I spilled fearful, frenetic talk of the incident to her mother until after midnight.

I heaved a sleep-laden body from the bed and slogged to the bathroom to wash my face, then tugged on pants and a shirt from Bobby's chest of drawers. Mrs. Cottrell was leaving Stacy's room when I entered the hallway. She carried a sewing case and a bundle of socks, and I knew she'd been in there all night. She left Stacy's door ajar and tiptoed down the long carpet toward me. "Morning," she whispered, face flushed with color after having seeped at the sight of us last night. "How do you feel?"

"It throbs," I said in a hoarse rumble. "What time is it?"

"Almost eleven. Stacy woke up a little while ago, but her head hurt and her stomach was nauseous—she needs to sleep. Are you hungry?"

"Not really. I could use something to get rid of this taste—maybe orange juice?"

She nodded and touched my arm as though to guide me as we descended the stairs; then she left for the kitchen.

Mr. Cottrell was heaped on one couch in the living room, flipping through the Sunday paper. When he saw me, he folded the paper in his lap. "How is it?" he asked.

"It doesn't hurt much now," I said stoically.

"Good. Get some sleep?"

"Thought I wouldn't need a pill, but I took one after all."

He motioned toward a chair. "Have a seat."

I obeyed, and Mrs. Cottrell presented a tall, sweating glass of orange juice. I swallowed thirsty gulps over a fuzz-covered tongue.

"I'll put these socks away," she said, leaving the room again.

Outside the living room windows the sun gleamed on the valley. The newspaper was strewn on the couch alongside Mr. Cottrell; he straightened this pile as I drank. He wore his trousers from last night and a T-shirt; he was unshaven, and his eyes were sunken from lack of sleep. Scratching the bristles of his cheek, he looked at me. "We didn't find much at your house last night," he said. "I'm afraid your horse is dead, Jeff."

I had known this, seeing Beast motionless on the ground. I felt my lips part, then realized I had no words to speak, finally nodding absently.

"We buried him early this morning," he said. "Behind the barn."

"Thank you, sir," I said.

"The blast hit him in the neck. You and Stacy caught some of the stray shot." He looked beyond me out the windows, frowning, then brought his gaze into the room once more. He said, "You could have been killed."

This reminder made me shudder, not only from fear for myself but also fear for him, that his family might have been shattered again, losing his daughter after losing his son. To me the danger still seemed unreal, lurking in a myopic visionlike dream. I found myself more concerned with the tangible effects before me— Mr. Cottrell slumped on the couch—and I wondered what hopeless thoughts had passed through his mind when the hospital called last night.

"The house wasn't broken into," he went on, "and we didn't find anything in the yard. Jeff, I need you to think about exactly what happened. Try to remember anything that might help us. You said you saw shadows. Did you see any faces? Did you see how many there were?"

I leaned forward in the chair, clutching the glass in both hands. "I remember those figures, those shadows, that's all. We thought they were some kind of animal."

"Did you hear any voices?"

"I think so. I'm sure I did. But I couldn't understand what they were saying. I heard them only for a second. They were running away."

"And you think there was more than one?"

"Yes sir. I want to say I remember more."

"Don't create something when you're not sure," Mr. Cottrell said.

I nodded, stared into the orange juice, then turned up the glass to my mouth.

"Your uncle came back to the house last night while

my deputies and I were there," he said, "so he knows what happened. He helped bury your horse."

A pause poured between us like cement. "He said he didn't know of anyone who would have a reason to be up there," Mr. Cottrell added, examining me intently, tone inviting a confirmation.

My heart seized the blood flow, then sent it racing, gastric acid burning my stomach as I remembered the break-ins at the house, and I dumped blame like hot coals on the image of Forrest. In my shame and anger I could not answer Mr. Cottrell or even look at him, gazing instead at orange pulp clinging to the inside of the glass.

At the periphery of my vision I saw Mr. Cottrell shrug, suspending his shoulders for a long moment before letting them fall again. "Well, for now we'll just have to keep looking."

No one went to church that morning. Around one o'clock Stacy, eyes red, head wobbling a little from side to side, limped down the stairs and dropped to the sofa. Mrs. Cottrell fixed sandwiches for lunch, but neither Stacy nor I ate more than a few bites—she was still queasy, and I could think of nothing but confronting Forrest.

When I mentioned—casually, hoping to avoid any argument—that I should be returning home, Mrs. Cottrell became distraught. "Jeff, I absolutely insist that you stay with us for a while. We don't know who those people were or whether they'll come back." She pleaded her case with her husband, who had showered and dressed for a trip into town. "Grant, it just makes sense for him to stay here. I can't go through another night like last night. I just can't."

Mr. Cottrell raised himself from lacing his shoe,

resting elbows on knees. "Jeff, we'd feel better if you stayed with us at least another night."

I did not want to debate the merits of Forrest's guardianship, for my defense of him would have been weak, and I did feel protected in this house. So I agreed to stay, and Mr. Cottrell left for town, followed later by Mrs. Cottrell on a grocery run. Stacy and I flipped through the paper for a while; we found nothing in it about the shooting (though an article did appear in the Monday edition). But after an hour I grew restless again, and hunting a new excuse, I said, "I'll need some things from the house if I'm going to stay over."

Stacy's eyes glinted fearfully. "Do you think you should go up there?" she asked.

"I don't have my own clothes, except what I had on last night, or a toothbrush or anything."

"You can wear Bobby's clothes."

"I need my *own* clothes," I said sternly, surprised at the irritation in my voice. This pressure they had exerted suddenly made me uncomfortable, as though I weren't free to leave of my own volition, and I found myself adrift on indecision. Maybe it was better to leave after all.

"Dad can pick up that stuff for you."

"Well, I forgot to ask him before he left. Nothing'll happen." Then I compromised. "I'll come right back."

"I'm going with you then."

"You're not supposed to walk. I'll be right back."

"No, I want to get out anyway. Let me come with you."

I was battling claustrophobia now. I had to talk to Forrest, to find out what he knew; it seemed that only he held the answer to where I belonged, for if he had been in any way responsible for what had happened last night, if he had brought this threat upon our house and family, I would not stay with him any longer. And I'd be damned if the Cottrells would keep me from this answer.

Rather than waste more time I helped Stacy to my car, which had been delivered during the night. When we reached my house, Forrest's pickup baked and glimmered in the drive. I told Stacy to wait in the car and went inside.

The kitchen was empty. I found him in the living room in his chair, eyes closed; in his lap he gripped the neck of a vodka bottle, almost empty. From years of observation I knew he'd started on that bottle many ounces ago. Flustered, looking for delay, I slipped to my room and packed a traveling bag, casting a glance through the window toward the backyard; the net and tire and a lawn chair were spattered with hot sun through the tree cover, but I saw no evidence of gunfire.

I walked outside through the back door and toward the barn, where treads of heavy machinery had churned impressions in dark clay. I followed this path around the barn and came upon a low mound of fresh-turned earth close to the tree line. This sight startled me, and I realized the absurdity of my notion that two or three men armed with shovels could dig a grave for a horse. Beast's burial had been serious work.

Resolve fueled by this discovery, I tramped back into the house and grabbed the traveling bag. When I returned to the living room, Forrest lay awake, still reclined in his chair. He blinked a few times, squinting, then focused his eyes on me and the bag in my hand.

"Where're you going?" he asked evenly, words unexpectedly well-formed.

The bag abruptly felt heavy, and I hefted it in my

hand, ashamed of it, and fleeing from my own home again seemed ridiculous. I wanted to toss the bag back into my room and say nothing. "The Cottrells'," I responded, almost whispering. "I'm going to stay there, maybe overnight."

His glare lingered on me, then he turned his head against the chair back, staring at the darkened TV screen. He brushed a hand clumsily across his mouth. "Your father-in-law was up here poking around a while ago," he said.

I dropped the bag to the floor; my hands found my back pockets and hid there. "He's not my father-in-law. He was trying to find out who was up here last night."

"You hang around that little tart of a daughter of his enough," Forrest said.

My stomach tightened; the back of my neck prickled. I knew better than to argue with him when he'd been drinking. But I held my ground, determined to drag an admission or denial, one or the other, out of him. "Did you talk to him?"

"He just wanted to know if he could look around," Forrest said.

I cleared my throat. "Forrest, listen to me. Do you realize what happened last night? Somebody shot at us. It tore a hole in my leg. Right now it feels like a hot iron against the skin, and Stacy is even worse. They killed the horse, Forrest. We need to know, do you have any idea who could've been up here last night? I mean, they *shot* at us—"

"How would I know that?" he burst out, turning his head toward me again. "First your father-in-law asks a truckload of questions, then you start in. Do you think I know something and ain't telling? Was that you putting him on to thinking I knew something about it?"

"No, that's not—"

"I'll tell you what, you're getting pretty know-it-all, Mr. Quarterback. You may be in college, and you may play on that praise-God-we're-so-great football team, but I'm the one," and he jammed a finger into his chest, "that got you into that in the first place, signed you up for a team when you weren't no bigger than a pork sausage and didn't even want to play. Gave you a home to live in. You wouldn't be *in* that college if it weren't for me."

"Taking a lot of credit, aren't you?" I blathered, wheeling away from him. He had knocked me off course with that one. But I circled the room and caught the current I'd been riding and again followed it to him. "Yeah, let's talk about football, Forrest. What was that you wanted me to do at the bowl game? Win by less than ten?"

He uncapped the bottle, turned it up, and drew a long swallow from it.

"You told someone you could fix the score of the game, didn't you?"

"That's over and done with and I don't want to talk about it," he said.

"We have to talk about it!" I exclaimed. "They came up here with a gun and they shot at us! They killed my horse!"

Struggling to raise the recliner, he propped himself with one elbow on the chair arm. Then, as if I were an idiot, he said, "How do you think I got you that horse, anyway?"

"I don't care how you got him! I want to know—"

"I *won* him."

"I don't care! I want to know who you told you could fix the game—"

Forrest sank again into the chair. "I ain't going to talk about it."

"You never talk about anything! Not unless there's something in it for you. Sure, you got me into football. But if I had done what you asked me, they would've thrown me out of football forever. I could've gone to jail and you with me. I can't believe you asked me to do that." I was trembling, afraid of this confrontation I had long avoided. "I can't believe you'd use your own blood relation for that. Go back a generation, Forrest, and we're from the same people. A part of us is the same. Would you cut off your own arm just for money?"

"If you were so worried about this *family*," he said, "you wouldn't have gotten your father-in-law sheriff involved. You'd have asked me first. Kept it in the family."

"Since when could I come to you?" I said, voice cracking under the weight of astonishment. Something was spreading through me, welling from recesses deeper than sensation, something dark I could not control, speaking for me, hazing my vision. "You let me down, Forrest. I'd want to talk and you wouldn't even be home. You drink too much, you gamble—"

"Clamp your mouth." He turned up the bottle once more, the last of the vodka bubbling and draining into his mouth. He wiped a sleeve across his lips, inhaling sharply as he surfaced from the plunge. "I don't need that kind of disrespect from a kid that's my responsibility."

"Your responsibility? What a joke! I'm just a burden you put on yourself for some reason. Why did you bring me here, anyway? You know what, Mr. and Mrs. Owens wanted me. Why didn't you let them take me? They could've brought me up. You didn't want me."

"There wasn't nobody after my sister died. Just me. I was the family. You belonged here."

The words could have come from my own mouth. The reason I had always accepted Forrest: he was the family. But hearing him say it seemed to shrivel my heart and stomach and flush blood from my body with some dense, impervious fluid, like mercury. His image came apart beyond a screen of tears. Chest squeezed by nausea, I shouted, "I don't *belong* to you. I don't belong to *any*body. I'll take care of myself with no help from you. And don't do your sister any favors, okay? She wouldn't want me here. She would've hated you for what you are." At that moment I recognized the blight inside me, realizing it had always been there without ever admitting it to myself: a bitter urge for reclusion, strong as the desire to build a family around me. If I couldn't have my parents, my rightful family, I wanted nothing. I wanted to be alone more than anything on earth.

"You—shut—your—mouth," he warned. "That's my sister you're talking about. You didn't even know her."

"She was *my mother*! I'm more like her than you can ever be. And she would hate you for what you are."

Forrest pushed himself from the chair, swaying under a rush of blood and alcohol to his brain, reddened eyes flaring at me. *"Shut up!"* he said, words thickening. He drew the empty bottle behind his head, aiming wide, and threw it, not forcefully but to intimidate me, and I ducked and heard the bottle glance high off the wall behind me. I spun to watch its flight and saw it bounce hard on the carpet without breaking. Then I saw Stacy.

She stood at the entrance to the living room, one hand gripping the doorjamb to steady herself on the wounded leg. Her shoulders were hunched, free hand pressing the side of her head, eyes squinting and mouth forming a tight circle. I lunged for her, heart springing into my throat, afraid she might teeter and fall.

"No, it didn't hurt." Then she added, as if it were more important to explain her presence, "I didn't know what was taking so long."

I wheeled toward Forrest and could think of nothing but pounding him senseless. I slammed my open palms against his broad chest, clutching his shirt front to wrestle him down. But even drunk he maintained remarkable balance, and his fist brushed over my arm and landed on my mouth like a mallet. Legs buckling, I sat hard on the floor.

Stacy shrieked, "Jeff, stop, please!"

The split lip stung and tasted salty. A thin smear of blood came away on my fingers. "Damn you!" I said, scrambling toward him again. He retreated a wary step before I shoved him against the chair arm, and he tumbled over in a clumsy heap, head striking the bare wood floor at the carpet's edge. He turned on his side.

I waved a quaking finger at him. "You keep your damn hands to yourself!"

"Jeff," Stacy pleaded. "let's go."

Forrest opened his eyes. "Get out of here," he said, voice tempered but thrusting like an oiled knife. "Get out of my house and take your little girlfriend with you. Both of you just get out."

I snatched the bag from the floor and furiously wiped my eyes with my shirt sleeve. "Who do you think you are? You just keep your hands to yourself."

I helped Stacy to the car. We said nothing. Blood simmered in my face and boiled water from my eyes, and as we descended into the valley I glared out the window, hoping she wouldn't watch me cry.

17

After three nights with the Cottrells, I decided for the sake of convenience to return home. As for Forrest, I simply would not speak to him at all. A stagnant, clinging August had arrived, and in three weeks football practice was to begin. Upon leaving for the university I would not be forced to confront Forrest again until Christmas vacation. The prospect of putting him out of mind for the entire autumn made me feel weightless.

When Stacy could walk with little discomfort, she decided to complete her internship in the attorney's office, and I put in every possible hour at McPherson's, including Saturdays and Sunday afternoons; in the evenings Stuart and I met at the high school to lift weights or run laps on the track or practice pass patterns on the football field. I roamed for suppers: one night with Stuart's family, the next with the Owenses, another with the Cottrells. At home I shut myself in my room and stayed there till morning. If Forrest happened to be in the house when I arrived, a burning lump rose toward my throat, but I'd swallow it and pass him hurriedly without even a glance at his face.

Thus I had achieved an almost perfect removal from him when I was summoned to the phone one afternoon at the lumberyard.

"Jeff, this is Mr. Cottrell."

"Hello, sir. How are you?"

"Well," he began, and the word seemed to disrupt the transmission and surge into my body like an electric charge, cauterizing nerve endings until I could not feel the receiver in my own fingers, dread for Stacy's safety numbing me. "An ambulance was sent to the mill," he continued. "They called to let me know what happened. They knew I could find you."

Confusion slowed my pulse and brought cold sensation to my skin. I could not fathom what such news held for me. "An ambulance—?" I said.

"Your uncle was complaining of a headache. He sat down, then fell to the floor. He's at the hospital, and I think you should see him right away. I can pick you up—"

"No," I said, amazed by my dispassionate reasoning. "No, but thank you. It will be faster if I drive myself."

I hung up the phone and pondered whether it was necessary for me to go, how close kin were expected to react in these situations. Mr. McPherson had been lenient in the past when we requested time off from work. I did not want him to believe I was taking advantage of his benevolence. But I had promised Sheriff Cottrell. That, more than any danger to Forrest, spurred me to my car.

On the way to the hospital I worried about Forrest,

but it was the detached concern I might experience on hearing of misfortune befalling a distant acquaintance. Something within me struggled against feeling more. Forrest had been wheeled into a treatment room, I was told, and I sat on a firm couch in the lobby with Mr. Cottrell, who met me there and asked my permission to stay until we were informed of Forrest's condition.

"I haven't told Stacy," he said. "I figured you'd want to know more before you talked to her."

"Thank you," I answered. He always had the right words or the proper self-restraint, or so it appeared to me. He was the only person whose presence would not have made me uncomfortable as I waited. I did not feel obliged to display false emotion or soothe anyone else's fears. Our complementary characters made me imagine that we could have been related, that I easily could have been his own son.

After an hour the treatment room door swung open onto the clamor inside, and a doctor in a lab coat emerged. He was an older man I'd never seen before, gray-templed behind wire-rimmed glasses; and he placed long, well-directed strides toward us, studying the dingy tile floor, as though he already knew where to find us. We stood as he approached.

"Sheriff," he said, head snapping up with a nod toward Mr. Cottrell. And to me, "Mr. Waters?"

I was unprepared for this formal address. I had expected "Young man?"

"Yes?" I responded.

"Your uncle's condition has stabilized, but there has been some bleeding in the brain. Such a thing is not common in men his age, but it's certainly not unheard of. We're going to move him to intensive care, and he'll probably need to stay there several days."

I suddenly felt foolish, as if I had not been paying attention in class and had been called on to answer a simple question. "Bleeding?" I asked.

The doctor looked at me for a moment, expression rippling outward as he understood that his was the first report I'd received. "Your uncle has had a stroke," he said. "A vessel has ruptured, and blood has escaped into the brain. He is still unconscious, so we can't be certain how extensive the damage is."

This revelation did not stun me. Instead I conjured an absurd scene in which we were all doctors conferring on a delicate case. "Couldn't you operate to relieve the pressure?" I said.

"I'm afraid an operation would not help and might create greater complications. The bleeding seems to have stopped, and this is something his body will have to heal by itself." His tone changed then, becoming more resonant, and he took a slight step back, speaking to both of us as though he'd mounted a podium to deliver a lecture. "Often there's very little we can do. This kind of thing just shows us how fragile our existence can be. Blood gives us life, yet the thin wall of a capillary or vein can rupture, and suddenly our own blood kills us."

"Is he going to die?" I asked, not from fear but because I felt it was my duty to know.

"I don't believe this episode will kill him. But I don't know what kind of life he'll be able to lead after this. There's such a wide spectrum of severity with strokes. Some people don't experience any permanent loss of function at all. It may take months of therapy to return to normal. Your uncle may have to be prepared to work very hard to overcome the effects."

"Sir?" I interrupted.

"Yes?"

"My uncle is a heavy drinker. Could it have been the drinking?"

The doctor inhaled through tightly drawn lips, then removed his glasses and pinched the bridge of his nose. "I don't know," he said, replacing the glasses. "It might have pushed him toward it. Has he mentioned any recent headaches or blackened vision or rushing sounds in his ears?"

I wanted to tell him I had not spoken to Forrest for days, but instead I said, "No sir. Not to me."

The doctor nodded. "He seems to be in good health otherwise. I can't say exactly what the causes were. It's as though something inside him"—and he passed a hand through the air—"let go."

Mr. Cottrell brought Stacy to the hospital at six o'clock that evening, and when she learned there was nothing more we could do, she pleaded that I leave long enough to eat at the diner in town. I refused to go home for the night, and the nurse finally relented, handed me a blanket, and allowed me to curl up on a short couch in the lounge next to the intensive care unit. I gloated over my noble sacrifice, a vigil of supreme charity that Forrest did not deserve. If he ever again had the audacity to doubt my loyalty to the family, I would not throw back at him all of the occasions when he had failed me. No, I would hold those memories in reserve and remind him first of this night.

But when I saw him stir the next morning, and I slipped into the room to see his open eyes, sunken and fearful, his frame frail against the stark linen, the insult of an oxygen tube running to his nose, guilt and fear

choked me. I whispered—the only breath I could man-
age—and tortured my face into a smile, "Well, what
have you gone and done to yourself?"

He stared at me, dry lips struggling to speak, and
a tear fell from my eye before I could turn my head. I
fiercely wiped it away, afraid he'd be disappointed that
I was behaving like a child.

His right side was stricken: arm crooked slightly, hand
unable to form a solid fist, leg a mere prop for his body
("Feels like it's asleep all the time," he said). His throat
rasped each word, and the corner of his mouth did not
flicker when he winced with the effort of motion. After
he was moved from intensive care, when he at last found
the strength to push himself from bed for an arduous
journey to the bathroom, he demanded to be let alone,
slowly sliding bare feet to the floor, gripping the edge
of the mattress, then reaching for the cane he'd been
provided, veins and muscles straining in his arm as he
shifted his precarious weight across the room.

In the ten days before he came home I would lie at
night in bed sweating, having struggled from the depth
of a shallow dream where I had been troubled about
what could be done, listening to absolute stillness in
the house and beyond open windows the hum of crickets
and a rare, faint breeze; and it occurred to me that true
reflection can come only at night, when nothing is left
to contemplate but your own being. Even the stars,
visible through one window in a sliver of blue-black sky
between the house and trees, were so incomprehensible
they turned wonder back onto my own insignificance.
As I lay there, I realized I already had the answer and
gave myself over to it again. This was Forrest's home.
He had nowhere else to go. I speculated whether, years

earlier when my parents died, Forrest had been tormented by these same thoughts, like heavy blocks on his chest. And lying awake, I understood why Forrest had brought me here, why he felt that he owed this to his sister: he was one of those people Bobby Cottrell had mentioned, people such as Bobby's parents, and Stacy—and myself—who always live within the family, the only segment of humanity that to them remains constant, familiar, explicable.

I revealed my decision to Stuart on the day Forrest came home. Fatigued from the exertion, Forrest had retreated to his bedroom in midafternoon when Stuart appeared at the kitchen door.

"Thought you were working today," I said.

"Got off early to see if you needed anything," he responded, but his attention quickly turned to his own stomach, and he swooped upon the chocolate cake Mrs. Owens had left for Forrest. "Sweetness," Stuart said, "succumb to me." He carved a huge wedge from the cake, plopped it on a chipped plate, helped himself to a glass of milk from the refrigerator, and followed me into the living room. The couch sagged when he dropped himself on it. I remained standing in front of him.

"You're starting to look like a grain-fed sow," I told him.

"Coaches wanted me to put on fifteen pounds this summer."

"I think they were hoping at least some of those pounds would be muscle."

"How is he?" Stuart asked, motioning toward the bedrooms down the hall.

"Tired. But he was glad to get out of the hospital. He kept asking them to let him go."

"That guy back there, he's a tough codger."

"Yeah, well, there's a lot of things he won't be able to do for himself now—"

"What, are you kidding? He's always taken care of himself."

"Stuart," I said, clipping his name under the force of consternation, "the man has had a stroke. He needs a walker. His arm is weak. Even his speech is affected—"

"Hey, I'm not denying that. I'm not arguing with you. What's the problem?"

"I'm trying to tell you something and you're not listening." I drew a long breath, inflating myself to full height. "I'm not playing football this year."

Stuart cocked his head absurdly, eyebrows arching in the affected manner of an English professor whose course we had taken together. "I beg your pardon, young man?"

"I'm not playing football this year," I repeated, parading these words solemnly to deny him any humorous avenue. He would try to joke us out of this spot together if he could. But this announcement was unpleasant enough already.

"You realize of course that the university athletic department frowns upon those students whose classes it pays for and who then don't show up for football practice each afternoon. How would your not playing football help Forrest?" He seemed to be probing my full intent, but I could tell he already knew.

"I won't be going to classes either. I'm not going to school at all this year. I'm staying in Assembly Shoals."

"Right. And what does Stacy think about this?"

"I haven't told her yet."

"You almost had your leg shot off. Now, my son,

you walk again. You must accept your calling. God wants you to play football."

A weight in my stomach tugged at the corners of my mouth and the words in my throat, leaving me to reply with a stare.

For the first time in our history I saw Stuart turn ill at the sight of food. He set down the half-eaten lump of cake on the coffee table. "There's got to be somebody else who can take care of him," he said, looking at me squarely.

"Who, Stuart? There's nobody—"

"The Owenses," he said, setting his jaw against the obvious retort.

"They have enough trouble taking care of her arthritis. They don't even *like* Forrest very much, not that they wouldn't do it if they could. But they've helped me enough already. I'm not about to shove this responsibility onto them."

"You shouldn't have to give up everything because of this."

"I'm not giving up everything. Even if I sit out this year, I'll have two years of eligibility left. Forrest should be better in a year, and we can work out something else then. Maybe I can even make it back for spring practice. But right now I'm all he's got. He took me in because I was part of his family. A small child was the last thing in the world he wanted to take care of, but he gave me a home. It wasn't much sometimes, but it was a place where I belonged. Now I have to take care of him. He's part of my family, and I shouldn't need any other reason."

The next day, a Saturday, Crazy Flea Sturkey visited the

house and insisted that he was taking Forrest fishing. I objected, but Forrest eagerly accepted, eyes glimmering at the invitation.

"Nothing wrong with me that I can't go fishing," he said.

"He don't need no mother hen," Flea said to me.

"Then I'm going with you." I told them.

So we loaded Flea's rust-eaten pickup truck and drove to the lake at the quarry. With his cane Forrest maneuvered himself to the rocks at the water's edge, then Flea and I lifted him to a flattop boulder and unfolded a lawn chair for him. I cast his line, then Forrest planted the butt of the cork handle against his stomach and steadied the pole across the crook of his weakened right arm, working the reel with his left hand.

"I got beer in a cooler on the truck," Flea said, stripping off his T-shirt, a meadow of hair on his chest rustling in a humid swirl of August air. "You want a beer?"

"No beer," I said. "He can't have alcohol, or caffeine, and he's got to watch what he eats because of the blood pressure. He shouldn't even be out here. He should be resting."

Flea stared at me as though I had just uttered the most incredible words he'd ever heard. "What about women?"

"Flea!" I scolded.

"Well, God Ah-mighty," he said to Forrest. "No beer, no women. Can't even drink coffee! Why didn't you just go ahead and *die*?"

Forrest's mouth curled into a wry half-smile but relaxed again, eyes intently focused on his fishing line where a plastic bobber quivered on the rippling surface.

Flea moved away from us, clambering over the rocks to establish his own enclave.

"That's a sick man," I said.

"Flea would do anything for his friends," Forrest said, voice hoarse. "That's why he don't have many; he chooses them carefully. But you remember he'll do anything for you."

I stood beside Forrest's chair, hands in my pockets, and we watched the glitter of sun and waited for a sudden plunge of the bobber—a fish striking the bait—until Forrest peered at me and said, "You fishing?"

"I wanted to talk," I said, surprised at my candor. I steeled against the temptation to tell him of my plan at the outset, knowing that before I could agree to stay with Forrest we had to purge hostile blood.

Forrest did not respond.

"You stuck a pretty good one on my chin the other day," I offered, feeling that same blush of anger and humiliation hotter than the sun on my face.

"You were coming at me."

"You were drinking."

I did not look at him, instead surveying the water, grateful that I was standing over him. It put me in a position of superiority. "All I wanted was to find out if you knew who could have been at the house that night. Somebody shot at us. They could've killed us."

With considerable struggle Forrest shifted in his seat, leaning against his left elbow on the chair arm. Long moments of silence seemed to solidify the space between us into a few feet of impenetrable mass. Finally he spoke through this barrier. "They ain't nothing. Thought I owed them something, thought I'd cheated them, so they came looking for money."

"Who came looking for money?"

"It don't matter. They're nothing. But it ain't hard to see what happened. They took a gun up there looking to scare somebody. You surprised them, that's all. They got scared, and they've disappeared like cockroaches into the woodwork."

"What are their names, Forrest? They could come back."

"They won't come back. Just take my word for it, you won't see them again."

Instead of growing impatient with Forrest, I wanted more than anything to believe him. I wanted at least once in my life to trust him without reservation. "Okay," I said, avoiding any inflection of warning that he'd better be right. "I'll take your word for it."

A glance from Forrest conveyed confusion at this unexpected allegiance. Finally he lowered his head again and said, "Oh, I had it figured, though," staring at the lake as if into his own genius. "If you'd lost the game, or won it by less than ten, I'd have gotten a cut of what they took. But then I decided you weren't going to give away the game. I just knew you'd go out there and play as hard as you could after what I'd said. I could see that in you. So I put my own money on you."

I was anxious to move from the subject, already leery of the conspiracy of silence I'd joined. "Forrest, we need to talk about some things. Have you thought about what's going to happen now, what you're going to do?"

"What do you mean?"

I had stepped around the chair where I could see his face. "About how you're going to take care of yourself?"

"You're in my way. I can't see the line."

"Forrest, someone's going to have to—take care of you for a while."

"I got money."

"It's not just money, and you don't have much of that. You can't move like before—"

"I know how I feel," he snapped. "You don't need to be telling me how I feel."

"I get good pay at the lumberyard. Mr. McPherson said I can work there as much as I want. Your insurance at the mill will take care of most of the hospital bills, and the house is already paid off. What I make can cover groceries and the utilities. I can help with your therapy. The doctor said you'll need therapy."

"It's not your concern. You won't be here, anyway."

"I'm taking this year off. I'm not going back to school."

He glowered at me, shaking his head, slowly but far to each side. "No. You play football."

"I will play, just not this season. I'll still be eligible for two more years even if I miss this one."

"I don't need you around."

"Yes, you do. I'm all you've got. You did it for me."

Forrest shook his head.

"I told Stacy last night. She's not happy about it, but she understands. Until you get stronger, you're going to need me. I've made up my mind." I turned from him and saw the bobber on his line dip below the surface, then pop up again. "Forrest, there it goes."

He waited until the bobber sank again, then jerked the rod toward him with his good left arm to set the hook and began reeling in the line.

"Cut it off!" Flea called, scrambling toward us. "Just cut off that lame arm. He don't need it!"

Flea scurried down the rocks to the lake level ten

feet below us and grabbed Forrest's line as the fish breached water, holding aloft a thrashing, glistening bass.

Forrest had tired from the effort, his face a worrisome red, and I took the rod from his unsteady hands.

"You go play football," he said quietly.

But I would not be dissuaded, and a long telephone conversation convinced the head coach I was serious about my intentions. Within a week Stuart had left Assembly Shoals to return to the university for football practice, pleading until the last minute for a different solution. When he was gone, his absence created a sense of solitude in me as heavy as hunger, and I knew that when Stacy left in less than a month for the start of classes I would at last shoulder the full weight of this decision. Alone with Forrest, my complete responsibility would be as caretaker of this family.

During the next two weeks I resigned myself to the work at McPherson's as a long-term prospect—not plunging in as I did each summer with temporary enthusiasm for a cash flow—leaving Forrest at home with the phone at hand so I could check on him throughout the day; and in the evenings we quietly ate generous meals delivered by the Owneses, or I would stir together the few recipes other than sandwiches I had ever mastered. Forrest mired himself in sullen introspection at these times, and I often asked how he felt.

"I'm stronger. You don't need to bother me about it every five minutes," he said.

Sensing that Forrest resented his dependence on me, I figured he'd just have to get used to it.

But though the earth had already begun to lose

more warmth in successive nights as August receded into September, I did not see the autumn of that year in Assembly Shoals. It was not unusual, even now, for Forrest to spend entire nights in his living room recliner. He found it as comfortable as his bed, and over many years the upholstery had shifted and the vinyl creased until a shallow imprint of his body was formed to accommodate him. I never sat there, an act that would have been unnervingly personal and assuming. It was Forrest's place of ultimate seclusion and greatest ease. And it was in this chair that Forrest died.

I found him in early morning. His skin had grown ashen and quite cold, eyes closed and face without expression; and though I recognized immediately that he was gone, my first reaction was to pull up the blanket to his shoulders in predawn air that braced the room through open windows. I felt no disbelief as I had when Bobby Cottrell had died. It seemed entirely logical, and I stood before him surprised that I had so sincerely prepared for a burden I would never have to carry, that I hadn't anticipated this result. Another ruptured vessel in the brain was always possible, the doctor had warned. But my ready acceptance seemed better explained by a deeper distinction between the twin tragedies of that summer: Bobby had thrust himself into the world, determined to find its continuity and meaning, only to become sudden victim to its capricious violence; Forrest had instead withdrawn from the world, unable to discover any grand scheme and unwilling to try, withdrawing into his own family and home and finally into himself, to finish his life awaiting its end. Though I truly missed Forrest, for a long time I entertained a notion that he had actually willed himself to die, allowing me to take my place among a larger family. At least, at his death this was the loss I felt: not of the last remnant of my family but only one member of it.

We buried him behind the weathered church in the same clearing where Bobby was buried. Flea Sturkey attended and did not say a word, stiffly attired in battered loafers and khaki trousers and tweed jacket despite thick heat—his only dress clothes and the unmistakable symbol of his respect. Stuart returned from the university for the afternoon, and his parents and girlfriend came, along with Mr. and Mrs. Owens and the Cottrells. The men joined me to lower the casket; then we shed coats and took shovels to cover it ourselves.

We never discovered who shot at Stacy and me that evening at Forrest's house (only Forrest, I suppose, knew the full truth), but after his funeral it did not seem important to find out. For me, those shadows faded as an independent menace and lingered simply as products of Forrest's own fallibilities, blights of evil and ignorance like those found on every soul, like my own dark and bilious bitterness over the death of my parents. Later I realized that with Forrest this bitterness had also been buried forever.

I felt glad that though Bobby and Forrest had never met, on that same hillside they would always be together. Bobby's death had shown me what he'd never had the chance to see himself, that if nothing else we shared the same destiny, the way the Cahala and every other river on earth inevitably, inexorably flow into the ocean. I, like Bobby, might never find humanity's purpose, but from that day forward I would proceed with the conviction that I belonged within it.

18

In two days I was packed and ready to leave. I toured the house with Mr. Owens, selecting furniture I wanted to keep, and he agreed to handle the sale of the rest and the house itself while I was away. My only contribution would be signatures at the closing. I moved my other belongings, those not needed at school, to the spare bedroom in the Owenses's house, where I lived until graduating from college. I strung up my net and tire in their backyard.

I have never again entered Forrest's house on the ridge. I don't know who lives there today, and that is how I will always think of it: Forrest's house. I wanted my final vision of it to be the one I'd known, not bare-floored and vacant or inhabited by strangers. That way, that home would continue to exist, at least in my mind, as the place where I was raised. If I did not let this image become covered under layers of time and resentment,

I would better remember what my years there taught me: that family is a tenuous and imperfect compromise and that Forrest had to be included within it. To escape the past is not to forget it but rather to accept it. I still possess my key to the lock, as if I could drive up to the house and open the kitchen door onto the familiar smell and arrangement, Forrest in his recliner or making sandwiches at the counter, sports on television, Beast in his paddock out back.

On the afternoon I returned to school, late for the beginning of my junior season, Stacy rode with me, eager to see the apartment she and her roommate had decided to rent for the coming year. She brought a sleeping bag to spend the night on the apartment floor; her father would haul up a load of her furniture the next day. We drove toward town, past poultry barns and the textile mills and the site where Emory Patrick's chemical plant once stood. The Assembly Shoals High School on the hilltop swept by, railroad then veering from the shoulder to traverse the Cahala River and run through town on the opposite side. Reflections of our car and faces floated across plate glass windows in brick storefronts along Main Street, and trees beside the riverbank fell behind; and we accelerated north until the main road and river intersected the white, heat-dazzled, four-lane highway that would carry us to the university.

I dropped Stacy at her apartment near campus, then drove to the athletic dorm. Our room was unlocked. Stuart's half was disheveled and strewn with crumpled clothing: my mattress lay stripped of linens, the study desk empty. On the bed he had left a note hastily scrawled in the block-letter printing he had used since elementary school:

ICE WATERS,

EFFECTIVE PLOY GETTING OUT OF SUMMER PRAC-
TICE, BUT THE RUSE IS OVER AND YOU'D BETTER GET
TO WORK.

SAVE ME! THESE OTHER QUARTERBACKS OUT HERE
COULDN'T THROW A FOOTBALL INTO THE OCEAN FROM
A ROWBOAT.

RENDEZVOUS AT DINNER, BUT MOVE IN FIRST!
THEY'VE HAD ME ROOMING WITH A FROSH LINEMAN,
LOOKS LIKE HE WAS RAISED ON RAW MEAT, BEEN
STARING AT ME HUNGRILY EVERY MORNING.

GUNSHOT WOUNDS, DYING RELATIVES—I SWEAR,
SOMETIMES YOU ARE MORE TROUBLE THAN YOU'RE
WORTH.

WELCOME BACK.

STUART

I piled my luggage on the floor and headed for the locker
room. Early evening was descending, and by now afternoon practice would have concluded, the team migrat-
ing toward the training table for dinner. The locker
room was deserted but for stragglers in the showers,
water spewing and voices distorted against tile walls.
Wadded athletic tape from ankles and wrists littered the
floor, canvas laundry bins sat heaped with towels and
soiled practice uniforms, the air was soaked with a
blended aroma of ammonia and perspiration and steam.
I felt unexpectedly foreign to this environment, suddenly uncertain whether I could make up lost time, and
decided I did not yet want to talk to anyone here. Our
equipment manager was efficient: he had already supplied my locker with a full uniform, shorts for light
workouts, a duffel bag of footballs. I pulled on the shorts,
a jersey, and cleats, and slung the duffel bag over my

shoulder, departing before anyone emerged from the showers, shoving through the locker room door into stifling, hazily diffused glare.

I crossed the practicefield, not stopping there, drawn instead toward the stadium along the path the team followed every home Saturday when cars jammed these streets and the tightly packed faithful heaved waves of obstreperous noise from the bowl and to our advancing column even before we reached the players' entrance. I needed to feel the stadium's familiar closure, the inspiration of focused intent. Circling through the main gate, I saw a solitary figure—black, tall, lithely muscular—sprinting forty yard dashes on well-groomed sod. I did not know him, but from his gliding strides I guessed he was a receiver, a freshman who had drifted here after practice, perhaps to anticipate his first game and the grand elevation of mere physical struggle. Having hoped that I would be alone, I hesitated before proceeding to the middle of the field and upending the duffel bag, footballs bumping and scattering on the grass.

The sprinter wore practice pants and a sweat-soaked T-shirt, shoulder pads and helmet discarded at the edge of the field; and though his face demanded recognition, I could not summon a name. Picking up a football, squeezing it in my hands to feel the grain of leather, I tossed it to him and said, "Here."

For a few minutes, without conversation between us, he ran pass patterns while I threw to him. Running, he seemed to flow, liquid energy radiating from shoulders and hips along limbs like whipcord, no awkward hitch in his joints as each motion of arms and legs ended in clean flicks of wrists and toes. Moist heat clung to us now, and his skin glistened like wet coal. At last I recalled his name from the newspapers.

"You're Anthony North?" I asked.

"That's right," he answered. A towel was folded over the waistband of his shorts, and he tugged it free, wiping his face and neck.

I extended my hand, and he shook it in a damp, powerful clamp. "I'm Jeff Waters," I told him.

He tilted his head, staring at me skeptically. "Thought you weren't playing this year."

"I wasn't, but—I had a change of plans."

"You going to be first-string?"

"Can't say. I'm a long way behind. Season opens in two weeks."

Anthony North had claimed a legion of pass-receiving records at a small high school in the state's southern woodlands. His decision to play college football at the university had been thoroughly publicized. The sportswriters had dubbed him North Wind—swift and lethal.

"How can you still be out here running in this heat?" I said.

"The more I run, the faster I become," he answered, rhyming these lines.

Blood surging, sweat trailing, I felt my competitive predilection restored under the approving observance of the empty stadium and this newcomer's brash assurance. "You could run backwards and beat me in a footrace," I said, "but I've got another idea. We play a little game sometimes. I'll give you thirty yards downfield, then I'll throw, and if you catch up to it, you'll be the first."

Without a word he trotted to my left and assumed his position on an imaginary line of scrimmage, and when I shouted "Go!" he darted from his stance. He didn't appear exceptionally fast leaving the line, and for an instant I was disappointed that he was not making a serious attempt, but gradually he accelerated. I stepped back, ready to throw, and after he'd raced thirty yards I hurled one high and long. Releasing it, I knew he had no chance; I'd never thrown one that far before. But as the ball spiraled through the top of its arc and started down again, he moved up through gears I'd never seen a human possess; his body leaned forward, and long arms flashed outward like arrows, ball dropping to rest softly on his fingertips. After three or four unbalanced strides he regained himself, tucking the ball under his arm, slowing, making a wide turn in the end zone to trot back to me.

I shook my head incredulously but felt no frustration at having lost this contest. In fact, I couldn't halt a smile from stretching across my face, though I turned so he wouldn't see it. My mind swam with the happy image of Anthony North performing impossible catches in a game.

As he flipped the ball to me again, I noticed Stacy standing inside the main gate, watching patiently with hands slipped into back pockets.

"Had enough?" I asked Anthony North.

"Sure," he smirked. "It's time to eat."

"I'll be there later."

He gathered his equipment and walked toward the main gate, nodding at Stacy, sliding through the turnstile and out of sight. Stacy waited for me to approach, loitering in the end zone as though her stepping onto the field would be a trespass.

"Who was that?" she asked.

"My favorite receiver, and I just met him. Did you walk here?"

"It's not far at all. I can walk to class every day. There wasn't much to see in the apartment, just a small kitchen, and a living area, and two empty bedrooms. But it has carpeting, and much more space. Anything would be better than a dorm room."

"How did you know I was here?"

"I didn't." She crossed her arms, stubbing grass with the heel of one shoe. "I wanted to see—where he talked to you."

Though I knew immediately what she meant, Stacy refused to look at me, apparently convinced I would not respect this desire or even understand the reference she had made. But in fact I felt noble in granting her this opportunity, a tangible connection with the irretrievable past that only I could provide. "I'll show you exactly."

She glanced at me with relief, and I led her to one side of the field where steps rose several feet to the first row of seats, and we climbed higher along tiered concrete. The bleachers had been swept and scrubbed and the seats coated with new paint and brightly numbered in stencil. I had not thought about it since the evening he had come, and I was startled to remember indeed which row it was and the precise points we had occupied along the curving aluminum bench. I ushered her to his place, and she sat, elbows on knees, feet propped on the bench below. With one space between, as before, I took my same seat and gazed at the field, already fallen under shadow, several footballs clustered at the center.

"I'm telling you," I said, "when the crowd sees that guy making those catches, they'll be up here dancing in the aisles."

"I hope so," she said distantly.

She had to be left alone in her own contemplation, I decided. I studied the laces of my cleats, then realized I had grown hungry and wondered what the serving line would be doling out for the team's supper. I was ready to suggest that we leave when Stacy said finally, "I feel closer to Bobby, knowing he was here and what he said. I can almost touch him. It makes me feel like I know him better." She drew a breath to complete her thought. "It seems like I know you better, too."

She continued to stare across the dimming expanse, and I did not respond, shaken now from distraction and caught in a larger tide generated by Stacy's suggestion. Everyone I had ever known well had been in this stadium at some time or another, and it was easy to imagine them all here together amid a throng as populous as any one person could apprehend, gathered in single purpose or cleanly defined opposition. Bobby had been right: I did appreciate the simplicity of this place.

We sat together on the long bench among parallel rows that mounted inner slopes of the bowl toward its rim, birds darting above where a circular band of late sun gleamed beneath an opening of sky and light retreating westward before darkness, and that day passed through night and into memory.

They Call Me Father

Recollections of the
Pioneers of British Columbia

The first volume is *The Reminiscences of Doctor John Sebastian Helmcken*, edited by Dorothy Blakey Smith. J. S. Helmcken was British Columbia's pioneer doctor, first Speaker in the legislature, and one of the negotiators of the colony's entry into Confederation.

The second volume is *A Pioneer Gentlewoman in British Columbia*, edited by Margaret A. Ormsby. The author of these recollections, Susan Allison, settled in the Similkameen Valley in the 1860's.

The third volume is *God's Galloping Girl*, edited by W. L. Morton. Monica Storrs's diaries describe her mission work on the Peace River frontier during the Depression.

The fourth volume is *Overland from Canada to British Columbia*, edited by Joanne Leduc. It contains the story of the Overlanders' trek from Ontario under the leadership of Thomas McMicking.

Letters from Windermere, edited by R. Cole Harris and Elizabeth Phillips, is the fifth volume in a series of editions of important documents of the colonial and early provincial history of British Columbia.

The sixth publication in the series is *The Journals of George M. Dawson*, edited by Douglas Cole and Bradley Lockner. The material included in the two volumes was written between 1875 and 1878.

They Call Me Father is the story of a Corsican-born Oblate missionary who worked in British Columbia for sixty-three years.

THEY CALL
ME FATHER

Memoirs of Father Nicolas Coccola

Edited by Margaret Whitehead

University of British Columbia Press
Vancouver 1988

© The University of British Columbia Press 1988
Printed in Canada
ISBN 0-7748-0313-4

Canadian Cataloguing in Publication Data
Coccola, Nicolas.
    They call me Father

(Recollections of the pioneers of British Columbia, 7)
Bibliography: p.
Includes index.
ISBN 0-7748-0313-4

1. Coccola, Nicolas.   2. Missionaries – British
Columbia – Biography.   3. Indians of North America
– British Columbia – Missions.   4. Oblates of Mary
Immaculate – Biography.   5. Oblates of Mary Immaculate
– Missions – British Columbia.   I. Whitehead, Margaret Mary,
1937–   II. Title.   III. Series.
BV2813.C62A3 1988   266'.2'0924   C88-091618-4

This book has been published with the help of a grant from the Canada Council.

CONTENTS

ILLUSTRATIONS

PREFACE

Prior to the late 1850's, the majority of British Columbia's native peoples had had no personal contact with missionaries. Most had become accustomed to the presence of white men through the fur trade, and many participated in an economic relationship in which both partners sought the advantage. Fur traders made few *direct* assaults upon native culture. Economic changes led to social disruption, but the Indians had proved that they could "hold their own" when confronted with an alien economic system. In the 1850's, however, they encountered Europeans whose sole purpose was to disrupt Indian society totally. With the arrival of both Roman Catholic and Protestant missionaries, the native peoples were brought face to face with men and women who were determined to revolutionize their world.[1]

In recent years, historians have attempted to present a balanced picture of native/white contact. But because scholars have tended to examine the lives of extraordinary men, "ordinary" missionaries, the faceless contingent who spent their lives among spiritual charges at once encouraging and frustrating, acquiescent and resistant, remain unknown. Unlike the rebels whose lives have been highlighted by historians,[2] the "typical" in-the-field missionaries worked by the rules of either churches or missionary organizations which both directly and indirectly governed most of their working actions. As a result, their daily working lives, their beliefs, motivations, and material concerns throw more light on Indian/white relations than the exceptional lives of the "great men" of mission history.

These "Memoirs" of the Corsican Roman Catholic missionary priest, Oblate of the Most Holy and Immaculate Virgin Mary, Nicolas Coccola, do not reflect a literary or philosophical bent, nor do they indicate a sense of self-importance, or a marking of his particular place in history. In 1934, after more than fifty years as missionary to British Columbia, Coccola wrote his autobiography "under obedience" to his bishop, Emile Buñoz. It was, at best, a reluctant undertaking—not a task of self-glorification but a bending to the will of a superior. As Coccola once wrote, "It is not an interesting task to write about oneself."[3] Like the majority of the province's missionaries, Catholic and Protestant, Coccola worked during his long career among the peoples of several Indian nations and served in a number of missionary roles.

The original "Memoirs" were written in pencil and are available for study at the Oblate Archives Deschâtelets, Ottawa. Several years ago (exact date unknown) someone—it was believed by the late Oblate archivist Gaston Carrière that it was a young seminarian—typed them up, completely editing them in the process into "good" English. This edited version is available both at the Archives Deschâtelets and at the Oblate Archives in Vancouver.

Father Coccola's reluctance to write his life story, combined with his advanced years, may have caused him to "cheat" a little. He appears to have supplemented his own recollections with material taken from mission records known as Codex Historicus—daily, weekly, or monthly records kept by each mission—and a notebook, apparently written during Coccola's years in the Northwest, a transcription of which is available at the Archives Deschâtelets and the Oblate Archives, Vancouver. The original notebook is at the chancellory, Diocese of Prince George. Consequently, parts of the "Memoirs" read like a diary. Moreover, Coccola may have had access to another important document. Ten years prior to writing his autobiography, Coccola was interviewed, while in hospital in Vancouver, by an interested amateur historian, Denys Nelson, who wrote up these interviews into a narrative.[4] Comparison of this interview data and the "Memoirs" reveals records of the same events, in almost the same sequence—although the narrative (which is considerably shorter and deals primarily with Coccola's earlier mission work) contains, in a number of places, more detail.

Presented here is the original pencil document. As Gaston Carrière expressed it, the document is "not a masterpiece of English literature." For example, past and present tenses are used indiscriminately; there is some repetition; and capitalization, punctuation, and spelling are inconsistent—sometimes Coccola spells the English word correctly, sometimes incorrectly, sometimes an "error" is simply the correct French word (for example, piquets/pickets). In the interest of the general readership (and for certain cost considerations), spelling, abbreviations, and capitalization have been made consistent. Quotation marks have been added to indicate direct speech and "silent" corrections have been made where deemed appropriate; but the editing has been done with respect for both scholarship and the French flavour of the text. According to Father Carrière, several pages of the original manuscript have been missing since 1959, and although he searched extensively, he was unable to locate them. Consequently, for Coccola's brief assessment of his early life and his first missionary assignment, we are indebted to the unknown seminarian who copied it.

I wish to express my gratitude to the Oblate Community for permission to edit and publish Father Coccola's Memoirs and my appreciation for the help and encouragement of family, friends, and colleagues. In particular, I am grateful for the unfailing support of my husband, Alan, the assistance and encouragement of Patricia E. Roy, the constructive criticism and sound advice of Jaqueline Gresko and Jean Barman, the enthusiastic help of archivists Sister Maria Santos (Nelson), Sister Mary Patterson (Bellevue, Washington), Sister Thelma (Victoria), Sister Louisa Dupuis (Edmonton), Sister Nora Cummings (Calgary), Monsignor Philip Hanley (Victoria), Father George Pflinger (Fernie), Tom Lascelles, Oblate Archivist, Vancouver, the staff of PABC, Victoria, and the Glenbow Archives, Calgary, the assistance of John Brioux, O.M.I. and Olive Gauthier (Ottawa, Archives Deschâtelets) with photographs, the editorial advice and copy-editing of Jane Fredeman, and the efficiency and dedication of my typist, my daughter Fiona Hafer. Above all, I owe a special debt to the late Gaston Carrière for his invaluable assistance and enthusiasm for the project, his wit, and his friendship.[6]

NOTES

1 Canadian church historians have delineated men as the movers and shakers of Canadian church historical development, and outside of the noted seventeenth-century church women of Quebec, little attention has been paid to women missionaries.
2 For example: Jean Usher, *William Duncan of Metlakatla* (Ottawa: National Museum of Man Publications in History, No. 5, 1974); David Mulhall, *Will to Power: The Missionary Career of Father Morice* (Vancouver: University of British Columbia Press, 1986); Patricia Meyer, ed., *Honoré-Timothée Lempfrit, O.M.I.: His Oregon Trail Journal and Letters from the Pacific Northwest, 1848–1853* (Fairfield, Washington: Ye Galleon Press, 1985).
3 Coccola to R.E. Casnell, 4 May 1909, Coccola Correspondence Outward, Archives Deschâtelets, Ottawa.
4 The pencilled manuscript is faded in parts, and sometimes the lines are cramped together; this makes it difficult at times to be absolutely certain of spellings and punctuation.
5 Denys Nelson emigrated to Quebec from England in 1912. After training in pharmacy, he worked at a number of hospitals including Winnipeg General and the Royal Columbian, New Westminster. After serving as a medic in World War I, Nelson bought a drugstore in Fort Langley. A keen amateur historian, Nelson's first publication was a history of Fort Langley published in 1927 by the Art, Historical and Scientific Association of B.C. Nelson also had an article, "Yakima Days," published by the *Washington Historical Quarterly*. He was one of the founders of the publication *Museum Notes*. His "Reminiscences of the Rev. Father Coccola" is available for study at the Archives Deschâtelets, Ottawa, and the Vancouver City Archives.
6 Father Carrière published two sections of the Memoirs in *Oblate Life* (formerly *Etudes Oblates*), Vol. 35, March 1976, and Vol. 39, 1980.

INTRODUCTION

In 1879, the French Republican government, under the leadership of Jules Ferry, planned to put into force laws aimed at curbing the power of the Roman Catholic Church. Ferry was convinced that at a time when "the rising claims of science, rationalism and free inquiry" were making an impact throughout Western Europe, the education of France's youth should be taken out of the hands of a church which openly opposed and attacked the new liberalism.[1] Ferry's plan to remove education from the church's ministry was seen as the opening salvo in what has been described as "France's last religious war."[2] Since the French Revolution, religious orders in general had lived an uneasy existence in France, and one, the Oblates of the Most Holy and Immaculate Virgin Mary, had especially strong reasons to fear Ferry's purely Republican government.[3]

The Oblate founder, Eugène de Mazenod, had always been a strong supporter of papal authority, a stance which guaranteed the enmity of any French government determined to subjugate the church to state control. When the Bourbon dynasty was overthrown in July 1830, for example, the beginning of the new régime was characterized by a violent anti-clericalism, and Oblate priests were driven from their establishment at Nîmes. In spite of hostility, de Mazenod committed himself to defending the church's rights regarding education, and he openly opposed government bills which moved to limit church involvement in higher education. Consequently, for a time, the Oblate superior was stripped of his French citizenship and deprived of his status.

The 1848 Revolution, which led to the Second Republic and the Empire of Napoleon III, at least partially restored educational freedom, and the religious orders breathed a little easier. However, the Third Republic of 1870, while initially seeming to support the church, became more and more anti-clerical; the Oblates saw in the election of Ferry a return to the bitter animosity of past years.[4] In the province of Burgundy, at the Autun scholasticate which housed young seminarians preparing for the priesthood, the administration feared that the government would close down the establishment and expel the Oblates from France.[5] Apprehension swept through the community, and the clergy discussed how best to protect the members and Oblate property against possible physical attack by local militia or police. A young seminarian, Nicolas Jourdain di Coccola, confronted his superiors with a solution: "give us guns and protection will be assured!"

A few days later, Coccola was en route to the mission fields of British Columbia.[6] For sixty-three years, this spirited young Oblate worked as missionary among the province's native peoples. After a brief posting to the Kamloops, Shuswap, and Nicola Valley Indian bands, Coccola spent eighteen years as missionary to the fiercely independent Kutenai before being transferred, in 1905, to Our Lady of Good Hope Mission, Stuart Lake, in north central British Columbia. Based at this mission, he ministered to Carrier, the secluded Sekani, and a few Tsimshians. His final posting as an active Indian missionary was as principal of Lejac Indian Residential School built for the education of northern Indian children. In addition to his missionary work, Coccola spent some time as chaplain to Canadian Pacific Railroad workers and as circuit priest to the numerous towns that mushroomed in the Kootenay region in anticipation of, or in response to, agricultural and mining enterprises.

BIOGRAPHY

Coccola was a Corsican. He was born on 12 December 1854 to Jean and Elise (née Peretti) di Coccola in the hamlet of Coccola, parish of Santa Luccia di Moriani.[7] The community was small and, like most of Corsica, rural. Born at a time when his church was combating an age of rapid political, economic, social, and cultural change, Coccola was raised during the years of clerical counterattack. To defend against liberalism, Catholic doctrine was taught in its full stringency. The clergy returned to the wearing of Roman and clerical dress, adopted the Latin liturgy, and through the use of elaborate religious rituals and the cultivation of such relatively new devotions as the Forty Hours Adoration and the Perpetual Adoration preserved and strengthened the faith of believers.

It was a time of romanticism in the Church. In France, miracles and visions culminating in the apparitions of Lourdes abounded. Conservative Catholic authors flooded the market with uncritical lives of the saints and devotional histories "so replete with supernatural occurances as to require of the reader an almost continuous act of faith."[8] Faith was strong in Coccola's family. In his only reference to his parents, Coccola notes that he had been born because his mother and father "had offered

prayers and visited shrines of the Virgin Mary to obtain a son." Moreover, two of the three Coccola brothers who attended the seminary became priests.

His early life most certainly determined by the teachings and rituals of
an embattled church, Coccola, after some private tutoring, entered the
lycée at Bastia—a commercial and military-dominated town. Techni-
cally under government control, the lycée was in reality run by strongly
ultramontane clergy who provided an unexceptional, humanities-
orientated, and highly disciplined education.[9] The Corsican's early
schooling was uneventful until the outbreak of the Franco-Prussian War
in 1870 threatened to disrupt his education. The French, badly over-
estimating the preparedness of their army, suffered numerous defeats,
and resistance to the Germans was maintained in French provinces (including Corsica) by hastily improvised and sometimes very young
volunteers.[10] Filled with patriotic fervour, the lycée students, including
Coccola and his classmates, rushed to enlist. However, only students
who got parental consent were allowed to join the military forces and
Coccola had to settle for studying both the German language and
geography—in case of a protracted war.[11]

A military orientation was the norm for many Corsicans. One historian claims that a fighting spirit is seen as an integral part of Corsican
heritage; "a love of firearms and an insistence even among the young
people, on carrying them about as a symbol of status and self-
assertiveness" was, and still is, a Corsican characteristic.[12] Certainly
many students leaving the lycée chose to join the military and went
directly to France for training; but others, like Coccola, chose to enter
the priesthood. In an economically restricted area such as Corsica,
choice of careers was severely limited.

However, Father Guibert, in charge of the Grand Seminary of Ajaccio
where Coccola began his training for the priesthood in 1873, noted certain problems with Corsicans. He wrote to his superiors: "The Grand
Seminary of Ajaccio presents a special characteristic which is that of the
difficulty involved in making young men of a very independent nature
conform to a rule, and of instilling feelings of piety and motives of Faith
into souls which are still dominated by nature with all its untamed energy."[13]

Coccola's choice of the priesthood at a time when the church was itself engaged in a battle of survival in France indicates that the Corsican
had not necessarily selected a non-violent vocation. And certainly his
first choice of China as the theatre for his priestly work reveals a certain
active courage; in the nineteenth century, missionaries were being ex-
ecuted in China.[14] Coccola was enthusiastic for a challenging missionary

post.[15] But, in nineteenth-century Europe, Coccola was only one of a multidenominational army of militant missionary enthusiasts.

MISSIONARIES

A nineteenth-century missionary was, by definition, a man of action, a soldier ready to conquer for Christ by delivering the Christian message to the world's non-Christian peoples: knowledge of an all-powerful, monotheistic God; of heaven and its joys and hell and its torments; and of the Christian precepts necessary to obtain the one and avoid the other. All missionaries were united in their determination to bring the pagan peoples of the world, at whatever cost to themselves or their spiritual charges, "to individual salvation through Christ."[16] But, in spite of their common intent, missionaries defy simple classification. They came from a variety of ethnic, economic, class, educational, and denominational backgrounds, and they brought to their mission work a variety of social theories advocated by their respective missionary organizations. All these factors influenced their approach to their work.[17] But, as has been argued elsewhere, it is also crucial to look at "what the individual agent actually did on the spot."[18]

Whether as individuals or as groups, since the 1960's the image of missionaries has undergone considerable change. In their own time, they were seen by many as heroes and heroines for having chosen to abandon the comfort and familiarity of their own cultured society for work within what was considered to be a primitive, often barbaric, and definitely pagan environment. Their mission was clearly understood both by the society they left behind and by those in the newly emerging frontier communities where they worked. In British Columbia, where missionaries arrived to begin permanent work among the native peoples in 1858, both government and settlers appreciated the missionary presence.[19]

Governor James Douglas encouraged and assisted all missionaries who came to provide "moral and religious training" for the Indians.[20] For settlers the missionary was often seen as the only white authority figure standing between them and the "uncivilized" Indians. Susan Allison, Similkameen Valley pioneer, wrote in her journal that "the priests were kindly neighbours and I am sure that it was to them I owed the goodwill of the Indians."[21]

As contemporary scholars began to focus on the missionary impact on native communities, the heroes became villains, agents of cultural destruction. As one writer argued: "Missionaries sought to change not only the ways of work and politics of native peoples but their innermost beliefs, feelings, and deepest held values as well; and because of this missionaries may be considered the most ambitious and culturally pervasive of all colonists, attempting social change and domination in their most radical form."[22] Missionaries certainly agreed that salvation outweighed the value of native cultures and demanded the total dismantling of native customs and tradition—regardless of their functional importance in aboriginal societies.[23] And, on the surface, the missionaries appear to have succeeded.[24] By the 1900's, most of British Columbia's Indians were at least nominally Christian. Indians such as the Chilcotin of the Cariboo region and the Kwakiutl of Vancouver Island who initially resisted missionary activity accepted the Christian message. Chief Pasala, a Kwakiutl hereditary chief, for example, had accepted Methodist missionary Thomas Crosby's offer to provide a teacher for his people, though he rejected Crosby's request that a missionary reside among them; but the chief eventually accepted Christianity, and a preacher arrived to assist the teacher.[25] However, despite missionary claims and official figures, missionary successes, particularly when judged by nonmissionary standards, were often more apparent than real. The missionaries operated under numerous handicaps, all of which severely reduced their effectiveness; and "success" depended as much upon pre-contact synchronization of Christianity and ancient beliefs—plus Indian willingness to proselytize for the new belief system—as upon missionary efforts alone. And Indian resistance to complete acculturation resulted in at least as many nominal as committed native Christians.

Many, if not most, European missionaries belonged to organizations. While they did provide spiritual and material support, these groups could also, by virtue of rigid rules, regulations, and expectations, limit missionary effectiveness.[26] In British Columbia organizations such as the Anglican Church Missionary Society, the Methodist Missionary Society, the Methodist Women's Missionary Society, and various Roman Catholic religious orders under the direction of the Congregation for the Propagation of the Faith (the Propaganda) in Rome provided, and supported, men and women determined to convert the native peoples.

Changes in Europe as well as missionary zeal had brought the Oblates. Between 1789 and 1870, as relationships between the Roman Catholic Church and the European states underwent stress and strain, a vast missionary army, supported by the papacy, strengthened and expanded the power of Rome in foreign lands. In 1814, the pope formally re-established the original "soldiers of the pope," the Jesuits. New orders such as de Mazenod's Oblates, Marianists, Fathers of the Holy Cross, and Missionaries of the Sacred Heart joined older orders, including the Jesuits, Franciscans, Capuchins, and Christian Brothers in the mission field. However, in spite of its original name—the Missionary Society of Provence—Coccola's order, unlike the guiding organizations of his Protestant missionary contemporaries, was not established to foster missionary endeavours in foreign lands.

De Mazenod's stated purposes to those men who would join him were: to "stir up the Faith which [was] dying among the poor";[27] improve the quality of the priesthood which, since the Revolution, had deteriorated to the point where instead of men of "quality," only "poor workmen, miserable peasants" were available to bring religious teachings to the people;[28] and to reform morally unworthy priests.[29] These formidable tasks required recruitment of an élite group of men, men who, like de Mazenod, were committed to the defence of the papacy. Such men were not easy to find.

In France, as in other European countries, the clergy were deeply divided. There were those whose reaction to the liberalizing changes of the French Revolution and subsequent political, economic, and social upheavals was to support the increased centralization of the church under a papacy of unlimited power.[30] Those of a less conservative persuasion believed that the church should come to terms with "modern men and modern institutions."[31] De Mazenod stood firmly in the conservative camp. This unstinting and sometimes dangerous support of the papacy was no doubt responsible for the willingness of Pope Leo XII to bend the rules which demanded that a new order prove itself over a long period of time and have numerous members before obtaining papal recognition. In February 1826, he approved de Mazenod's still small society and agreed to the founder's choice of name.[32]

Initially, the only practical objective of the Oblates was to preach to the rural poor of Provence in the form of "missions." A "mission" consisted (and still consists) of a set formula of prayer and preaching over a specific number of days or weeks, and the preaching concentrates on the basic tenets of the Catholic faith. This type of "Home Mission" had its roots in the seventeenth-century work of men like Vincent de Paul and John Eudes and had been outlawed by Napoleon in 1809. But the Restoration saw the revival of the format throughout France. Between 1815 and 1830, the Oblates gave over one hundred "home missions."[33] But while the work of his small group centred on Provence, de Mazenod's ambitious mind was already on establishing his missionaries throughout the world as "co-redeemers [with Christ] of the human race." While in Rome in 1826, he wrote to Cardinal Pedicini that "when subjects were more numerous, the Superiors would send them to America, either to aid the poor Catholics deprived of all spiritual goods, or to make new conquests for the Faith."[34] During his lifetime, de Mazenod (not always without opposition) gave his small, locally oriented society a world-oriented mission. Under his administration, the Oblates accepted the direction of major seminaries (such as the one at Ajaccio), became directly involved in education, took over parishes or established new parishes in missionary territory, and, perhaps above all, entered the field of foreign missions. By 1859, the Oblates had expanded into Switzerland, Corsica, England, Eastern Canada, the eastern United States, Western Canada (the prairie territories), Ceylon, Oregon, James Bay (Canada), Texas, Algeria, Natal, Ireland, Mexico, and British Columbia.

Their first missionary work actually among native peoples was in Eastern Canada. In June 1841, Monseigneur Ignace Bourget, bishop of Montreal, stopped at Marseilles en route to Rome, and requested Oblate priests, both in their capacity as preachers of missions and as, when required, missionaries among the native peoples. It was natural that Bourget approach de Mazenod.[35] Quebec clergy, particularly Bourget's predecessor Bishop Jean-Jacques Lartigue, actively promoted ultramontanist ideology; "papal and Church supremacy in secular as well as religious matters was adopted with a vengeance by Monseigneur Lartigue and the bishops of Quebec were not unreceptive."[36] Bourget, "a genius in central Church organization," completed Lartigue's plan to bring like-thinking priests (nuns and teaching brothers also) from Europe.[37] He was determined that Protestant Ontario would not assimilate Catholic immigrants and that the Catholic Church of Canada would be controlled from Rome.[38] Such wishes could not have fallen on more responsive ears. Bourget got his Oblates.

Eugène de Mazenod saw only success for his missionaries and pressed them on in spite of their small number to extend themselves as far as possible;[39] "you cannot expose yourself to... losing the advantage which you are rightly and very well exploiting to evangelize all of North America by ministering to the Diocese of Montreal, Quebec, Kingston and the Red River. A little courage and confidence in God is needed."[40] The words were encouraging, but de Mazenod did little to ease his missionaries' workload. When he promoted the move to missionary work among native peoples, de Mazenod added a new section to the order's *Constitution and Rules.*

The original Oblate statutes clearly stated that the aim of the society was not only to work towards the salvation of others but, "above all else," to provide its members with the means of practising religious virtues. De Mazenod drew up constitutions, rules, and vows worthy of a contemplative order devoted solely to a life of prayer. For the missionary, each day's activities included several periods of meditative prayer, scripture study, visits to chapel, recitation of the rosary, examination of conscience and "Divine Office" (which could in exceptional circumstances be modified, but never omitted). There were weekly and monthly retreats and spiritual conferences to reinforce his faith and his sense of community. Oblates were ordered also to read scripture and to study papal writings and what de Mazenod termed "selected literature." Far from absolving missionary Oblates from this rigorous and time-consuming routine, the new section stressed that those distant from the Congregation should be more disciplined and even stricter in observing all the points of the rules, "especially those that concerned spiritual exercises."[41]

Accepting mission work in the Oregon Territory in 1847, de Mazenod was filled with enthusiasm: "Behold a new mission opening up before us... our family will preach Jesus Christ from one ocean to another in these immense regions which have never known Him; what an apostolate!"[42] But when Brother Nicolas Coccola arrived on the Pacific Coast, it was in Victoria, not Portland, that he landed. The Oblates were to know defeat in Oregon. But the lessons they learnt there merit consideration since they not only influenced the life and work of Coccola and all Oblate missionaries to British Columbia, but also reveal the way in which organizational problems and objectives could hinder in-the-field missionary accomplishments.

DENOMINATIONAL RIVALRY

The first problem encountered was denominational rivalry. What had begun with the Reformation could not be escaped even in the wilderness of the Pacific Northwest. The first missionaries to the Oregon Territory were Protestants. In the 1830's Methodists Jason and Daniel Lee and Presbyterians Marcus Whitman, Henry Harmon Spalding, and William H. Gray, with their wives, settled throughout the area. While in many parts of the colonial world missionaries of various denominations frequently socialized and assisted each other, this was not the case on the Northwest coast. It was as essential for Catholic missionaries to save the Indians from the heresy of Protestantism (in the case of the Protestants, it was from "papist ways") as it was to save them from "paganism." Close on the heels of the Protestant missionaries, on 24 November 1838, the territory's first Catholic priests, French-Canadians François Norbert Blanchet and Modeste Demers arrived to begin their task of establishing the Catholic Church "in that part of the Diocese of Quebec situated between the Pacific Ocean and the Rocky Mountains."[43] By sending the two priests, Bishop Joseph Signay of Quebec was responding to the requests of French-Canadian settlers, mostly employees or ex-employees of the Hudson's Bay Company settled in the Willamette Valley, for priests to serve them. But Signay stated quite clearly that the "prime objective" of their mission was to Christianize the Indian peoples living in the vast diocese. Until 1842, the two priests worked alone. Between September 1842 and July 1846–when the Northwest was elevated by Rome to the status of an ecclesiastical province and divided into three dioceses—two other French-Canadian priests, Fathers Langlois and Bolduc, five Jesuits, a few Jesuit lay brothers, and six nuns, Sisters of Notre Dame of Namur, tried to cover an area where white settlers were increasing and where Indians were numerous. Blanchet (now archbishop of Oregon City) appealed to de Mazenod for help. Because he had already committed many men to North America, the founder was reluctant, but Magloire Blanchet, bishop of Walla Walla (later Nisqually), appealed to the Oblate superior in Canada, Bishop Bruno Guiges, for help, and he was promised Oblates.[44] De Mazenod acquiesced, and on 2 January 1847, the first Oblate missionaries to the Pacific Coast, Father Pascal Ricard (superior), Brothers Casimir Chirouse, Charles John Felix Pandosy, Georges Blanchet, and lay Brother Celestin Verney, arrived at Walla Walla. In October, after initial contacts with the local Indians, they established St. Rose Mission near Fort Walla Walla on land provided "somewhat reluctantly" by Piopiomosmos, a Walla Walla chief. Equally soon, they were caught up in denominational rivalry intensified by their presence.

They had been at St. Rose Mission approximately six weeks when the infamous Whitman massacre occurred on 29 November 1847. Minister and missionary Dr. Marcus Whitman and his wife were among the fourteen Americans killed by Cayuse Indians at the Presbyterian mission near Walla Walla. The Reverend Henry Spalding accused the Catholic clergy of inciting the massacre. Even before the massacre, proselytizing the Indians had proved difficult. Ricard believed the Presbyterians were "telling lies about the Catholics" and advising the Indians not to receive them. After the massacre, missionary work was nearly impossible. The resultant warfare between the Cayuse Indians and whites, along with Protestant accusations of "Catholic complicity" in the massacre and the consequent American resentment of the French priests, all took their toll.[45] And as a result, to ensure that the Catholic priests established themselves ahead of Protestant rivals, Louis D'herbomez* O.M.I., who arrived with the second contingent of Oblates in 1850 and became acting superior of missions in March 1857—his permanent appointment was made in 1859—was to push his missionaries to the limit, for in British Columbia, as in Oregon, Protestant missionaries posed a threat. Anglican Bishop George Hill of Victoria pressured missionary societies to send bishops, ministers, teachers, and catechists to prevent the expansion of the Roman Catholic Church.

Because of his concern over the Protestant thrust, D'herbomez

* Although this spelling seems incorrect, this is both how D'herbomez spelled his name and how it appears in Carrière, *Dictionnaire Biographique des Oblats de Marie Immaculée au Canada*, Vol. 1, pp. 285–86

pleaded with de Mazenod to allow the establishment of missions in mainland British Columbia. "Time is pressing," he urged, "the English Church have already an Episcopal See; their ministers are travelling in all directions and they know as well as we do how to choose the best places for the success of their purpose."[46] To a man who had come to envision the province as a "second California" where the Catholic Church would flourish among the increasing numbers of French, Irish, Canadian, Italian, Spanish, and Mexican immigrants, the spread of Protestant faiths was a very real threat.[47]

POVERTY

A second problem encountered in the Oregon Territory was poverty. The 1848 Revolution in France prevented the Society for the Propagation of the Faith, the principal fund-raiser for the Oblates, from sending aid. Missionary work suffered as the Oblates struggled "to keep their heads above water." Ricard explained to a fellow priest, "our poverty prevents us from becoming missionaries, we have become simple tillers. We have hung our crosses at the sides of our beds and we have taken up the hatchet and pickaxe." A vegetable garden and "small supplies" on credit from Hudson's Bay Chief Factor William Fraser Tolmie helped the missionaries at St. Joseph's Mission, near present-day Olympia, Washington. But missionaries working among Indians in eastern Oregon were often reduced to trading "such items as handkerchiefs" with the Indians in exchange for food.[48] This experience no doubt influenced D'herbomez's pattern in British Columbia of opening Indian missions where there was a white Catholic population established—or soon expected—to help support the missionaries' works. This dependence upon white subscriptions was one reason why missionaries, including Coccola, sometimes supported white policies at the expense of the Indians.[49]

INTRADENOMINATIONAL CONFLICT

A third problem encountered was the animosity between the Oblates and the French-Canadian clergy, particularly between Ricard and the Blanchets. This discord was multifaceted. At one level it was purely cultural: a French/French-Canadian conflict. However, almost from the day of their arrival, the Oblates clashed with the Blanchet brothers on both personal and administrative levels. Personal hostility began in 1847 when the newly arrived French missionaries met Magloire Blanchet at St. Louis, Missouri, en route to the Oregon Territory. Blanchet had understood that the Oblates would not be arriving for several months, and since he had made no travel arrangements for them, he was not entirely pleased to see them. Upon their arrival on the coast, in both canon law and the Oblate constitution, Ricard and his priests had to accept the directives of Oregon's ecclesiastical leaders. However, what the Oblates felt was necessary to achieve their missionary goals and what the ecclesiastical leaders felt was imperative for the good of the entire Roman Catholic church in Oregon were not always compatible. Money, land, and recruitment were the three basic areas of discord.

Always short of money, the Oblate superior demanded that the Oblates use any money they received from the Society for the Propagation of the Faith simply to support the missionaries and that the bishops pay the expenses of building and upkeep of mission property. Land preempted by the Oblates for development of missions and mission farms had to be registered in the name of individual members, since American law did not recognize the rights of religious groups to own communal property. The bishops insisted that though it was registered by Oblates, the land belonged to the Catholic church rather than to the order. Since both the Oblates and the Oregon church were in financial need, neither would give up what they considered to be their due right.[50] Compounding the problems was the defection in 1849 of François Blanchet's secular priest, François Jayol, to the Oblate order. The Oblates always worked in pairs, and apparently "the timid Jayol was attracted to this system out of fear of being alone." Blanchet, angry at this apparent "pirating" of his priest, demanded his release and threatened to suspend the unfortunate Jayol from the priesthood.[51] Both the Blanchets and de Mazenod, not to mention Ricard, who was determined to justify himself, made frequent appeals to Rome for justice. Although eventually matters calmed down somewhat, the deep-seated antipathy between the Oregon bishops and the Oblates was not resolved.

Better working conditions were available north of the border and Louis D'herbomez determined to gain autonomy for the Oblates in the new territory. This was not an easy task. Bishop Modeste Demers, who had no diocesan priests to help him, initially welcomed the Oblates to his immense diocese. He was not prepared, however, to hand over control to the French missionaries. But D'herbomez was still determined on autonomy. He believed it essential that New Caledonia be taken from Demers' jurisdiction and placed in the hands of a missionary order. Demers and D'herbomez took their quarrel to Rome, and a political struggle ensued. In 1864, Rome granted the Oblates the autonomy they desired. Demers was left in charge of the truncated diocese of Victoria while D'herbomez, given the honorary title Bishop of the Melitopolis, was made ecclesiastical leader of the mainland Vicariate of British Columbia. The new situation, which had grown out of the Oregon experience, placed D'herbomez and his missionaries in dual roles. Already combining the roles of ecclesiastical leader and director of Oblate missions in the Pacific Northwest, D'herbomez now had to combine mission extension with the creation of an adequate financial base to build churches, residences, schools, and charitable institutions. The Oblates were the vicariate's only priests and thus had to combine mission work with responsibility for white parish developments, a situation detrimental to Indian work.[52] While some of these organizational difficulties were peculiar to the Oblates, other difficulties were more universal.

IMAGE OF INDIANS

Today's missionaries receive linguistic training and spend time in the field learning native languages and other aspects of native culture—although it has been suggested that this training is less an appreciation of native culture than an attempt to find more efficient methods of transmitting Christianity.[53] Until recent decades, however, missionaries in general were ignorant of the cultural values held by native societies. Many missionaries were of the working or lower middle classes and had limited education.[54] But even where they were of élite status and had received considerable schooling, Europeans had limited knowledge of societies whose structural features differed so radically from European norms. As one scholar has pointed out: "traditional Europe had central government in territorial states, world religion, coined money, market places, cities, literacy and written documents... large and dense populations, settled agriculture, external commercial trade, professional soldiers and very sharp social stratification."[55] Given this cultural background, even though early missionaries from peasant and working class backgrounds would have a limited appreciation of subsistence economies, none would appreciate the pervasiveness of Indian spirituality or such widespread prestige and status-oriented activities as the potlatch.[56]

By the time Nicolas Coccola reached British Columbia, the Oblates had already made contact with the native peoples the Corsican was to convert and hold to the Catholic faith. Coccola could have had some knowledge of these Indians prior to his departure from France through reading *Missions de la Congrégation des Missionaires Oblats de Marie Immaculée*. Published from 1862 to 1972, the *Missions* consisted of letters and reports from Oblate mission administrators and in-the-field workers around the world. However, even into the twentieth century, some Catholic missionaries entered British Columbia knowing virtually nothing of the Indian peoples. Upon her arrival at Sechelt in 1911, Sister Patricia of the Sisters of the Child Jesus knew only that the natives were known as "Red Indians" and that "they would not be civilized." During World War Two, missionaries trained to work in Africa or Japan found themselves working among the province's native peoples of whom they had no knowledge. And in the 1950's, an Oblate teaching brother knew of the Indians only what he had seen in the movies.[57] Although Coccola met missionaries who had worked among those who were to become his spiritual charges, these men most likely suffered from the ethnocentric blindness which affected all missionaries to some degree, and it is unlikely that prior to his arrival he had more than a very superficial knowledge of native culture. Even after years of contact, there is an absence in his writings of significant cultural descriptions; the only people whose past seems to have aroused his interest were the Kutenai. However, lack of knowledge did not cause missionaries to hesitate in their attempts to bring about massive cultural disruption among native communities; and Coccola, like his Protestant rivals, had a "perfect" conversion system.

MISSIONARY METHODOLOGY

The Corsican was not free to develop his own missionizing techniques or to make adjustments for local conditions or even for the strength or weakness of native response.[58] His order had prescribed a strict, rigid plan for both conversion and control of Indian spiritual development. Formulated initially as a result of local missionary conditions in Oregon, the plan was based on instructions from the founder and successful Jesuit methodologies used in Paraguay and the Pacific Northwest. Its aim was to create missionary-controlled Indian communities, ideally isolated from white contact and contamination and governed by almost puritanical laws; laws implemented to keep the Indians free from sin and faithful to Catholicism.

Missionaries of all denominations regarded Christianity as a zero-sum proposition; their bid was for total influence and control.[59] Essentially this attitude was fostered by ethnocentricity. For all missionaries, the starting point in their relationship with native peoples was their belief not only in the superiority of white civilization, but most particularly in the superiority of Christianity over indigenous religions. With God's blessing, the right formula, and spirited presentation, the Indians would be brought to see this superiority. Unfortunately for missionary expectations, such elements as native economic needs, their nomadic lifestyle, the detrimental effects—to Indian spiritual and material well-being—of Indian/white contact and the persistence of native spiritual beliefs all countered missionary efforts. To counteract the first two problems, missionaries of all denominations encouraged indigenous peoples, regardless of their cultural development, to settle in one place and follow agricultural pursuits. To counteract problems three and four, the missionaries envisioned building separate native Christian communities which would—as cities "set on a hill"—by example draw others to the faith.

Protestant missionaries, particularly Church Missionary Society workers, established these communities on the premise that they would eventually be expressions of a native church. In effect, the white evangelical's role was to be one of guidance until such time as the community, complete with its own native clergy and native lay leadership, could stand alone. By the 1870's and 1880's, the northern coastal regions of British Columbia abounded with newly created Christian communities, all established by white clergy or lay evangelicals of various denominations: the names Greenville, Aiyansh, Kincolith, and, of course, the supreme example, Metlaklatla, are witness to the popularity of the model society ideal.[60] But the Roman Catholics were also captivated by the "city on a hill" concept—although, in spite of Church efforts to encourage native vocations, Catholic missionaries intended to retain control over such communities.[61]

Although not unconcerned with the "civilizing" process, Catholic missionary efforts aimed to produce not so much pseudo-Europeans as devoted Roman Catholics, and permanent missionary control was an important component of this plan.[62] The Oblate missionary who initially drew his superior's attention to the need for an organized method both to counteract the frustrations of working as circuit missionaries among nomadic Indians and to gain Oblate conversion objectives was Paul Durieu. He noted that regardless of the apparent responsiveness of groups of Indians, without constant attention and supervision few kept their promises to give up "superstitious practises," polygamy, gambling, and liquor.[63] A practical solution could be found, in part, in the "Instructions on Foreign Missions" which Eugène de Mazenod had added to the *Constitution and Rules* in 1853 and which stressed the "civilizing" aspect of missionary work. The founder wrote:

> far from thinking it incongruent with their ministry to train the Indians to the duties of civil life, the Oblates will consider it as intimately connected with the mission's welfare and as most fit to the obtaining of better results. Every means should therefore be taken to bring the nomad tribes to abandon their wandering life and to build houses, cultivate fields and practise the elementary crafts of civilized life.

De Mazenod specified—without explaining how—that the missionaries should keep traditionally warring tribes peaceful and promote interior tribal harmony, industry, and labour. Although he stated firmly that the

Oblates should "never take upon themselves the government of the tribes," nevertheless, when tribal elections were held, they were to procure votes for those capable of fulfilling the office, "namely of governing according to the dictates of Religion and Justice."[64] In spite of de Mazenod's caution, Durieu and his superior, who appeared to favour more direct missionary control, based their system primarily on Jesuit methodology.

Oregon's Jesuit missionaries used as a blueprint for their missionary developments the "réduction," or model self-supporting agricultural Christian mission village established by Spanish Jesuits in seventeenth-century Paraguay. By isolating Paraguayan Indians from European contacts, suppressing polygamy and the use of alcohol, using native officials to help control and punish immorality, and stressing the celebration of feast days to strengthen both faith and Indian commitment, "the Jesuits made model Christian peasants of nomadic pagans." Durieu had personal experience of Jesuit attempts to instigate a similar system in Oregon among the Flatheads and the Coeur d'Alenes. During the Yakima Indian war, he was forced to take refuge with the Jesuits at Colville. Moreover, it is possible that the Jesuit "classical historical concept" might have appealed to the highly educated D'herbomez and Durieu.[65] It must be noted however, that the nineteenth-century Jesuits held a far more liberal attitude towards religious practice than the more Jansenistic-directed Oblates, and the "laws" governing Jesuit communities may not have been as stringent as those imposed by the Oblates.

"Durieu's system," as it became known, created in every willing Indian village an administration under the direct authority of the bishop with local missionaries acting as the initial and ongoing supervisors.[66] The administration consisted of the chief and sub-chief, who were responsible for keeping undesirable white men (for example, bootleggers) away from their people; one or two watchmen, who ensured that both adults and children attended religious instruction and did not return to now-forbidden Indian practices; policemen, who carried out punishments—fines or, occasionally, physical punishment for frequent repeaters—passed down by the chief on those who lapsed into the old ways (although drunkenness was one of the gravest transgressions); catechists, who were responsible for teaching religious knowledge to both adults and children, and "la cloche" men, bell-ringers, sometimes known as "ting ting" men, who summoned the people to church three times daily.

Watchmen were crucial to the system. In one sense they perpetuated the British and European system of "monitoring," which was prevalent in the school systems. But their duties were far more widespread. One watchman related what his role entailed: "The Watchman woke the people in the morning before church. When the church bell rang he stood by the door and waited for the people to enter the church. If they smelled like they were wearing perfume, hair cream or face lotion, they would be reported and punished, sometimes the punishment would be to stand in front of the altar with your arms out to the side. If you didn't want the punishment you could pay a fine." Watchmen would report on such diverse actions as not helping the elderly or throwing stones at the church. Consequently, they were a force to be reckoned with. But, as one Indian noted, "in those days the men were very humble and never questioned the Watchmen's word."[67]

In accepting the new administration, the Indians had to reject forever all tribal celebrations, all patronage of the medicine man or shaman, intoxicants, and gambling. Sunday observance was strictly enforced. Weekday attendance at mass (whenever possible) or at daily prayer and catechism sessions was mandatory.[68] Marriages had to have the priest's consent, and leisure activities were frowned upon unless all necessary work was completed. Every aspect of life operated under puritanical restrictions. For example, boys and girls could not play together, women and girls could never be alone (especially at night), any man or grown boy who entered the room of a woman when she was alone and engaged her in conversation had to be punished, and the Indians were forbidden to sing love songs or songs associated with gambling or medicine men. The system also encouraged pomp and ceremonial aimed at undermining Indian ritual while catering to the Indians' highly developed appreciation of symbolism, mysticism, and solemnity.[69]

In the 1880's Durieu, influenced by European trends to strengthen the faith, added the "action de formation" to the system; "it was designed to curb pride and produce a fearful respect for the Sacraments."[70] "To bring the Indian to lead a Christian life," Durieu wrote, "the missionary must exercise upon them a twofold action. A destructive action, in destroying sin wherever it flourishes and a formative action, in moulding the inner man by instruction, preaching and the reception of the sacraments." He went on to say that sin had to be destroyed by "repressing and punishing it relentlessly as an evil, horrible, and degrading thing." The missionary had to inculcate "horror, fear and flight from sin" and the repression of evil among people whom Durieu believed would easily revert to pagan ways if not attended to unceasingly.[71] An important and controversial element of this control was the use of physical punishment, in particular the practice of whipping those found guilty of serious sin. The missionaries did not introduce this aspect of control, but many saw it as a useful method of keeping the Indians to the faith.[72]

Corporal punishment for serious offences was part of nineteenth-century European thinking, and government officials as well as mis-

sionaries approved its use. In 1873, for example, when white settlers in
the Clinton area tried to prevent a local chief from punishing his
peoples' transgressions, both Judge Matthew Baillie Begbie and future
premier and lawyer George Walkem advised them to desist from inter-
fering; Walkem was "most anxious to see the Indian chiefs use the whip
in earnest" and even considered introducing a motion in the legislature
to have a law passed on the subject.[73] Not all Oblates were enamoured of
the Durieu system, but Coccola appears to have given it his unqualified
support.[74] Its success, however, obviously depended as much, if not
more, on the Indians than on the missionary.

The Indians assigned to the spiritual guardianship of Nicolas Coccola
and who accepted Durieu's system were not, as one missionary expressed it, "simple pagans,"[75] an unconverted, undifferentiated mass
with similar cultural backgrounds and traits, common customs and traditions, universal arts and skills.[76] These native peoples were of three different ethnic backgrounds. Moreover, they spoke different languages.
And the differences between the languages of the Interior Salish,
Kutenai, and Athapascans was equal to the differences between European languages. Fortunately for missionaries without a talent for linguistics, many Indians were either familiar with the Chinook jargon, a
hybrid language developed for use in the fur trade, or were multilingual
and able to act as interpreters—skills developed in pre-contact times
during tribal trade negotiations.[77] The native peoples did hold certain
cultural manifestations in common. All held traditional animistic world
views and utilized supernatural explanations to interpret their daily
lives. The spirit world was all-embracing and explained such events and
experiences as economic successes and failures, illness, accidents, and
natural phenomena.[78] The extended family and the community guided
the Indians through rites of passage—birth, puberty, marriage, death—
and marked these events, and others, with ritual and ceremony.

Still, to Coccola the Indians appeared willing to jettison all these
traditions—although, he notes, not always without some resistance.[79]
For example, on his first circuit among the Nicola bands, during his
nine-day stay with the Coldwater Indians, Coccola persuaded them to
accept the Durieu system. He "organized" the camp according to
Durieu's instructions. Chiefs were elected as captains (unfortunately, no
information is given on how this election was achieved). These men were
chosen to "keep up the discipline and continue the teaching." He
selected "intelligent men" to teach the Catholic catechism in his absence
and others, "strong men," were appointed as watchmen. The following
day the competition asserted itself as the camp's medicine man began
and at first succeeded in intimidating Coccola's "converts." According
to Coccola, he began "howling... imitating owls, coyotes and other

creatures." This was done to create "awe in the hearers," and it succeeded in sending a shiver down Coccola's spine. The missionary responded by refusing to say mass since "God cannot reign with the devil." He berated the newly elected officials for not keeping order as promised and shamed the two watchmen into tying up the luckless medicine man, who apparently promised "to keep quiet in future."[80]

The reasons for Indian acceptance not only of culturally repressive Christianity itself but of the harsh Durieu system in particular remain elusive—although several possible explanations have been advanced.[81] In a secularized society (the extent of secularization being an area of scholarly debate) more people are less willing to accept the idea that the appeal of the Christian message and the charisma of certain missionaries had some bearing—although from the days of the first Christians these two factors have played an important role in the spread of Christianity. More "acceptable" reasons are: the old gods and spirits had betrayed them, "just as the gods of the tribal Gauls had been powerless to prevent the Romans from conquering them"; the Indians, their culture shifting and changing as the white population increased, saw a need for new knowledge to help them cope with their new situation; Christianity offered access to the white man's world and might also lead to sharing of white power and wealth; Christianity, in particular Christian conversion systems such as Durieu's, increased the prestige of those elected or selected as leaders in the new power structure; marriage between Indian women and either Catholic French Canadians or Catholic Iroquois fur trade personnel precipitated conversion; and their numbers decimated by new diseases (for example, it is estimated that the Interior Salish numbered 13,500 in 1835 and only 5,800 by 1885), the Indians were anxious to use any new method that might save them from sickness and death.[82] The willingness of large numbers of Indians to both accept and promote not simply Christianity but a culturally repressive white religious system is a historical puzzle perhaps best resolved by the native peoples themselves.

INDIAN RESPONSE: INTERIOR SALISH

In spite of efforts by tribal shamans or medicine men, more and more Indians came to accept Christianity, and whatever their reason for so doing, they became an indispensable part of the proselytization process. The scarcity of priests and the vastness of the territory remained constant problems; and, of course, the Protestant ministers had to be kept at bay. Whether they accepted Christianity in toto or simply "added the Christian god to the existing pantheon as a kind of insurance policy,"[83] the Indians themselves had to keep the Christian message alive between missionary visits. It was therefore important for Coccola to establish and train neophytes as soon as possible.

Among the majority of Interior Salish, including the Nicola bands, the imposition of a new power structure was made easier by the absence of clan systems or secret societies. The foundations of these Indian societies were the family and the band, the latter a group of families more or less related by blood and marriage. Each band had an hereditary chief, "but real authority lay with an informal council of the elder men." Although a special chief was elected to lead the Indians in times of war, his authority ended with the conclusion of a particular raid.[84] Some Interior Salish religious beliefs were quite compatible with Christian, sometimes specifically Catholic, beliefs—a stroke of luck for missionaries struggling to transcribe Christian theology into languages which lacked the necessary vocabulary. The Indians believed in ghosts and guardian spirits and also that on leaving the body souls travelled to a far place, "somewhere beyond or at the edge of the world," a spirit world where it was always warm, where berries were always ripe, grass always greener, flies and mosquitoes non-existent. Most believed in two great spirits they called the Old One and Coyote. The Old One, chief of the ancient world was all-powerful and created the world in much the same way as the Christian God. Coyote, the Old One's chief assistant, was sent by the Old One to travel over the world and put it to rights—a role not unlike that of Christianity's Jesus. Each person had a guardian spirit which protected him from physical harm.[85]

Although this spirit took the form of birds, animals, or other natural elements, the idea could be synchronized with the specifically Catholic belief in guardian angels. The Interior Salish's most notable festival was the mid-winter (or mid-summer if a band received a message from the spirit world) ghost or circle dance. On the morning of the dance they fasted and washed. At noon they feasted and prayed to the chief of the dead to preserve them from all harm. In the afternoon they danced, and in the evening the men held a pipe-smoking ceremony; "so greatly did they reverence this Chief of the Dead that at the coming of Europeans several bands elevated him to the rank of a sky-deity and identified him with the God of the Christian missionaries."[86] These beliefs, which synchronized so well with Christian beliefs, were at least partly responsible for any positive Salish response.

INDIAN RESPONSE: THE KUTENAI

Coccola's first major missionary work was among the Kutenai, and in spite of the relative isolation of these native people, there is evidence that many had already accepted and practised the Roman Catholic religion since the days of early contact. The Kutenai pre-contact religion, which resembled in some respects that of the Plains Indians, included beliefs about heaven, the origin of the world, and a destructive flood. Moreover, Kutenai experience as a nomadic people subsisting in a wilderness, their sense of a transcendental realm, their use of taboos, and their acknowledgement of the necessity to thank a creator all combined to encourage convergences.[87]

Kutenai knowledge of Catholicism began in the eighteenth century when a Flathead prophet called Shining Shirt foretold the coming of "Blackrobes" to the Kutenai nation. After the turn of the century, when the Hudson's Bay Company sent Catholic Iroquois to the Pacific Northwest to teach the Indians the economics and techniques of the fur trade, the Kutenai experienced another source of Christian knowledge. By the 1830's religious observances blending native and Christian rites began to appear; "sabbath observance and daily prayers gained ground." By the time the first white missionary, Father Pierre De Smet, made contact with the Kutenais in 1845, he found them "delightedly open to the new faith."[88] Without missionary contact or direct white pressure, the Kutenais had gradually synchronized native beliefs and Christianity.[89]

Indian Commissioner Dr. Powell, in a letter to the minister of the interior in 1873, portrays the Upper Kutenai as "prudent, brave, unrevengeful and most of them devoutly religious and good Catholics."[90] Chief Isadore, when speaking with the commissioners, explained how, in his youth, he had become a "watchman," a role he had continued in when he became chief. But he went on to explain that the "watchmen" were no longer as "active or vigilant," because of recent Indian association with the "Chinese and bad Whitemen"; the Durieu system was losing its impact.[91] It fell to Coccola to induce the Indians to return to the system, and to judge by externals, he appears to have been singularly successful.[92]

Like his predecessors, Coccola—as indeed all missionaries throughout the province—experienced difficulty in teaching Christian theological concepts to the native peoples. Particularly difficult for Catholics to explain was the central act of the mass—and of the Catholic faith—in which the priest, by the power of God, changes bread and wine into the real presence of Jesus Christ. With familiar European condescension, he explained his difficulty to a bishop already familiar since his days in Oregon with this very real problem:[93] "You know my Lord how hard it is to drive ideas of the immaterial order into their intelligences, both by reason of the coarseness of their minds and of defects of their language which does not contain any expressions corresponding with these ideas... It was thus that I have grappled with the question of the institution of the sacrament, the question of the Real Presence, of the requisite disposition for Holy Communion."

Part of the problem was infrequency of priest/Indian contact. The teachings of the Catholic Church were offered both in the twice-yearly visits of the missionary to individual Indian villages and on the great feast days of the church when Indians, some travelling close to a hundred miles, would gather at St. Eugene's Mission. It was the visible presence of so many Indians, both Catholic and non-Catholic, at these gatherings that was so gratifying to Coccola. As at the Indian villages, the Durieu system was in place during these ceremonial events. Coccola assembled the chiefs, watchmen, and catechists of each band, and together they "made a census" of all those guilty of drunkenness and gambling. Those listed were asked to accept public penance for their "sins" of intoxication or gambling; "the Chiefs and the Watchmen judged and sentenced the drinkers without sparing those among the watchmen themselves who had succumbed to temptation. The fines were paid in money or in nature and amount I think to $56. Moreover, the whip functioned for two days." An outsider who witnessed one such gathering wrote: "Isadore and his four sheriffs [watchmen] seized all who had been guilty of any offence, such as gambling, drunkenness or theft. They were tied down on a robe, hands and feet secured by rawhide thongs to stakes placed in the ground, and soundly flogged, regardless of age or sex. By some means or other the chief knew the culprits, but, in spite of that fact, and the consequences of that folly, they never failed to appear at the Church to take their medicine."[94] Under the Durieu system, the negative aspect, confession and punishment, was to be followed by positive affirmation of faith. What this involved can be best described in the missionary's own words.

Coccola's letter to Bishop D'herbomez described the events of the 1888/89 Christmas, New Year's, and Epiphany (January 6th) celebrations, his sense of accomplishment, his hopes for the future; it also illustrates how crucial for missionary success was the use of ceremonial.

We are at the end of the festive night, the young men bring in pine branches, the more skilful women draw out of them all sorts of decorations for the Church, the men garnish their cartridge pouches for the purpose of saluting the Nativity of the Great Chief, a recollected joy is manifest everywhere and on all faces, should you enter the houses you will see displayed the fine feast day suits left in reserve for the days of communion, the costly blankets of diverse colors wherein a Kootenay brave drapes himself like a Roman in his Toga, the smell of toilet soap replaces the smell of sulf with [sic] so much the savages habitually smear their hands and faces. This is because I have promised to pass the review. The review is passed. All is well in the exterior forum, and after a while when the last absolutions will be

given, all will be well also, all will be glistening with God's grace in
the interior forum.

A few whites, officers of the camps, others are coming to take part
in our solemnity: Father Richard and Brother Burns do them the honour of the house while awaiting the hour of the office and I on my
side, I put the finishing touches on the preparations of the feast. The
altar is covered with improvised flowers, above the tabernacle and
above the stand surmounting it for the exposition of the most Blessed
Sacrament, stand out in large characters formed out of pine cones, the
hymn of the angels, Glory in Excelsis Deo. A pendant charged with an
abundance of lights and suspended from the middle of the Church
lights up all these beautiful things to the amazed eyes of our native
population, and since the spectacles of this world have only a relative
importance, since above all the merit of this all is due to the Birth of
the Infant God, visible to the eyes of faith and tangible in pure hearts,
ours was magnificent in comparible [*sic*]. At 11-30 the public crier
gives the signal to the carbineers who have just drawn up in line in
front of the Church in battle array. On its side the bell calls the faithful. Midnight sounding, Male and female singers intone the hymn of
the angels... which we have translated into sauvage while conserving
the same rhythm and it is sung on the air as in French. Three salvos of
musketry accompany these chants and announce to the whole country that the celebration of the mystery begins. The doors of the
Church are thrown open and about three hundred persons enter in
perfect order and recollections. Father Richard is at the Altar. The
sung mass begins and proceeds amid a holy enthusiasm only interrupted at the Gospel by an instruction in English for the Whites re-
produced in Kootenay for the sauvages. ... One hundred and seventy
communicants approach next with respect the holy table and receive
with their hearts, to bear away to their dwellings, the most High
God. ... I was blessing God who had refused his light to the arrogant
and lavished it upon the lowly and the humble.

The officer of the police present at our ceremony as simple spec-
tator has often said to me that he would never have believed the Indians capable of such devotion and of such order in their movements.
Before, during and after communion every one was in his place and
preserved this recollection till the close. The Christmas feasts are for
our Indians essentially religious feasts; the civil holiday and the rejoicing going along with it take place only on new Year's Day. Noel
[Christmas] had grace like those days one would willingly prolong
forever and seem the shorter because the more enjoyed. But my work
was not finished because of that. Like a good family head I felt it in-

cumbent of me to organize honest amusements for my grown up children. Moreover there were beggars, penitents in need of a third confession, new arrivals who have had to go a distance of 100 miles or more over unbroken roads who had been detained by the snow and came late. They were coming like the Magi guided by the light of faith, but more fortunate they received into their hearts the God of Love, unique object of their search. Among the latecomers were some families of the Shuswaps whose singing and language contrasted with that of the Kootenays, theirs soft and harmonious, that of the latter in a accent harsh and more rustic. . . . Our sauvages inaugurated the New Year by bonfires and which men and women cooks prepared appetising banquets. At midnight the bell having rung the signal, all the men in the village that might carry a gun drew together around the Church. At a second signal the singing begins and three platoons firing saluted and rendered homage to the Great Chief of Christmas, it was a Happy New Year to the King of Kings to the Lord of Lords and to all who love him. The crowd in a procession next came and sung beneath our windows. They sing for the Holy Father, they sing for His Lordship the Bishop, they sing for the Reverend General, they sing for Father Fouquet whose devotion the Indians have not forgotten, finally they sing for all the Fathers and Brothers of the House where after took place the traditional hand shaking. . . . During the whole of this time the temperance flag floats over the heads of the feasters.[95]

It is a grand day for the poor, they take up a good collection and they are permitted to bring along with them their appetite and their stomarchal [*sic*] capacity, sacks and pots for the surplus. . . . Our sauvages are very fond of one another and some of them without ostentations perform very praiseworthy acts of Charity. The mother of the Chief Isadore nourishes five or six orphans and this example is not lost, the others without doing as much because they have not the means at least show themselves compassionate and helpful towards this unhappily too numerous class. Our sauvages have decided to build a catechism hall and they are very actively engaged in the forest cutting and hauling out thick planks and joists for this purpose. The other day one of them who is not the most fervent came to make a request, as he said, on behalf of the young people. For them and for himself he requested permission to execute traditional dance. Gravely I answered that when he had to treat a matter as grave as this he should take it up with the Chief and Watchmen. Away he hurried to the intermediaries indicated who present themselves and give their opinion. Now of his own accord the Chief declared there should be no dance for several reasons, first because the previous year they had not followed the rules laid down by the priest, for second place when they were privileged to have a priest sacrificing himself for them it was unseemly to act like fools and to return to former superstitions; those who had received the Eucharist should above all abhor the dance. I had only to say amen to this sapient speech.

To Coccola, the conduct of the Indians, their continued acceptance of the Durieu system, their participation in Catholic ritual, their preparation for and reception of the eucharist, and their rejection—though by no means total—of their past ceremonials all indicated a strengthening commitment to the Catholic faith. He felt great satisfaction. In concluding his letter to the bishop, he wrote: "After all I can say my Lord that I am the spoiled child of God since I have been missionary, perhaps with a few exceptions I have had only consolations in all the works apostolic which have been given me to do."[96]

Because much of what they wrote to administrators would be published—a technique to raise funds for missions that had been in use since the Jesuits arrived in Canada in the seventeenth century—missionaries of all denominations seldom mentioned their failures or disappointments. Moreover, fervour and enthusiasm inspired by ritual is difficult to differentiate from genuine faith. Coccola, however, appears satisfied and admits to missionary difficulties with only one band of Kutenai. These were the Lower Kutenai of Tobacco Plains. Powell, following the usual tendency among whites to classify Indians by their appearance and adaptability to white culture, once referred to them as "squalid and miserable in appearance, quiet and sullen in manner, destitute and starving."[97] On his first visit to these Indians, Coccola tried to encourage the young men to turn to farming instead of being totally dependent on fishing. He was not too optimistic about keeping these Indians on the straight and narrow. The Lower Kutenai mixed freely with the American Indians, and the missionary considered this as damaging to Kutenai "advancement." When the Indians who had attended the 1888/89 Christian festivities were leaving, Coccola expressed the hope that the Christian Kutenai, "like the Magi," would influence the unconverted; "God grant their souls may be an accessory of conversion for the sauvages of Tobacco Plain and of some others who are going helter-skelter and have become the devil's slaves."[98] Within a few years, the Kutenai of Tobacco Plain had their own church, and Coccola wrote to his superior that he visited them regularly, not only in the spring and fall, but "sometimes in the intervals there are sick calls for my Indians do not want to die without receiving the sacraments."[99]

INDIAN RESPONSE: ATHAPASCANS

Like the native peoples of the Kootenays, the northern Athapascans, Coccola's next, and final, missionary charges, had accepted Roman Catholicism prior to his arrival. Predating miner, settler, or surveyor, in 1842, a priest of the Roman Catholic Church made direct contact with the Indians of the northern interior. At that time, this region was considered part of the Diocese of Quebec, and the mandate given by Archbishop Signay to Blanchet and Demers as they left for the Oregon Territory to "withdraw from barbarity and the disorders which it produces, the Indians scattered in that country" applied equally to New Caledonia.[100] Consequently, on 16 September 1842, after travelling north with the fur brigade, Modeste Demers arrived at Fort St. James. After spending three days at the fort, celebrating mass and meeting some of the Indian peoples, Demers returned south as far as Fort Alexandria. There he wintered, and he preached daily to local and visiting Indians. Before returning to the Oregon Territory, Demers had the Indians of Fort Alexandria construct a small chapel; of little practical use without the continuous services of a missionary, the chapel served notice to all of the Catholic church's jurisdiction. Two years later, according to Archbishop Blanchet, a deputation of Indians from New Caledonia arrived at Fort Vancouver asking for a missionary. In response to this request, in June 1845, a Jesuit missionary, Father John Nobili, travelled north to Okanagan Lake. From there, with the assistance of a second Jesuit who joined him in 1846, for two years the missionary kept contact with those Indians previously visited by Demers. But twenty years passed before the church made any major effort to Catholicize these Indians. It was the founding of St. Joseph's Mission, Williams Lake, in 1867, that gave impetus to this work.

From the mission, Oblate priests travelled to the northern forts where they met Carrier who travelled to trade at the forts or were employed as fur-trade personnel. These brief meetings between Oblates and Carrier encouraged the missionaries to greater efforts, for the Indians appeared to be interested in Oblate preaching. In the spring of 1867, for example, Father James Maria McGuckin met fifty local Carrier plus approximately a dozen northern Carrier from Fort George and Stuart Lake at Quesnel. Not only were these Indians attentive to his preaching, they also responded enthusiastically—so it seemed to Father McGuckin—to suggestions that they follow the Durieu plan and elect church officials among their bands. The Oblate wrote to his bishop that one of the chiefs wished to elect two watchmen and two policemen immediately and that after aiding them in their choice, he gave them such instructions as he deemed necessary. A spokesman for the Stuart Lake band, a number of whom appeared to have French-Canadian blood, told McGuckin that he was under instruction from his people to take back a priest "by force if necessary." Notwithstanding possible Indian enthusiasm consequent on novelty, this interest was an encouraging sign to the Oblates. Indian interest might also have been aroused by Father McGuckin's concern about education for their children.

Like other native peoples, these Indians were not slow to recognize the advantages to be obtained by equipping themselves and their children with new knowledge, and the missionary may have been exaggerating only slightly when he informed the bishop that "all the Indians from the Junction [Fort George] to Stuart Lake were anxious to send their children to school."[101] In spite of this Indian enthusiasm for some form of white-style education for their children, over fifty years would pass before this was achieved. However, the movement of miners from the Cariboo region into Carrier territory stimulated the Catholic church to provide at least a permanent mission in the north. Numerous Catholic miners, predominently Irish and Italian, whose spiritual needs had been met by the missionaries from St. Joseph's Mission began, as rumours of new gold strikes to the north began to circulate in the late 1860's, to move out of range of the mission centre. Father McGuckin advised his bishop to open a mission further north to accommodate both miners and Carrier, and in June 1873, Bishop D'herbomez sent Fathers Jean-Marie LeJacq and Georges Blanchet to open Our Lady of Good Hope Mission at Fort St. James.[102]

Like those who worked among the Interior Salish, missionaries who worked among the Carrier must have found that their work was made a little easier by the presence of certain elements in Carrier pre-contact religion that synchronized with elements of Catholicism. According to anthropologists the Carrier believed in a supreme spirit—the Wet'su-wet'en, Bulkley River Carrier, named this superior being Udakke or "that which is on high"—to whom they offered gifts of food and to whom they prayed for help in times of famine;[103] they practised group worship; they believed in a soul and in an afterlife for the soul in a "shadowy underworld" or far place somewhere in the east; they believed in personal spirits, both good and evil, and they believed in the power for good in confession of faults to a medicine man. Although the first three of these beliefs were said to have been lightly held, they nevertheless gave some sense of familiarity to missionary talk of God, the necessity for church attendance, and the importance of the soul.[104] Since the Carrier offered food and drink to their sky god when asking for favours, the priests' actions of offering bread and wine at the mass would be at least partially understood. The strongest Carrier belief was belief in a multitude of spirits whose help they sought through certain rituals. As with the Interior Salish, the Catholic concept of the role of guardian angels and Satan's army of devils could be incorporated into Carrier belief in protective and harmful spirits—even though, like the Salish, Carrier spirits took the forms of animals, birds, and other natural elements. A purely Catholic concept was that of confession to a priest for expiation of sins. Daniel Harmon, a clerk with the North West Company who lived among the Carrier from 1810 to 1819, wrote in his account of those years: "When the Carriers are severely sick, they often think that they shall not recover unless they divulge to a priest or a magician every crime which they may have committed which has hitherto been kept a secret."[105] This custom may have been natural to the Carrier; mention of it certainly predates any direct contact between the Carrier and Catholic priests. But it might also have been introduced into Carrier religious tradition through what was known as the prophet movement.

The prophet movement manifested itself in British Columbia in the early decades of the nineteenth century.[106] Some of the province's Indians had travelled out onto the prairies or down into the Oregon Territory and had come in contact with either missionaries themselves or, more likely, missionary-contacted Indians. On their return to their own people, these "native prophets" acted out the role of missionaries and imitated aspects of Christian ritual. The northern Carrier had their own prophet, an Indian called Beni, who, after disappearing from his community, returned with knowledge of prayer, the sign of the cross, repentance, and salvation. Beni may well have had contact with Russian Orthodox priests who proselytized among the northern coastal regions of Alaska.[107]

About 1834, a movement that effected a larger area spread rapidly among the more southerly Lower Carrier bands. Five years earlier, two Indians, one a Spokane, the other a Kutenai, returned to their homes after being baptized and instructed by Oblate missionaries in the Red River area of Manitoba. Spokane Gerry preached his newly acquired knowledge among his people, and information on this new religion was passed from tribe to tribe throughout British Columbia. John McLean, a trader at Fort St. James, wrote of the movement reaching his area "where it spread with amazing rapidity all over the country."[108] The use of Christian rituals and gestures were, in this manner, incorporated into Carrier religious observances. For whatever reasons, between the opening of the Fort St. James mission and the arrival of Nicolas Coccola in 1905, the majority of the Carrier and an unknown number of Sekani accepted Christianity. In his 1893 report to the Department of Indian Affairs, Indian Agent Ernest Loring claimed that the Indians in his charge were moral, honest, law-abiding, and respectful towards authority and implied, with supreme ethnocentric arrogance, that this was owing to their membership in the Roman Catholic church.[109]

INDIAN-SETTLER CONTACT AND CONFLICT: THE NICOLA

Although the Indians appeared sympathetic to the Christian message, by the time Coccola reached British Columbia, they had become downright hostile towards white civilization. Missionaries of all denominations confronted the difficulties created by Indian economic changes and Indian/white contact and conflict. Coccola's first posting was brief, 1880 to 1883, and was among the Shuswap-speaking Indians of the Kamloops district and the Okanagan-speaking Nicola Indians of the Nicola Valley. When the Corsican arrived in 1880, Kamloops had been a white commercial centre for close to seventy years. But long before the arrival of white traders, Kamloops and district had been home to several bands of Interior Salish peoples. In the vicinity of present-day Kamloops were the Shuswap of Deadman's Creek and the Shuswap of Kamloops. The Shuswap-speaking Interior Salish occupied a large area which stretched to Lillooet in the southwest and the Okanagan in the southeast and included the Shuswap Lake, Adams Lake, and Spallumcheen Valley regions. The Kamloops area Indians were nomadic in summer, when clusters of teepees of various sizes were scattered throughout the Kamloops district as the people hunted, fished, and gathered berries. In winter, they inhabited permanent or semi-permanent winter homes, living in keekwillie houses, underground circular pits approximately five feet deep (the diameter varied) over which stood a teepee framwork covered against the winter cold. One band had an extensive winter village on the north shore of the South Thompson River between Monte Creek and Campbell Creek and was generally regarded as "the most war-like and powerful." This group was particularly well-placed to take advantage of the new trading opportunities that opened up with the coming of the fur traders.[110]

These traders arrived in November 1811, when Alexander Ross and David Stuart of the American Pacific Fur Company wintered in a keekwillie house on the Thompson River. The following year, Ross returned and established a permanent trading post at a spot on the south side of the river junction called by the Indians "cum cloups," Kamloops. In November 1812, Joseph La Rocque, trader for the Montreal-based North West Fur Trading Company, set up a rival post. When the North West Company purchased its rival in 1813, the post was enlarged and carried on a very lucrative trade with the Indians. In 1821, the North West Company amalgamated with the Hudson's Bay Company, which remained in control of the post until 1861, when the young colony allocated six hundred acres to the company.

For several years the growth of Kamloops was slow but steady, and the native peoples experienced minimum cultural stress. One of the first white groups to settle in the area were survivors of the great Overlanders Trek. The one woman among the courageous (or foolhardy) people who, heading for the gold fields, travelled overland from the eastern seaboard, was Mrs. Catherine Schubert. Shortly after arriving at Kamloops, she gave birth to the first white girl born in the area with the assistance of an Indian woman. With others of the group, the Schuberts settled down to ranching, but the numbers of settlers remained relatively small. Kamloops received a boost in 1865 when gold was discovered in the Big Bend region and eager miners arrived at the fort. Although the mining boom was brief, some successful—and not so successful—miners settled in and around Kamloops.

One such settler (who was also a "trekker") was John Andrew Mara.[111] Entrepreneurs like Mara saw a great future for Kamloops and when the first Canadian Pacific Railway surveyors arrived in 1871—causing frenzied activity—Mara was one of a number of businessmen who built steamboats which operated on the Kamloops waters and which, during the railway construction, transported materials and supplies over the long stretch of country between Savona and Eagle Pass.

The impact of the proposed railway fostered a building boom in Kamloops and provided expanded economic opportunities for the native peoples. Numerous stores and sawmills as well as several hotels were built, and men began to purchase land around the Hudson's Bay Company land holdings. The Canadian Pacific Railway built Montreal House (later used as the Anglican church) as a centre for housing, equipping, and feeding its growing numbers of employees. This must have been somewhat disappointing for local entrepreneurs, but the C.P.R. never lost an opportunity to recover what it paid out in wages. Employment opportunities for both Indians and whites developed rapidly. People were needed for survey crews, as packers to transport men and equipment into the wilderness, and as messengers for communication between the various groups. In this type of work the Indians, so familiar with the region, had an advantage.

In 1874, the land survey teams completed their work and drew up the boundary lines of the first township. Six years later, construction began on the railway section between Emory Bar and Savona's Ferry. This encouraged more settlers, and Kamloops began to develop as much as a supply centre for ranching and farming as a construction centre. The permanent white male population only grew from 74 in 1874 to 102 in

1882, hardly constituting a population boom, but there was also a large shifting population of railway construction workers. One possible reason for the delayed boom was that it was not until the end of 1882 that the C.P.R. officials discarded the Nicola Valley route which would have bypassed Kamloops.[112] However, with the beginning of railway construction, Kamloops' future as a developing community seemed assured, and the area's native peoples faced massive disruption.

Although Coccola learnt to speak Shuswap so that he could attend to local Indians, his first missionary circuit was among the Okanagan-speaking Nicola, where the young and still inexperienced missionary encountered not the friendliness of the Shuswap but hostility, indifference, and even active resistance. Only his willingness some weeks earlier to attend and treat, successfully, the sick son of Tziliktza, a man of some influence among both the Okanagan and Shuswap Indians, guaranteed him some hospitality and protection.[113] While Coccola's companions at Kamloops called the Nicola Indians "wild," they most likely meant unresponsive to Roman Catholic missionary overtures. The Nicola bands, like the Shuswap—and most Indians Coccola would work with—had already (some to a greater or lesser extent) kept pace with the economic and social changes created by the invading whites. The Nicola had actively and successfully participated in the fur trade, had begun subsistence farming, started reserve cattle-ranching, worked as cowboys on white-owned ranches, mined for gold, and begun freight-hauling.[114] Nevertheless, since the 1870's white ranchers, some of whom had come originally in search of gold, were constantly increasing their land holdings, and the Indians were feeling the squeeze. By the time of Coccola's visit, these Indians, like many Indians in British Columbia, harboured bitter feelings towards the growing white population, and particularly towards government officials. They were angry and frustrated by the government's policy of reducing Indian lands to accommodate the increasing numbers of settlers. The Nicola Valley reserves clearly illustrate the government's indifference to Indian attempts to cope with the rapid changes.

The reserves were established by government surveyor Peter O'Reilly in 1868. Immediately, one Nicola chief complained to Anglican missionary John Booth Good that O'Reilly had "ignored his expressed wishes and excluded his favourite living place, with its burial sites, water courses, and potato patches from the reserve." Moreover, O'Reilly then levied heavy fines against the Indians when their cattle, accustomed to wandering at will, crossed a settler's wheat field.[115] In 1879, the Nicola met with a large number of the tribes and bands of the southern interior to discuss their mutual problems. Working in consultation with the Indian agent, the Indians agreed upon a number of measures: they would seek education for their children; improve sanitary and medical facilities in Indian villages; subdivide arable land on an individual basis (the land practice of their white neighbours); work a set number of days per week; fine Indians who got drunk or gambled; abolish the potlatch—although one suspects that many Indians did the Indian equivalent of "finger crossing" when agreeing to this.

A head chief and council of thirteen was elected by all the representatives to administer these regulations. This obvious Indian desire to make concessions, to educate their children, and "to train themselves for citizenship" horrified the settlers. Any Indian effort to unite had to be discouraged. In this particular case, the head chief must not be recognized, and the new regulations not be confirmed by either the provincial or federal governments. The best way to achieve white domination, at a time when the Indians were still numerically superior, was to keep them divided.[116] Understandably, having borne injustice after injustice, the Nicola Indians could not be expected to welcome with open arms men bent on causing further social disturbance, and Coccola received a mixed reception although, as noted earlier, he blamed the machinations of the Indian medicine men rather than prior contact problems. But Coccola was not to spend long among the Nicola. He was sent to the Kutenai people as conflict between these proud and independent Indians and white settlers threatened to escalate.

CONTACT AND CONFLICT: THE KUTENAI

Europeans who came in contact with the Upper Kutenai found in their fine appearance, hunting skills, and proud dispositions all the qualities of "the noble savage," an image created in nineteenth-century literature.[117] Coccola had great admiration for the warlike Upper Kutenais and noted their successes in conflicts with the Blackfoot. The Lower Kutenai, a more sedentary group, appeared less glamorous and received no missionary accolades. Both groups once lived on the plains, but according to some anthropologists, they had been driven across the mountains by other Plains Indians. One Kutenai tradition holds that the people migrated six hundred years ago from around Lake Michigan. Initially, all Kutenai settled in U.S. territory, but natural migration and Kutenai disillusionment in 1855 with American efforts to restrict their land claims drove some to settle in Canada.[118] As in their religion, in dress and customs the Kutenai still resembled the Plains Indians. They were few in number. It has been estimated that in 1835 there were only 1,000; by 1885, this number had been reduced to 625.[119] Proportionally, the Kutenai appear to have lost fewer people to white-introduced diseases than other native groups, but the 1835 figure could be misleading. The earliest trading post in the Kootenay region was Kootenay House, built in 1807 north of Lake Windermere by David Thompson. Traders were responsible for taking the 1835 census, and by that time disease could have already been introduced either by the traders themselves or by Kutenai contact with Plains Indians.

Pre-contact society and economy has been described as "simple," a euphemism popular among ethnocentric Europeans who were blind to the richness and complexity of native life.[120] Even before the Europeans settled in the Kootenays, many bands were already raising horses and cattle; but they were contemptuous of farming. During the early years of white expansion into the region, the Kutenai were relatively undisturbed. However, during Coccola's eighteen-year ministry, the Kootenays became a booming and prosperous region with subsequent Indian dislocation.

Interest in the Kutenai land began in 1863, when a gold rush was triggered by the discovery of gold on Wild Horse Creek; in less than a year approximately five thousand fortune hunters took approximately $20 million worth of gold dust and nuggets out of the creek. Because part of the route from the new gold diggings to the coast went through the United States, American customs officers were collecting a fortune. Governor James Douglas decided to extend the Dewdney Trail—a pack route connecting the Similkameen Valley to the coast—two hundred miles eastward to Galbraith Ferry, giving the prospectors an all-Canadian route. Because transportation problems limited effective exploitation, the majority of miners left the area as easy gold pickings disappeared. But some who had made good remained behind to take up land in the Kootenay. One of the first to purchase land in the Cranbrook area was John Galbraith. An Irishman who had arrived too late to stake a placer claim, Galbraith built a ferry at what became known as Galbraith's Ferry and made his fortune charging passengers five dollars for the crossing—plus one dollar a head for horses and mules. When Galbraith expanded his enterprise to include a store and freighting supplies to the mine, his brothers Robert and James joined him, and all three purchased ranch land in the area.[121] Still, until the late 1880's and 1890's, white settlement remained sparse. In 1882, the Blue Bell silver-lead mine was staked on the Riondel peninsula, but as the local Nelson newspaper complained, "Though we piped to the world, the world would not dance to our music."[122] Because of the tremendous expense involved in mining in the Kootenays, the Indians were not initially unduly disturbed. They had in fact expanded their economic activity by hunting and packing for the miners and by serving as guides for white hunting parties. But this reasonably peaceful co-existence between the Kutenai and white settlers was shattered in the late 1880's as a new mining boom, centred in the Kootenay and Boundary regions brought vast, rapid change.

American businessmen had created a mining empire which was based in the western American states of Utah, Colorado, Idaho, and Montana. Lead, silver, and zinc mines "studded the mountain states," and Spokane, Washington, developed as the key smelting centre of mining enterprises. Soon the mountains of the Kootenay and Boundary areas swarmed with American prospectors. Most of these men lacked the capital to develop underground mining or smelting centres. They hoped to make money by selling their discoveries to American capitalists.[123] Exploration uncovered significant lode mines. For example, in 1889 on Red Mountain (near Rossland), two former placer miners found copper and staked five claims. Lacking the fees to register the claims, they offered Eugene Topping, Nelson's mining recorder, one of them if he would pay the fee on all; "ironically, Topping's claim, called the Le Roi, proved to be the richest of the group." In 1890, it changed hands for $4 million. The shares of another of the original five, the War Eagle, rose from 10 cents to $15.20

Nelson, Rossland, New Denver, Slocan City, Sandon, Kaslo, Grand Forks, Phoenix, and Greenwood "emerged overnight as boom towns." Trail became a smelting centre, and Fernie developed as a major coal-producing centre, providing coke for the hard-rock mines and smelters. British Columbia became Canada's mining province, "producing more copper, silver and gold than the rest of the country combined."[124] All this activity could not fail to have a tremendous impact on the native peoples. Even as Coccola set out to take charge of the Kootenay mission, the Kutenai Indians were already feeling the pressure of the new era and began to resist white pressure.

One band of Kutenai in particular, led by Chief Isadore, openly defied the white man's law. And because of his prestige among the Kutenai people, if he so wished, Isadore could enlist the help of Indians on both sides of the border in an all-out war against the encroaching whites.

Canadian officials kept a close eye on happenings in the United States. In the 1850's, during the Cayuse and Yakima Indian wars in Oregon and in the mid-1870's during the valiant struggle of Nez Percé Chief Joseph and his people in Idaho and the success of the Sioux against the American army, the government of British Columbia was uneasy.[125] The province's Indians might easily imitate their American brothers and turn to war as a means of retaining their land.

There is no doubt that Kutenai sympathized with the pressured Indians across the border. But Isadore had two specific grievances. In 1886, two of his band were captured and jailed for the 1884 murder of two white placer miners whose remains were discovered at Deadman's Creek. This arrest enraged Isadore. He charged that when Indians were killed no investigations were made and that if his men had done wrong, he, as chief, should punish them according to Kutenai law. In addition to the arrest of his men, Isadore was also angered by white attempts to steal his land. Colonel James Baker, described by one historian as "a man of splendid physique and fine presence, a distinguished empire soldier, brother of the famed Pasha Baker, long-standing member of the Athenaeum Club and speculator extraordinaire,"[126] had recently purchased what became the townsite of Cranbrook—which Baker named. Included in the deal was land staked originally by John Galbraith. This area, known locally as St. Joseph's Prairie, belonged to Isadore and his people; it had been Kutenai land for generations.[127] Moreover, it was valuable land since, in an area which needed massive irrigation, the prairie had a natural stream running through it. Baker had ambitious plans to raise quality breeds of cattle there, but he was unable to persuade Isadore to vacate it. Soon after his arrival in the Kootenay, Baker had "bought the 219 votes necessary to win the borough of Kootenay West [South] in the legislature." He was a man of some influence, and for several years he had been agitating to have a garrison of the North West Mounted Police stationed in Kootenay.[128] Not all settlers agreed with him that such a move was necessary. Primarily because the police would have to be paid, they thought it "useless to spend so much money for a place which had been so long quiet." When Isadore and some of his men broke open the jail and released Kapula, one of the captives, he played into Baker's hands. Baker's son, along with surveyor Frederick Aylmer and provincial policeman Anderson saw in Isadore's action a declaration of war. Foolishly, they plotted to capture Isadore and hold him as hostage "for the life of any whiteman who might be killed." This plan of action provoked some settlers to plan to drive the three would-be kidnappers out of the district.[129]

The federal government responded to the uneasy situation in January 1887 by sending Lieutenant-Colonel Lawrence Herchmer to investigate and report on the situation in Kootenay. A commission consisting of A. W. Vowell, provincial gold commissioner and local justice of the peace, Dr. I. W. Powell, Indian commissioner for British Columbia, and Herchmer visited Isadore. The chief used the occasion to present a list of grievances to the white officials. Looking "very fierce in an attitude of independence," Isadore spoke of the injustices suffered by the Indians: "Look over the land. How many white men have the Indians killed? Look at this place, there is the blood of a Kootenay. It is the white men who spilled it, we have seen this with our own eyes. The white man [murderer] went down below [Victoria] for trial. We thought he would be killed [executed] the white chiefs said so, not long after he returned. Another white man struck and killed an Indian. . . . I don't know how long ago on the prairie [at Fort McLeod] white men killed two Indians because they thought the Indians had fired the prairie." While the commissioners succeeded in getting Isadore to hand over Kapula, they noted that the Kutenai had "several hundred fighting men well-armed and supplied with ammunition."[130] This information led the federal government to dispatch to the Kootenay district a detachment of Mounties under the command of Major S. B. Steele. In June 1887, the detachment arrived at Galbraith's Ferry where they set up a temporary fort on ten acres of land leased from Galbraith. Since the break-out, there had been no further Indian activity, but Steele, who had been "detailed to restore order among the Kootenays," discovered that without Indian co-operation his task would be extremely difficult.

The Indian territory was almost inaccessible to the police; "there was no way in in the summer except by pack mules and no way in in winter except on snow shoes." Under the circumstances, it paid to be diplomatic. Steele recognized that Isadore was a power to be reckoned with, and the major was impressed with the Indian leader. According to Steele, who had become well acquainted with the Plains Indians, "neither Chief Red Crow nor Chief Crowfoot of the Blackfoot exercised at the height of their power the discipline that Isadore exercised." In a preliminary hearing which Isadore and his people both attended and followed "with keen interest and great intelligence," Steele found that there was not enough evidence to bring the Indians to trial.[131]

Dr. Powell received numerous letters on the subject from settlers, including several from Colonel Baker, from the government-appointed Indian Agent Michael Phillips, from the missionaries, and even from Major Steele.[132] Steele asked for justice for Chief Isadore:

> By all the laws of right and wrong the place belongs to him and for me to tell him that his place belongs to another was for me most unpleasant . . . there is not one white settler in the district that would not feel that a wrong had been done. Isadore is vigorous and energetic. He butchers and sells his cattle up town and asks no favour of anyone; simply to be left alone on his farm.[133]

Powell passed on all information received to his superiors in Ottawa, and the results of these pleas for justice—although not all settlers agreed completely with Steele—illustrate very clearly that justice for the Indian was a rare commodity.

In September 1887, the federal government sent a commission consisting of Forbes George Vernon, the provincial commissioner of lands and works, Dr. Powell, and Peter O'Reilly, the surveyor responsible for laying out the Kutenai reserves three years earlier, to deal with the disputed land question. Both Vernon and Powell were sympathetic to the Indians' needs, but they were helpless in the face of a provincial government policy aimed at keeping the settlers happy. The votes of Kootenay settlers were often crucial to a provincial government holding onto power with a small majority.[134] Moreover, Colonel Baker was himself a member of the legislature. Although Isadore and his band were away and could not be heard from or consulted, the commissioners revised the reserves in the interests of the settlers and confirmed that St. Joseph Prairie was now Baker's property. Major Steele was instructed to inform Isadore of the decision and assure him that the government would pay monetary compensation. As Steele anticipated, Isadore objected most strongly. The chief "launched forth into an eloquent account of the wrongs against his people," and not trusting the government, he refused to vacate the land unless he was paid in advance for improvements—such as irrigation—the government promised to make on newly allocated Indian land.[135] In the spring, matters came to a head when Steele sent Isadore an ultimatum. Isadore had spent the winter sending out word to all the Canadian Kutenai and to Kutenai and Flathead Indians of Montana and Idaho, all of whom promised their support in all-out resistance to white encroachment.

CONTACT AND CONFLICT: THE ATHAPASCANS

But the Nicola and Kutenai were not the only spiritual charges of Nicolas Coccola to face massive disruption. The Corsican seemed destined to work among Indians who actively resisted white encroachment of Indian land and culture, for the missionary's second long-term charges were the Athapascans of New Caledonia, who, after years of acquiescence, finally took a stand against white-administered injustice. The region of New Caledonia was given its somewhat romantic name by Scots explorer Simon Fraser, who was captivated by the beauty and Scottish highland character of its lakes and mountains.[136] Natural beauty notwithstanding, it was a harsh land consisting of endless miles of mountain barriers, wild, hazardous rivers, lakes that were placid one moment, storm-struck the next, weather extremes, muskeg, mosquitoes, and blackflies.[137] But to the Indian peoples it was a land of abundance. All summer long the rivers teemed with salmon—spring, sockeye, coho, humpback, and dog salmon—and the lakes contained numerous other fish, including an abundance of carp, which could be caught both in summer and, by ice-fishing, all winter long. Bear, deer, beaver, rabbits, and marmots provided meat, and berries and roots rounded out the food supplies.

The region's native peoples were primarily Carrier, an Athapaskan people: the Lower Carrier—Algatcho, Kluskoten, Tauten, and Nazkoten—the Upper Carrier—Tanotan, Tachickwoten, Nulkiwoten, Cheslatta, Necosliwoten, Tachiwoten, Natliwoten and Stellawoten—and the Babines—Nataotin or Babine Lake Carrier, Wet'suwet'en or Bulkley River Carrier.[138] The region was also host to the nomadic Sekani, the Tahltan, Kaska, a band of Slave, and two bands of Beaver. Coccola's new spiritual charges lived in the Upper Fraser, Blackwater, Nechako, and Bulkley River valleys and around the regions many lakes. These Indians traded with the coastal tribes from whom they acquired not only trade items but also, in ages past, a political system and several cultural innovations.[139] The population was divided into three classes: nobles, commoners, and—although relatively few in numbers—slaves. But there was no "royal class" of rulers, and a commoner who could gain the support of enough friends and who gave the required number of potlatches (a custom the Carrier had adopted from their coastal trading partners) could become a nobleman. Although within each community there was a chief, decisions regarding Carrier life were reached through consultation among all chiefs, so that the Carrier "never possessed any unified government."[140] The Sekani, with whom missionaries had minimal contact for several decades, were year-round hunters whose political organization and social life were simple. Each band had a chief, but apparently he possessed very little, if any, authority.[141] Prior to European contact, it is estimated that the Carrier numbered approximately 8,500 and were reduced, primarily by white-introduced diseases, to 2,000 by the 1930's; the Sekani had numbered approximately 1,000 and were reduced to 160 by 1923.[142]

The history of contact between Indians and whites in New Caledonia began in 1792 when, on his historic journey to the Pacific, Alexander Mackenzie met with both Sekani and Carrier bands. Mackenzie introduced them to the value of trading directly with Europeans by offering "looking glasses, beads, and other alluring trinkets," and he introduced them also to the power of the newcomers by illustrating the use of guns.[143] But it was Simon Fraser who made the more notable and permanent impact. Under his direction preparations were made for the construction of a fur-trading post on Stuart Lake in 1806. Anthropologist Diamond Jenness discovered that at their first encounter with Fraser and his party, the Carrier of the Stuart Lake area believed the newcomers were "reincarnated shades of cremated Indians, because they not only came from the east, up the Nechako River, but they blew smoke from their mouths."[144] The Carrier appear to have made a quick re-evaluation because, after it was completed by the summer, Fort St. James succeeded immediately in attracting large numbers of Indians and "trading and bartering" were started on the spot.[145] Fort St. James became in time the administrative centre for the lucrative northern fur trade.

Both Mackenzie and Fraser found evidence that the Sekani and Carrier had trading links with the coast.[146] Fraser's aim was to put an end to this former trade pattern and substitute a fort-centred one. The Indians, who received what one historian called "illusury substitutes" for their fur coats and robes, were instructed by Fraser to exert themselves and procure as many as possible of the specific skins enumerated by the white trader.[147] However, the Indians proved to be far from gullible. Both Carrier and Sekani continued to trade with coastal Indians whenever the price offered by their former trading partners was higher than that offered by the Europeans. To counteract the lure of this coastal trade, the North West Company introduced the debtor system. Indians were sold a variety of trading goods and hunting equipment in the fall and had to pay for them in furs in the following spring. In spite of this attempt to tie them to a monopoly trading situation, the Indians continued to sell to the highest bidder.[148]

As Fraser was the first to discover, life could be precarious in this northern region. Natural disasters such as forest fires that depleted meat supplies or a poor salmon run could be fatal. By August of his first northern summer, Fraser and his men were close to starvation. Partly to reduce demands on what little food there was and partly to establish a second trading post before winter, Fraser sent John Stuart to establish a fort on what Stuart named Fraser Lake.[149] There were Indian villages at both ends of the lake and at least seven other communities in the vicinity. Fort Fraser became the trading centre for these people. In 1821, the Hudson's Bay Company fell heir to this rich fur-bearing territory. A year later, the company built Fort Babine (or Fort Kilmaurs as it was also known) on Babine Lake, northwest of Stuart Lake, one of the main spawning grounds of the Skeena River salmon. The new fort was situated on an old Indian trail from the lake to the Skeena River. It was founded partly as a salmon supply depot—the company needed four salmon per day, per company worker, every day of the year—and partly as the company's first, and unsuccessful, attempt to lure the Babines from their coastal trade allegiance. The fort, "rather a miserable place, not without it share of murders and revenges," was soon abandoned as the company found it more economical to build at the Babine Indian village where many Indians congregated during the salmon season.[150]

Like the other Indians of British Columbia, the Indians of the northern interior enjoyed economic benefits from the developing fur trade as new wealth, in the form of trading goods, was injected into their economy. All that was required of the Indians was acceptance of a new partnership and, particularly among the Carrier, who traditionally had not hunted in winter, an increase in time spent hunting.[151] The traders and the

Indians were "part of a mutually beneficial economic symbiosis."[152] Moreover, since the traders were always in need of game and fish to supplement their often meagre, sometimes non-existent food supplies, the Indians could be said to have had, at least for several decades, the economic edge.

Until the turn of the century, these northern peoples remained relatively isolated from rapid white population growth. However, they could not escape entirely the ravages to their society caused by the importation of European diseases, which travelled throughout the province via the trade routes.[153] Nor could they escape the acculturation resulting from fur-trade contact. By the late 1880's, Carrier men had become trappers equipped with European-style clothing, and many had abandoned traditional communities to build square-timbered homes in the vicinity of trading posts. They planted vegetables to supplement their traditional foods and acquired a taste for luxury items such as tobacco, tea, and sugar. Because there was no white population to provide labourers for work around the forts, the Hudson's Bay Company hired Indians as carpenters, fur-packers, and farm labour.[154] When the company built a schooner on the 101-mile long Babine Lake to transport goods from one end to the other, Indians were hired as deckhands. From the early 1860's, another avenue of employment opened up, one that was to bring more than one dimension of change to the northern bands.

As it had in other parts of the province, the search for gold brought the first wave of European non-fur-trade population. In 1861, gold strikes on the Stikine and adjacent rivers led Governor James Douglas to organize what he named the Territory of Stikine, with himself as administrator. In the late 1860's, the Omineca gold rush attracted hundreds of prospectors, many from the Cariboo placer-mining area where lucky strikes were now rare. Gold seekers arrived in Carrier country via Hazelton on the west coast and Fort St. James to the south. Although the rush peaked around 1871, the Omineca attracted placer gold miners until after the turn of the century. A third major strike at Dease Creek, and the rich claims of Thibert and McDame creeks, began the Cassiar gold rush of 1872. Most of those who came north in response to gold strikes were transients. The less fortunate sometimes remained in the country to pack supplies in to the more successful. Placer miners and packers either returned to the coast during the harsh winters or tried their hand at trapping. All these newcomers infringed upon Carrier territory, although some Indians took advantage of their presence to earn income by packing or supplying foodstuffs.

Some of the gold seekers who remained in the country and some of those attracted to farming to meet the demands of miners for all kinds of food established pockets of settlement. Fur traders had been the first to explore the possibilities of crop-raising in New Caledonia, but harsh weather conditions, spring frost, wild animals, and insects mitigated against success.[155] But primarily because transportation routes through the rugged terrain were either non-existent or extremely difficult, white stock-raisers and farmers remained relatively few. A boost to settlement was provided by the laying of the Perry Collins Overland Telegraph Line. This line was to link the United States to Europe using a telegraph wire across northern British Columbia, Alaska, and Russia. During 1865 and 1866, approximately 150 men led by Colonel Charles S. Bulkley were at work cutting a road for the line twenty feet wide through previously inaccessible wilderness. The successful laying of a trans-Atlantic cable in 1866 made the line at least temporarily obsolete—although it was possible, if one desired, to communicate with New York City from a remote northern Carrier village.[156] Since it provided an easier access route for would-be settlers, the line did serve some useful purpose. Another sign of changing times was the appearance, beginning in the 1870's, of railway surveyors.

Sandford Fleming, the well-known Canadian Pacific Railway surveyor and engineer, was the first to point out that a natural railway route lay across the northern interior. After following the Yellowhead route from northern Alberta, from the headwaters of the Fraser, the railway could travel along the river to Fort George, then go along the Nechako and Endako Rivers to Dease Lake, across the Bulkley mountains to the headwaters of the Bulkley River, follow it northwest to the Skeena, and then pass along the Skeena to the coast. Fleming believed that along this route lay the "chief belt of settlement in Central B.C."[157]

Some had an even greater vision. A botanist with a Canadian geographical survey team visited the northern interior between 1872 and 1875. Professor John Macoun saw a tremendous future for the region, one that included neither Indians nor wildlife: "When the forest is cleared, by whatever cause, the soil will become drier, and the climate will be considerably ameliorated... as Germany was to the Romans, so much of our North West to us—a land of marsh and swamp and rigorous winter. Germany has been cleared of her forests and is now one of the finest and most progressive of European countries. May not the clearing of our North-Western forests produce a similar result?"[158] Fortunately, no one responded to this vision.

None of these early white-promoted activities brought the Carrier peoples into close relationship with the white population. Indian Agent R. E. Loring, who had charge of what was called the Babine Agency, sent the following 1893 report to Ottawa: "These Indians are nearly entirely dependent on the results of the pursuits of their forefathers; they are too remote from the intercourse of white men to gain more remunerative employment."[159] The late 1890's changed this situation. In the spring of 1896, interest revived in the Omineca mines, and although most miners travelled up the coast to the interior, a constant trickle of men, women, and pack animals made its way north through Fort St. James; in 1898, the discovery of gold in the Klondike turned "this transient trickle" into a torrent.[160] Both the Canadian government and local newspapers—in particular, the *Ashcroft Journal*—promoted what became known as the 1,700-mile "poor-man's" route to the Klondike. This trail began at Ashcroft and followed the earlier telegraph route through Quesnel, Stony Creek, Moricetown, and Hazelton, then on through Atlin and Whitehorse to Dawson City.

Throughout the summer of 1898, a steady procession of fortune-seekers trudged slowly northward through Carrier territory.[161] Indians now found work transporting miners and their supplies. But the gold strike brought more than miners. In the spring of 1898, for example, the North West Mounted Police Klondike expedition stayed over a month at Fort St. James.[162] Between 1899 and 1901, the Yukon Telegraph, "born of the Klondike Gold Rush" and following much of the earlier Collins Telegraph Line, established a link between Dawson City and Vancouver, giving the rich goldfields their first all-year-round communications with the outside world.[163] "Civilization" was inching its way north, and, accordingly, miners provided Indians with liquor, raped Indian women, and returned Indian hospitality by stealing animal traps and food from Indian caches, "something other Indians would never have done."[164] When they were packing for miners, the Indians neglected their hunting and fishing, and hunting was often also disrupted by miners who caused fires or, with their noise, drove game away. The miners, however, were only a temporary aberration; a more permanent threat to the Indian lifestyle arrived at the turn of the century—the promise of a railway.

Canada's era of prosperity, 1896 to 1913, generated primarily by a population boom on the prairies, found Canadian railways inadequate to handle the increased grain trade. Charles M. Hays, general manager of the Grand Trunk Railway, ordered a survey of northern British Columbia and, on 2 November 1902, submitted to the federal government a proposal to build a line from North Bay, Ontario, to Fort Simpson on the Pacific Coast; "the federal government readily approved, and it was expected that the Grand Trunk Pacific would build through one of the more northerly passes," either the Pine River or the Peace River Pass.[165] Although it would be some years before the railway became a reality, the prospect of it attracted increasing numbers of settlers to the

interior valleys. The scene was set for Indian-white conflict over ownership of land and large-scale disruption of the Indians' trapping-,
hunting-, and fishing-based economy.

CONTACT AND CONFLICT: THE MISSIONARY'S STANCE

Like most of British Columbia's missionaries, Coccola found himself
drawn into the economic world of his spiritual charges.[166] But the extent
of missionary involvement in temporal affairs differed according to both
missionary inclination and organizational policy.

One of Christianity's supreme ironies has been the ongoing difficulties
its messengers have encountered deciphering their role regarding the material welfare of their spiritual charges. Most missionaries deemed it part
of the proselytization process to raise the living standards of their native
converts to acceptable European levels, but should they, or would they,
involve themselves in counteracting the often destructive effects of white
encroachment? Through religious teaching which minimized the importance of suffering in this world and maximized the justice and equality
of the world to come, the churches at large reinforced the economic and
social status quo and encouraged passivity. Forced to confront the negative realities of Indian-white contact, however, missionaries frequently
responded as much on a personal as a theological level. Some simply
pleaded the Indians' case by bringing poor conditions to the attention of
government agents; others advised the Indians to hasten cultural change,
to establish viable agricultural pursuits, lumbering, canning, brickmak-
ing, and so forth, and to compete in the new economy.[167] Missionaries
also taught the Indians the due process of law by which they might appeal unsatisfactory government decisions regarding their land. The
Tsimshian at Metlakatla, taught by William Duncan, "were well versed
in those mechanics of petitioning and letter-writing that characterized
the relations of dissatisfied citizens with their government."[168] Oblates
advised Indians to pre-empt land, wrote letters both to government officials and the press, composed and distributed petitions, and kept the Indians informed of changes in the law. The contentious issue of native
rights to the land and to maintenance of traditional practices versus
settler and industrial needs drew Coccola into a series of personal in-
volvements and choices—some of which illustrate the conflict inherent
in the missionary's dual role as spiritual guardian to both combatants.

During his years in British Columbia, Nicolas Coccola was far more
than a missionary to the native peoples. Owing to Bishop D'herbomez's
insistence that Oblates be given autonomy in the Vicariate of British
Columbia, each missionary priest was expected to act as pastor to an
ever-increasing number of settlers. Although some Protestant mis-

sionaries also served a white constituency, in general their missionary organizations did not promote dual roles. It was vital for the Oblates that contact with white settlers be maintained because they were a major source of financing. Although initially the Society for the Propagation of the Faith provided money for expansion, Rome expected the new vicariate to become self-supporting as quickly as possible. Each missionary had to collect donations from both Indians and whites not only for the support of his individual mission but also for the support of ecclesiastical programmes. In a rapidly developing area like the Kootenays, the church had to erect parishes in each settled mining town. And although in the long term such parishes provided regular income in the form of special collections for a variety of causes, initially they were an expense. The construction and furnishing of a church building itself was a costly business. The Oblates had early recognized that cultivating the friendship of influential men could be beneficial to the material success of the church. Without the financial and political assistance of such men, the bishop could not hope to build all the institutions necessary to keep the Catholic church a viable presence in the province. With this in mind, upon his arrival at St. Eugene's, Coccola sought the friendship of the Kootenay businessmen. The Oblate saw no conflict in his dual role of missionary to native peoples and priest to the growing white communities, but the Indians were aware of it. As Coccola's "Memoirs" reveal, they were realistic enough to see that their interests and the interests of settlers were totally opposed. Two disputes over Kootenay land illustrate how missionaries were sometimes forced to deal with this conflict of interests.

When Coccola arrived at St. Eugene's Mission in October, the land question was still unresolved. According to the missionary, as confrontation between Isadore and his people and the Mounties appeared inevitable, Major Steele sent for him to prevail upon the Indians to accept the inevitability of defeat.[169] Ironically, a young Corsican who had been willing to take up arms to defend his order's property against a hostile majority, now, successfully, counselled Indians trying to protect their land from encroachment by a hostile white majority to accept the government's terms. In the face of white solidarity, Isadore acquiesced. But it was not the only time that Coccola was to become involved in Kutenai/white land disputes; a second incident occurred several years later.

By 1895, the Corsican missionary was no longer visiting the West Kootenay bands. Rapid population development had put too much strain on the resources of St. Eugene's Mission, and the bishop had divided the territory in two sections: East Kootenay, still served primarily from St. Eugene's, and West Kootenay, where Oblate priests in white parishes visited local Indians. An Oblate priest in Nelson was responsible for visiting the boundary reserves, but because of the weight of white parish activity and involvement, his visits to the Indians were few. In the Creston area, the Alberta Company was draining marshy land along the Kootenay River to produce a viable agricultural resource. The Kutenai had a village along the river bank, and when workmen attempted to drive machinery through their land—in particular, through their cemetery—the Indians stood them off with guns. According to Coccola, the Department of Indian Affairs wrote to Bishop Paul Durieu asking that a missionary be sent to resolve the conflict.[170] Coccola persuaded the Kutenai to accept the company's offer of a new village site (to be selected by the government not the Indians) and a new church.

Coccola believed that the Indians desired a new church as strongly as he did. There was some truth in this, for the majority of them had, by this time, accepted Catholicism. A church in the village meant that feast days such as Christmas and Easter could be celebrated at home. The people no longer needed to make the long trek to the central mission for these events. Moreover, a church had become a status symbol in the new social order. It is unlikely, however, that it was as central to the Indians' needs as it was to their missionary's, and Coccola's statement that having accepted the company's proposal, "all their [the Indians'] troubles were over" was more than a little naive. When speaking with Denys Nelson, Coccola added an interesting and telling comment: "But to the credit of the Company, he never got any money at all for the building of the church, nor did he want it, since the Indians might easily be brought to think that he had been paid more than he allowed that he had received."[171] This statement clearly illustrates two important points: that influences other than that of the church were at work on the Indians and that the Indians were indeed suspicious of their missionary's motives.

To Coccola, the futility of Kootenay resistance in either case at this time and in a violent manner was clear; they might win a battle, but they were sure to lose a war. Moreover, the lessons of Oblate history in the Pacific Northwest were not lost him. Oblate missionaries in the Oregon Territory had remained with the Yakima Indians during the natives' last stand against the injustices of the American government's Indian policy. This apparent support of the Yakima earned the Oblates both government and settler hostility, a condition which played a large part in Oblate missionary failure in Oregon. When he decided to intervene in the Isadore/Baker conflict, Coccola asked Father Richard to accompany him "so that he might hear what was said and be a witness lest [Coccola's] words might later be distorted and misrepresented as had happened to Father Pandosy in the States at Yakima." Moreover, in accordance with 1877 Oblate policy regarding Indians and government proposals, the missionaries were to remain neutral.[172] Coccola's caution and his weak defence of Indian rights, however, did not remain a constant throughout his missionary life.

Coccola had not been many years in the north when Indians who had previously been protected by their inaccessibility from the destructive effects of white encroachment began to experience population pressure. In a letter to Bishop Emile Buñoz, Coccola explained the rapid and destructive changes:

> The building of the Grand Trunk Railway was attracting seekers of agricultural lands, seekers of timber for the saw mills and seekers of gold and other precious metals. . . . The country was invaded by the land surveyors of both government and the industrial companies. The solitude of our valleys and mountains was replaced by the goings and comings of intrepid pioneers studying the resources of a new country which they intended to exploit. For consequence game and fur animals vanished before the invaders who by either design or accident burned the huts of the Indian hunters and of the surrounding areas, the new farmers planted their pegs and tents beside the meadows of the sauvages and the latter who hitherto considered themselves sole masters and lords of the country found themselves hemmed in on all sides.[173]

The Indians complained that "careless land stakers and prospectors" had caused forest fires and driven the game away.[174] Coccola made Ottawa aware of these problems also. In a letter to the Department of Indian Affairs, in October 1909, he stated that the Indians were starving, at least partially as a result of white influx,[175] although he suggested that only Indians "unable to provide for themselves" be helped.[176]

Gold-mining had brought the first industrial threat to these isolated northern peoples, and it was followed by other industries which posed long-term economic hazards: the canning industry, lumbering, and farming. What was at stake was a commodity vital to Indian survival—the salmon of the northern lakes and rivers. In spite of increased trade opportunities and the availability of some wage labour, salmon remained the staple tribal diet of most of the interior Indians. In 1906, after making a two-and-one-half month journey through the northerly regions of his extensive diocese, Bishop Augustine Dontenwill told a news reporter than since his last visit to the north five years previously, the Indians had made little headway in agricultural pursuits: "they still cling to their fishing as a means of subsistance," the bishop commented.[177] Unfortunately, all the new activities in the north placed stress upon this major source of Indian food.

Placer-mining had been the first white-instigated activity to have an impact upon the salmon runs. Waters flowing from the diggings had increased the amount of silt suspended in the streams. This reduced penetration of the light necessary to the growth of the aquatic photosynthetic micro-organisms which fed the fish. Heavy silting could simply smother salmon spawn, preventing young salmon from emerging. Lumbering by individual farmers or companies had an even greater potential for damage. By removing forest cover which bordered streams and rivers, farmers and loggers exposed the shallow waters to direct sunlight; this raised the temperature and destroyed cold-water fauna. Once again the balance of nature was disturbed. Moreover, lumbering caused erosion and flash floods, which, together with timber debris, obstructed the migration of fish to their spawning grounds. Farming had an equally devastating effect. The plowing of land, or even animal-grazing, increased water run-off, which again led to flooding or the blocking of streams with soil and debris.[178] Thus, mining, logging, and extensive farming had the potential to affect the salmon-spawning grounds seriously, but the canning industry proved to be a more direct threat to Indian welfare.

As early as 1877, a San Francisco-based salmon-canning company tried to exploit the potential of the Skeena River. It proved to be a growth industry. By the 1880s, several plants were established on the Skeena, Nass, and other coastal rivers.[179] A few years after the turn of the century, fourteen canneries operated on or in the vicinity of the Skeena River alone.[180] The reason for the development of the industry was the market for canned salmon in industrial Europe—primarily England. Salmon-canning had begun in Europe, but by the nineteenth century most of the major salmon rivers there had been either fished out or had been blocked by "man-made alterations to the river environment," which prevented salmon reaching spawning grounds.

Britain's industrial population needed supplies from new areas, and initially its demand was met by the eastern North American regions of Maine and New Brunswick. Discovery in 1864 of the teeming Pacific Northwest rivers brought American businessmen to this new type of "gold field" of northern British Columbia.[181] The early canneries were wasteful enterprises. They indiscriminately hauled in salmon, giving little if any thought to conservation, even as a good business measure. Often far too many salmon were pulled from the rivers and had to be dumped because the canneries ran short of cans. These operations did provide many Indians with wage labour, but the cannery operators blamed the Indians when the salmon run was light. They complained to government officials that the Indians' method of fishing—the building of basket-type weirs—was responsible for the scarcity of salmon. The result was new fishing regulations prohibiting the ancient methods and allowing the use of nets only. This had a devastating effect on the Indians. It led Bishop Dontenwill to comment that "unless the fishing regulations with regard to trap fishing are altered, the Indians in the North will not be able to live at all in two or three years."[182] When the cannery operators brought pressure to bear on Ottawa to enforce federal laws and prevent the Indians from operating their traditional fishing weirs, Father Coccola took what could be considered his first strong stand on behalf of Indians' cultural rights; he travelled to Ottawa to protest.

Settlement had remained slow, but the promise of two, possibly three, railways changed the situation. The Grand Trunk Pacific charter of 1903 provided for the completion of its projected railway by 1911. The company had announced that its Pacific Coast terminus would be Prince Rupert, Kaien Island, about thirty miles south of Port Simpson, and in 1908 began clearing a townsite, building wharves, and constructing warehouses. Contracts for the building of the first section eastward from Prince Rupert were let that year. In 1906, Charles Clifford, M.L.A. for the Skeena Riding, formed a company to construct a railway from Kitimat Arm northward to Hazelton. Known as the Pacific Northern and Omineca Railway (but to locals as the Kitamaat, Hazelton and Omineca), the railway, to be completed from Lake Superior to Edmonton, was not bound by its charter to complete its line to the coast within a specific time, but it was rumoured that, within a few years, the line would go north to an outlet on the Pacific.[183]

By 1908, the northern interior had been well-publicized by the provincial government. In the summer of 1901, Gold Commissioner F. W. Valleau reported that from Fort St. James to Fort McLeod the land was "well-timbered with pine, spruce, and poplar and dotted with innumerable beautiful lakes." Valleau found the soil for at least thirty miles east of Fort St. James "very fertile, pear-vine and wild timothy growing to a height of four feet in many places." The gold commissioner also proclaimed the Bulkley Valley ideal cattle country and the Parsnip River Valley good for farming and promising as a coal-mining area. Valleau believed that if the Grand Trunk Pacific selected the Pine River Pass route, it would open up "undulating, park-like country... destined to become a paradise for sportsmen" as well as rich farmland, between the Pine River and Fort St. James. From reports such as these, the provincial government advised would-be settlers that: "in the northern interior... which it defined as lying between parallels 52 degrees and 60 degrees north latitude... there [were] large areas of fertile land well-suited to mixed farming, dairying and cattle-raising." But they stressed the value of stock-raising as there was a profusion of such natural fodder as "peavine, vetch, red-top, wild timothy, rye and blue grass." Settlers were

warned that until the promised railways were in place transportation facilities would remain limited. The principal route to the new farming
areas was by the three steamers plying the Skeena River between Port
Essington on the coast and Hazelton—from Hazelton people would
have to travel overland. An alternative route was available: Ashcroft to
Quesnel, 220 miles; Quesnel to Blackwater River, 40 miles; Blackwater
to Tsinkut Lake in the Nechako Valley, 50 miles; a trail from this point
led to the junction of the Bulkley and Telkwa Rivers, a further 145
miles. The government warned settlers that until the railways went in,
they must be prepared to "rough it." Surveyors' reports also led the government to tell would-be farming pioneers that although the winters
could be severe, Indians had informed government officials that chinook
conditions prevented deep freezing in some areas and, consequently,
that few horses or cattle were lost.[184]

Government promotion succeeded in attracting some new pioneers to
the northern interior where they began clearing land. But often individual farmers were the least of the Indians' problems. After the Grand
Trunk Pacific purchased Kaien Island, land syndicates purchased thousands of acres in the Nechako, Bulkley, and neighbouring valleys and
sent out surveyors to mark off their claims. In addition, the provincial
government leased out northern timber lands, placing no limit on the
number of leases an individual or company could hold. Faced with
diminishing supplies from the United States and Eastern Canada and
with a railway boom predicted, timber barons looked eagerly on the un-
tapped resources of the northern interior.[185] For the first time, many Indians faced the reality that their claims to the country based on traditional village and winter and summer campsites were dismissed by the
encroaching whites. Since Indian communities often stood at the most
advantageous spot with regards to transportation or the fertility of surrounding areas, the native inhabitants were pressured to move. The experience of the Fort George Indians, who were among Coccola's spiritual charges, provides a good example both of such pressure tactics and
of Coccola's continued involvement with Indian material welfare.

Until the promise of railways drew attention to the northern interior,
Fort George attracted few settlers. The fort was erected in 1807 and
stood at the confluence of the Fraser and Nechako Rivers. For several
years it was a major trading centre for Carrier Indians and Chilcotin and
Shuswap of the Cariboo region. From 1821, Fort Alexandria and Quesnel appear to have been more active fur-trade posts. In spite of railway
rumours, even as late as 1909, Fort George had few buildings other than
a sawmill erected a year earlier to provide cut timber for local farmers.[186]
In 1909, John McInnis, former Kootenay miner and ex-M.L.A. for the
Boundary Riding, arrived with his family.[187] A carpenter by trade,

McInnis built the first non-fur-company store and began supplying farmers with general merchandise.

By 1910, railway fever, which instigated a rush of American, European, and Canadian capital into the province, produced a burst of frenzied activity in Fort George, which appeared to be a likely divisional point for the Grand Trunk Pacific. Land and colonization companies in the fast-developing Vancouver promoted the sale of town lots; three or four possible townsites were surveyed. Premier Richard McBride, accompanied by his friend Sir Harry Brittain, made the first motor-car journey to Fort George via the old Cariboo Road. Brittain commented that, on their arrival, the men found "a very riot of enthusiasm. In fact there were three Fort Georges, each one claiming to be the greatest city of the future." One entrepreneur, George J. Hammond, established the Natural Resources Commission, which promoted throughout Canada, the United States, even Europe, the townsite his company had surveyed. Hammond predicted that Fort George would be "the railway hub of inland British Columbia" and advertised that "ten railroads building or chartered—some surveyed—all headed to Fort George."[188] One Grand Trunk Pacific agent informed Ottawa that four or five townsites were laid out and that people were being duped.[189] However, the early interest shown by Grand Trunk Pacific officials in the 1,366 acres of Indian reserve was a strong indication of the favoured site.

When approached by agents of the Grand Trunk Development Company, the chief of the Fort George Shuswap refused to negotiate. His answer was: "For more than 200, perhaps 300 years we live here, we die here, we bury here, we fish, hunt and trap here, by and by we make gardens here. We like this place. All our people no like to sell this place."[190] Along with the Grand Trunk, other companies applied for parts of the Indian land. The B.C. Express Company argued that the Indians did not require the land the company needed to build "warehouses, offices, docks, stables and equipment." One entrepreneur, J. A. Cosgrove, offered the Indians $500 per annum for life in exchange for their land.[191] The Department of Indian Affairs, which supported the Grand Trunk Development Company, sent a department representative, the Reverend John McDougall, to negotiate with the Indians, and McDougall found them now divided on the question of the sale. McDougall offered $68,300, one-quarter to be paid immediately, in cash, another quarter to be paid on removal. The rest would be "funded to the credit of the band and be paid to the Indians annually." An extra $10,000 would be provided for building costs and the Indian graveyard would be preserved.[192]

At first the Indians agreed that Father Bellot (Coccola's assistant) could negotiate with the department for them, but by April 1911, the proposed deal fell through, and the Indians requested that Coccola be allowed to speak for them.[193] The Natural Resources Commission, pressing the advantages of its own site, advised the Indians to refuse the $50 an acre offered by the department on behalf of the railway company. Acting on this advice, the Indians demanded $1,000 an acre. The local Indian agent, convinced that Coccola would influence the Indians to be more reasonable, suggested that the deal be put on hold until the missionary arrived. Unfortunately for the department, Coccola negotiated his own deal with the representative of an Ottawa company, who offered $100,000 in cash, a house for each Indian family, churches and recreation halls for each new reserve site, and $1,000 towards the removal of the dead to another location; the Indians accepted this offer unanimously.[194] The department, determined to sell to the railway company, refused to allow the deal, but Coccola advised the Indians to stand firm.[195] The result was the surrender of Indian land for $125,000, of which $25,000 was to be used for new buildings.[196] Although this was a far better deal than had been originally offered, the Grand Trunk Development Company sold the resultant town lots for as much as $10,200 each.[197]

Coccola's more aggressive stance on behalf of the Indians and Ottawa's willingness to acquiesce (although admittedly the department succeeded in defrauding the Indians) could both have been influenced, at least in part, by an emergent militancy among some northern tribes. Unlike the case in the Kootenays, where missionaries could ill afford to gain the displeasure, if not enmity, of prominent businessmen, in the northern regions where settlement was more isolated and where policing on a large scale was both impractical and impossible, the government officials needed the support of the missionaries.[198] Arbitrators of influence were increasingly needed as some Indian bands began to respond to white intrusion with threats of violence.

In 1908, Chief Capilano of North Vancouver,[199] "perhaps the earliest native activist in the province," travelled to Ottawa with other Indian leaders to question the federal government on the impact of the Grand Trunk Pacific Railway on native habitat.[200] Some Indians had firsthand knowledge of the impact of the railway. As the railway moved down the Skeena and Bulkley Valleys, Carrier Indians were employed in "packing and freighting, on survey crews, and as producers of ties, timber and other goods and services."[201] The Indians asked about the rights of native peoples to timber on their reserves, an important issue given the railway's need for and, by charter, its right to obtain lumber as it moved across the province. Indian concerns over their hunting and fishing rights and their land claims, as well as timber rights, were met with verbal assurances that native interests would be given consideration.[202] The evasiveness led to unrest. Several chiefs from the Skeena region threatened to massacre all the settlers in the Hazelton area as soon as the winter freeze-up blocked communication. This threat of violence brought a commission consisting of federal and provincial representatives to the north to hear Indian grievances and to establish where further reserves were needed to protect Indians from further white encroachment.[203] The arrival of the commission did not put an end to violence or threats of violence. In the remote and difficult terrain of the northern interior, the Indians were free to act for their own protection.[204] Although the Carrier, perhaps partly owing to the influence of their missionary, appear to have been more accepting of the inevitability of the white presence, a party of armed Indians in 1909 forced farmers in the Kitwanga Valley to abandon their homesteads, and Indians harassed and physically attacked white workers building a new road in the Hazelton area.[205] Conditions remained tense for several years.

The Carrier achieved some success in having more reserve land set aside. According to Indian Agent Ernest Loring, the Indians of the Stuart Lake Agency, "only recently brought in touch with civilization other than as represented by the Northern frontier trader, trapper and prospector," received thirty-seven reserves.[206] Receiving and keeping, however, were not synonymous. An editorial in the *Omineca Herald*, 20 January 1913, reflected the attitude of many northern whites: "In justice to the settler and to the country, a large portion of the land already held by the Indians should be taken away from them and thrown open to settlement. This district requires all the agricultural land available and unless the Indians will cultivate it, the white man should be allowed to take up the land for that purpose." The government was always willing to oblige. Indian protest was muted—although not totally silenced—as the First World War and the completion of the railway "brought a virtual end to the campaign for traditional rights; not until the passage of two generations did the active prosecution of native land claims resume" among the Indians of the northern interior.[207]

The ongoing problem of Indian/white contact was, for the missionaries, multifaceted. As white settlement increased, many worked to keep contact between their Indian converts and whites to a minimum. There were several important reasons for this: minimal contact meant that the Indians continued their dependence on the missionary for interpretation of the new social order; increased contact meant that Indians would realize that whites seldom practised what their missionaries preached; and continuous contact meant Indian exposure to those who mocked religion and denigrated the mystique of the missionary. How-

ever, part of the missionary role was to prepare Indians for full participation in a white-dominated society, and cultural contact was deemed
an important part of this process.

MISSIONARY AS ROLE MODEL

Initially, the missionaries themselves acted as role models for their charges. Although they were few in number, missionaries spread themselves
even more thinly by becoming not only ministers of religion but also administrators, farmers, doctors, social workers, and teachers. While at St.
Mary's Mission to complete his course in theology (which had been interrupted so abruptly in France), Coccola had his first lesson in Indian
subsistence living when his companions taught him how to fish for
salmon. For the young Corsican, salmon-fishing was enjoyable, but he
had also to cure the fish, which was less enjoyable; "the smell of it was
awful, enough to knock a bull down."[208] But given the constant shortage
of money, learning to live off the land became an integral part of missionary work. Moreover, as farmers and ranchers—and also as
artisans—missionaries hoped to encourage the Indians by example and
direct instruction to emulate their efforts.[209]

All missions were expected to produce at least enough agricultural
commodities to make them self-sufficient. Many Protestant and Roman
Catholic missionaries, both men and women, attempted small-scale
market gardening. Some missions developed extensive mixed-farming;
others developed as both farms and ranches. St. Eugene's was no exception, and Coccola was proud of the mission's achievement in that direction:

> Looking at the temporal side of affairs for a minute, it must be noted
> that the Mission at St. Eugene was the first to bring machinery and
> farm implements into the district. Mowers, binders, threshers and
> other kinds; besides the beautiful garden that they created, [the mis-
> sionaries] had all kinds of fancy stock, Holsteins and even Jersey
> cows. People wanting milk cows knew where to go to get them. It was
> the same with the horses. A percheron Stallion was obtained from the
> Guichon's stable, which after a while was exchanged for a "Clyde" of
> 2,000 lbs. weight. This in turn gave place to a "shire." They were
> spreading this stock throughout the country. They would exchange a
> colt for a cow, and thus supply every part of the country with good
> horses. They had about 100 acres under cultivation and experimented
> with different kinds of grass to see what was the most suitable for the
> district. Seeds suitable for their purpose were also obtained from Ot-
> tawa. The seed was distributed to all who came to ask for it, the ar-

rangement being that they return the same quantity when they had got it back from what was sown.[210]

Missionaries like Coccola hoped that the Indians would profit by their good example. Cut off from their former hunting grounds, their land fenced in by whites, the Indians often had little choice but to farm, and sometimes this had unforeseen negative effects. Reporting on the Kutenai, their Indian agent noted: "The general health of the Indians has been good though consumption and scrofula seem to be much on the increase. Formerly these Indians lived almost exclusively on a meat diet; now they use flour as their staple article of food and the children are certainly less robust than formerly."[211] This clearly indicates that change in lifestyle, perhaps as much as direct contact with contaminated whites, could have contributed to the prevalence of certain diseases among the native peoples.

MISSIONARY AS MEDICO

As well as providing role models as farmers and ranchers, missionaries also applied themselves to the medical welfare of their Indians. Most missionaries repudiated the theory held by many whites that the Indians were doomed to extinction. They determined that by teaching "progressive" hygiene practices along with Gospel truths they would halt the deterioration caused by the Indians' low resistance to newly encountered, highly contagious diseases brought on or accelerated by Indian/European contact. Fur traders were the first to bring new medical knowledge to the Indians. At a time when diseases capable of mass destruction such as smallpox, measles, and influenza were decimating Indian bands and tuberculosis was destroying whole families, the missionaries also brought medical information. The Indians continued to use traditional medicines to try and counteract the new illnesses—for example, the Bella Coola Indians treated the Spanish influenza epidemic of 1918–19 with the traditional medicines devils' club, swamp gooseberry, and water hemlock[212]—but, in general, traditional healers were confronted with situations alien to their experience.[213] While Indians seldom totally rejected the traditional healing arts with their emphasis "on supernatural inspiration and magic knowledge," they began to turn to the missionaries for help.[214]

The medical background of the missionaries was varied. Some were qualified doctors and nurses who had trained specifically to practise medicine among indigenous peoples. Others were semi-skilled or had studied medicine independently, aware that such knowledge would be valuable, perhaps vital, to them in remote regions. And there were those who, although educated, had little or no medical training and had the role of medical missionary thrust upon them. But however complex or superficial their medical knowledge, missionaries did contribute to Indian physical welfare. For example, in 1862, William Duncan saved his followers from a smallpox epidemic that ravaged Port Simpson by isolating those showing early symptoms of the disease. Similarly, in 1882, C.M.S. missionary Robert Tomlinson helped to save Indians from the village of Kitwanga on the Skeena River from a measles epidemic.[215]

Unlike Tomlinson, Coccola had no medical training.[216] However, as he notes in his "Memoirs," soon after his arrival in British Columbia he acquired a medical reputation. Coccola was not the only Oblate to perform medical services. Father Charles Pandosy, the Oblate who opened the first mission in mainland British Columbia in the Okanagan Valley, left a medical dictionary full of detailed descriptions of diseases from pregnancy disorders to broken bones, prognosis, and remedies.[217] And herbs and roots (treatment familiar to the Indians) were used effectively by Father François-Marie Thomas, missionary in the Cariboo region.[218] But Coccola was involved in a rather unusual medical experiment. His predecessor at St. Eugene's, Father Léon Fouquet, had established a women's group among the Indians known as the "Kenouktklakalka Palki," or "The Women who Watch," to guide the health of children from birth to the age of seven. Coccola took over the society, although he appeared to think that the organization was simply a midwifery society. Troubled that the thrust of the society was "not sufficiently spiritual," Coccola drew up new rules for the group which included both concern that pregnant women not carry heavy burdens and that examples of cleanliness be given to children and the dictate that the women go to communion on all major feasts and wear special blue veils.[219]

Despite missionaries' good intentions and their willingness in many cases to offer practical as well as spiritual guidance to native peoples, they met with limited success. By reason of geography many bands remained isolated, and missionaries spent years simply covering and recovering the basics of Christianity.[220] Moreover, in spite of evidence that some Indians—either in spite of or because of their isolation—remained faithful to religious practices, others were questioning and falling away from the faith.[221] As settlement increased in some areas and expanded economic opportunities for the Indians, missionaries became alarmed by the negative impact of increased Indian/white contact.[222] Their efforts to establish model Indian communities had met with limited success; a second response to threats to missionary efforts, which also fulfilled the missionary mandate to "civilize," was the Industrial Boarding or Residential School.

THE RESIDENTIAL SCHOOL

The idea of industrial schools for Indian children also had a long history in North America. In 1743, an American missionary, the Reverend John Sergeant, suggested that Indian educational institutions should divide the Indians' time between study and manual work—a farm attached to each school would provide the opportunity for farm work and also "sustain the scholars." In 1803, the American Presbyterian Assembly, echoing the "city on a hill" theory, supported a school among the Cherokees where Indian children who learnt practical skills were to become "beacons" by which the parents might gradually be conducted into the same field of improvement.[223] Sixteen years later, the American secretary of war, John C. Calhoun, established a fund for Indian education, but it was to support only those undertakings which stressed "agriculture and mechanical arts" for boys and "spinning, weaving and sewing for girls."[224] In Canada the theory that Indians would be more quickly assimilated into white society by the promotion of agricultural, trade, and domestic arts was followed with equal determination.

In southern Ontario, Methodist missionaries in the 1820's and 1830's had manual labour schools at Alderville and Muncey. Attached were model farms equipped to teach Indian children the fine arts of farming—European-style.[225] Methodist leader Egerton Ryerson advised the assistant-superintendent of Indian Affairs to give Indian children "a plain English education adapted to the working farmer and mechanic... agriculture, kitchen, gardening, and mechanics, so far as mechanics is connected with making and repairing the most useful agricultural implements."[226] Regardless of cultural background, every Indian boy was to be raised as a farmer or, more likely, a farm labourer. Ryerson's advice was not the only influence on subsequent government policy. In 1879 Nicholas Flood Davin, "an Irish-born poet, lawyer and journalist" who later became Conservative M.P. for Assiniboia West, was commissioned by Ottawa to investigate American Indian Industrial Schools, the principal feature of President Ulysses S. Grant's Indian policy of "aggressive civilization."[227] In spite of American difficulties with the system, Davin was impressed and recommended that the Canadian government follow American methods of using religious organizations to implement a part-academic, part-trades' training programme.[228] Consequently, in British Columbia, Roman Catholic, Anglican, Presbyterian, and Methodist churches established industrial schools with the active co-operation of the federal government.[229]

To federal Indian policymakers who assumed control over the previously church-dominated Indian education after Confederation, the idea of industrial/boarding schools was eminently practical. Student residence ensured both isolation from home influence and also regular attendance; moreover, one establishment could be situated so as to accommodate students from a large geographical area. It was also a matter of sound economics to have missionary organizations subsidized by a federal per capita grant run such schools. Churches were seen to have the means to supplement government funding when necessary, and the difficult task of recruiting teachers for isolated Indian schools could be left in church hands.[230] By the time Coccola became involved in Indian education, the residential school had become a favoured Catholic tradition.

The education of native peoples has long been part of Roman Catholic Church history in Canada; as early as the 1630's, the Jesuits were sending Huron boys to be educated at their Quebec seminary, and the Capuchins, a Franciscan order, educated Micmac children at Port Royal, Acadia.[231] The Oblates continued that tradition by building a day school for Indian children at their first mission in the Okanagan. This institution encountered the same problem most Indian day schools across Canada faced, irregularity of attendance.[232] Whenever children were needed to participate in Indian economic activity such as hunting, fishing, or harvesting, parents kept their children home. In addition, the virtues of punctuality and regularity so desirable to whites are not prized in Indian culture. A French-Canadian missionary who established a day school on Anaham Reserve in the Chilcotin country in 1944, clearly stated the difficulties; according to Sister Teresa Bernard:

> These people were not used to stay on the reserve. They had meadows far away, and they had cattle and they used to hunt. When they used to go, they used to bring the whole family. They didn't know when they had asked for a school that they would have to stay down and look after the children, or keep the children home. . . . But Christmastide came, and the snow, but they said they had to go and feed their cattle. So after Christmas, we had maybe six in the school.[233]

In a letter pressing for a residential school for Carrier Indians, Coccola stressed that day schools had limited success. He argued: that Indian children needed what he referred to as "general training" before they could be made to "look at books"; that Indians would be loath to stay behind and look after children during the hunting season; that children left alone would ignore the school; that a school in each village would be too expensive; and that teachers would be hard to find.[234] For the early missionaries, a more severe disadvantage of day schools was the continuing close connection between children and their ancestral culture. While the churches agreed with the government that education placed a "civilized culture" within Indian grasp, they were also convinced that religious indoctrination was equal to, if not more important than, job preparation.[235] While research on the Anglican Church suggests its clergy gave equal weight to moral and cultural modification, the annual reports of the Methodists "leave no doubt" that schools were intended primarily for converting Indians to Christianity.[236]

The Roman Catholic Church regarded Catholic education as essential to its continued existence. French Oblates subscribed to the central tenet of French Catholic schools that true civilization lay not in technology but in the practice of true religion.[237] And the Oblates of British Columbia regarded the residential school as "the ideal set-up" for retaining and strengthening the Indians' Catholic faith; this goal, not assimilation, was the Oblates' primary concern.[238] In spite of Catholic missionary determination to make of every native village a dedicated Catholic community, they were realistic enough to see that only in a very few instances had they come close to achieving success;[239] residential/industrial schools ensured that Indian children would be raised in a totally Catholic environment. Bishops sought the services of orders of teaching nuns to instruct and care for the material well-being of the girls;[240] priests and religious brothers performed the same services for the boys. Schools in British Columbia under the direction of the Oblates were built close to a mission centre and, where possible, relatively remote from both Indian and white communities. Away from the negative effects of both Indian community life and white settlement, the children would become exemplary Catholics. Although of secondary importance in the minds of the Catholic missionaries, Indian children would also be "forcibly initiated into the social and occupational patterns of white life";[241] they would acquire such attributes of white civilization as personal cleanliness, a neat and orderly appearance, table manners, punctuality, and deference to authority.[242] Missionaries and government officials agreed that in a controlled environment apart from both Indian and white communities, young Indians would be totally assimilated.

Over time, both the churches and the government recognized the limitations of Indian educational efforts, particularly with regard to preparing the children for a new economic life.[243] But a reading of Coccola's 1893 annual report to the Department of Indian Affairs leaves the impression of complete success:

> The additional number of twenty-five pupils admitted to this school during the past year has much contributed to enliven the already cheerful little band. This general happiness must also be attributed to the good health of the children which they now fully enjoy. Their good spirits and forbearance towards each other may likewise be

mentioned. The qualities are a powerful assistance in the general work of the institution for if the children are "at home" and feel happy and contented, their progress will in every respect be more rapid. Their behaviour is certainly excellent, owing much to the continual watching and constant care of the devoted sisters. The diet is excellent, also the clothing, which is changed to suit the children's wants in the various seasons. The parents are anxious to send their children to school; thus we have the opportunity of taking more children than we are allowed to admit. The older boys have learned carpentry and some of them have become quite expert at the trade. They have also helped all spring in gardening, ploughing, harrowing and sowing about fifteen acres of land. A good durable flume was put up by the boys under the supervision of a carpenter. Now their principle occupation is weeding and irrigating. Excellent progress has been made by most of the pupils, especially in dictation and arithmetic. Many visitors to the institution in the course of the year express, after inspection, their astonishment at the progress made by the children in so short a time. Their intelligent cheerful appearance and their courteous and polite manners were always highly praised. The special instructions given to the girls embraces all branches of housework, sewing, knitting, mending and cooking. In concluding I am happy to state that the school has been most successful since its opening; the pupils speaking English quite fluently.[244]

What this glowing account hides is that initially Coccola had used trickery to get many of the children into the school!

RESIDENTIAL SCHOOL: INDIAN RESPONSE

Recognizing that with the rapid growth of white settlement and development of a new economic order their young needed new knowledge to survive social change, many Indians had sought education for their children. However, they desired this new learning to be a supplement to, not a replacement for, traditional learning processes. In addition, not only did the residential school totally remove children from parental guidance and control, it also tended to take in children from a wide geographic area, mixing native peoples who took great pride in their individual cultures and who resented being lumped together under the heading "Indians"; in some cases, the children came from tribes who were traditional enemies.[245] But there were graver Indian concerns.

Native peoples, both adults and children, confronted an educational régime imported from Europe and implemented without modification throughout North America. Missionaries knew only one form of education. Schools were operated under strict controls. School staff expected order, strict obedience, total attentiveness and disciplined behaviour, and if a child failed to act according to the expected norm or exhibited behavioural problems, the answer was physical punishment. This method of education, which stressed formation of character, was common to all schools, public, private, or parochial, and when residential schools were established, it was applied without any consideration given to cultural clash. An Indian child was simply a child. It was inconceivable that the system be altered to accommodate children whose personality traits included enjoying the present and, under community advice, exercising personal freedom of choice. Indian children, inexperienced in close confinement, educated in the closeness of the extended family group, seldom, if ever, physically punished for misdeeds, and uncomprehending of the commonly held European belief that fear was the beginning of wisdom, had to conform to the alien education pattern.[246]

Confronted by a daily routine controlled by bells, which consisted of hours spent sitting in classrooms or chapels, and outdoor activities restricted to either agricultural pursuits deemed learning experiences or to collection and preparation of firewood for the school heating system, many children rebelled in a very basic way: they ran away. Running away became the most common and most consistent way in which Indian children expressed their dissatisfaction with their new life. Commenting on the runaway situation, Bishop Dontenwill pinpointed what he considered the conflict between Indian and white cultures that resulted in aversion to the schools. While the schools were endeavouring to inculcate the principles of religion and morality, he argued, the children found moral directions "irksome" and had a "holy horror" of anything that was systematized. (How then explain Indian "acceptance" of the Durieu system?)

Consequently, when Indian children had to face the necessity "of going against their hereditary inclinations to indulge in their love for independence and [were] constrained in their habits of disorder, it [was] not surprising that they should wish to throw off the yoke of discipline."[247] Father Joseph Allard, a French-Canadian Oblate who preceded Coccola as principal of Stuart Lake boarding school, noted in his diary some of the problems both he and Coccola encountered:

On the 4th February at nine o'clock in the morning the boy boarders started to come in. Thirty-seven of them demanded my immediate attention and caused me no little preoccupation. In the unique bedroom in the semi-storey of the log building I had prepared only 25 little collapsible iron beds. I was short twelve. Beds came from Vancouver, nearly 1000 miles away. . . . Happily I had a single board wall partition between the boys' beds and mine I said to Pete the carpenter "Go upstairs right away with Leon and Felix, tear down that partition, use the two-by-four and the boards, and make twelve bunks on the north wall." It was done, and the 37 boys had each a bed for the first night.

But not all problems were so easily resolved. Like Indian children throughout the province, Father Allard's pupils were not enamoured of their new school:

> The watching of 37 Indian boys, all of them deprived for the first time in their life of their usual general freedom, was quite a problem, especially during recreation. They knew no amusements and they seemed to have no disposition to enjoy anything. Boys of Stuart Lake bunked together. So did the boys of Stony Creek or Fraser Lake and of Hazilget [sic]. They stood sullen in the corners of the recreation room and gave the impression that their greatest desire was to get out of their prison. I set the portable harmonium in the recreation room and I played it, accompanied by O'koni [a Belgian who had taught day school at Stuart Lake reserve] playing the cornet. They listened, but they stayed in the corner.... It took a few days of paternal care to generate the spirit of home life. A few remained wild and missed no chance to run away into the woods close by the school and then to their homes, and even to the far-away hunting grounds where their parents had gone.[248]

In this diary entry is revealed the missionary ethnocentricity so evident among most missionaries of all religious persuasions throughout the province; how could a missionary generate the spirit of a home life natural to Indian children in such an alien environment? What the missionaries cultivated was *their* perception of what a child's home life should be. And, as they had done in the first Oblate school in the Okanagan decades earlier, the Indian children rebelled. Running away remained a perennial problem for all schools and the deaths of three children attending the Lejac Residential School who froze to death trying to reach their parents was representative of experiences elsewhere.[249]

While children expressed their unhappiness by running away, their parents expressed their dissatisfaction with the type of education offered their children by keeping them at home. Despite the best efforts of church and government officials, even at the peak of their popularity, residential/industrial schools enrolled no more than 10 per cent of Indian children of school age.[250] Indian resistance was based on a number of factors: natural parental feelings, school repression of native culture, reports of cruelty and hardships, and the prevalence in some schools of poor conditions and, consequently, disease.[251]

Separation from their children was totally unnatural for Indian parents, and most refused to part with them even under government threats. In 1902, Bishop Dontenwill complained that parents and relatives were "abettors of the truancy" and that the support adult Indians gave to the runaways prompted the children to "launch forth with more vigor."[252] Indians who for years had struggled to adjust to loss of land, loss of tribal government, loss of social and cultural patterns, and in many, though not all cases, loss of independence, were now told to give up their children. Faced with the choice of keeping the children close to ensure continuity with the past or giving them up completely into the hands of the whites, many Indians chose the former course. At Stuart Lake, Indians had desired education since 1867, and they had helped to pay for and build their own school.[253] In 1921, after years of missionary pressure, the government funded a residential school but insisted that it be built at distance from existing Indian villages. When the Lejac School opened in September 1923, parents resisted. Coccola complained: "the month of Sepber [*sic*] was spent in collecting children from the different camps for the school, the parents doing nothing towards the education unless coaxed and threatened."[254]

One of the most controversial aspects of native education was the suppression of native languages by force. Soon after his arrival in British Columbia, Coccola learned a little of the English language from some Indian boys at St. Mary's Mission. One irony of early Catholic missionary-Indian contact was the struggle of both to learn the intricacies of English. Communication in the schools was initially a major problem. Residential schools tended to mix language groups. At St. Mary's Residential School, Stalo children mixed with Thompson and Chehalis, and at the Williams Lake Indian Residential School, the Shuswap, Carrier, and Chilcotin children all spoke different languages. At Williams Lake, the teachers, the Sisters of the Child Jesus, had come from France and spoke only French.[255] Since under government directives lessons had to be given in English, both teachers and pupils had to learn a new language. Had they insisted on the use of English only during the classroom time, the churches might have avoided many Indian attacks on their system. However, teachers and administrators insisted that native children speak English at all times and punished, often severely, those who were caught speaking their native tongues.[256] But it was not language loss alone that concerned Indian parents.

More destructive of native culture was the breakdown of "tribal family cohesion and its replacement with peer group allegiance."[257] Indian children were taught to reject their own culture or, at least, to see it as inferior. As one student remembered: "They were always degrading us because we were Indian. We didn't come from homes, we came from *camps* and we didn't know how to live. We ate rotten fish so they didn't seem to be particular in what they gave us to eat. They never let us forget that we were *Indian,* and that we weren't very civilized, that we were more or less savage."[258] More insidious was the institutionalization effect.[259] After spending ten months of each year organized and routinized in the company of other children, the Indians began to lose their attachment to their own homes. A Lillooet woman noted: "When you went home you missed the companionship of the others. You felt alone. Although the family was there, my brothers were there, my older brother, my uncle, my grandmother... but you were lonely. At least I was. And the children on the reserve were not of your... oh they were *people* you know, but they weren't like the ones you had in the convent." On returning to school, "We never felt that we were leaving somebody that we loved. We were glad to get away."[260] Because this distancing occurred over time, it was probably not noticed immediately by Indian families. Of more instantaneous impact was the loss of children to disease.

In his 1893 report, Coccola noted that several school children had died or were dying of tuberculosis. Living conditions had become one major reason for the prevalence of this disease. Indian parents, however, saw the school environment, which herded children together in both classrooms and dormitories, as a contributing, even primary, factor. It was not until the Depression years that Indian parents, under economic stress, began to appreciate at least one role of the school. As a Chilcotin Indian, member of a tribe that had strongly resisted white education, wrote to his son; "I didn't make much money this year, just enough to buy grub to live on. You are lucky to be in school where you get plenty to eat. If you were home you would get hungry many days."[261] But regardless of their culturally destructive aspects, the schools were not totally negative environments.

In a world that was rapidly changing for most Indians, the missionaries were the only people consistently willing to provide the education necessary to help them deal with this change. Finding staff willing to work on Indian reserves in remote areas was a major problem for Indian educators. And although missionaries brought Indian children together in residential schools to assist their Christianization efforts, by educating young Indians about one another they inadvertently "spread a pan-Indian identity... and politicized them about their place in the larger society."[262] As one writer has argued, "However dismal the record of church-run Indian schools... it remains a fact that most of today's Indian rights leaders are products of these very schools."[263] Coccola's estimate of the impact of his Kootenay school may have been overly optimistic, but, in the long term, all missionary schools proved to be of some value to native peoples.

MISSIONARY AND THE WORKERS

Although most of Coccola's writings deal with his work among the native peoples, he does also note the attention he gave to one important segment of his white constituency, the railway workers of British Columbia. The Corsican's records of his life are largely unadorned by reflections on the economic and social upheavals that took place during his ministry. Yet Coccola was clearly aware from personal observation of the difficulties, the extreme hardships, endured by those who constructed the province's railways. Soon after his first missionary circuit among the Nicola, he was assigned the spiritual care of the Canadian Pacific construction workers who had been attended by the famous prairie Oblate, Father Albert Lacombe, prior to crossing the British Columbia border.[264] Coccola's contact with the construction workers in the Fraser section of railway building had been minimal. His companions, Father Edmond Peytavin and Father LeJacq, had attended these camps whenever a call came in for a priest—usually a sick call. But Coccola's curiosity about railway construction appears to have overcome prudence on at least one occasion, and the missionary briefly encountered difficulties workers experienced on a day-to-day basis.

After leaving the Nicola, instead of returning directly to Kamloops, he made his way in extremely cold weather, via North Bend (where he shared frozen chicken, frozen potatoes, and frozen peas with the hospitable Indians) to the town of Yale. Coccola followed the tracks already laid. He made his way down under extraordinary difficulties, crossing trestle bridges covered with ice where the planks were so far apart that it was necessary at times to cross on hands and feet. Coccola and his Indian companions passed through tunnels so damp that ice was hanging overhead in a threatening way. Eventually, not far from Yale, he came upon a camp of Chinese workers where he wished to stop and rest. The Indians, however, did not think the camp safe because the Chinese had begun smoking opium pipes. Coccola heeded their advice, and they walked on to the Indians' camp at Spuzzum, where the sleeping Indians were unceremoniously awakened by the Indian guides. The missionary had reason to regret listening to his guides when he was given a plank to lie on for the night!

Railway construction had injected new life into Yale. On 14 May 1880, "a blast of dynamite" marked the beginning of railway construction by Andrew Onderdonk, a railway builder with "unlimited backing from an American syndicate and a reputation for pushing ahead with great engineering projects."[265] Yale, a dying town since the end of the gold rush, sprang to life. The Hudson's Bay Company opened a store, "the Italians opened fruit stands and the Chinese opened restaurants." Onderdonk was responsible for the presence of the Chinese Coccola had met. The demand for labour could not be met locally, and after hiring "clerks out of employment, broken down bartenders and others of that ilk" from San Francisco, Onderdonk brought two thousand men from China—although the Chinese, kept below decks with the hatches closed (supposedly because of bad weather), developed scurvy, and on their arrival in British Columbia close to two hundred were dying.[266]

At Yale both Indians and whites received Coccola with enthusiasm, although the missionary questioned the sincerity of the white congregation who attended his mass. He knew very little English, yet his audience (among whom he heard "the unaccustomed sound of the 'frou frou' of silk skirts") was enthusiastic about "the best sermon they had ever heard." Coccola's reaction? He noted, "Shows how crazy people are."[267] From Yale Coccola returned to Kamloops and worked among white people living around the city until Bishop D'herbomez sent him to the construction camps. His district covered Kamloops to Calgary (giving Father Lacombe a welcome break). Construction workers, Indian camps, and developing white centres came under his care. Coccola moved along the railway route carrying his "chapel" as he called the bag containing articles necessary for the celebration of mass. Initially, he received a cool reception from the construction workers, a reception he detailed in a letter to a friend in France written on 10 February 1886. Coccola wrote about his arrival at Eagle Pass in the company of a "non-Catholic" friend, presumably someone he met on the trail. The letter is worth quoting as it fills in detail left out by Coccola in his "Memoirs":

> My non-Catholic friend insisted that he pay for my room at the best hotel in the place. He wished me "good night." This wish was not as effective as I would have wished it. I was asked to share a room. Politeness and necessity caused me to say "yes." My room-mate was an American—a little the worse for whisky. Nobody pays attention to drunks around here, there are so many of them. I went to bed but he went out promising to return soon. I was stretched out on my bed, it might have been midnight but people walked the streets as if it were mid-day. I had hardly closed my eyes when my room-mate returned, this time dead drunk. Began to swear, then to snore. No hope of sleep for me, then about 3 A.M. the shouts "Fire, Fire" made me jump from bed. Fortunately the fire was quickly extinguished. At dawn I left my room—a room of fatigue rather than of rest and got ready to leave by the 6 o'clock stage coach. I arrived at one of the camps where the

foreman told me there were many Catholics. He gave me every opportunity to speak to them. The men did not seem friendly. Some questioned, "are you a priest?" When I said "yes," they said "impossible a priest would not venture alone on such a mission in such a country." Others shouted, "He is here to beg for our money." They did not intimidate me. I waited until they settled down. I spoke first in English, then in Italian wishing success to all in return for the curses that had been hurled at me. When the Italians heard me speak their language they were ashamed. They probably thought I had not understood. The news of the arrival of an Italian priest spread quickly along the line. The following day I had a very small congregation. I was not discouraged. Experience had taught me that beginnings in this work are difficult. When I found myself among French workers I sang "The Lament of the Exile." It was enough to move the hearts and gain the confidence of these poor workmen really exiled in this forgotten section of the country. The Austrians and the Poles were the ones who showed the noblest traits and the greatest generosity. The Irish, proud of their Catholic heritage, not influenced by human respect in the presence of non-Catholics, wanted to go to confession and receive the Holy Eucharist.[268]

Coccola spoke of "noblest traits," but he must have realized that it was extremely difficult for the construction workers to manifest any such traits when they lived in such inhumane conditions. The environment itself was one major enemy. By the fall of 1883, the railway had reached from Calgary to near the summit of Kicking Horse Pass. Twelve thousand men were needed in the mountains once winter had passed, and by June men were pouring off the trains and walking along the right of way to the construction camps. The summer of 1884 was miserable; cold and wet, men struggled to get supplies and equipment along a tote road that frequently flooded with water from the Kicking Horse River. The continual blasting along the line caused frequent avalanches. One witness saw an avalanche descend about five thousand feet from a summit and with such force that "it tore directly across a valley and up the opposite side for another eight hundred feet." Construction work also caused forest fires which made working conditions even more unbearable. The workers were also at the mercy of their employers, who insisted that work went on "at a killing pace" between ten and fourteen hours a day, every day, for weeks at a time; when rain slowed down construction, some workers had to work by moonlight to catch up.[269]

They lived in every kind of accommodation, including roughly made bunkhouses, log huts, old box cars, tents, and large marquees with hand-cut logs as the floor. Wooden accommodation was often "poorly

ventilated, dirty and verminous."[270] Coccola described how the young
men "would lie down on the planks. They had laid down branches from
the trees, but the leaves were long since worn off, and they were lying on
the bare sticks for the most part; the men scratching themselves all night
long, keeping the rest awake with their music." For this accommodation, the men paid exorbitant prices. Sanitation was primitive, and often
water supplies would become contaminated. As Coccola noted, "a good
deal of sickness prevailed among the workers, but this was not spoken
about much outside. There was a good deal of typhoid and what was
known as 'mountain fever' and other epidemic diseases."[271]

Construction was dangerous as well as hard work. One author gives
the following vivid description:

> Near one of several tunnels along the Kicking Horse the cut in the hill
> was so deep that the men worked in three tiers. At the very top, the
> route was being cut through gravel; in the centre the gravel gave way
> to blue clay; below the clay was hard rock. The men on the lowest
> tier, working just above the layer of rock (which would have to be
> dynamited), attacked the clay from beneath. Twenty to thirty feet
> above them a second gang worked, chopping out the gravel and
> wheeling it away in barrows. The high gang removed the top layer of
> sand and stumps. Those at the very top worked in comparative
> safety; the middle gang was in some peril because they had to watch
> out for rocks that might topple down on them; but the lowest gang
> was in constant danger—from both benches above them came a con-
> tinual shower of rocks. Morley Roberts, who worked on the lowest
> tier, reported that he never felt safe for a single moment. Every sixty
> seconds or so, all day long, a warning cry would be heard and a heavy
> stone or boulder would come thundering down the slope, scattering
> the men on both sides. On his third day on the job the impact from an
> eighty-pound rock put him out of action for five days."[272]

The men who lived and worked in such dangerous conditions were
also entirely financially dependent upon their contractor. The "bilking
of workers by railway contractors" goes back to the earliest days of railway construction. A common practice was to deduct payment for food,
clothing, tools, and so forth sold at monopoly prices at the company
stores; this left little or nothing for many of the workers.[273] Although in
his "Memoirs" Coccola mentions only delay in the payment of wages as
cause of a strike (the C.P.R. was in yet another critical financial position), to Denys Nelson he gave a clearer picture of the workers' problems:

They [the workers] were entirely dependant upon the contractor and had to purchase all their supplies from the company's stores, paying with tokens which would be cashed on pay day. They were for the most part illiterate men and had to trust to the honesty of those in charge that they would not cheat them. Then, when payday came round, sometimes they found that their pay cheque was almost swallowed up by the charges against them, and they were unable to tell if they really had had all that they were charged with, or to check the account up in any way nor, if they were being charged a fair price for what they had had. So sometimes there was much ill feeling, which occasionally developed into a strike. One such case was that at Donald, the company's Head Quarters west of the Rockies, that is of the Western Lines. Another was that at Golden. The Paymaster was accustomed to pay by cheque with a pair of guns lying on the table by his hand, which did not tend to promote feelings of trust and confidence on the part of the men.

In spite of what he knew about working and living conditions, about the dangers and diseases the construction workers faced, Coccola still believed that "the men were treated fairly well on the whole... for those days, things were not so bad."[274] This scant comment is a veritable outpouring compared with the missionary's silence on the protracted, often violent, strikes in the Kootenay region.

During Coccola's years in the Kootenays, white as well as Indian society underwent great social upheaval. Because the ore was of a high grade, and extraction was low in cost, the hard-rock mines in the region were prosperous. Extensive silver and copper deposits, the mechanized nature of the mining industry, and cheap railway transportation also combined to keep profits high. In 1897, one observer noted that in spite of a slump in the silver market, "the ores were usually of such high grade, as to leave, even at the lowest price, a good margin of profit."[275] Increased mining meant increased smelting and, consequently, a constant demand for coal. But mining was not the only extractive industry flourishing in the Kootenays. Rapid prairie development beginning in the late 1890's led to a demand for lumber.

To meet this demand, American lumbermen extended their operations northward from Oregon into East Kootenay—in particular, the Fernie region. Since 1894, the Canadian Pacific Railway, in need of lumber to build and repair track, had been cutting timber in the Fernie area. But it was the Americans who exploited the region's timber resources. While some lumbermen obtained provincial government timber licences for purely speculative purposes, others built large lumber mills powered by

modern machinery which enabled them to produce between 75,000 and
100,000 feet of lumber per day; "one single American firm took out
25,000,000 feet in the Fernie district."[276] By 1905, most mill-owners had
retail stores in prairie towns, and the lumber went east, travelling on the
new railway lines. In a province gone railway mad, speculators lobbied
the provincial government for massive land grants in exchange for new
lines throughout the Kootenay region. James Jerome Hill, American railway magnate, purchased the Nelson-Fort Sheppard Railway, the Red
Mountain Railway, and the Kaslo and Slocan Railway, all built to facilitate the transportation of ore.[277] The Canadian Pacific Railway, spurred
on by Hill's plans to divert the Kootenay mining wealth to Washington
State, persuaded the federal and provincial governments to grant land
subsidies for the extension of a line from Lethbridge, Alberta, through
the Crow's Nest Pass to Kootenay Lake. By the end of 1897, Kootenay
industrial development led not only to a profusion of short-lived mining
and railway communities but also to the incorporation of such major
cities as Nelson, Rossland, and Grand Forks[278] But while many
prospered, others fought to survive. As with all rapid industrial development, the Kootenay extractive frontier took its toll in worker exploitation.

Labour historians have portrayed a grim picture of life for the average
worker on the western mining frontier. As each new mine and smelter
went into production and each new railway produced divisional points,
company towns grew up around them. Among them were towns like
Mother Lode, a community of approximately one hundred where the inhabitants as well as the miners lived a hazardous life because surface
deposits were blasted out of the nearby mine—on one occasion, a
mother and child were killed by a piece of ore that crashed through the
roof of their home; Boundary Falls, near Greenwood, which grew up
around a copper smelter; Hosmer and Morrisey, coal towns with populations of two thousand and three thousand respectively—by 1913,
Hosmer was shipping two thousand tons of coal a day from its mines;
larger communities such as Rossland, which developed around the Red
Mountain gold mines; and numerous, mostly temporary, railway towns
such as Eholt, a Canadian Pacific divisional point between Phoenix and
the Granby smelter. Many of these instant communities were destined to
become ghost towns.

The populations of the frontier communities ranged from a hundred
or so to several thousand, and the quality of life varied from dangerous
and squalid to dangerous but relatively comfortable. Most were both
built and controlled by a company. It has been noted that some
Kootenay company towns were, like their Alberta counterparts, "a
wretched place, with stinking outhouses, no fresh water supply,

dilapidated shacks, and cold, damp bunkhouses. There may have been no medical facilities, no schools, bad food, lice-ridden blankets, and frequent attacks of typhoid." Other companies offered cottages with electricity, running water, and adequate sanitary conditions, recreation and meeting halls, libraries, sports facilities, even, in later years, movie theatres. Whether their physical living conditions were good or bad, the men were totally dependent on the company for the necessities of life and worked long hours for little pay.

Although many miners came from the coalfields or hard-rock mining fields of the United States, Britain, or Europe, there appears to have been a singular lack of expertise. For example, "it was not discovered until after several major disasters, in which hundreds of miners were killed, that the coal of the East Kootenay region was fifteen times more gaseous and therefore much more likely to cause explosions than comparably-graded bituminous in Pennsylvania."[279] Faced with a provincial government willing, under pressure, to pass but not enforce safety legislation and with employers determined to maintain high profits at all costs, the miners turned to militant unions for help; the strike, often violent, became part of Kootenay social experience.[280]

There is as yet very little evidence of how the Catholic church responded to the rapid development and social unrest.[281] The large numbers of Catholics among the immigrant miners into the region taxed the church's limited resources as the bishop established parishes in the new communities. According to canon law, it was incumbent upon the bishop to erect a parish wherever "a community of Christ's faithful" was stably established under the authority of a diocesan bishop, and the Kootenays came under the authority of the Oblate bishop of New Westminster.[282] Coccola's "Memoirs" suggest that parishes consisting of Roman Catholics and Eastern Orthodox Catholics appear to have been provided with their own ministers, if not their own churches. After churches came the need for schools and hospitals. The bishop turned to missionary orders to open schools and hospitals. In the Kootenays, the Sisters of St. Joseph of Peace arrived in 1896 at Rossland to establish a hospital; the Sisters of Providence, already running the Indian school at St. Eugene's Mission, opened a hospital at Cranbrook.[283] The suggestion by one historian that in the Kootenays the only hospital for miles "was apt to be owned and financed by the union" needs qualification.[284]

It has also been suggested that where priests, teachers, and other professionals made up part of a mining community, "they too were company employees."[285] This also needs revision or, at least, more research. It is true that, as already noted, the Catholic church sought and obtained funding for its institutions from influential men. Coccola, for example, was willing to accept money towards a hospital at the mission from a

panicking Catholic railway contractor, Mr. Haney, whose poor and un-
sanitary working conditions had led to outbreaks of typhoid among his
workers and to accept a gift of land from Colonel Baker when the hospital was moved from the mission to a more central location at Cranbrook. Interestingly, at the official opening of the hospital in April 1898,
a spokesman for the Canadian Pacific Railway stressed that the company had not furnished the funds for the building.[286] Do these transac-
tions mean that Coccola was "employed" by Haney and Baker? Or was
he simply taking advantage of one man's fear and another man's ego?

Certainly the Sisters of Providence, who were called upon to find operating costs, were not capitalist employees;[287] nor were the Sisters of St.
Joseph of Peace.[288] These sisters had received a request at their convent in
New Jersey from a Rossland priest asking for nuns to open a hospital
among the mining camps. Donations from both local businessmen and
miners had been collected before the sisters arrived, but the two nuns,
Mother Mary Teresa and Sister Mary Stanislaus, moved among the
miners making their own collection. Operating at first out of a rented
two-storey building, they later built a new hospital which opened on 4
November 1896. Initially, the running costs of the hospital were raised
by payroll deductions of one dollar per month, but in 1898 the provincial government gave the nuns a $3,000 grant, the first of its kind in the
province.[289] This enabled the order to expand its facilities. Were these
nuns in the employ of the mine owners or the miners? Or were they
simply following their mandate to care for the sick? Until more research
is undertaken on the role of the churches of British Columbia in industrial developments, the answer remains elusive.

But Coccola's "Memoirs" do give some brief glimpses of social developments from the viewpoint of the church's "man-in-the-field." The
only "disturbance" in the Kootenay mining towns Coccola comments
on in his "Memoirs" is the animosity that developed between Polish and
"Slovakian" [*sic*] Catholics and English-speaking Catholics in Fernie.
Although this clash obviously reflected the work-oriented clashes that
became part of the European immigrant experience in the Kootenays,
Coccola makes no reference to this social turmoil. Between 1900 and
1903, the missionary visited Rossland, a prominent mining town and
the centre of much miner unrest, several times. A six-month strike began
at Rossland in July 1901, but Coccola's sole comment on the town was
that the Sisters of St. Joseph of Peace had opened a hospital there.

Coccola could not have been ignorant of the social unrest or of the
violence connected with the strikes; he was called upon to mediate several. But such events do not appear to have interested him. As a member
of an ultimately conservative church, Coccola undoubtedly supported
the economic status quo. As his "Memoirs" reveal, he was convinced

that men such as railway contractors and engineers, and particularly railway builders like William Mackenzie—hated by labour for worker exploitation and harsh anti-union actions but seemingly admired by Coccola for his profitable business practices—appreciated the influence of the church over working men. However, the extent of that influence remains to be determined. Ultimately, as priest among a white consti-tuency, Coccola remained focused on the religious services necessary to the saving of souls.

Towards the end of Coccola's missionary career, the missionaries in general had begun to lose their influence. For the Oblates the major goal still remained saving Indian souls. But constant contact with whites often had devastating results, and alcoholism and community break-downs became commonplace among former Durieu-controlled bands. Moreover, government officials began to usurp missionary power. The Oblates tried "to minimize the impact of governmental agencies on the Catholic population," but except in the case of still-remote and in-accessible bands, they could not stem the tide.[290] Agents explained to In-dians that the physical punishment proclaimed by the Durieu system was illegal; that adultery and drunkenness might be immoral, but they were not against the law; that, through the agent, the government would provide such items as medication and also money to enable Indians to begin their own businesses; and, as time passed by, that the agent did the paperwork that brought family allowances and old-age security bene-fits.[291] Contact with whites also brought an awareness of "work for pay," and, as he notes, Coccola found his Indians asking for money in ex-change for repair or improvement work on their churches, work tradi-tionally donated—although not always without prodding.

For several decades following contact, the reactions of the Indians of British Columbia to the teachings of all the missionaries appears to have been for the most part quite positive. According to the 1939 census, 57 per cent of British Columbia's Indians were Roman Catholic, 20 per cent Anglican, 20 per cent United Church, and 3 per cent other denominations—mostly Salvation Army. Only twenty-eight Indians were recorded as still holding aboriginal religious beliefs.[292] But however strong the conversion statistics appear to be, many, if not most, Indians retained their old beliefs even while they practised Christianity. The sur-vival of the potlatch, which all religious denominations condemned, and the continued influence in many areas of traditional healers and medicine men are witness to this[293] as is the failure of the Catholic church to attract native peoples to the priesthood and women's religious or-ders.[294]

To the end of his life, Coccola's faith in his church's errand to the na-tive peoples of British Columbia remained constant, even though he

could not have failed to notice that the passing years brought little headway. Many Indian communities lost the momentum that had characterized initial Indian enthusiasm and desire and appeared uninterested in
progressing further,[295] hence the lack of Indian vocations. Coccola continued to travel from band to band, offering what one missionary
referred to as "a cultic service," saying mass, and administering the
sacraments, and with this he seemed content. His writings do not reveal
any change in his relationship with the Indians; it remained paternalistic.

Shortly after his arrival in the north, the Indians began to give Coccola
a tumultuous welcome. Martin Starret recalled the first time he wit-
nessed the arrival of Father Coccola at Fort Babine:

> Indians were shoving cartridges into their magazines to fire a salute.
> They must have fired off all of twenty boxes of thirty cartridges to
> welcome the priest, and there were answering shots from the boats
> coming in, too... just as they were landing the Indians started to sing
> in Chinook: and it seems to me right now I can sing you that song
> right perfectly. This is the way they sang it.

> Ay, Pell Cola! Ay mesika papa!
> Ay, Pell Cola! Ay mesika papa!
> Mamook Klahowya mika tenas
> Mamook klahowya kuna mokst mesika.

"Hi Pere Coccola, hi our father! Make greetings your children, make
greetings altogether we."[296]

Coccola noted in his diary that at Easter, in 1940, when he was already retired from missionary work and was acting as chaplain at the
Sisters of the Child Jesus Hospital in Smithers, the Moricetown Indians,
their priest being absent, came to Smithers for him. They took him to
their village in order not to be without mass and communion on this important feast. This Coccola found extremely satisfying; he commented:
"distributed some 86 communions and returned home a little fatigued
but glad to make my old Indian children happy."[297]

This paternalistic attitude, which was accepted by both priests and Indians, would from the turbulent 1960's on come under scathing attack
as Indians blamed the Christian churches for destroying Indian culture
and encouraging Indian dependency. A historian wrote recently that
today's Indians will decide their own religious future, "and their decisions will inevitably be affected by unhappy memories of missionary
father-figures and regimented residential schools."[298] That is too large a

generalization. The Indians always have determined their religious future. As they have been rightly credited with business acumen, enterprising attitudes towards new employment developments, and selectivity when proffered white culture, they should be credited with the ability to accept or reject Christianity in terms of its spiritual advantages. And while some native peoples have bitter memories of some missionaries and certain aspects of their schooling, they have affectionate and grateful memories of others.[299] Evidence of Indian ambivalence can be found in the words of an Indian leader. When interviewed and asked about the role of the church among his people, Sechelt Chief Clarence Joe stated: "Well I think if it hadn't been for the church, the white man's church, I think there would have been a total destruction here among the Indians, because they were getting wiped out, you might say, by sickness and by liquor brought in by the white men. The white man was invading their villages and they were taking their women away when they were on their drinking sprees. In my deep thinking, I think the church was responsible for saving the Indian nation in this country. The more I look at it, the more I'm convinced, regardless what church they are."[300] Moreover, the implication that past generations—and, indeed, those Indians today who travelled hundreds of miles to meet their spiritual leaders—Pope John Paul II and Archbishop Runcie—existed in a father-child relationship that was somehow demeaning, does a disservice not only to the native peoples but to all Christian peoples who for centuries accepted this relationship as the norm; presumably, historians are fully aware that the paternalism of the church goes back to the beginning of Christianity. As Nicolas Coccola's "Memoirs" reveal, unlike the surrounding white society, and sometimes the missionaries themselves for whom the "man of God" was equated only with the "man of good," the Indians, displaying acute discernment, accepted their missionaries, "warts and all."

NOTES

1 Ernest John Knapton, *France: An Interpretive History* (New York: Scribner's, 1971), p. 438.

2 Gordon Wright, *France in Modern Times* (Chicago: Rand McNally, 1974), p. 233.

3 Founded in 1816 by Eugene Charles Joseph de Mazenod, the order was known originally as the Missionary Society of Provence; later, in 1825, when the order moved its central establishment to Nîmes in the Languedoc, it was renamed Oblates of Saint Charles. The name Oblates of the Most Holy and Immaculate Virgin Mary was selected by de Mazenod in December 1825.

4 The Roman Catholic Church in France had long been split between those who supported a national or Gallican Church under the control of the state and those who championed an Ultramontane Church under the supreme authority of the papacy. For information on conditions of the Roman Catholic Church in France, see: H. Daniel-Rops, *The Church in an Age of Revolution, 1789–1870* (London: Dent, 1960); Adrian Dansette, *Religious History of Modern France,* trans. John Dingle (New York: Herder and Herder, 1961); Derek Holmes, *The Triumph of the Holy See* (London: Burns and Oates, 1978); on specific incidents, Donat Lavasseur, *History of the Oblate Congregation* (Ottawa, 1959)—although an in-house account, much of Lavasseur's material is useful because it is based on personal clerical correspondence.

5 This concern was fully justified. The Autun Scholasticate was closed, and teaching staff took refuge with the local bishop while most scholasticates were sent to finish their training in Inchicore, Ireland (Lavasseur, *History of the Oblate Congregation,* p. 130).

6 "Memoirs," p. 4. By juxtaposing his "call to arms" and his departure for the mission field, Coccola leaves the impression that his militaristic attitude led his superiors to despatch him to a less volatile milieu. Interestingly, another "troublesome" Oblate, Adrian Morice, also a seminarian, accompanied Coccola to B.C. (see Mulhall, *Will to Power*).

7 Coccola gives very little information about his childhood in his "Memoirs," but I do not subscribe to the idea, argued by Mulhall (re Morice) that this could have indicated an unhappy childhood (p. 1). Coccola was asked to write about his work and may have considered his early life redundant. The exact date of Coccola's birth is unknown: Coccola gives it as 6 December, yet Oblate records list it as 12 December. Attempts by an Oblate archivist to obtain a birth or baptismal certificate from Corsica met with no success. Although his mother's name is given as de Veretti in the *Dictionnaire Biographique des Oblats de Marie Immaculée au Canada,* vol. 1 (Ottawa: Editions de l'Université d'Ottawa, 1976), it is an error—information from the author, Gaston Carrière.

8 Holmes, *The Triumph of the Holy See,* pp. 138–39; see also Robert D. Cross, *The Emergence of Liberal Catholicism in America* (Chicago: Rand McNally, 1958), p. 4.

9 Although Coccola refers to Bastia's schools and colleges as "quality institutions," the overall calibre of France's lycées and colleges was not high. Tom Lascelles, "Leon Fouquet and the Kootenay Indians, 1874–1887" (M.A. thesis, Simon Fraser University, 1987); Martha McCarthy, "The Missions of the Oblates of Mary Immaculate to the Athapascans, 1846–1870: Theory, Structure and Method" (Ph.D. diss., University of Manitoba, 1981), pp. 31–32. However, according to his "Memoirs," Coccola had the ability, and will, to learn numerous Indian dialects, and soon after his arrival in British Columbia, he was able to preach in English. Knowledge of English was encouraged in Oblate-directed schools.

10 A. W. Palmer, *A Dictionary of Modern History, 1789–1945* (England: Penguin, 1971), p. 128.

11 Nelson, "Reminiscences," p. 1.

12 Ian Thompson, *Corsica* (Newton Abbot: David and Charles, 1971), p. 165.

13 *Rapports historiques et statistiques sur la Congrégation des Missionnaires O.M.I. et compte-rendu de 1853–1854* (Archives Deschâtelets, Ottawa), p. 6. On the Ajaccio seminary, see Theodore Ortolan, O.M.I., *Les Oblats de Marie Immaculée devant le premier siècle de leur existence* (Paris: Librairie Saint Paul, 1914).

14 For the hardships of missionary work in China, see Paul A. Cohen, *China and Christianity: The Missionary Movement and the Growth of Anti-Foreignism, 1860–1870* (Cambridge, MA: Harvard University Press, 1963), p. 262.

15 Foreign missions were attracting men who saw in them the possibilities of new beginnings for the Roman Catholic faith away from increasingly godless European society (McCarthy, "Missions of the Oblates of Mary Immaculate," p. 69).

16 Philip Goldring, "Religion, Missions, and Native Culture," *Journal of the Canadian Church Historical Society* 26 (October 1984): 47.

17 Thomas O. Beidelman, "Social Theory and the Study of Christian Missions in Africa," *Africa* 44 (1974): 237–38.

18 Robin Fisher, *Contact and Conflict: Indian-European Relations in British Columbia, 1774–1890* (Vancouver: UBC Press, 1977), p. 131.

19 Although it is possible that Russian Orthodox missionaries entered British Columbia prior to settlement, the first European missionaries were Franciscan friars who came with the Spanish exploration vessels in 1774 and 1775. On the public image of the missionary, see Max Warren, *Social History and Christian Mission* (London: SCM Press, 1967).

20 Fisher, *Contact and Conflict*, pp. 68–69.

21 Margaret Ormsby, ed., *A Pioneer Gentlewoman in British Columbia: The Recollections of Susan Allison* (Vancouver: UBC Press, 1976), pp. 42–43. Resistance to missionaries tended to come from traders. See Margaret Whitehead, *The Cariboo Mission: A History of the Oblates* (Victoria: Sono Nis Press, 1981); Usher, *William Duncan of Metlakatla*.

22 Thomas O. Beidelman, "Contradictions between the Sacred and the Secular Life: The Church Missionary Society in Ukaguru, Tanzania, East Africa, 1876–1914," *Comparative Studies in Society and History*, 23, no. 1 (1981); 74. For a similar argument, see also Judith Shapiro, "Ideologies of Catholic Missionary Practice in a Post Colonial Era," *Comparative Studies in Society and History*, ibid., pp. 130–49; Robin Fisher, *Contact and Conflict*; J. M. Bumstead, "The Grand Old Canadian Skin Game Revisited," *Bulletin of Canadian Studies* 3 (Edinburgh, 1979): 62–70.

23 Goldring, "Religion, Missions and Native Culture," p. 47. Even Father Morice, whose passion for ethnography and linguistics might have made him more sensitive than most to native culture, demanded almost total capitulation (Mulhall, *Will to Power*).

24 On problems created for missionaries by lack of native cultural knowledge, see Shapiro, "Ideologies of Catholic Missionary Practice."

25 Information on Chief Pasala, see "Billy Assu (Chief Pasala) File," PABC.

26 For the varied results of missionary rejection of organizational controls, see Usher, *William Duncan of Metlakatla*; Mulhall, *Will to Power*. For difficulties incurred by organizational inflexibility, see Whitehead, *Cariboo Mission*.

27 A major problem for the church in France was to keep the urban and rural poor loyal to their religion, particularly after the Catholic Church's charitable institutions, teaching and nursing religious orders, and church lay societies were suppressed during and after the French Revolution.

28 In letters to his family and in a "Memoir," de Mazenod was scathing about the lack of interest in the priesthood among the distinguished families of France now that the church was no longer able to offer them "rich benefices" (Lavasseur, *History of the Oblate Congregations*, p. 13). See also McCarthy, "The Missions of the Oblates of Mary Immaculate," p. 31.

29 The government of the Revolution set out "The Civil Constitution of the Clergy" on 12 July 1790 without consulting the papacy. By this constitution, the state administered the church in France and appointed bishops. Those priests who would not sign this constitution were banished or killed. The government also attempted to have priests "voluntarily" give up their duties and marry. A certain number of priests gave in to this pressure. Either by death or banishment or assimilation, France lost approximately thirty thousand priests. Many of those remaining "lacked zeal, confidence and courage" and often lived

morally questionable lives (Pierre de la Gorce, *Historie réligieuse de la Révolution française* [Paris: Plon, 1938], 5: 248, 403).

30 Cross, *The Emergence of Liberal Catholicism*, p. 4; see also Holmes, *The Triumph of the Holy See*.

31 Cross, *The Emergence of Liberal Catholicism*, p. 10.

32 In November 1825, the Society consisted of fifteen priests and eight scholasticates (Lavasseur, *History of the Oblate Congregation*, p. 35).

33 McCarthy, "The Missions of the Oblates of Mary Immaculate," pp. 78–85.

34 *Missions de la Congrégation des Missionaires Oblats de Marie Immaculée* (Paris: A. Hennuyer, 1862–1900; Rome: Maison Générale, 1900–1972), 1872, p. 278.

35 On the relationship between de Mazenod and Bourget, see Leon Pouliot, "Mgr. de Mazenod et Mgr. Bourget," *RHAF* 15 (11 June 1961): 3–23.

36 Fernand Ouellet, *Lower Canada 1791–1840: Social Change and Nationalism* (Toronto: McClelland and Stewart, 1980), p. 334.

37 Murray W. Nicolson, "Ecclesiastical Metropolitanism and the Evolution of the Catholic Archdiocese of Toronto," *Histoire sociale/Social History* 15, no. 29 (May 1982): 144.

38 Ouellet, *Lower Canada 1791–1840*, p. 335.

39 In 1841, the congregation numbered fifty-nine; of these seventeen were to go to Canada. Bourget continued to press de Mazenod; he wrote to the founder: "Do not forget Burlington, the Red River, the shanties, Bytown, the Saguenay, Temiscaming, Abitibi, the St. Maurice, the whole Diocese of Montreal." 26 Dec. 1945 (Gaston Carrière, O.M.I., *Recherches historiques sur la province du Canada-Est* (Ottawa: Ed. Etudes Oblates, 1954), 2: 38.

40 De Mazenod to Father Bruno Guiges, O.M.I., 5 December 1844 (Lavasseur, *History of the Oblate Congregation*, p. 95). In 1847, Father Guiges was named bishop of the Diocese of Bytown (Ottawa). In 1853, Father Alexander Taché, O.M.I., was named bishop of St. Boniface. The Diocese of Quebec had jurisdiction over the Oregon Territory, Vancouver Island, Alaska, and the Queen Charlottes until 1846 when Rome divided the territory into three dioceses—Oregon City, Walla Walla, and Vancouver Island and New Caledonia. The Diocese of Vancouver Island still included Alaska and the Queen Charlottes at this time.

41 *The Constitutions and Rules of the Congregation of the Missionary Oblates of the Most Holy and Immaculate Virgin Mary* (Rome, 1936), p. 21.

42 De Mazenod to Father Guiges, 25 September 1944 (Lavasseur, *History of the Oblate Congregation*, p. 50).

43 Instructions of Bishop Signay to Blanchet and Demers, 17 April 1838, Register M. fol. 96v–99r, p. 1, Archives of the Archdiocese of Quebec.

44 Magloire Blanchet was the brother of François Norbert Blanchet; he was a former canon of Montreal Cathedral who had been imprisoned for alleged activities in the Papineau Rebellion—although the charges against him were never proved.

45 Wilfred P. Schoenberg, *Paths to the Northwest: A Jesuit History of the Oregon Province* (Chicago: Loyola University Press, 1982), p. 46; David Nicandri, *Olympia's Forgotten Pioneers* (Olympia: State Capital Historical Association, 1976), p. 4.

46 Bishop D'herbomez to de Mazenod, 6 April 1859, D'herbomez Correspondence, Archives Deschâtelets, Ottawa.

47 Report of the Vicariate of British Columbia, 1861, File PB517, Archives Deschâtelets, Ottawa.

48 Nicandri, *Olympia's Forgotten Pioneers*, pp. 6–8. Because of the missionaries' obvious money problems, the Hudson's Bay Company was reluctant to extend them credit.

49 This is not to suggest that it was the *only* reason why missionaries supported whites at the expense of their Indian converts, but it would obviously be an important reason.

50 Whitehead, *Cariboo Mission*, pp. 16–17; Nicandri, *Olympia's Forgotten Pioneers*, pp. 44–45.

51 Nicandri, *Olympia's Forgotten Pioneers*, pp. 42–43.

52 For evidence of difficulties presented by this dual role, see Whitehead, *Cariboo Mission*.

53 Shapiro, "Ideologies of Catholic Missionary Practice," p. 147.

54 McCarthy, "The Missions of the Oblates of Mary Immaculate," p. 32; Usher, *William*

Duncan of Metlakatla; Lascelles, "Leon Fouquet and the Kootenay Indians," p. 82; Arthur N. Thompson, "The Wife of the Missionary," *Journal of the Canadian Church Historical Society* 15 (1973): 35–44.

55 George Dalton, "The Impact of Colonization on Aboriginal Economies in Stateless Societies," *Research in Economic Anthropology* 1 (1978): 56.

56 Ibid., pp. 136–37. The potlatch is a traditional Indian feast, a formal function, given for a serious socio-economic reason. Essentially a coastal tradition, it was transmitted to Interior tribes through trading relations. The Carrier, for example, held a potlatch to validate the claim to a title given by the provider of the feast. People from other groups (not related to the celebrant) bore witness to the succession and were rewarded with food and gifts. Without a potlatch, there could be no legitimate claim to status. Missionaries and government officials attempted to prevent the potlatch celebrations which they completely misunderstood. For some missionaries, the potlatch represented an opportunity to indulge in gluttony, energy, and pride; other missionaries permitted "small and regulated feasts" (Mulhall, *Will to Power*, p. 49; see also Philip Drucker, *Cultures of the North Pacific Coast* [Scranton: Chandler, 1965]).

57 Interviews with Sister Patricia, Sister Eileen Bernard, Alex Morris, O.M.I., and Orland O'Regan, O.M.I. (Whitehead Collection, PABC). See also McCarthy, "The Missions of the Oblates of Mary Immaculate," p. 99.

58 Those missionaries who were innovative or who exhibited an independent attitude towards missionary methodology tended to clash constantly with authority figures or groups (see, for example, Usher, *William Duncan of Metlakatla*; Mulhall, *Will to Power*).

59 Bryan Wilson, *Religion in Sociological Perspective* (New York: Oxford University Press, 1982), p. 61.

60 For information on the success and failure of this concept, see: Usher, *William Duncan of Metlakatla*; Whitehead, *Now You Are My Brother: Missionaries in British Columbia*, Sound Heritage Series, no. 34 (Victoria: Provincial Archives of British Columbia, 1981).

61 On Roman Catholic problems with Indian vocations to the priesthood and women's religious orders, see Whitehead, *Now You Are My Brother* and *Cariboo Mission*. On efforts of the Propaganda to encourage native clergy, see McCarthy, "The Missions of the Oblates of Mary Immaculate," p. 24.

62 McCarthy, "The Missions of the Oblates of Mary Immaculate," pp. 56–57.

63 P. Besson, *Un Missionaire d'autrefois: Paul Durieu O.M.I.* (Marseilles, 1962), p. 215.

64 "Instructions of our Venerated Father," insert in *Constitutions and Rules*, p. 13.

65 Jacqueline Gresko, "Roman Catholic Missions to the Indians of British Columbia: A Reappraisal of the Lemert Thesis," *Journal of the Canadian Church Historical Society* 24 (October 1982): 52. According to Gresko, missionaries who admired Durieu tended to write of the system as if it were created by their Oblate superior, whereas, in reality, D'herbomez directed Oblate efforts to implement the Jesuit-style missionary scheme.

66 Information from Besson, *Un Missionnaire d'autrefois*; Edwin M. Lemert, "The Life and Death of an Indian State," *Human Organisation* 13, no. 3, (1954); Bishop E. N. Buñoz, "Catholic Action and the Durieu System, 1941," MS, Oblate Archives, Vancouver.

67 Dorothy Kennedy and Randy Bouchard, *Sliammon Life, Sliammon Land* (Vancouver: Talonbooks, 1983), p. 122.

68 Mass is a complex of prayers and ceremonials that make up the celebration of the Eucharist. High mass (which in past centuries used to be the norm) is celebrated on special feast days; there is more ceremonial, incense is used, most often important prayers are sung, and there is a special blessing. A catechism was an official book which provided for children and potential converts the basic tenets of the Roman Catholic faith in a "question and answer" format.

69 There is some evidence that the stress on solemn ceremonial was advocated by de Mazenod and was rather the imposition of the virtually unchanged European home mission system rather than a system aimed at accommodating the native peoples (McCarthy, "The Missions of the Oblates of Mary Immaculate," pp. 80–86, 105).

70 Rod Fowler, "The New Caledonia Mission: An Historical Sketch of the Oblates of Mary Immaculate in North Central British Columbia," *New Caledonia Heritage Research Report*, 1986, p. 34. See also Mulhall, *Will to Power*, p. 78.

71 Durieu to LeJacq, 27 November 1883, Durieu Correspondence Outward, Archives Des-châtelets, Ottawa.

72 For a full discussion of how the whipping complex became incorporated into the cultural fabric of Northwestern tribes, see Thomas R. Garth, "The Plateau Whipping Complex and Its Relationship to Plateau Southwest Contacts," *Ethnohistory* 12 (1906): 141–93.

73 Father James Maria McGuckin to Bishop D'herbomez, 10 November 1873, McGuckin Correspondence, Archives Deschâtelets, Ottawa. For clashes between Oblates and settlers re whipping, see Whitehead, *Cariboo Mission*, pp. 46–97; Mulhall, *Will to Power*, pp. 80–82.

74 For antagonism towards Durieu system, see Whitehead, *Now You Are My Brother;* Mulhall, *Will to Power*, pp. 58–60.

75 Interview with Sister Patricia, S. C. J. (Whitehead Collection, PABC).

76 Kennedy and Bouchard, *Sliammon Life, Sliammon Land*, p. 19.

77 Ibid., p. 22. Some older Shuswap Indians I interviewed could speak some French as well as Shuswap and English, but it was unclear whether this language had been handed down from the fur-trade period or had been learned from French-speaking priests and/or nuns (see interviews with Shuswaps, Whitehead Collection, PABC).

78 Elmer S. Miller, "The Christian Missionary, Agent of Secularization," *Anthropological Quarterly* 5, no. 43 (1970): 14–22.

79 For arguments about the limited success of the Durieu system, see Gresko, "Roman Catholic Missions to the Indians of British Columbia"; for the importance of Indian active participation in the Christianizing process, see Margaret Whitehead, "Christianity: A Matter of Choice," *Pacific Northwest Quarterly* 72 (July 1981): 98–106.

80 Nelson, "Reminiscences," p. 12.

81 For examples, see Whitehead, "Christianity: A Matter of Choice"; Lemert, "The Life and Death of an Indian State"; Hilary E. Rumley, "Reactions to Contact and Colonization of Religious and Social Change Among the Indians of B.C." (M.A. thesis, University of British Columbia, 1973); Fisher, *Contact and Conflict;* Dalton, "The Impact of Colonization on Aboriginal Economies in Stateless Societies"; Whitehead, *Cariboo Mission*.

82 For statistics, see Wilson Duff, *The Indian History of British Columbia*, vol. 1, Anthropology in British Columbia (1964), p. 39.

83 Fisher, *Contact and Conflict*, p. 123.

84 Diamond Jenness, *Indians of Canada* (reprint, Toronto: University of Toronto Press, 1977), pp. 352–53.

85 Information on Shuswap religion is taken from James Teit, "The Shuswap," in Franz Boas, ed., *Memoir of the American Museum of Natural History* (New York, 1909).

86 Jenness, *Indians of Canada*, pp. 358–59.

87 Bob Bettson, "Native Spirituality Blends with Christianity," *Indian Record* (January 1985): 48.

88 Father Pierre Jean De Smet, S. J., was a noted missionary to the American Plains Indians. He began his work among the Dakotas of Iowa, then moved to establish missions among the Flathead Indians. De Smet travelled extensively in Europe recruiting personnel and soliciting funds to build a mission network throughout the Northwest (Henry Warner Bowden, *American Indians and Christian Missions: Studies in Cultural Conflict* [Chicago: University of Chicago Press, 1981], pp. 185–86). For more on the prophet movement, see pages following.

89 Lascelles, "Leon Fouquet," pp. 33–34.

90 Powell to Hon. A. Campbell, minister of the interior, 3 November 1873, Record Group 10, vol. 28013, file B302, PABC. Other officials praised the Kootenay (Major Sam Steele to Powers, 16 July 1887, RG 10, vol. 4038, file B302, PABC; Alexander F. Chamberlain, "Report on the Kootenays of Southeastern British Columbia," British Association for the Advancement of Science, London [1892]: 552–55).

91 Powell to superintendent general of Indian Affairs, 13 July 1887, RG 10, vol. 28013, file B302, PABC.

92 Coccola's predecessor, Father Leon Fouquet, suggests in his letters that the Kootenay were not adversely affected by white contact and did not succumb to alcoholism or prostitution (Lascelles, "Leon Fouquet," p. 29).

93 Coccola to Bishop Paul Durieu, 28 April 1889, Coccola Correspondence Outward, Archives Deschâtelets, Ottawa.
94 Powell to A. Campbell, 3 November 1873, RG 10, vol. 28013, file B302, PABC.
95 Oblates, particularly Bishop Durieu, promoted temperance societies. For example, at a celebration at Sugar Cane Reserve, Williams Lake, in 1895, Bishop Durieu took the opportunity to inaugurate an Indian Total Abstinence Society of British Columbia (Whitehead, *Cariboo Mission*, pp. 95–96). According to Gresko, knowledge of French-Canadian temperance societies was carried to Oregon by French-Canadian missionaries and picked up by the Oblates (Gresko to author).
96 Coccola to Bishop Paul Durieu, 28 April 1889, Coccola Correspondence Outward, Archives Deschâtelets, Ottawa. The missionaries often used the French term "sauvages" to describe the Indians; it was not necessarily a derogatory term although the French meaning is "wild" or "untamed."
97 Powell to A. Campbell, minister of the interior, 3 November 1873, RG 10, vol. 28013, file B302, PABC.
98 Coccola to Bishop Paul Durieu, 28 April 1889, Coccola Correspondence Outward, Archives Deschâtelets, Ottawa.
99 Coccola to superior general, Rev. Cassien Augier, 6 February 1900, Coccola Correspondence Outward, Archives Deschâtelets, Ottawa
100 Rev. F. N. Blanchet, *Historical Sketches of the Catholic Church in Oregon and the Northwest* (Washington, 1910), p. 8.
101 Information on early contact via St. Joseph's Mission in Whitehead, *Cariboo Mission*, pp. 46–47.
102 Information on establishment of Fort St. James Mission taken from ibid.
103 Maureen and Frank Cassidy, *Proud Past: A History of the Wet'suwet'en of Moricetown, B.C.* (Moricetown: Moricetown Band, 1980), p. 22.
104 Jenness, *Indians of Canada*, p. 367.
105 Daniel Harmon, *Sixteen Years in Indian Country, 1800–1816* (Toronto: Macmillan, 1957), p. 251.
106 McCarthy stresses the importance of the prophet movement in the Athabasca region and also the persistence of prophets long after the introduction of Catholicism.
107 A detailed study of the prophet movement can be found in Rumley, "Reactions to Contact and Colonization."
108 A. G. Morice, *History of the Northern Interior of British Columbia* (Smithers, B.C.: Interior Stationery [1970], 1978) p. 225.
109 Indian Agent R. E. Loring, Report of Babine Agency to D.I.A., 30 June 1893, RG 10, vol. 4038, file B302, PABC.
110 On ethnicity, language, and geography, see Duff, *The Indian History of British Columbia*, p. 31; on Kamloops history, see Mary Balf, *Kamloops* (Kamloops: Kamloops Museum Association, 1969), and Donovan Clemson, "Kamloops: Hub of South Central B.C.," *British Columbia Digest* (December 1963), pp. 19–24.
111 John Mara was elected to the B.C. legislature and represented the Kootenay region for five years. With partners such as Francis Barnard of stagecoach transportation fame and Forbes George Vernon, one of the first Okanagan settlers, Mara built railway branch lines in the Okanagan (Mara, Barnard, and Vernon files, PABC).
112 Balf, *Kamloops*, pp. 18–31.
113 According to Wilson Duff, there is no one correct spelling of an Indian name; in most cases a number of alternative spellings are used (Duff, *Indian History of B.C.*, p. 10). Coccola's spelling of Tziliktza is different from the spelling given by Nelson, "Chilhitsa" (presumably based on Coccola's pronounciation), and James Teit's "Teilaxitca" in Franz Boaz, ed., *Reports of the Jesup North Pacific Expedition*, Memoirs of the American Museum of Natural History, New York, 1900.
114 Rolf Knight, *Indians at Work: An Informal History of Native Indian Labour in British Columbia, 1858–1930* (Vancouver: New Star Books, 1978), p. 145.
115 The Indians made strong complaints about every reserve O'Reilly laid out, yet, in 1880, he was appointed by the provincial government as Indian reserve commissioner (see Fisher, *Contact and Conflict*, pp. 199–201).

116 Ibid., pp. 178–79.
117 For details on how the image of the Indian changed from Elizabethan times to the eighteenth century, see Gary B. Nash, "The Image of the Indian in the Southern Colonial Mind," *William and Mary Quarterly* 29 (1972): 197–231. In the nineteenth century, the popular novels of James Fenimore Cooper reflected a "romantic" view of the Indian that had begun in England with the Romantic poets and been perpetuated by American poets, writers, artists, scientists, and natural history buffs—mostly easterners who had limited if any contact with the West (see, for example, Roderick Nash, *Wilderness and the American Mind* [New Haven: Yale University Press, 1967]).
118 Robert H. Ruby and John A. Brown, *A Guide to the Indian Tribes of the Pacific Northwest* (Norman and London: University of Oklahoma Press, 1986), p. 100. In the introduction the spelling *Kutenai* refers to the Indians and *Kootenay* to geographical locations.
119 Duff, *Indian History of B.C.*, p. 39.
120 Jenness, *Indians of Canada*, p. 339. Each band had its own hereditary chief, and this chief was supported by an informal council of older men.
121 On Galbraiths, see Galbraith File, PABC.
122 Margaret Ormsby, *British Columbia: A History* (Toronto: Macmillan 1958), p. 315.
123 Martin Robin, *The Rush for Spoils: The Company Province, 1871–1933* (Toronto: McClelland and Stewart, 1972), pp. 15–17.
124 Elsie G. Turnbull, "Rossland Camp," *Pacific Northwesterner* 6 (Winter 1962): 9–11.
125 Kutenai Indians of Montana were also being pressured by white population, and many were related to the Kutenai in Canada.
126 Robin, *Rush for Spoils*, p. 68.
127 The Prairie is evidently named after Chief Ka Ka Kilth, who took the Christian name of Joseph, a Kutenai referred to by Powell as "a fine looking Indian, intelligent, shrewd and one of the most pious men of his tribe" (Powell to A. Campbell, minister of the interior, RG 10, vol. 4038, file B302, PABC).
128 Robin, *Rush for Spoils*, p. 68.
129 Leon Fourquet, "Memorandum on the Troubles in the Kootenay," MS, Archives Deschâtelets, Ottawa.
130 J. W. Powell to superintendent general of Indian Affairs, 13 July 1887, RG 10, vol. 28013, file B302, PABC.
131 S. B. Steele, *Forty Years in Canada: Reminiscences of the Great North-West with Some Account of His Service in South Africa* (Winnipeg: R. Long, 1914), p. 246.
132 RG 10, vol. 28013, file B302, PABC. This record group contains a large number of letters both to Powell and from Powell to Ottawa re Kutenai land claims.
133 Steele to Powell, 16 July 1887, RG 10, vol. 28013, file B302, PABC.
134 Fisher, *Contact and Conflict*, p. 197.
135 Steele, *Forty Years in Canada*, p. 250.
136 Morice, *History of the Northern Interior of British Columbia*, p. 64.
137 Audrey Smedley-L'Heureux, *Northern B.C. in Retrospect* (Vanderhoof, 1979), p. 4.
138 Duff, *Indian History of B.C.*, pp. 33–34.
139 Jenness, *Indians of Canada*, pp. 363–64; Marius Barbeau, "An Indian Paradise Lost," *Canadian Geographical Journal* 1, no. 2 (June 1930): 147.
140 Jenness, *Indians of Canada*, pp. 365–67.
141 Ibid., pp. 379–80.
142 Ibid., p. 382; Duff, *Indian History of B.C.*, p. 60.
143 Morice, *History of the Northern Interior*, pp. 38–40, 42, 148.
144 Diamond Jenness, "The Carrier Indians of the Bulkley River: Their Social and Religious Life," *Bureau of American Ethnology Bulletin 133*, Anthropological Papers, no. 25 (1943): 539.
145 Morice, *History of the Northern Interior*, p. 63.
146 Fisher, *Contact and Conflict*, p. 31.
147 Morice, *History of the Northern Interior*, p. 63.
148 Fisher, *Contact and Conflict*, p. 33.
149 Morice, *History of the Northern Interior*, p. 67.
150 Imbert Orchard, *Martin: The Story of a Young Fur Trader*, Sound Heritage Series, no. 30

(Victoria: Provincial Archives of British Columbia, 1981), p. 4, 51; Coccola mentions the murder of a H.B.C. manager at Fort Babine (Nelson, "Reminiscences," p. 104; and "Memoirs," p. 93).

151 Jenness, *Indians of Canada*, p. 364; Duff, *Indian History of B.C.*, p. 85.

152 Duff, *Indian History of B.C.*, pp. 55–56.

153 For example, in 1862, smallpox was brought to Victoria probably by a sailor coming from San Francisco. When it became apparent that many Indians had been stricken with the disease, the city authorities evicted them and burned their houses. As the northern Indian visitors among them returned home, they carried the infection with them spreading the disease throughout the interior as well as up the coast (Fisher, *Contact and Conflict*, pp. 115–16).

154 David Mulhall, "The Missionary Career of A. G. Morice, O.M.I." (Ph.D. diss. McGill University, 1978), pp. 100–1.

155 Margaret A. Ormsby, "Agricultural Development in British Columbia," *Agricultural History* 19 (1945): 11–20.

156 Cassidy, *Proud Past*, p. 21.

157 J. A. Lower, "The Construction of the Grand Trunk Pacific Railway in B.C.," *B.C. Historical Quarterly* 4 (July 1940): 163.

158 Bureau of Provincial Information, *New British Columbia*, Official Bulletin no. 22 (1908), p. 59, PABC.

159 Indian Agent R. E. Loring, Report on Babine Agency to D.I.A., 30 June 1893, RG 10, vol. 4038, file B350, PABC.

160 Mulhall, "The Missionary Career of A. G. Morice, O.M.I.," p. 294.

161 Ibid., pp. 307–8.

162 Ibid., p. 318.

163 Diamond Jenness, "The Yukon Telegraph Line," *Canadian Geographical Journal* 1, no. 2 (June 1930): 695; Smedley-L'Heureux, *Northern B.C. in Retrospect*, p. 37.

164 Mulhall, "The Missionary Career of A. G. Morice, O.M.I.," pp. 317–18.

165 T. D. Regehr, *The Canadian Northern Railway: Pioneer Road of the Northern Prairies, 1895–1918* (Toronto: Macmillan, 1976), p. 285.

166 Few missionaries ignored the material welfare of the native peoples; for an argument that Morice was an exception, see Mulhall, *Will to Power*.

167 See, for example, Whitehead, *Cariboo Mission;* Usher, *William Duncan of Metlakatla*.

168 Usher, *William Duncan of Metlakatla*, p. 128.

169 There is little mention of Coccola's role in Steele's account of the uprising (*Forty Years*). One might suspect that Coccola exaggerated his part. But Steele's book deals also with missionary activity in Alberta, and although he gives prominence to Protestant missionaries, he ignores the vital work of Father Albert Lacombe, who is credited with calming the angry and unjustly treated Blackfoot. Denominational partiality appears to be a possibility.

170 Efforts to locate this letter have, to date, been unsuccessful.

171 Nelson, "Reminiscences," p. 36.

172 Ibid., n. p.; Lascelles, "Leon Fouquet," p. 109.

173 Coccola to Bishop Buñoz, December 1908, Coccola Correspondence Outward, Archives Dechâtelets, Ottawa.

174 Letter from the chiefs of Stuart Lake, Pinchi, Tache,and Yecoche to the minister of Indian Affairs, RG 10, vol. 4027, file B347, PABC.

175 Coccola to Frank Pedley, D.I.A., 12 October 1909, RG 10, vol. 4027, file B347, PABC.

176 Coccola to D.I.A., 11 November 1909, RG 10, vol. 4027, file B347, PABC.

177 *New Westminster Daily News*, 17 August 1906, p. 8.

178 Gordon W. Hewes, "Indian Fisheries Productivity in Pre-Contact Times in the Pacific Salmon Area," *Northwest Anthropological Research Notes* 7, no. 2 (Fall 1973): 144–46.

179 Keith Ralston, "Patterns of Trade and Investment on the Pacific Coast, 1867–1892: The Case of the British Columbia Salmon Canning Industry," in *British Columbia: Historical Readings*, eds. W. Peter Ward and Robert A. J. McDonald (Vancouver: Douglas and MacIntyre 1981), pp. 300–1.

180 A. L. Pritchard, "The Skeena River Salmon Investigation," *Canadian Geographical Jour-*

nal 34, no. 2 (August 1949): 60; Charles F. Broches, "Fish, Politics and Treaty Rights: Who Protects Salmon Resources in Washington State?," *BC Studies* 57 (Spring 1983): 86.

181 Ralston, "Patterns of Trade and Investment," pp. 298–300.

182 *New Westminster Daily News,* 17 August 1906, p. 8.

183 Bureau of Provincial Information, *New British Columbia,* Official Bulletin, no. 22 (1908), PABC.

184 All information on settlement conditions, ibid., pp. 3–21.

185 Robin, *Rush for Spoils,* p. 92.

186 Coccola to Bishop Buñoz, December 1908, Coccola, Correspondence Outward, Archives Deschâtelets, Ottawa.

187 Information on John McInnis, John McInnis File, PABC.

188 Above information taken from Ormsby, *British Columbia: A History,* p. 359.

189 Wainright (G.T.P. official) to Pedley, deputy superintendent of Indian Affairs, 31 May 1910, RG 10, vol. 4038, file 325, PABC.

190 Rev. John McDougall to Pedley, 25 July 1909, RG 10, vol. 4038, file 325, PABC.

191 Requests to federal government from B.C. Express Company and from I. A. Cosgrove, RG 10, vol. 4038, file 325, PABC.

192 McDougall to the D.I.A., 20 December 1910, RG 10, vol. 4038, file 325, PABC.

193 Bellot to Pedley, 14 January 1911; Pedley to Bellot, 16 January 1911; E. J. Chamberlain (?) to D.I.A., 12 April 1911; MacDonald to Pedley, 14 April 1911, RG 10, vol. 4038, file 325, PABC.

194 Coccola to Pedley, 29 August 1911, RG 10, vol. 4038, file 325, PABC.

195 The man in question, Durnford, had no legal right to deal with the Indians, although Coccola was unaware of this. It was suggested by the local newspaper that Durnford was the agent of a "slick individual in Vancouver—who shall be nameless" (*Fort George Herald,* 28 October 1911, p. 1). The newspaper also notes Coccola's efforts on behalf of the Indians.

196 Ramsden, D.I.A. representative to D. C. Scott, D.I.A., Ottawa, 16 November 1911, RG 10, vol. 4038, file 325, PABC.

197 Ormsby, *British Columbia: A History,* p. 359.

198 For detail on how at least some traders and government officials sought the help of missionaries in the north, see Mulhall, *Will to Power.*

199 For information of Chief Capilano, see Chief Capilano File, PABC.

200 David R. Williams, *Simon Peter Gunanoot, Trapline Outlaw* (Victoria: Sono Nis Press, 1982), p. 76.

201 Knight, *Indians at Work,* p. 140.

202 Williams, *Trapline Outlaw,* p. 76.

203 Coccola to Bishop Buñoz, December 1908, Coccola, Correspondence Outward, Archives Deschâtelets, Ottawa.

204 As David Williams makes clear, Indian crimes could be difficult if not impossible to solve, particularly if Indians refused their assistance.

205 Williams, *Trapline Outlaw,* p. 80.

206 Loring to D.I.A., 1909, RG 10, vol. 4038, file 325, PABC.

207 Williams, *Trapline Outlaw,* pp. 81–82.

208 Nelson, "Reminiscences," p. 5.

209 For variety of missionary roles, see Whitehead, *Now You Are My Brother* and *Cariboo Mission*; Elizabeth Graham, *Medicine Man to Missionary: Missionaries as Agents of Change among the Indians of Southern Ontario, 1784–1867* (Toronto: Peter Martin Associates, 1975); Usher, *William Duncan of Metlakatla.*

210 Nelson, "Reminiscences," p. 32.

211 Phillips, report to the D.I.A., 1 July 1893, RG 10, vol. 4038, file 325, PABC.

212 Grant Thomas Edwards, "Bella Coola, Indian and European Medicines," *The Beaver* (Winter 1980): 5.

213 Fisher, *Contact and Conflict,* p. 131.

214 Louise Jilek-Aall, "The Psychiatrist and His Shaman Colleagues: Cross-Cultural Collaboration with Traditional Amerindian Therapists," paper presented at the World Congress of Psychiatry, 1977, Honolulu.

215 Whitehead, *Now You Are My Brother.*
216 Tribute to Coccola's medical skills was given by a Nechako Valley pioneer, George Og-
    ston, who noted: "If medical attention was required, no matter where and by whom, Fa-
    ther Coccola would reach the sufferer, if it were humanly possible to do so" (*Nechako
    Chronicle,* 17 July 1954).
217 Father Pandosy's Medical Dictionary, Archives Deschâtelets, Ottawa.
218 François-Marie Thomas, "Memoirs," MS, Oblate Archives, Vancouver; Sister Patricia in-
    terview (Whitehead Collection, PABC).
219 Lascelles, "Leon Fouquet," pp. 60–61. For Oblate efforts to improve status of Indian
    women, see McCarthy, "The Missions of the Oblates of Mary Immaculate," pp. 250–51.
    On Oblates as promoters of homeopathic medicine, ibid., p. 217.
220 For problems of missionaries re geography, see Whitehead, *Cariboo Mission*; Mulhall,
    Will to Power.
221 For evidence that Indians remained faithful despite neglect see William Christie interview
    (Whitehead Collection, PABC). For evidence of Indian questioning of missionary system,
    see RG 10, vol. 28013, file B302, PABC; also Mulhall, *Will to Power.*
222 During his years at St. Joseph's Mission, Williams Lake, Father James Maria McGuckin
    was particularly disturbed by what he termed "the deplorable state" of Indian girls living
    near the mining areas. McGuckin emphasized the desirability of teaching these future
    Catholic mothers: "in vain shall we teach the boys as long as the girls are ignorant and
    wicked" (Whitehead, *Cariboo Mission,* p. 53). See *Memoirs,* p. 66.
223 Robert Berkhofer, Jr., "Model Zions for the American Indians," *American Quarterly* 15
    (1963): 177.
224 Ronald N. Satz, *American Indian Policy in the Jacksonian Era* (Lincoln: University of
    Nebraska Press, 1975), p. 248.
225 Elizabeth Graham, *Medicine Man to Missionary,* p. 65.
226 "Report of the Welfare and Training Service of the Indian Affairs Branch, 1946," RG 10,
    vol. 6811, PABC.
227 E. Brian Titley, "Indian Industrial Schools in Western Canada," in *Schools in the West:
    Essays in Canadian Educational History* eds. N. M. Sheehan, J. D. Wilson, D. C. Jones
    (Calgary: Detselig Enterprises, 1986), p. 135.
228 John Webster Grant, *Moon of Wintertime: Missionaries and the Indians of Canada in En-
    counter since 1534* (Toronto: University of Toronto Press, 1984), pp. 30–35.
229 For the opposition of some government officials to the industrial/residential concept, see
    Ken Coates, "'Betwixt and Between': The Anglican Church and the Children of Carcross
    (Chooutla) Residential School, 1911–1954," *BC Studies* 64 (Winter 1984–85): 27–47.
230 For constant financial disagreement between the federal government and one religious or-
    ganization, see Correspondence between School Principals of Williams Lake Residential
    School and the D.I.A., RG 10, vol. 6438, PABC. In 1917, the government grant to the
    Williams Lake school was $8,222; school expenditures totalled $8,757 and the local mis-
    sion ranch, which provided meat, fuel, and vegetables, carried the deficit—Accounts of
    Williams Lake Industrial School, year ending 31 March 1917, file XVII-H-54, Archives
    Deschâtelets, Ottawa.
231 Grant, *Moon of Wintertime,* p. 159.
232 Titley, "Indian Industrial Schools in Western Canada," p. 134.
233 Interview with Sister Teresa Bernard, S.C.K. (Whitehead Collection, PABC).
234 Coccola to J. D. McLean, D.I.A., 17 January 1916, RG 10, vol. 4027, file B347, PABC.
235 For the argument that the government and the Roman Catholic Church worked in
    harmony, see Diane Persson, "The Changing Experience of Indian Residential Schooling:
    Blue Quills, 1931–1970," in *Indian Education in Canada, Vol. 1, The Legacy,* eds. Jean
    Barman, Yvonne Hébert, Don McCaskill (Vancouver: UBC Press, 1986), pp. 150–68;
    for a different perspective on the relationship between Church and government, see
    Coates, "Betwixt and Between."
236 For the Anglicans' views, see Coates, "Betwixt and Between"; on Methodists' views, see J.
    Donald Wilson, "'No Blanket to be Worn in School': The Education of Indians in
    Nineteenth-Century Ontario," in *Indian Education in Canada,* eds. Barman et al., pp.
    64–83.

237 McCarthy, "The Missions of the Oblates of Mary Immaculate," p. 55.
238 This long remained the Oblates' primary objective (see "Report of the Canonical Visitation of St. Peter's Province, Canada, October 1950–May 1951," Oblate Archives, Vancouver).
239 The best known, and considered the most successful, Oblate missionary work was done among the Sechelt Indians. Native peoples from other regions were taken by their missionaries to the Sechelt Reserve so that they might observe a "model" community and profit spiritually by the contact (Father LeJacq to superior general, 21 October 1895, Archives Deschâtelets, Ottawa).
240 The most successful mission work was achieved where missionary nuns established schools and hospitals. Not enough attention has been paid to the impact these women—and, in fact, all missionary women of all denominations—made on the history of Indian/white contact.
241 Titley, " Indian Residential Schools in Western Canada," p. 141.
242 On the value placed by missionaries on hygiene, punctuality, and the work ethic, see Usher, *William Duncan of Metlakatla;* Coates, "Betwixt and Between"; Whitehead, *Now You Are My Brother.*
243 See for example, interview with Orland O'Regan, O.M.I. (Whitehead Collection, PABC); Coates, "Betwixt and Between"; Gresko, "White 'Rules' and Indian 'Rites'"; "White 'Rites' and Indian 'Rites': Indian Education and Native Responses in the West, 1870–1910," in *Shaping the Schools of the Canadian West,* ed. N. M. Sheehan and R. M. Stamp (Calgary: Detselig, 1979), pp. 84–106.
244 Coccola to Superintendent of Indian Affairs, 1 July 1893, RG 10, vol. 4038, file B350, PABC.
245 For opposing views on the "problems" of mixing native children from different tribes and bands, interviews with Alex Morris, O.M.I. and Orland O'Regan, O.M.I. (Whitehead Collection, PABC).
246 See interviews with Indian people, Whitehead Collection, PABC; correspondence between school principals and D.I.A., RG 10, vol. 6436, PABC; François Marie Thomas, O.M.I. to Jean Marie LeJeune, 23 September 1901, Thomas Correspondence, Archives Deschâtelets, Ottawa; McCarthy, "The Missions of the Oblates of Mary Immaculate," p. 55.
247 Dontenwill to A. G. Vowell, Indian superintendent, 26 February 1902, RG 10, vol. 6436, PABC.
248 Father Joseph Allard's diary as quoted in Kay Cronin, *Cross in the Wilderness* (Vancouver: Mitchell Press, 1959), pp. 216–18.
249 Interview with Bill Christie, former Indian agent (Whitehead Collection, PABC). See also Whitehead, *Cariboo Mission,* p. 124.
250 Titley, "Indian Industrial Schools in Western Canada," p. 149; Whitehead, *Cariboo Mission,* p. 125.
251 Titley, "Indian Industrial Schools in Western Canada," p. 145.
252 Dontenwill to Vowell, 26 February 1902, RG 10, vol. 6436, PABC. See also Chas. Moser, *Reminiscences of the West Coast of Vancouver Island* (Victoria: Acme Press, 1925), pp. 154–55.
253 Rod Fowler, "The New Caledonia Mission," p. 45.
254 Original "Memoirs," p. 101 (pagination by author).
255 In 1895, Bishop Paul Durieu approached the Sisters of the Child Jesus at Le Puy, France, hoping to persuade them to staff Indian schools in British Columbia. The first group arrived in 1896 at St. Joseph's Mission, Williams Lake (P. Coron, *Messengers of the Holy City* [Lyon: Lescuyer, 1969], pp. 145–46).
256 For Indian perspectives on language suppression, see Indian interviews, Whitehead Collection, PABC; Robert Levine and Freda Cooper, "The Suppression of B.C. Languages: Filling in the Gaps in the Documentary Record," *Native Languages and Culture,* Sound Heritage Series, vol. 4 nos. 3 and 4 (Victoria: Provincial Archives of British Columbia, 1976); Andrew Paull (Indian activist) in *Oblate Missions* no. 21 (Dec/Mar. 1950–51).
257 Marie Battiste, "Micmac Literacy and Cognitive Assimilation," *Indian Education in Canada,* Barman et al., eds., 1: 36.
258 Interview with Mary Englund (Whitehead Collection, PABC).

1   Father Nicolas Coccola, date unknown. Courtesy Archives Deschâlets, Ottawa

2 Nicola Indians, date unknown. Courtesy Provincial Archives of British Columbia

3 Nicola Valley Indians, date unknown. Courtesy Provincial Archives of British Columbia

4   St. Eugene Mission, Cranbrook, B.C. Courtesy Provincial Archives of British Columbia

5   Father Coccola as a young priest with Kootenay Indians. Courtesy Archives Deschâlets

6   St. Eugene Indians at Cranbrook, B.C., 1902. Courtesy Provincial Archives of British Columbia

7   ON HORSEBACK, LEFT TO RIGHT: Phillip Wa-Tam (Philip Beaver Tail), Alipine Gustave (Alpine Gus), Joe Joe-Nina (Joe Nana), Skaakum Joe (Skookum Joe), Kootenay Pete (Joseph Kootenay Pete). STANDING ON LEFT: Sabastien Ole Joe (Sebastian Joe). STANDING IN CENTRE: Chief Isadore-Keith Go Woyia (Isador). KNEELING, LEFT TO RIGHT: Billy Paul (William Paul), Storken (Louie Storiken), Kapilo Gustabe (Kapulo). Courtesy Provincial Archives of British Columbia

8   St. Eugene Mission, including industrial school run by Sisters of Providence. Courtesy Provincial Archives of British Columbia

9   Photo believed taken about 1890. BACK ROW, LEFT TO RIGHT: Chief Piere Thunderbird, Government Chief of St. Mary's Band; Chief Able Three-Feathers, Church Chief of Creston; Chief Aleso Alexander, Government Chief of Creston. FRONT ROW, LEFT TO RIGHT: Chief Able Morning Star, Chief of Columbia Lake Band, Windermere; Chief Fran Franciscus, Chief of St. Mary's Band, Cranbrook; Chief Pierre Kinbasket, Chief of the Shuswaps, Athalmere

10   Kootenay women with Father Coccola on the right.   Courtesy Archives Deschâlets, Ottawa

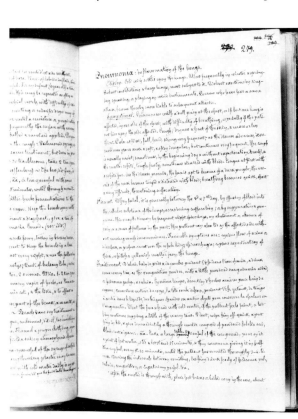

11   Page from medical dictionary used by Father Coccola.   Courtesy Archives Deschâlets, Ottawa

12   St. Eugene Mission, Cranbrook, B.C., Feast of Corpus Christi, 1899. Courtesy Provincial Archives of British Columbia

13   The hospital at Rossland, B.C. Courtesy Sisters of St. Joseph, Newark, Bellevue, Washington

14 First visit of Father Coccola to Taché Village, B.C. Courtesy John Brioux, O.M.I.

15 Our Lady of Good Hope Church, Fort St. James, with Oblate priest standing in front of it.
Courtesy Provincial Archives of British Columbia

16 Smoking salmon, Fort St. James, Stuart Lake, B.C., 20 August 1909. Courtesy Provincial Archives of British Columbia

17 Bishop Bunoz visits the north, date unknown. Courtesy John Brioux, O.M.I.

18   Father Coccola with Babine Indians (believed by Gaston Carrière to have been the Indians who accompanied Father Coccola to Ottawa).   Courtesy Archives Deschâlets, Ottawa

19   Father Coccola and Ft. George chief (from Frank C. Swannell diary, 1908-9). Courtesy
Provincial Archives of British Columbia

20   Father Coccola and Indian children, Lejac School, 1938 (?). Courtesy Archives Deschâlets, Ottawa

21   Father Coccola with Sisters of the Child Jesus, Lejac School, 1938. Courtesy Archives Deschâlets, Ottawa

22   Bishop Bunoz, Father Coccola, Bishop Coudert (Coadjutor), Lejac, 1939. Courtesy Archives
Deschâlets, Ottawa

23 Father Nicola Coccola, o.m.i. Courtesy Oblate Historical Archives, Ottawa

259 For arguments re institutionalization of Indian children, see Persson, "The Changing Experience of Indian Residential Schooling," pp. 150–67.

260 Interview with Mary Englund (Whitehead Collection, PABC).

261 This note was included in a letter of Father George Forbes, O.M.I., to the deputy superintendent general, D.I.A., 7 March 1936, RG 10, vol. 6438, PABC.

262 Jacqueline Gresko, "Creating Little Dominions Within the Dominion: Early Catholic Indian Schools in Saskatchewan and British Columbia," in *Indian Education in Canada*, Barman et al., eds., 1: 102.

263 On positive effects of residential schooling, see Wilson, "'No Blanket to be Worn in School,'" p. 64; Gresko, "Creating Little Dominions Within the Dominion," p. 102.

264 Coccola appears to have had a great admiration for Father Albert Lacombe, O.M.I. Lacombe was one of a team of four Quebec priests sent to the Red River Colony to minister to the Indians and métis. Not originally an Oblate, Lacombe joined the congregation some time in 1853. He is probably the most famous western Roman Catholic missionary.

265 Nelson, "Reminiscences," pp. 15–16.

266 Ormsby, *British Columbia: A History*, pp. 280–81.

267 Nelson, "Reminiscences," p. 16.

268 Coccola to an Oblate friend at Belcamp Scholasticate, 10 February 1886, Coccola Correspondence Outward, Archives Deschâtelets, Ottawa.

269 Information on environmental conditions taken from Pierre Berton, *The National Dream* (Toronto: McClelland and Stewart, 1974), pp. 416–18.

270 A. Ross McCormack quotes one miner as complaining that after deductions, "they were working for 'overalls and tobacco'" (*Reformers, Rebels, and Revolutionaries: The Western Canadian Radical Movement, 1899–1919* [Toronto: University of Toronto Press, 1977], p. 12).

271 Nelson, "Reminiscences," p. 18.

272 Berton, *The National Dream*, pp. 418–19.

273 Irving Abella and David Miller, eds., *The Canadian Worker in the Twentieth Century* (Toronto: Oxford University Press, 1978), p. 59.

274 Nelson, "Reminiscences," pp. 20–23.

275 David Bercuson, "Labour Radicalism and the Western Industrial Frontier, 1897–1919," in *Readings in Canadian History: Post Confederation*, R. Douglas Francis and Donald B. Smith, eds. (Toronto: Holt, Rinehart and Winston, 1982), p. 162.

276 Ormsby, *British Columbia: A History*, p. 339.

277 Fort Pend d'Oreille, built in 1856, was later named Fort Shepard (E. T. Clegg, "Ghost Towns of the Kootenays," *British Columbia Digest*, December 1963, p. 18).

278 Ormsby, *British Columbia: A History*, p. 317.

279 Information on living conditions taken from Bercuson, "Labour Radicalism and the West," p. 168.

280 For more information on unrest in the Kootenays, see, for example, Bercuson, "Labour Radicalism and the West"; Paul Phillips, *No Power Greater: A Century of Labour in British Columbia* (Vancouver: B.C. Federation of Labour, 1967); Stanley Scott, "A Profusion of Issues: Immigrant Labour, the World War, and the Cominco Strike of 1917," *Labour/Le Travailleur*, 2 (1977): 44–78.

281 Bercuson has recognized the importance of the Catholic church's influence among Cape Breton miners and notes that the Italian community in Trail constituted a conservative element (without reference to its Catholicism), but 25 per cent of Kootenay miners were European and what needs to be examined is the influence of the Catholic church on these men, as also on the Irish, English, and American Catholics. McCormack, in his discussion of Ukrainian immigrants, ignores their Catholicism and the values it transmitted.

282 *The Code of Canon Law* (English translation)(London, 1983), pp. 92–93.

283 *Rossland Miner*, 3 January 1969; *Cranbrook Herald*, 12 April 1898.

284 Bercuson, "Labour Radicalism in the West," p. 167.

285 Ibid.

286 *Cranbrook Herald*, 3 May 1898.

287 The Sisters of Providence order was founded in Montreal in 1848. Although the order worked in the Oregon Territory, it was not until 1886 that the first Sisters came to British

Columbia from Quebec; their first undertaking was St. Mary's Hospital, New Westminster.

288 The Sisters of St. Joseph of Peace order was founded in England in 1884. The nuns' first concern was to help impoverished women and this concern led them to the immigrant women of North America. Their first U.S.A. establishment was in Newark where they opened an orphanage, hospital, school for the blind, etc. In 1890, two nuns were sent to Washington State to found a hospital in a region desperately short of social services. Within six months, they had a thirty-bed hospital at Bellingham. Other nuns from both England and the eastern states joined them, and in 1896, sisters travelled to the Kootenays to open a hospital (information from Sister Mary Patterson, Bellevue, Washington).

289 *Rossland Miner,* 3 January 1969.

290 Grant, *Moon of Wintertime,* p. 198.

291 Interview with Bill Christie (Whitehead Collection, PABC).

292 Duff, *Indian History of B.C.,* p. 87.

293 Whitehead, "New Missionaries, Old Problems," in *Now You Are My Brother,* pp. 69–87.

294 In a newspaper interview Father Alex Morris, O.M.I., reflected that: "In Africa after anything from five to 10 years, natives have been running their own schools and became bishops. And right here we have achieved nothing comparable. And it has been found that Indians are more tenacious at holding onto their ancestral way of life than any other race we have met" (*Williams Lake Tribune,* 21 March 1957).

295 Grant, *Moon of Wintertime,* p. 253.

296 Orchard, *Martin Starret,* p. 52.

297 Coccola Notebook, Archives Deschâtelets, Ottawa, p. 33.

298 Grant, *Moon of Wintertime,* p. 264.

299 See Whitehead Collection, PABC—in particular, interviews with Mary Englund, David and Celestine Johnson, Lily Squinahan, and, although the quality is not as good, Indians of Alkali Lake; see also Imbert Orchard Collection, PABC, interview with Chief Clarence Joe.

300 Interview with Chief Clarence Joe (Imbert Orchard Collection, PABC).

They Call Me Father

MEMOIRS

On the Island of Corsica, called "the pearl of the Mediterranean,"is the hamlet of Coccola. The hamlet was built on high rock six miles from the shore, when centuries ago the Corsicans were jealous of their independence. Like a watch tower, it had an immense view of the sea and at the moment that suspected boats were seen the blowing of the horn and the smoke of a fire gave the alarm, the next village did the same and in a short time the whole Island was busy bringing women, children and stock to the Interior where the men would be armed to repulse any attack. The Island was coveted by French, English, Spanish and Greeks as a strategic point in European wars for the navy. Twelve families had their homes in the hamlet with a chapel dedicated to St. Sebastian. The slope of that rock was surrounded with orchards and gardens while the plains were covered with vineyards and fields of grain or alfalfa. In this hamlet in the parish of Santa Lucia, I was born on the 6th day of December, 1854. My parents wanting a son had offered prayers and visited shrines of the Blessed Virgin to obtain the object of their desires, promising that the name of Nicolas would be given to that son.

Education began early. After two years at the village school I was entrusted to the private teacher to prepare for my entrance into the Lycée of Bastia. The discipline there was a military one professors imbued with ultramontane principles. I followed the courses as far as Rhetoric—after that was sent to Ajaccio for Rhetoric and Philosophy. Humanities completed, time had come to see what course in life I was to take. To the surprise of my school associates at the age of nineteen I entered the Grand Seminary of Ajaccio, Father Santani, O.M.I., Superior.

For the first few months I felt very happy to find that I had devoted myself to the service of God. After a while I began to think that I could do still more for God in that service. The desire of foreign missions with the hope of martyrdom appeared to me as a higher calling. On a promenade with the students, talking of the most excellent way to please God, someone said that the religious life was more pleasing to God than the missionary one, even with the looked-for martyrdom. To go to foreign missions in search of martyrdom is a life of an adventurer taking risks indeed, but yet man has control of his free will. And free will is the only thing that man has as his own and the only thing then he can offer to God, for everything else, body, health, fortune, is in God's hands. "Then religious life is what I must have," I said to myself.

In the second year of my Grand Seminary, my mother died. She was the strongest tie that kept me in the world, having lost my father before. I made my desires known to my director Father Semeria who did not pay much attention to them.[1] The third year my desire to join a Religious Order grew stronger but my director said that I was necessary to my family. Being the oldest of the boys, I could not leave them. In my fourth year in the Seminary already ordained Deacon I asked my director to pronounce whether I had a religious vocation or not. "You have," he said, "What Order do you choose?" "The one having a special devotion to the Blessed Virgin." "All the different orders do that. The Oblates are enrolled under the banner of Mary Immaculate. Will that be your choice?" "It is. When may I leave?" "The Oblate Father who preached the Seminarians' retreat is to leave within a week for Marseilles." "With him shall I go." Writing my adieu to my people in Santa Lucia, I was off.

In November 1878, I was at the Novitiate of Notre Dame de L'Osier. Father Gandor, Master of Novices, would send one of the novices to spend the recreation with them.[2] Without their knowing I would learn from them all the ways and rules of the house. One night we had a heavy fall of snow about two feet. Father Gandor thinking that such a sight would discourage me, coming from Ajaccio where occasionally a little flurry of snow comes in the morning disappearing at the first rays of the sun, came to my room and said, "We have some snow." "Yes," I remarked, "it is really beautiful and I like it." He left my room, as he felt assured that nothing could frighten such a type. On the 8th of December, feast of the Immaculate Conception, I received the habit, and then the novices looking at me as their confidant and adviser because I was deacon and older than the majority of them, would tell me their little troubles, getting words of encouragement.[3] Our Novice Master had a severe appearance and his scrutinizing eyes could almost read our hearts. Not the least infraction of the rules or discipline was unnoticed. Many times I was cut and the novices did not spare me at the Culpa, but our sympathetic Master would excuse me, attributing my mistakes to ignorance of the rules.[4] A new novice coming from Seminary of Frejus was admitted to the Novitiate in the absence of Father Gandor. At the return of the Father this novice was so frightened by his cold appearance that he said to me, "If I knew that such was the Master of Novices, I would not have come to this house." Being at that time the admonitor, I told him, "Consider all that as Providential.[5] If you had found a charming Master you might have remained in the Novitiate for the sake of him, but now if you persevere, it will be for God and for your soul, without any other consideration."

On the 8th of December, feast of the Immaculate Conception, I made my perpetual vows and was sent to Autun to finish my theology and receive priestly ordination.

But I was not very long there. The French Government was about to put in force the laws regarding the expulsion of religious. The Superiors were planning how to protect the members of their Community and the property against the gendarmes. I happened to say, "Give us guns, and protection will be assured." A few days after, I received my obedience for British Columbia. To prevent severe criticism from those of my people who were ready to accuse religion of cruelty and of ingratitude, I went to Corsica to see and to console those who had made so many sacrifices for my education. From there I went to Paris to see the Superior General, Father Fabre. On June 6, 1880, I left Havre on the SS. *Gascoigne,* with F. F. D. [sic] Chiappini and a novice. After thirteen days we landed at New York, took the train for San Francisco, where we waited for five days in the Arch-Alemany Palace for the boat which was to take us to Victoria.[6] The small side-wheeler boat on a choppy sea rolled us up for five days, trying severely the endurance of my two seasick companions.

We landed in Victoria the capital of B.C., which then had a population of 5800.[7] I did not find the Bishop at home, but the Fathers from Belgium and Holland, stationed there, were very kind to us during the three days spent with them.[8] From there another small boat brought us to New Westminster on the Fraser River on the 26th of July, 1880, just a month after leaving France. Bishop D'herbomez welcomed us very affectionately. We were there only a few days. St. Mary's Mission, 40 miles east on the Fraser River, was our destination. Rev. Father Carion, the Superior, was to be our Professor of Theology.[9] Fathers Enger, Chirouse, and Martin were good to us.[10] There was a school for the boys and from them I learned some English vocabulary, especially when they quarrelled, which happened often enough. Brother Devries [sic], formerly captain of the boats on the Fraser, was their teacher.[11] There was also a school for the girls under the direction of the Sisters of St. Ann.[12] Between the two institutions was the parish church where the farmers of the neighbourhood white or Indian gathered on Sundays. Two Brothers attended to the garden and nice orchard. Our kind teacher Father Carion at the request of Bishop D'herbomez would give us occasional holidays which we enjoyed in hunting and fishing, but when the haying season came we were at work in the fields. On one occasion one of the boys, be-

ing sent to the house to get the lunch, came back with the pot empty.
Asked why, he answered that when coming with the bucket full the
horse balked [*sic*] him off and spilled the contents and now the pot is
good only for a hole in the bottom! When the salmon season came, we
hooked them and brought them home to salt and to cure in barrels for
the winter; we thought it to be a good apprenticeship for missionary life,
earning our living after the example of St. Paul. The day of seriousness
had come after a silent retreat. On Passion Sunday 1881, Father Chiappini and I were ordained priests and, the brother-novice-Deacon-by
Bishop D'herbomez.[13] Our obediences were not slow in coming, Father
Chiappini left for Okanagan and I for Kamloops.

The little white village of Kamloops was built on the south side of the
confluence of the South and the North Thompson Rivers. The village
was composed of two hotels, two stores, a blacksmith shop and a few
Chinese huts. The Indian Camp with about 30 houses and a church and
a day-school was on the opposite side, farms and gardens extending
along the North Thompson to the foot of St. Paul Mountain. The Mission was located three miles west of the white village on the Thompson
River. I found there Father Lejac [LeJacq], Superior, Father Edward
Peytavin and Brother Surel living in a log house 24 × 32. The Sisters of
St. Ann had a nice boarding school for white and halfbreed girls; a con-
struction started to be a school for the boys. Mass was said in the Sisters'
Chapel where the white people of Kamloops came Sundays, Father
Peytavin officiating. Father LeJacq when home went to the Indian Camp
for Sundays.

The carpenters building the boys' school were first class mechanics. I
saw the opportunity of making myself useful and learning the trade,
which has been of great help to me everywhere I went, building houses,
schools, church and hospitals. All the spare time I had was spent with
the carpenters or with Brother Surel in his new garden and orchard. But
learning the Indian language and going with Father LeJacq to some of
the camps was my principal occupation. When the two Fathers were absent I had to say Mass and preach in English to the whites on Sunday.
Though possessing very little English I dared to speak, not always knowing myself what I was saying. On one Saturday wishing to finish a piece
of work that the carpenters had left undone, I cut my thumb so badly I
did not know if I should say Mass wearing a bandage before the whites.
But having some tincture of arnica I applied it all during the night and in
the morning the bleeding had stopped and the wound had closed,
though I shall carry the scar to the grave.[14] That gave rise to the rumor
that I was a doctor, and from that time whites and Indians came for
medicines. We had no doctor in the district at that time. Having quite
often to replace Father LeJacq in Kamloops' Indian Camp, the young

men became very attached to me. Perhaps because of my being young they offered me beautiful horses and asked me to run races with them and at times seeing that I liked a particular horse they would present it to me. My home-coming with a new horse gave Brother Surel great pleasure for it meant that he had a horse to plow and to haul the waggon [*sic*] he himself had constructed. The boys would also bring a fresh milch [*sic*] cow to help our new mission and school. In a word, the Kamloops Indians were doing their best to make my life pleasant. On Sunday the church floor was covered with roses filling it with sweet perfume. That would not say that they were without defects, which forced me to administer severe reprimands and chastisements. Gambling was prevalent. Bernard, the one most attentive to the priest, supplying fire-wood and water, always ready to do work around the house, asked me for the use of a saddle for a few days to go to the next camp. He came back after a week but without the saddle and explained that he lost it in gambling; that he had even gone so far as to gamble his own person! Being a slave he could not return until the winner (his master) had a dream in which he found himself trampling the blood of Christ and realizing that Bernard being baptized was sealed with the precious blood, he ordered him to leave the camp at once.

Living in that log house mentioned above, used for kitchen, study and bedroom was not very good for my lungs, though I would often run outside, even in a temperature of 20 below, for fresh air. My health began to fail, and when Father Martinet Visitor of the Vicariate came to Kamloops he ordered me to go to Okanagan Mission for a complete rest.[15] The distance between the two places was about 200 miles. Losing my trail and my horse not being shod it took me five days, reaching the Mission on a Sunday afternoon. Father Chiappini being alone was glad to see me. He had announced to the whites a week's instructions for the Jubilee and just now he had a sick call.[16] In his difficulty he said, "If I send you on that sick call I would be blamed, since you are ordered to rest; it is better to have you preach and I will go." "Adsum," I answered.

Father Chiappini returned on the fifth day and everything went well. After two months of rest, and feeling well, I returned to Kamloops. The school for the boys was opened with Father LeJeune in charge. An Indian from Nicola Valley came to take a priest for the son of the chief, Johnny Tziliktza, who was dying. As none of the Fathers could go, I decided to go, taking some medicine with me. I covered the distance in one day, over fifty miles, heard the confession of the boy sick with pneumonia. On the following morning I wanted to go back but the older brother said; "You cannot go, your horse is dead. Stay here until we see what effect the medicine will have." I consented to stay on condition that they would give me a good horse and guide to explore the country.

This they promised to do. Coming back to the sick man in the night, I found the people rejoicing because he was much improved. "Tomorrow we will give a horse with which you can make ten miles an hour." So it happened. Father LeJacq was pleased to hear of my success as a doctor of soul and body, and sent me on another sick call to Fountain, and Lillooet, some hundred and fifty miles. The messenger having waited we travelled together, arriving on the evening of the third day. Fifteen people had already died of the influenza and many more were dying. Getting off the horse my first visit was for the Catechism Hall where the dead son of the chief was lying on the floor surrounded by people praying and crying. After some prayers I told the people to have confidence for the priest, Christ's representative, was with them and in the morning by the offering of Mass, Jesus Himself would be with them. I instructed them that those who were sick should stay in bed, as I would see all after Mass. What was my surprise to see so many skeleton-like forms standing in church, for everyone young and old, well and sick, wanted to attend. From that day nobody died in the camp and the sick quickly recovered. After fifteen days of Instructions I left the camp in a happy and healthy condition.

From Fountain I went to another small village at the foot of Pavillion Mountain the following day as I turned around to preach I saw a large number of the Fountain people coming in. Afterwards I asked what had brought them there. They answered: "When we went to the church to pray and saw the Tabernacle locked and you not there, we could not pray but cried; and that is why we came here to assist at Mass once more and see you." It was in this district that two years before this Father Chirouse was brought to court by some of the white people, who were jealous of the influence of the priest and opposed to his efforts to stamp out the immorality of some wicked white settlers among the Indians of Fountain. Father Chirouse was accused of inflicting a severe punishment upon a woman of the tribe guilty of immoral conduct.[17] I had occasion to meet some of those same white people and I did not hesitate to tell them what I thought of them when they praised me for my success in stopping the "flu." The Indians were not the only ones to profit of the visit of the priest through the district. White people had the opportunity to approach the Sacraments when Mass was offered in their houses. I went also to another small camp called Highbar perched on the brink of a precipice on the high bank of the Fraser River, visited long before this by Father LeJacq. There the Indians told me an amusing story of this missionary. A white settler had said that he was to slap the Father when he would come around. They reported this threat to Father LeJacq at his next visit. Father told the Indians; "Come along with me to that white man." When there, Father said: "I come to receive that slap which you proposed giving me." The poor man excused himself and showed great kindness to the Father! There is nothing so effective with the adversaries of religion as to face them. As a rule they are cowards when standing before one of persuasion and courage though they may talk much in a crowd with no one to oppose them.

Returning to Kamloops I gave an account of my trip to Father LeJacq who said; "You had easy success with people practically well disposed, many of them good Christians. Now go to the wilds with the pagan Indians, matters may not be so pleasant." There I went, calling first at the camp of Tziliktza Johnny, the boy cured almost miraculously of pneumonia. His brother Alexander and a few others received me cordially but the rest of the camp still half pagan and influenced by Indian medicine men did not seem disposed to accept Christian teachings though they followed the Instructions I gave in a house, there being no church yet in the camp. The seed was cast the future will tell whether it took root. To show his gratitude Johnny gave me his own saddle horse, considered the best in the district and for which he even refused big money from white people anxious to buy it. Alexander his brother put silver spurs on my heels. When hesitating to accept them, he said; "If you do not want to take the risk of camping outdoors, you must have them." I found the truth of that some days after when caught in a dark night with snow on the ground. I saw a light at a distance and wanted to go to it but my horse facing a creek would not advance. Remembering the silver spurs I applied them and in one jump he cleared the creek, and we arrived in safety.

Accompanied by Alexander as a guide, I stopped the first night at Laurent Guichon's house, where I gave these good people an opportunity they seldom had to approach the Sacraments. Next call was at the large camp of Indians at Douglas Lake. It was already getting dark. The young men knowing the case of Johnny Tziliktza came around me took charge of my horse and gave me supper. Right after, a big man whom I took for an Indian doctor brought me to the largest house which was filled at once by the people and said in very eloquent style: "Men of this camp, listen and understand how thankful we should be to have with us a learned man who knows everything about heaven and earth. He is the light to shine in our dull eyes and tell us what we must know. Explain to us why white people build churches. Is not the earth with the canopy of heaven more pleasing to the Great Spirit who fills the world than all the churches?"

"Surely" I answered "and churches are not built for the Great Spirit but for us poor men. If I would tell what you want to know on the outside, when speaking to the people many would be looking at somebody passing by or at the dogs barking and not pay attention to my speech;

but in a church all eyes and ears would watch me and learn good things.
That is why churches are built." All the audience approvingly exclaimed, "Ah! Ah!" His second question was: "Why jails?" Answer:
"When your dog steals or bites, you tie him up so he cannot steal or bite
any more, so the white people confine in jail any man who does harm,
that people may not be annoyed and peace disturbed by the wicked
ones." "Ah! Ah!" Third question: "Are there any Spirits presiding over
created things, human, animals and plants; are they good and bad
spirits?" Answer: "Before making man God created Angels all of them
good, beautiful, intelligent. After a while some of them thought themselves equal to God and refused to obey Him and those were cast away
and thrown in the big fire where they are to stay forever. And those are
the bad spirits now jealous of the good men destined to take the place
they have lost by disobedience." "Ah! Ah!" Fourth question: "What
Spirit is in me?" I saw at once the trap in which he was hoping to catch
me. I could not say that the good Spirit was in him if I did he would say:
"Having charge of this camp I can look after it and you are not
needed."If I would answer the bad Spirit is in you he would have jumped
on me being such a big man convinced of his strength and the support of
the people. The audience, no matter how numerous, was waiting for the
answer. Then I looked at my watch and said: "It's getting up past
twelve." and with my elbow making sign to the boys around me: "Let us
go to bed, tomorrow we will have time to talk again." The boys saying,
"Father is tired," left the room and the rest followed.

Providence helping, I had the tact to win the affection of the young
men who sympathized with me, being young like myself, and they
showed me kindness in this instance, knowing that the old Indian Doctor did not like my presence in the camp. Tired and uncertain of what
good could be accomplished when these Indians looking more like
brutes than men I rolled in and let the morrow be what it may. It was not
very long when violent knocks shook the door fastened from the inside. I
heard a voice: "Leave that door alone, the priest is sleeping." "If I cannot get in by the door, I shall by the window." Close to me there was an
axe and I had my mind made up that if anyone would show his head he
was not to get in. The intruder went, and I learned in the morning that
the son of the Medicine Man was the guilty one.

In the morning, looking for a decent place where I could say Mass, I
was startled by the tramping of the horses. Going outside I saw my Indian doctor on horseback in paint and feathers, leading all the camp in
the same style, evidently on the warpath passing by where I was, to show
me I suppose his greatness and power. I saw then that it would be a
waste of time to stay there any longer, hoping better for the future. My
guide, Alexander Tziliktza looked disheartened and without many

words brought my horse and so we left for the next camp.

We landed there about four o'clock. It was snowing and getting dark, being the month of November. The canine family announced our coming by loud barking, likely displeased by our intrusion. One after the other the men getting out from their wigwams—as there were no houses or tents to be seen—surrounded me. I stood on my horse so that everybody could see and hear me, showing myself bigger than any of them and independently said: "I heard what you said in this camp, that the priest did not want to stay with you because he does not care for you, or he is afraid of you, and goes direct to white people. Now I will show you that I care for you and am not afraid. I will stay with you if you offer me a wigwam " I waited for an invitation, still standing on my horse. Then an old man said: "Here is my wigwam for you." I came down from my horse, went inside, spread my horse blanket on the ground and fixed the saddle for a pillow. They gave me something to eat and left me alone. Once more I was planning a programme for the following day. I could not sleep and so I said the Rosary.[18] About midnight a man came to me in the dark and whispered: "I do not belong to this camp and I am a Catholic. There is a young man dying, do you want to see him?" Up at once I was brought to a boy of about sixteen in the last stage of consumption, prepared him and fearing that he would die at any moment baptized him—first reward for my trip. Close to there I could hear a noise like a band of coyotes barking. As there were no wigwams around I asked my Catholic guide where the barking was coming from. He said: "There is a Kicoule [sic] house under the ground, they are having the great potlatch" (distribution of blankets and food by a rich proud man aspiring to be chief). I went back to my wigwam and found the fire had nearly gone out. After a while a man came and spread his overcoat over me thinking that I was asleep. I wanted to see that benefactor but before daylight he had taken the overcoat. Seeing no prospect to do any good for the present I accepted in the morning the offer of an Indian living not far from there to go with him to a comfortable house where I could say Mass, instruct and baptize the children. Being told that a Spaniard, named Garcia Crasus, was living a little distance from there with his family, I went to say Mass on Sunday. The Mass was attended by a few Catholics among them a Portuguese who exclaimed: "Thanks be to God; I heard 'Dominus Vobiscum' and believed myself back in my country Portugal from where I came twenty-five years ago!" Shortly after, Crasus located a coal mine, now the city of Merritt.[19] His daughters after that were educated at the Sisters' School in Kamloops. Many a time I invoked the remark of the Portuguese to prove the wisdom of the church in saying Mass in Latin.[20]

The Coldwater Indians hearing of my presence in the Valley came for me. I spent ten days with them organizing the camp, a mixture of Catholics and pagans. As the weather was very cold we had to live in the Kicoule [*sic*] house with nineteen families in it. To describe a building of that kind: the ground was dug four or five feet deep, poles placed in a circular form with an inclination to represent a cone with an opening in the top for entrance and ventilation, going in by a strong pole with notches used for step-ladder. The outside was lined with bark from the trees and a layer of dirt making the walls impermeable to rain and wind. How could we expect to smell rose perfume? On the 8th of December the altar linen was far from being snow-white, as I said Mass every day for the nine days I was there. My poor pony who for the nine days had been pawing through the snow to get the scanty grass around the camp could scarcely stand on his feet. Besides being very cold, frost had formed around his eyes so that he could not see the trail covered with snow. Every time I think of it I reproach my cruelty to the horse in urging him through. Reaching the hotel Koutly I was warmly received by the owner and family, all Catholics. They were surprised that I was not frozen having only ordinary clothing when travellers with fur coats were touched by the frost. From there I visited an Indian camp not far off but found no Catholics except a few who had been baptized years ago in other camps by missionaries passing by.[21] Pagans as they were and living as such in polygamy and superstitions of all kinds, what could I do? When teaching them catechism, they enjoyed that as far as I spoke of the goodness of the Supreme Creator, but as soon as I exposed his Justice and the punishment of Hell there was nothing heard but "Hist! Hist! You must have come from there since you know so much about it." But as I said above some had been in Catholic camps and heard of the Incarnation of Our Lord and a woman had a church in the town with an opening in the roof through which the Great Spirit was expected to come to incarnate in her. Every morning when I rang the little Mass bell she would blow the horn calling the people to their meetings. Having asked to see the old chief who was dying I found him lying down well surrounded by Indian doctors performing their incantations. I told his son who had given me marks of affection if he would not have me to prepare his dying father to go to heaven; but the lad, afraid of the doctors, did not say a word. The chief of Coldwater, Paul, who had followed me, was there behind the Medicine men. As he understood their language and what they were saying he was making me signs to go away from the tent. Seeing that nothing could be done I left and Paul coming with me said: "It was Providential that you went, for the four Medicine men were to kill you right there." The camp is now Catholic, having a nice church. I then took trail towards Suspension Bridge and being alone and getting dark I saw a light through the woods, made for it and knocked at the door. An old man with long white whiskers seeing that I was a priest greeted me in French. After prayer, he told me that he had not seen a priest for thirty years, but always said his prayers. "Tomorrow I will say Mass for you and it is advisable for you to make your confession and prepare for Communion."[22] "We will leave that for your next visit,"he replied. I told him, "God sends you a priest now, profit by the occasion, for you or I may die at any time." After Mass and Communion I left my old Frenchman in tears of joy and gratitude. When returning to Kamloops by way of Savona's Ferry three weeks after, a letter announced his death.

Father LeJacq was glad to see me back after 3 months and attend for him the sick calls on Shushwap [Shuswap] and Adams Lakes. In July when the days were hot and the sandy roads dusty to spare myself and more so my horse I would leave in the evening travel all night till about two o'clock in the night getting off from the saddle and rolling the long rope of the horse to my arm he would have an hour of grazing and I sleeping. And [the horse] going too far for more grass pulling the rope woke me up and then on the trot to my destination attend my sick person, giving the Sacraments, encourage all around and in the evening start again for Kamloops, depending on my unusual horse, gift of Johnny Tziliktza of Nicola to find the trail. When uncertain if I was on the right one when at different crossings, the horse would hesitate to go. I had only to throw the reins on his neck and soon he was on the trot in the right one.

In August 1883, Father Lacombe wrote that the missionaries of Alberta had been attending the construction camps of the Canadian Pacific Railway but the missionaries of B.C. should attend to them as the said camps were now extending in their Province and had the responsibility of them. Father LeJacq told me: "Here is your field of labor go to it."I went on, my first stop was Eagle Pass. No construction work there yet except surveyors and engineers' camps locating the best pass for the R.R.R. [*sic*] but there was much activity on the part of the forerunners of the men to be employed on construction consisting in gamblers, whisky sellers and toughs of every description. Saloons and dens of all sort were going up waiting for the railway builders to come with their wages and spend the last dollar they would earn at the cost of so many hardships. Those saloons keepers lived by preying upon the navvies who might appear amongst them on pay day and get drunk. The expression "rolling" was well known, originating from the practice of rolling around a drunk man, incapable of protecting himself. His pockets were searched and anything of value taken from him. I had difficulty in finding a bed for the night, and when I was in, a drunk man came to lay down in it. Alarm was given in the middle of the night. Fire! Fire! Glad to see the morning light so that I could get out of such an inferno.

Things were better when I came to the construction camps. If there were men who would dissipate and throw their money away, the majority of the men in those camps were coming from good Catholic families anxious to earn enough to send their cheques to their parents. I would write their letters and enclose the cheques before they were cashed, that was a part of my work. Saving money and souls.

The contractors were glad to see me offering hospitality in their offices and tables, but prefered to stay with the men in the bunk houses, giving me the opportunity to speak to them, say the evening prayer with them, give instruction, hear confessions until midnight, say Mass at five and give communion, everything over at 6, ready for breakfast and go to work at 7. When Mass & Communion was for the cooks it was offered at three, giving them ample time for their work. On Sundays we had high mass at 9 o'clock, men coming from the surrounding camps. The men [built] the altar at the foot of large trees with 200 assisting. To not annoy the contractor, I would never keep the men from being on time for work. Never remained in camp more than three days though asked to stay longer. Going from camp to camp I very seldom missed Mass. At Rogers Pass, where I was calling often on account of the many men employed in rock work, the buildings were carried off in the following spring by avalanches of tremendous force and power bringing along trees and immense rocks. The continual blasting was the cause of it. Glaciers which had never moved from their rocky beds above the clouds came down with a tremendous roaring; by the pressure of the air one of those avalanches not touching the ground below of the valley rose up many hundred feet on the other side burying a construction train with 19 men. At times I had to encourage some of the young surveyors afflicted with nostalgia, coming to their meals they would put their elbows on the table, their heads in their hands and not eat: "See young men, in a few months the construction work will be over and, returning to your homes in the East, the glory of opening a new world shall be yours. I am young as you are and the work over I have to remain in this Province without any praises to my address and yet I am happy as a man doing good should be." One thing worth mentioning was so few accidents. The handling of the explosives were in charge of experienced men, but the mountain fever or rather typhoid was prevalent. Small hospitals were crowded here and there, giving the patients all possible help. The Medical Department was under Doctors Orton and Brett with a staff of young doctors visiting the camps regularly trying to keep down disease caused by dampness and bad sanitation.[23]

In the fall of 1883, tracks were laid as far as Donald [which] was expected to be the divisional point of the railway. There were the offices and residences of the principal officials of the company, with a good hotel. A little farther west on the same flat, saloons and stores were operating. Trains ran regularly loaded with supplies and men from the East for the camps in the west. There must have been a population of 300 souls, carpenters, engineers, electricians, track men etc living in shacks, tents or in box cars. Mass was said in any of those habitations according to people wanting to have it. One afternoon there was some excitement; the track men declared a strike. A train loaded with gravel was on the main track and a freight with passengers was due in the evening. I was asked to speak to the men, which I did, but they complained of not being paid for the past month and would not work unless settled at once. I assured them that settlement would be made soon, but by wasting time their cheque would be only smaller on the next pay day, that the company had no desire to defraud them of their dues. The Mounted Police came also to speak to the men having heard of threats to set fire to the station under construction, but what could five or six police do in a crowd of desperatos [*sic*]? I showed the harm they were doing to themselves: striking would deprive them of return tickets to go East and going in their own account how costly it would be. After a moment of silence one said: "I am willing to go to work if the others consent." "Go on," I said to him "the others will follow," and the same evening the cars were unloaded, men singing at their work. That made the foreman, a Protestant, say: "I would rather have a priest at my side, in time of trouble, than a general of army."

In Donald I taught catechism to the children preparing for their first Communion.[24] Among others I had the McDonald and McKenzie children to instruct. Met them years after, always proving grateful and affectionate to me and to the Church. After occupying positions in railways ownership, McKenzie [Mackenzie] and Dan [Donald] Mann, constructors on the C.P.R. became railway magnates building roads of their own in many parts of the world.

The little town of Golden at the foot of the Rocky Mountains on the Kicking Horse River kept me busy for many days, having there besides the railway men the employees of a large sawmill under the management of the Carlin Brothers.

The name of Kicking Horse given to that portion of the tote road between Field and Golden during construction came from the number of accidents to men travelling on horse back. There the famous Doctor Hector exploring the Pass with a party of Indians was kicked by a wild horse breaking several ribs and rendering him unconscious.[25] The Indians thinking him dead had dug a grave. When burying him they saw the signs of life and restored him to consciousness. Another accident was [that] of H. S. Holt a prominent engineer.[26] Ahead of his party and seeing his horse slipping [he] managed to dismount but then the horse hit him in the chest knocking him over the side of a precipice about 60 feet perpendicular to the river below. Rolling down he was caught in a dead tree. His party lowered to Mr. Holt a lariat which he tied under his arms and they pulled him up. Many other horse kicked there for the last time.

The construction camps at Field and Logan through the Rocky Mountain were closing down, only the men occupied with the balasting of the tracks were left. Gave me the opportunity to visit what families were located there and I went to Canmore, almost a town, the trains coming that far regularly from the East. The hotel was kept by a Catholic family whose kindness I can never forget. The parlor was turned into a chapel and Mass was said every morning for the many glad to assist. There was a large crucifix, and a statue of the Blessed Virgin, and coming from the pagan West where the emblems of religion were seldom seen I believed myself in heaven. From there I visited the Sanatorium at Banff owned by Doctor Brett whose guest I was. He put a horse at my disposition to see the surroundings. Rheumatic cases had already come there, among them some Catholics glad to have the priest with them. Calgary was nearer to me than Kamloops, where I could renew my supplies for Mass. Father Lacombe received me very cordially. It was at his instigation that I was in charge of the construction camps.

Calgary built on the bank of the Elbow River was promising to be a big town. The Catholics had there already a little chapel and a priest house, a large school under the direction of the Faithful Companions of Jesus,[27] and a splendid hospital under the management of the Grey Nuns.[28] Practical lessons Father Lacombe gave me. When in the chapel reading our office, the door bell ringing, Father went. Coming back it would not be long that another ring would call him up. I could not help but remark: "What meant all these ringings, and continual going?" He answered: "Are you in this country for your comfort or for the people? Those people are newcomers in town and come to the priest for information or to ask for a letter of introduction to get work. Could I hesitate to help them?" From that I took the resolution to act the same; I believe I did and have been well repaid for it. It might be well to note here of what help Father Lacombe was to the C.P.R. When the construction advanced on the prairies around Calgary, the Blackfoot Indians armed, stopped the men who did not care to face the guns.[29] Father Lacombe wired to Van Horne manager of the C.P.R. to send a car load of flour and beef. When the car arrived Father Lacombe called the Indians to come and help themselves, saying: "This is what the Railway will bring to the country; why then wish to prevent its coming?" And the work went on, thanks to Father Lacombe. He was considered as a great friend of the C.P.R. and always treated as such.

My repeated visits to Calgary gave me the opportunity to meet nearly all the missionaries of Alberta. I thought myself very small in company of Fathers Lestanc, Leduc, André, Doucet, [and] Legal, afterwards a successor of Bishop Grandin, who assisted at his consecration in St. Albert.[30]

In November 1884, I was on my way to Kamloops when a heavy fall of snow blocked the road and I had to stop at Rogers Pass. I was living in a box car with the telegraph operator for many days. The tremendous avalanches roaring at night kept us from sleeping fearing that at any moment we might be blown away. By good chance orders were given for a number of men to come to clear the road for the special train of the principal directors of the C.P.R. coming to drive the golden spike announcing the completion of the road. It was on November 7, 1884 at the point called Craigellachie that the last rails from the East and West were laid and Donald Smith seized the sledge hammer to drive the spike which united the Dominion of Canada from ocean to ocean. There were present James Ross manager of construction, Van Horne C.P.R. president, James Dickey, Dominion Engineer.

From there Kamloops once more. The Railway construction being over, I would have to attend only to what people took charge of the stations and little towns started along the Selkirks and the Rockies, but travelling was now on trains and once in a while on hand cars or speeders. Revelstoke, Donald, Golden and Field were the most important points of my visits. During construction the spiritual field was left to me, but as soon as trains were running then ministers of different sects were about. One of them came to me saying: "Are you Father Coccola?" "Yes that is what is left of my name." "I praise you for the work you have done in the mountains, but I must say that no matter what country we go, we find the priest ahead of civilization and Christianity. Only this I find strange in your church is the celibacy. When I was not married [I] had experienced hesitation of the people towards me, but after I was married was welcome everywhere." I remarked: "You praised me for the work done; how could I do it if married? I had to be with sick or dying of tyfoid [*sic*] and smallpox; how could I go after that to my family and bring the germs? It would be cruelty and injustice. Then you see one of the two had to be neglected, the work or the family. Leaving aside St Paul, Napoleon who had a good knowledge of human nature said that his best generals were unmarried. The married ones when the bugle called to march would hesitate thinking of their family but [those] not married would lead their men to victory or death. I see what is your point that man cannot live without the woman; here is a comparison. When a man is not in the habit of smoking he does not care for it or has a disgust for it, but the man who has the habit, if he has the misfortune to forget his pipe he will borrow the pipe of his friend." The minister left me alone never to speak to me.

When I returned to Kamloops my Superior Father LeJacq said: "Whites and Indians at Enderby, Armstrong and even Vernon had no priest for some time, will you go to them?" Off I was, this time on sleighs. [It] turning very cold had to camp at the first roadhouse, 40 miles; other travellers had to do the same. For three days no one could face the north wind. There was only one stove in the house and a man froze his toe in bed. A change in the weather came and we were all on the road. Calling on the farmers and seeing many children growing without education, I offered the parents to send them to our schools in Kamloops but prizing their cattle more than the children, though white people, said "we have no time having to attend to the stock." I offered to take them myself on my sleigh, and on my way back I had a full load to the agreeable surprise of the Sister Superior of the convent of St. Ann. In the last 4 years what transformation in the Okanagan Valley, with the beautiful orchards replacing the wild sedge fields, and the prosperous town of Vernon. Vernon was called formerly: Priest Valley. When the Oblate Fathers came to locate in the Interior [they] picked up that point, but after exploring of the country did not find it central enough and moved not far from where Kelona [Kelowna] is at present. Father Richard and Pandosy were the first priests in that new location. Father Pandosy died in giving a mission in Penticton but was brought back and buried at the mission. At our regret the mission land was sold but the beautiful church dedicated to Marie Immaculate built by Father Carion at the blessing of which I took part is still in existence.[31]

In September 1887 I was in Golden growing to be a nice town with a population of 300 souls requiring my spiritual attention. Mass was celebrated in a large apartment of Green's Hotel until a church could be built. Received there a letter from Father LeJacq calling for my return to Kamloops where our beloved Vicar Bishop D'herbomez had come wishing to see me without delay, stating that something under the wind was not pleasing. What could it be? the anticipating pleasure of seeing the Bishop prevented any consideration. When landing in Kamloops in the night I went to my room and found Father Bedard in my bed. Then realized that I was to be transferred. To where I did not stop to guess. In the morning the Bishop handed me the letter of obedience, watching what impression the reading of it would make on me: "I send you to Kootenay, St. Eugene Mission, and you have to start as soon as possible."

"Will tomorrow be soon enough?" I remarked.

"No I want you with me for a while. No matter what is said about St.

Eugene, the Indians on the warpath at present, it is a nice mission with a great future."

"I do not mind what it is or what it shall be. You send me there, and there I shall go; it is not the country that makes a man, but it is the man who makes the country."

"The two Fathers Fouquet and Richard have been there a long time and need a change. Father Baudre will go with you as Superior and you will be in charge on the missions."[32]

The white people of Kamloops at the eve of my departure expressed their regrets in a beautiful address and presented as a reminder of their affection a costly watch. Golden was our nearest point by rail to St. Eugene, but from there it was 200 miles away. Getting off the train what was our disappointment to learn that navigation was closed for the season, the water in the Columbia River being very low. Inquiries were made to get horses and guide, so to go by trail. No one would venture to go to cover the distance through a bad trail. After three days, a family of Shuswap Indians who years ago immigrated to Columbia Lake came to Golden to sell their furs. I spoke to them in their language saying that I came from Kamloops to go to St. Eugene Mission and asked them to take the two priests. "We have only one horse to spare and we will take you as far as our camp 100 miles and from there the Kootenay Indians will bring you to the mission." I wired to Bishop D'herbomez who answered to send Father Baudre to Kamloops and go alone.

What a trail and what a bill of fare for the three days: porcupine cold meat boiled a week ago, bannock baked of long date and tea. Though hungry I could not swallow but a little of it, enough to keep me alive. We reached the village on Columbia Lake on Saturday. What a joy for the 8 families to hear me speaking their language and giving fresh news of their friends of Kamloops and Shuswap camps. All came to the Sacraments and would have been glad to keep me for a few days, but on Sunday afternoon Captain Wood of the Mounted Police going to the Barracks at Fort Steele handed me a telegram urging me to go ahead without delay.[33]

The Shuswap hearing that I was to look after the Kootenays pitied me. Twelve miles farther North there was a camp of the Kootenays and I was hoping that some of them would come to take me for the rest of the journey but none showing up on Monday I told the people there that I had to go. They said: "We have done our share of the work now is the duty of the Kootenays to do the balance." I asked then where was the road? and I left on foot alone. Then the Shuswap jumped on their horses with one for me to ride and we went to Baptiste Morijeau's farm with a large family and induced his father-in-law to give me a horse and take me to the mission.

Major Steele with whom I was well acquainted during the construction of the C.P.R. and who knew the influence of the priest in the strikes of the working men had, with his hundred mounties, gone over some weeks ago and had told the few white settlers along the way frightened by the uprising of the Indians: "Do not fear, a Priest is coming behind who will have order established." Those whites would watch me coming to see what kind of man I was. Trusting my guide I followed him across the Kootenay and St. Mary's River at moon light, and after nine we knocked at the mission door. Fathers Fouquet and Richard were glad to see me but disappointed to see only one priest when two were expected to replace both. Told them my difficulties and that they should be glad to see one. Father Fouquet did not waste time, profiting by my guide and horse to go by the road I had just covered.

Father Richard though desolate at first reconciled himself with circumstances. The question came: who is the Superior? I said: "You are by rule because you are the older and know all about the place." Brother John Burns about 65 years of age was very kind to me and so always was to the last. He was prospecting for gold when he joined the Oblates and meeting with all kinds of men had a good knowledge of human nature. Witty, he had a ready answer to any question or remark. Being our cook and forgetting salt in the soup I would say:

"Brother the salt must be getting dear and you are saving it."

"Well you are always so thirsty in these warm days that a salty soup would not be good for you." The next meal by mistake he put salt twice. I would remark:

"Salt is getting cheap again"

"But in this dry summer, salt will lubricate and no need to take any other physic."

The Fathers had done wonderful spiritually and materially. The Indians loved their priests and the little log church whose ceiling was of [a] big sheet of canvas flapping at all winds and allowing plenty of ventilation. In winter I had to bring the chalice to the red stove pipe to prevent freezing.[34] The log house was divided in four apartments with the interior chapel communicating with the sitting room by a large door, and an addition for kitchen and bunks for visitors superposed offered necessary comfort. A good size garden in front of the house supplied vegetables and not only for the Fathers but also for the gold miners of Wild Horse and Perry Creeks. The outside buildings consisted in a little store house, as the supplies for a year had to be secured from the American side every fall by packhorses, then stables for horses, cattle, pigs and chicken. The flour mill running by water power was close to the St. Mary's River and used for grinding the wheat of the farm and of the two neighbouring farmers. 30 acres of land under cultivation would, besides the grain, provide feed for the 15 head of cattle. There was work enough done to demonstrate to the Indians what could be got from the land. But the Kootenays were meat eaters and as long as the game would be plentiful they were not going to turn their eyes to the soil; they even considered it degradation for man to till the land. Trapping, hunting, packing for the miners or serving as guides for white hunters of big game was their occupation. By it they were earning all the money to buy ammunition, tobacco, tea, sugar and blankets so necessary to them, having not yet adopted white people's clothing. A young buck coming from across the American town [border] with costly trousers was turned in ridicule and he had to mutilate them. The Kootenays had no love for white people for the reason that the majority of those they had seen were drunkards, blasphemers, trying to corrupt the women, being themselves religiously inclined, sober and moral. On one of their gatherings, the question was: "Where are the white people coming from? not from God surely to judge by their ways of living." Then François a faithful friend of the priest remarked: "Is not the priest a white man and why is he a priest if not because his father and mother are good Christians, then there must be good white people somewhere."

What made the Kootenays good in reality but so rough and wild in their manners with their blankets and long hairs was their mode of living. Until some twenty years ago, they would [go] to hunt buffalo across the mountains at the great displeasure of the Indians of the plains and great fighting occurred then. It took four Blackfeet [Blackfoot] for a Kootenay. One of those, Joseph Nanna, who at home would not hurt a fly, finding that one of his horses had been stolen by the Blackfoot went to them to return his horse, but they only laughed at him. He located the band where the horse was; he drove the whole band keeping with his gun the Blackfoot in pursuit. Some of the Kootenays would lose their scalp or their life, but soon their friends sought their revenge; that is what gave to the Kootenays that belligerent spirit.

Persons who heard that the Buffalo was seen by millions on the prairies, wonder that not one is to be seen now, and even only a few bones may be found. The answer is that after the Indians were supplied with guns and the hides were sold to a great advantage both to Americans and Canadians the animals were slaughtered and the bones collected and thousands of tons were shipped to the sugar refineries and bone dust factories in the States. There are some herds in the Peace River which protected will increase rapidly.

Of the many whites who were in this country only a few were left. After taking from the creeks what gold they could find on the surface, and the impossibility of bringing heavy machineries [*sic*] [they] had gone back to other gold fields. What brought in now the garrison of Mounted

Police who established their quarters at Galbraith Ferry, known now as Fort Steele, named by their commander Col. S. B. Steele later promoted for distinguished services in the world war to the rank of Major-General? Remains of two white men had been found murdered on the Wild Horse-Golden trail in 1884, showing that they had been murdered at Deadman's Creek two young Kootenay Indians suspected had been arrested and locked in jail at Wild Horse. Chief Isadore infuriated that his two men had been arrested without evidences and without his knowledge went at the head of 30 of his warriors armed all though, broke open the gaol and turned the two Indians free, saying: "If it can be proved that these men are guilty, I will be the first to punish and deliver them. How many Indians have been found killed and white men were not arrested?" At the same time he (Isadore) ordered Provincial Constable Anderson who had made the arrest and Hon. F. Aylmer the judge and land surveyor to leave the country in 24 hours.

This action caused much alarm to the few scattered settlers who applied to the Provincial Department for protection. The Indians had other grievances, one of them was the sale of St. Joseph Prairie, a beautiful spot free from mosquitoes with a creek running through. The spot had been occupied from immemorial times by past generations. It was now purchased by Colonel Baker who ordered Isadore and his people to vacate it. This they flatly refused to do.

The Colonel being a member of the B.C. legislature and with much influence obtained from Ottawa the help of the Mounted Police to establish order in the Kootenays. In the fall of 1887, the police were located in their comfortable quarters at Galbraith Ferry, about 7 miles from St Eugene Mission.

My first work in coming to St. Eugene was to visit the white settlers. Colonel Baker, who in course of time proved to be a good and useful friend, had my first call and then Major Steele and his men, making arrangement with him to say Mass at the Barracks from time to time. The major ordered his men to avoid any intercallation [sic] with the Indians and things were going smoothly, but certainly the Police were an ombrage [sic] or a menace to the Indians who never went about unless well armed; even coming to church [they] had revolvers and knives at their belt, until I told them that the church was not a hunting ground, and I would not allow armed men in it. It was like burning coals under the ashes, ready to sparkle at the first wind. The Indians did not like to see me going to say Mass at the barracks, or the officers coming to spend an afternoon with me.

Having prepared some 50 children for their first Communion to take place on Corpus X [Christi], a large shelter was made of trees, a big steer killed, the children sitting around a well loaded table had breakfast with me, chiefs of different camps with their watchmen assisting.[35] After the children were through much being left on the tables I asked them to eat. All looking very happy I said: "Is not this a grand day?" "Sure it is" was the answer. "Every day for us good children of God should be like that, the presence of the mounties should not mar our happiness. The police are here only to keep order in the country and prevent white people to do you wrong or any of you to do wrong to the whites." Chief Isadore, though a good Christian and a man of good judgement remarked in a grumbling tone: "You say so because the major is your friend." Vexed at that remark so unexpected, I gave a blow on the table the dishes rattleing, [*sic*] said: "Sure the major and all his men are my friends; they call me father as you call me so. The priest takes God's place on earth who is the father of all. So must be the priest But when you say that the Major is my friend you mean that I love the police more than I do you. See when I go to the barracks my horse is taken up, fed, groomed, and when ready to leave, the horse is saddled, [and] is brought to me, but when you call me for some of your sick people, I have to have my horse ready and returning home I have to look after my horse in shape for the next sick call; and with whom do I stay, with you or with the police? So if I love any one in preference it is you. What have you to say now?" All were dumb.

Not foreseeing imminent troubles, I began the visit of the outside camps. After Easter 1888, the Shuswaps on Columbia Lake who had been so good on my way from Golden were expecting me. I found first a band of the Kootenays located at the head of the Columbia River with Mathias for chief and Tame, Captain, both faithful Catholics having strong authority upon their men. As they were scattered on farms, I told them to gather the people and coming back from the Shuswap camp I would remain with them for a few days. There were no churches in those two camps and the first work was to build them. All agreed to that and decided to collect money and buy the necessary material so that on my next visit we could start to build. Until then mass was offered in the largest house.

To reach the above camp it took days and hardship in those times. In leaving the mission we had to ford the St. Mary's and Kootenay Rivers, unbridged, cover 40 miles trail to Canal Flats, cross again the Kootenay River, climb a mountain by a rocky trail, like a step ladder, where drops of water trickling from rock to rock would form a rivulet down the valley, this being the head of the Columbia River which seen down at Portland is like a sea. The name of Canal Flats is due to the attempt, by a rich company, to divert some of the Kootenay waters into the Columbia with the prospect to make the two Rivers navigable from Golden B.C. to the United States. I had the opportunity to make use of that navigation, but the settlers along the Columbia, having their farms flooded raised complaints and after a year the canal had to be closed.

Going down the slope on the other side of the mountain the trail tapped the hot springs where Sam Brewer and his wife kept a roadhouse. Their only son they had, about 9 years old, had been baptized by a miner when at the Perry Creek Mines a fire broke out and the child badly burned was not expected to live. A few years after, I took the boy to Spokane College.[36] Ten miles from there was the first Kootenay camp under the leadership of Mathias, eight miles farther a white settlement Windermere on the Columbia Lake, the Shuswap camp on the same lake six miles west. The trail is now replaced by a national road joining B.C. to Alberta across the Rockies.

Returning to St. Eugene we were busy with the harvest, the crops on account of the drought not very good. Father Richard being a practical farmer and good gardener and depending on him for the material part of the work, I left for West Kootenay. Crossing the mountains with no one living to be seen except wolves; roasting under the sun, if not raining, during the day, and freezing at night; landed after the fourth day at Port Hill boundary line between the States and B.C. on the bank of the lower Kootenay River. We found there the family of McLoughlin, son of a doctor and governor in Oregon.[37] Well educated, married to a Kootenay woman. From him we learned where the Indian camp was to be seen across the Kootenay River. We swam our horses, and after four miles through swampy ground at the risk of getting stuck we located the camp. No houses, no tents only wigwams, made of reed-cane 5 feet long joined together like straw mats.

Found there about 80 souls. On account of the distance and the condition of the trail, the priest had not been in the camp for years, but the Indians themselves, at least the majority, would go to St. Eugene once a year for the feast of Corpus Christi. They knew some prayers, but addicted to gambling[38] their time was spent at that when forced by hunger they were not out hunting or trapping; the fishing was left to the women. No flour in the camp and consequently no bread, and not much clothing. They were glad to see the priest and the boys would bring me ducks and fish which were plentiful. With the reed-canes they fixed a place large enough for all to assist at Mass and follow the instructions. In one corner of it, I planted 4 piquets, spread my travelling tent on it and that was the altar. Underneath I fixed my bed putting saddles and other articles for the trail close to it, to keep everything from the hungry dogs. One of them came in the night to drag the pack saddle; gave him such a blow that my hand was swollen, but kept it away for good. Another night I saw the skunks around the fire I had in the wigwam eating the remains of my supper but considered it prudent to let them alone.

These people are simple, moral and well disposed towards religion, if kept away from mixing with the Americans on the other side of the boundary line. Organized the camp appointing watchmen to keep order and assist the chiefs. The head chief Sampierre is getting very old, but the sub chief Justin is energetic and promised to keep in force the regulations given.

I asked the young men: "Why are you so poor physically and financially? here is the cause. You spend your time night and day gambling and no work or prayer done. Now every night at nine blow the horn say the prayers in common go to sleep, and at 6 in the morning at the call of the horn have prayers, and work your gardens on the high ground and provide plenty [of] food for yourself and family. Save what money you make in trapping, buy cows from white settlers that your children will have milk; in a large prairie like this it will be easy to raise stock." The general impression I had of the Kootenay bottoms after looking at [the] immense acreage around, I considered that a hundred families could make a splendid living if the land was kept from flooding. Now, in September, the water had gone leaving rich pastures.

Taking advantage of the little steamer *Galena* coming from Bonner's Ferry on the Kootenay River going to the outlet of the Kootenay Lake 80 miles to a point called Kootenay Landing, and after the city of Nelson, I went to see what the place was like. Found there a city of tents. By chance I located the Latremouille family whom I had known on the construction of the C.P.R. and I had opportunity to say Mass for those willing to attend. Many mining claims were located all around waiting for capital to purchase and develop. There I met James Cronin coming from the Coeur d'Alene mining fields. Being an expert miner, he was looking for investments for American capital. The gentleman became, three years after, our partner in Moye [Moyie] Mine.

Having no communications with St. Eugene, I was anxious to see how things were. Not many days after one of the Indians, Pierre, came to the Father's house with a wild look, as a demented [man]. This is the same Pierre who two years after was the originator of the St. Eugene Mine at Moyie. Without introduction he said: "You must leave the country. Three years ago we ordered the surveyors and Provincial constable to leave and they did it or they would not be living today."

Coolly I said: "If surveyors of land and constable went, they did well. They had come here to make money and when they saw no money in sight and their life in danger they left, but for myself I have not come for money or good time but to help the Indians to live well and show them the way to heaven, and as long as there is any Indian living or myself living I shall not leave the country." "Then we will kill you." Opening by breast [and] getting vexed stood up went to him and said: "Go ahead, it is better to die than live with men like you. I have been so far taking care of your bodies and souls and you, worse than dogs, do not appreciate it; I give a bone to a dog and he licks my hand. Know this: should all the Indians come to kill me I shall not make a step back, no one can hurt me, and only one I fear, God." Pierre went telling the people outside: "That priest is an old soldier, faced many guns and can handle a gun better than any one of us. The Whites love him, the Indians fear him and God takes his word, better to let him alone." There was in the camp an old man, Allan, peaceful and a good Christian, who secretly kept me posted on the dispositions and plans of the tribes. "I fear and foresee great troubles: at the signal given, the American Indians will come from the boundary lines, Montana and Idaho joining the Kootenays and set fire to the Barracks in the night." Chief Isadore who had agreed to abandon the place occupied by the Indians in Cranbrook, Joseph Prairie, under certain conditions proposed by Major Steele and Colonel Baker, objected to [leaving] when the Colonel started to fence the whole estate in provision of selected breed of cattles to be brought in.

In May, the major sent his interpreter to Isadore with the ultimatum to vacate Joseph Prairie on the conditions proposed and accepted consisting in beautiful piece of land on the Kootenay River bank with an irrigation ditch, and that cash would be paid for what buildings the Indians had on the prairie according to [the] value estimated by arbitrors [sic] of Isadore's choice and if he refused to do so willfully he would be made to do by force. The messenger came to me asking me to go with him. I told him to go alone, but if badly received then I would go. Few minutes after, the messenger returned saying: "Isadore does not want to listen to me, that he would rather die of a bullet than to vacate." I went then, told Isadore: "The offer made to you by the major of so many acres of good land with water on it and $700.00 for your buildings in Cranbrook is very advantageous. If the mission with the church had not been built here where the soil is poor and gravellous [sic] I would go and start our mission on the spot offered to you in compensation of what Cranbrook is. You say that you would rather die of a bullet than consent, but if you refuse and open battle with the police you may easily have the best of the hundred men here, but thousands will come after them, kill and destroy your camp and before God and men you will be responsible for the destruction and blood shed by your proud obstinacy. How will you stand it?" Isadore quietly said: "You are our boss. As you say it will be done." Turning to the messenger: "Go and report to Major Steele what Isadore said." All shook hands and the troubles were over to the great satisfaction of everybody. Before leaving Kootenay with his garrison Major Steele arranged for sports on the flats of Four Mile Creek inviting all the inhabitants of the district white and red to take part in them to cause friendly feelings with the Whites and Indians. A large subscription list for prizes and refreshments was made up by the Whites. We had from Major Steele, wagon, sleighs, 2 sets of harness 3 stoves and other useful articles.

On August 7, the Mounties left for Fort Macleod and at once I wrote to the Indian Department, Ottawa to give us a boarding school for the children stating that the Indians would never after that give any trouble to the government. We had then mail once a month and very irregular. Correspondence was slow. The answer was favorable and we were asked to find a suitable location. Could not find any on the Indian reserve ground; gravelous [*sic*] and no water. Then I offered 30 acres of land near our house which could be irrigated by St. Joseph Creek flowing through. There was no lumber to build until a sawmill was erected five miles north of us. It was to take 2 years before three buildings could be completed, a central building for the staff, chapel, kitchen and dining room, the 2 other buildings on each side one for boys, the other for girls.

Now that calm and order were established we could give attention to improvements around the place. The fence of the graveyard falling down had to be renewed. No bell for the church, no belfry for it. The work on the belfry started and a 400 lb bell ordered. Money was collected for the purpose and Whites, Protestants or Catholics, willingly and generously contributed with the Indians.

Doctoring—Here I was called to play the Doctor *malgré lui* at the mining camp of Wild Horse Creek. In a row, one of the miners had the frontal bone cut by the blow of an axe, the brain protruding, pressed the brain back and by antiseptic application he was able to return to work after 4 months. Not long after the customs officer at Fort Steele had the right hand poisoned and decaying. I had to dissacate [*sic*] it and after six months new flesh covered the bones and the hand [after] being a little stiff for a while became normal. No doctors in the district I was called day and night by White or Indians in all kind of accidents and sickness. Returning home one day after having [been] called in the middle of the night to attend the only son of the manager of the North Star Mine, I was asleep on my horse when a group of men burning charcoal woke me up. I excused myself of passing by without noticing them, they said: "This does us more good than a sermon in three points." And I went on.

Tobacco Plain was the only part of my district that had not been visited yet. Found the Indians in August located on the boundary line between Montana and B.C. Their reputation was not very good. They had no church and only a few shacks. They were accused of murdering three White men and killing no less than 14 head of cattle belonging to White settlers. But it was found that the crimes were the work of the Montana Indians coming to B.C. to avoid the United States justice; but our Indians were not free from blame. With roaming dispositions they were lazy, addicted to gambling and drinking. I had some difficulty to gather them around, and after the mission they showed better disposed, burned down their cards and other gambling articles and resolved to build a church. Returning to St. Eugene the white people free now from anxiety were coming to church on Sundays. Mrs. Colonel Baker though Anglican called herself Catholic and was with us on Sundays and festivals. Took advantage of the Colonel's friendship to speak and propose some improvements in the district, and to use his [influence] as Member of Parliament to bridge the St. Mary's River. Remarked also that we had, so far, no way to dispose of our farm produce and our beef, but if a trail was open along the St. Mary's River down to the Blue Bell Mines on Kootenay Lake we would have an easy outlet for all our produces.[39] I represented also of what an advantage it would be to reclaim the immense prairies of the lower Kootenay Valley where a number of families could be located. The Colonel entered in my views; the following year the bridge was built, a company was formed to reclaim the lands on lower Kootenay and steamshovels with other machineries [*sic*] used for the canal to join the Kootenay with the Columbia waters were transported to the spot.

The autumn was spent in breaking a few more acres of virgin land and pulling stumps. Finding too slow and expensive the use of tackles and stump pullers, we tried to blow them by dynamite. The experiment was so successful, that we ordered a few cases for the next season. Our men got so expert at it that even by a light charge had the best of the large stumps even of the Tamarac tree whose roots spread far with a centre one going deep in the ground. The stump being shattered, we let it dry for a month, and taking the fragments or kindling and setting fire would burn all roots under the ground. In spare time we were translating the prayers before and after Communion into Kootenay from the chinook composed by Bishop Durieu, also the hymns in preparation for Christmas. The week before Christmas all the Indians from Columbia Lakes, Tobacco Plain and even many of the lower Kootenay had come to St. Eugene to follow the exercises in preparation for the feast. The subject of the instructions for the 8 days was Pride, and its consequence.

The Feast was celebrated with the greatest devotion. Just before midnight Mass to which many Whites of the surroundings attended, the Indians who had guns fired volleys after volleys in honor of the coming of the King of Peace, burning the ammunition piled up in preparation for war with the Whites. The altar looked beautiful with a new Gothic Tabernacle, work of an artist, and bouquets of artificial flowers arranged by the hands of Mrs. Colonel Baker. The night was calm with a bright moon. Numerous communicants, and though the Kootenays have not melodious voices, they showed the strength of their lungs in rendering the hymns they had learned.

We were not to neglect or let drop a society of midwives Kenootlakatla [*sic*] Palka, established by Father Fouquet to assist in confinement cases. It was composed of a President with three assistants and had rules to follow: 1. Had to meet twice in the year, or oftener at the request of the President. In those meetings the 3 assistants had to give an account of their work. 2. The visitation to be their principal feast.[40] 3. To receive Holy Communion in all the feasts of the Blessed Virgin. 4. To approach the Holy Table in their uniform, consisting in a blue veil with white trimmings. 5. Have to give example of cleanliness to their children. 6. To notify the chief of women with child carrying heavy loads. 7. To assist their members in sickness and provide temporal comfort and send for the priest if [patient] seriously ill. 8. On the death of one of the members, must have mass offered at which all shall receive communion. 9. 6 months of trial before admittance. Immorality cause of expulsion and degradation in public.

1889. The new year ushered in very mild with sunshine, permitting our Indians to have their traditional dinner in plain air in which every one had to take part to prove that harmony existed in the camps, all enmity and misunderstanding had been buried with the old year. The material for the dinner was provided by those who had means to do so, consisting in home made cakes, bread, tea, sugar, meats, dried fruits etc. The priest was invited to bless the table and the crowd. What was left was distributed by the watchmen to the widows, orphans or blind. In imitation of St. Stephen and his 7 helpers, a collection of food or money was collected by the said watchmen to be distributed among the needy enough to last for months without obliging [them] to humble themselves to beg or the generous givers to be exposed to pride.[41] The bell so long waited for was brought at last on sleighs from Golden R.R. station by willing Indians proud of the 700 lb bell which all wanted to see and hear. With the assistance of white carpenters the tower was ready to receive it.

The stables falling in ruin occupied the winter months. Taking advantage of 2 feet of snow, logs were cut and hauled in place for the fences needing repairs. Spring coming I left for the Shuswap camp on Columbia Lake, the roads were in bad condition and on six miles from the camp my horse played out went to camp with a family not far from the trail. It was providential, found the children in tears their father of 60 years was dying. Said Mass in the house and administered the Sacraments to the sick man who died three days after. The Shuswaps received the priest with the same joy as usual having the prayers taught in Kamloops in their own language, they learned them without difficulty and many were admitted to make their first communion.

On the 2nd day of April 1889, started seeding the wheat in the 70 acres of prepared soil at St. Eugene. The feast of Easter approaching, our time during the Holy Week was taken by preparing the candidates for first communion. The subject of instruction for the 6 days was the virtue of purity. In our spare time the cleaning of the village had to be done, but I suppose on account of the spring warm sun my people were indolent and slow to work. I had to use all kind of stratagems threatening to refuse to bless on Holy Saturday the houses with unclean yards.[42] Easter Sunday the first communicants marched to the church, the boys dressed in black made from the cloth of the Fathers' old cassocks, the girls in white with a blue sash, present of Mrs. Col. Baker. The new Gothic candlesticks present of Mr. Norris customs officer, adorned the altar,[43] never before [had] the sun shone on a happier day in St. Eugene.

Mass over, the Whites, Protestants or Catholics, with all the Indians shook hands with the first communicants, there were representants [sic] of the Indian camps even some of the Wild Tobacco Plains, who offered to take me to their plains 80 miles away, but only a few families were to be seen, the rest gone across the line on the American side. Father Richard had the wheat ready for the flour mill, and we ground the best flour we ever had

On May 1889 before the high water visited the lower Kootenays, the Indians were progressing there, their gardens are promising and with the money from selling their furs have secured cattle and horses from the American settlers; Chief Justin handled his men with an Iron hand. The prayers and catechism are taught and learned, many well-prepared made their first communion. Mrs. Rykert sent bouquets of flowers for the occasion. Mass was said this time in the new house of the chief. Before leaving camp I gave to each communicant one flower of the bouquets on the altar to keep as souvenir of the day. When in the fall coming again and people going to confession, one of the penitents asked me: "What shall I say." "You confess your sins." And then showing a little sack he said: "How could I commit sin having always before me the flower of my first communion. Jesus gave Himself to me and I gave myself to Him."

One day boys frightened ran to my wigwam saying two whitemen in rags are around the camp. "Bring them in," I said. Exhausted they dropped down, gave them a cup of tea and let them sleep until I had something ready to eat. Then they told me that having left Spokane a week ago with food for three days they had been without anything to eat for four days and not able to pack they had left their blankets and outfit behind. Gave them only little food and had them to sleep before giving any more. Such is the life of the prospectors through these mountains, how many that are not heard of, prey of the wolves or grizzlies?

On my return to St. Eugene I found the fields suffering for want of ir-rigation. Many a time I mentioned to Father Richard that without irriga-tion we were planting in vain, but always he answered of the im-possibility of it and of the cost of it. Though I was the superior I did not like to act for fear of displeasing him, but secretly I turned the water on the grain. A fortnight after told the Father, "Let us go and see how things are growing." Surprised at the green and rich spots, I said: "What does this contrast come from?" "Surely from the water," he remarked. After that we built a dam on St. Joseph Creek and our fields, hay and grain had better aspect. In June Father left for his retreat preached in New Westminster by Father Augier.[11]

The sawmill built by Mathers brothers four miles from the mission was a boon not only for the schools but for the country around. Plans and specification given, the erection of the schools and adjoining build-ing was going ahead. Material also for our sheds—our stock growing in number—was hauled on the spot. Our travelling was at that time on horseback through all kind of rough trails. I had picked for my riding the best horse of the country but finding that the more I was feeding him and with the best care he was very dull I asked Father Richard what could be the cause of that, who said: "Horses here are interbreeded [*sic*]." Then I wrote Father LeJacq to send us the percheron colt stallion I had from the Guichons when in charge of Nicola Valley—He was good enough to send it to us and I went to Golden to take him from the train, as I was afraid that in other hands he was not safe on the trail of 200 miles. After that we improved our band of horses. The summer passed very quickly. On the 24th of September 1889, I left for Nelson and found the town much developed. Hotels, private residences going on fast, some of the mines starting to operate, but capital slow to come to the country known only by prospectors who had no means to develop their claims. Mass was celebrated in private, but the inconvenience of that is easily understood. The necessity of church and school is already felt and I notified the Bishop [of] that. 8th of December was the feast of the Immaculate [Conception]. With Brother Burns made our annual retreat in preparation.

With the month of November comes the snow. The summer high water had brought quantity of cedar trees on St. Mary's shores, made many thousand of shingles to cover our barn and cattle sheds. All manual work gave place to the spiritual exercises in preparation for Christmas, the Indians in a body from every other camps had come to St. Eugene. The subject of instruction was God Almighty, absolute master of man, created for no other purpose but to know Him and serve. "What have the chiefs and watchmen done during the summer?, of how many disorders have some been guilty, of gambling all what they should have saved for their family even to their shirts, of drinking and fighting—all that is displeasing to God, and the chiefs and watchmen have made no efforts to prevent that. I am afraid a severe punishment is hanging over your heads. The hand of God who has lavished blessings upon you may lay heavy upon you." Of the five missions preached to the Kootenay this seemed to have the greatest effect. Chiefs and watchmen rose up and promised to act more effectively in the future. The Christmas Crib, present of the white Catholics, attracted the attention of young and old, the children pointing during prayer to the little Babe, the ox or the horse.[45] In the night when saying my prayers unseen, some of the wild bucks came to kneel before the crib asking pardon and making resolutions for doing better.

1890, the new year ushered in very cold and stormy. Summer was hot and no rain, consequently shortage of feed. In February violent blizzard 40° and 41° below zero gave a sad blow to the stock. White and Indians were losing cattle and horses and hay getting scarce. Ourselves began to ration our stock. During mars [*sic*] wind was blowing in all direction. Of man's memory no winter like this had been experienced. Chief Isadore lost all his horses of pack and 60 cattle. Others were in the same condition. People come to ask us for a little hay for the only horses left. The women were preaching to their children: "Do not be sorry for losing your horses. God Who had been good to you has been offended by your gambling and laziness, now you cannot go out gambling and drinking and you are obliged to stay home and pray if you do not want God to take your life also and let you go to the big fire." Some of the Indians humbled themselves before God, others blasphemed and said: "The priest is the cause of our misery. He called the wrath of heaven upon us." When they met me riding on my fat horse they refused to speak to me. But I was telling them: "When I was under the burning sun making hay you were flying around looking for fun, now you walk and I ride."

Easter did not bring the usual crowd. Having no horses to ride and to pack food supplies many had to remain at home. The subject of instruction was the vanity of the goods of this world, cause of God's forgetfulness. The story of Job had the effect of reviving the morale and they promised not to cry or complain any longer. The feast over I was leaving for Columbia Lake to give the opportunity to those who could not come to the mission to make their Easter duties. The high water on the Elk River forced me to return home without reaching Tobacco Plains. The school buildings were painted and soon ready for occupation. Nobody having come for the priest from the lower Kootenay, the St. Pierre Indians had not the usual spring mission.

In June 1890, we cleared 10 more acres of virgin soil. The land surveyors having come to survey five square miles of land for the coal mine's company, I obtained from them to survey 368 acres adjoining the mission which they were good enough to do free of all charges. The sad news of the death of our beloved Bishop D'herbomez cast sadness and the Indians who knew him joined in prayers for the repose of his soul. On the 20th of the same month I went to New Westminster for the annual retreat of the Fathers and brought back with me a mower and seeder machines to facilitate the work on the farm.

The Sisters of Providence taking charge of our Indian School landed at St. Eugene on the 15th of August. Having no furniture yet they had to sleep on the straw until the necessary equipment arrived, but like good missionaries no word of complaint. They had with them, a white orphan girl, Mary Raunch, who rendered great services in sewing and cooking and even in classroom, learning quickly the Indian language and having authority upon the children.

Thanks to the frequent rains of summer we had a splendid harvest and with the thrashing machine of Colonel Baker the grain was put in safely for the flour mill to provide bread for the school. We ground 10,900 lbs of first class, 3400 of second, 3200 of third besides the many tons of bran for the stock and market.

Antipathy of the Indians toward the White race. When everything was ready for the opening of our Indian School, the faithful old man Allan came to tell me secretly that the Indians were not to trust their children to white women though called Sisters.[46] The priest was not considered as a white man by them, but as some one sent to them direct from heaven. I thanked my old friend and prepared my plans. Sent three of my best watchmen to Columbia Lake with an order to bring to the mission the children I named for the Saturday 18th of October; then on Sunday the 19th after Mass in the church, I called and filed up the children of the mission of those parents favorably disposed toward the school, added to the file those children arrived from Columbia Lake and marched them to the school houses only a few hundred yards from the church. The parents or all the congregations followed to see where the march was leading. The Sisters were on the porch to receive the children who entered and closed the doors. [I] told the crowd to go back to camp, and so the school opened with 20 pupils on October 19th 1890. Other children jealous of the selection made asked to be received the following days. The plan was successful and triumph complete.

We planted 8 acres of all wheat, but we found that the climatic conditions were against it, and did not experiment any more in the future.

A sick call brought me to Tobacco Plains. Once more I crossed the boundary line to give to the Catholics of Montana the opportunity to approach the Sacraments.[47] As a rule I would call at the store for information about any newcomers and meet so many of the settlers as possible to make them know that I was in the surroundings. Strange to say people who never spoke of religion, but to turn it in ridicule, stopped to do so. Leaving my team outside, the passersby would ask whose team it would be. Children would answer: "That is the God's man team." For the word priest was unknown in the valley.[48]

December was very mild and the Indians flocking around St. Eugene for Christmas: Justice was the subject of the preaching during the 8 days in preparation. Honesty in dealings, obligation of contracts, paying debts, stealing or helping to steal, obligation of restitution etc. . . . The instructions were followed with interest. The Kootenays different from many other tribes are thinking people. After the instruction, the men gathered to discuss the preaching, even they ask their children to give an account of what the priest had said. About 200 approached the Holy Table. The whites are influenced by the faithfulness and behaviour of the Indians, day and night the crib has visitors, the parents bring their children close and explain to them what is seen in the crib. The training of the schoolchildren caused the admiration of Whites and Indians.

1891. January with its mild weather allowed us to do some slashing and prepare more ground for the plow. On the 27th of February a sick call took me down to Tobacco Plain. The weather turning cold suddenly brought the thermometer down to $-35°$ and I had to remain there until it changed. Took advantage of my stay with all the tribes around me to enforce the discipline.

The School gave great satisfaction to those in charge [and] was also an attraction for the Indians of the different camps, and at Easter we had a great attendance. On the 21th of April I was called to the Lower Kootenay. The influenza was raging among the Whites and Indians. How true it is that suffering brings men to God more than prosperity. After spending a week with the Indians, I went to Ainsworth on the Kootenay Lake. Good number of miners came to meet me to attend their religious duties and expressed the desire to have a monthly visit, willing to pay the expense of the priest. They spoke also of building a church on that spot. Capital was investing and development was employing a number of men. The church was built later on the Kaslo end of the lake, in that direction. Nelson growing also was visited and the Catholics formed a committee and started collections for church, school, and hospital. Permission was asked from the Ecclesiastical authorities to go ahead with the work. It was thought my plan was premature, and the Bishop answered that he would be coming soon and see for himself what was to be done.

The 31th of May 1891 we had for the first time at St. Eugene the procession of Corpus Christi. The streets were beautifully decorated with

trees and buntings of all colors, and the weather being all what could be
desired we had the largest gathering we ever had. Besides the first communicants 250 approached the Holy Table. On June 30 the Shuswaps
and the Kootenays of Columbia Lake had the visit of the priest. The influx of the Whites, land seekers or prospectors are an alarm for the
priest. The Indians are more disposed to take example from the bad than
the good. All are in earnest to build their churches, offering cattle or
horses, but I prefer to have cash to buy the material. There are good carpenters among themselves to do the work. The rains though rather a
little later promising good crops, and with the month of August we began our harvesting, giving 14 tons of wheat and three of oats.

The superintendent of Indian Affairs came to visit the school and had
only words of praise for all what he had seen and heard. Father Richard
who in August had gone to New Westminster for his retreat came back
on the 14th of September with Reverend Father Fayard Vicar General
taking the place of Bishop Durieu as visitor of the district. The Vicar
found the necessity of building a larger and more convenient house for
our residence, which may require more priests, for the growing of the
district. The principal object of the visit of Reverend Father Fayard was
to find out if my plans of building church, school and hospital in Nelson
proposed to Bishop Durieu sometime ago were justifiable.

On the 18th of September we left on horseback for the Lower
Kootenay the trip was full of adventures and hardships. The Sisters had
prepared the kitchen box with food supply enough for four days across
the mountains without habitations [*sic*]. It was Friday time to start but
my Superior was in a great hurry, the Bishop having limited the days of
such a long trip. Told us that the big boats had just made their last trip
for the season the water being too low; but a small boat now under repair may make few more runs. To put to profit the time we had to wait I
took Father Fayard to the Indian camp across the river. The trail being
soft through the swamps, Father's horse sunk in, told the Father to
stretch his legs. The horse rising up quickly threw off the rider. In those
swamps horse and rider have to be accustomed to the ground; getting to
soft spots go on quickly, not given time to sink. The sight of a camp of
wigwams made not a good impression on the Visitor.

Returning to Port Hill, no news of the expected boat. Father Fayard
anxious to go asked: "Why not take a canoe?" "Impossible," I said,
"The might of the lake, the sudden storms would not give any hope of
seeing Nelson. Let us go down to Bonner's Ferry and find if there is any
chance of the steamer making another trip." No boat going, was the answer to our inquiries, the last chance is to go by train to Spokane from
where we may find a way by land or water to Nelson. No better result.
Father Fayard said: "The time of my return to New Westminster is due

and the Bishop is waiting for me." Then I put him on the train for B.C.
When by myself, went to Coeur d'Alene to visit the Indian School at St.
Ignace in charge of the Jesuits and profit of their experiences.[50] Once
alone I found my way to Nelson that fall. The disappointments and
hardships will show to outsiders and priests in cities of the trials of missionaries in these new countries. The visit of Father Fayard was fruitless,
at least for what had regard to Nelson and its environs.

A railroad line was in construction between that city and Robson or
Columbia Landing where the C.P.R. steamers plying on the Arrowhead
Lakes of the Columbia River connecting with a C.P.R. branch from
Revelstoke were opening the interior of West Kootenay. That railway
construction took some of my time saying Mass at the different camps.
On a Saturday I came to the principal one for the Sunday. The walking
boss or the principal man there, greeting me said: "You could not come
in better time. Though not a Catholic I know the good effect of the
priest's presence. Here is my tent, in it you make your home for the days
you will afford to stay with us. The men are on strike and look ugly. The
police from Revelstoke are here too, but I depend more on you to keep
order." Spent the afternoon with the men who told me their grievances.
Promised them to see that they would be rectified with the company and
at midnight I returned to my tent. When taking off my coat a man pointing his gun raised the flap. Asked him what he wanted. He said, being
himself surprised, "Where is the boss?" Could not tell but "surely he
must be in the camp."

On Sunday I said Mass in the open and Monday all went to work. My
presence there no longer required I left and coming to shack where the
druggist was dispensing medicine I stopped for a rest and be acquainted.
Shortly after, the chief engineer of the construction Dushuney
[Dushesney] entered complaining of pain in the stomach. Quickly the
druggist gave him a mixture to drink, being close I saw what it was.
Then I was introduced to Dushesney who asking where I was going said:
"We will travel together." Being a Catholic the conversation was
friendly until we came to his headquarters and he invited me to supper.
When we were at the table he said: "I am sick to die." "No wonder," I
remarked "what you drank at noon was enough to kill a bull. If you accept, I have something to help you." Having with me some emergency
medicine. He went to bed, the first thing in the morning he said: "I feel
gay as a bird." Some days after we met again this time he had sore eyes. I
asked him if I could help him: "Go ahead, you cured me before, do it
again." This railroad from Nelson to Robson was after extended to
Trail Smelter, Rossland to Grand Forks, Okanagan and finally to Vancouver.

The falling of leaves from the trees made me think to return to St.

Eugene before the snow blocked the trails. My horses being with the Saint Pierre reserve, I had to stop to give the Indians one more opportunity to approach the sacraments. I found them progressing, houses had been built on dry land and their stock increased. To give an idea of the pharasaics [*sic*] disposition of the Indians, I quietly remarked that some of them were well disposed and attached to the priest, others jealous to see the priest going so much with the Whites were keeping off and not giving any help thinking that if the priest was well off he would despise them.[51] They knew that I had to depend on them to catch my horses. I had to humble myself before them. I went after them rather strong telling them that if I had no pity on them or love them as I did, [I] would never come back to them: "See what you were before I came to see you, and compare to what you are now?"

The prosperity and happiness of our Indians of St. Pierre attracted the attention of the American Indians who three times made application to come to our meetings by representatives of their tribe. I consented on condition that they had to submit to the regulations of our camp and accept any punishment deserved. Considering [it] too hard, two times hesitated, but consented at last. After taking part in our reunions they begged me to visit their camp and do there what was done on the Canadian side. Bishop Durieu at the request of the Bishop of Idaho, then B. Glorieux, had asked me to take charge of the Bonner's Ferry Indians, not imposing me to do it, having more than enough to do among our own people, but to see what good I could do to them.[52]

Consenting to go, they could not do enough to appreciate my visit. Found in their camp church and school buildings, but the Jesuit Father in charge never had any control; children never put a foot in the school and when Mass was going on some gambling was going on in front of the church and the priest, disgusted, had refused to come back to them. Chief was elected, watchmen appointed and for the two years I visited that camp, everything was in order.

Returning to St. Eugene in November I find the influenza raging. Already 40 had been the victims, soon I was gripped myself and the feast of Christmas was silent. But death spoke more eloquently than any priest could do. In 1892 the winter was not severe, [if] it had been the atmosphere would have been purified and put a stop to sickness.

Last fall Joseph Bourgeois with two prospectors had located the North Star Mine.[53] What gave occasion to the discovery is this. Women were looking for berries along the St. Mary's River; having found a shining rock they put it on their basket, coming to a patch were the berries were plentiful they dropped the shining rock rather too heavy and taking useless room in their basket. Bourgeois coming along shortly after noticed it and looking on the hill side from where it could have detached located the North Star. The property was sold to Donald Mann of Montreal one of the great contractors on the C.P.R. line around Revelstoke, in whose camp I spent many days. That was more than enough to bring prospectors in the district, the hills were white with tents.

Profited by this to tell my Indians: "You see White people taking the mineral of your country under your eyes. Long enough you are complaining of the poverty of your church and expect me to build you a new one, but busy as I am with your spiritual interest and having to run from camp to camp for your sick people I cannot do it. Why don't you locate some mines as the White do, then we will build. With all your pride, the White people come from far off and get rich and you, too lazy to improve yourself, remain poor. What are you good for?" My words were not lost, though I had not much confidence in them.

After Easter on the 22nd of April I left for Columbia Lake; the roads were in bad condition. On reaching the Shuswap camp, felt another touch of the grippe. Went to bed when at two in the morning some violent knocks were heard at the door. I was all in perspiration and did not answer but the people upstairs answered: "What do you want?"— "The Priest"—"The priest just came and is tired, you will see him tomorrow, go away"—"Why do you not let the priest go for sick people?" When I heard that without asking who was sick or where, I said: "Saddle my horse, I shall be ready at once." Two Whitemen were at the door. Left with them and my horse who was tired out last night was now flying so that the other men could not keep up. Came to the hotel at Windermere, they brought me to a man with broken arm. Made bandages of a sheet, took shingles for splinters, put the bones in place. They gave me a bed to sleep and at daylight I asked for my horse and returned to Shuswap to say Mass it being Sunday. I was cured of my grippe. How good is God. Mass said began the instructions as usual. White and Indians were in admiration at the strength given by God to his priests. Arnie Small not a Catholic showed his gratitude by his kindness to priests or Sisters especially when he was the Indian Agent in Kootenay.

The presence of the Whites is a detriment to the Shuswaps. Regulations were put in force to keep the Whites out of the Reserve after dark. The Rivers rising I had to hurry for Tobacco Plains before the water got too high; having no bridge we put our clothing on our back and trusting in our horses we cross them, but the water is so cold that at times my heart ceased to beat. The Indians were well disposed and we went to find the best location for a town site and a church. The Indians being poor we made plans accordingly.

On the 22nd of June Father Richard was replaced by Father de Vrient. We were sorry to see the former leaving us, he being so useful for the temporal welfare of the mission. Having been notified to preach the annual retreat of the Fathers had to leave for New Westminster in August. At my return the harvesting was done followed by thrashing, and flour mill, put in operation, gave about 3 tons of good flour and so many of second and 3rd quality. The North Star Mine was sold to D. Mann by J. Bourgeois for $40 000. The news stimulated our prospecting Indians but so [far] no one has anything found. The fall being mild we began on the 3rd of November to plow the piece of ground around the graveyard, it is practically paved with roots from the trees cut last year. We had bought a new horse 2000 lbs heavy and with our other strong teams no doubt of success. The proximity of that field and the facility to irrigate it—St. Joseph Creek running through—determined us to go to work. For many years such mild fall had not been seen in the Kootenays. We had planned also to build our new house, but we had not all the material needed. Besides the old house of logs might be more comfortable if not so nice for the winter. The school giving great satisfaction but we cannot exact much application in the classroom, for confinement is hard on the health of the children. The white people made present of an organ costing $150. Mr. Galbraith was the collector of that amount. The Indian superintendent visited and praised the school for the progress made in every line. The *Colonist* of Victoria was the echo of the superintendent, a copy of which was mailed to us.

It began to snow on the 14th of November and did not stop snowing until we had 3 feet of snow. Frightened by so much snow the Indians wanting to celebrate the Immaculate Conception with the exposition of the Blessed Sacrament all day, returned from their huntings. 7 large steers were butchered to approvisionate [sic] the school for the winter.

Christmas was a feast of recollection. The 8 days in preparation had for subject the 7 gifts of the Holy Ghost.[54] The Bishop having gone to Europe had authorized me to confirm Whites and Indians, 64 in all.[55] Never had our people given marks of better dispositions. A chinook storm reduced the snow to 6 inches.

1893. At midnight the guns announced the new year. The day was spent in rejoicing. Health good, food provisions in abundance, the weather fine. Anxious about their stock, all went. The mission camp was deserted. We thrashed what wheat was left from last fall. 5 tons of first class grain was handed to the granary and the rest was kept for pigs feed, having about 40 of them. On the 26 of January turned cold, 25° below, and our cattle that had left in the chinook storm came back to be fed. The 1st of February the mercury dropped to 28° with 20 inches of snow on the ground and more in perspective. Stock dying all around by the blizzards. On the 6th of March was called to Tobacco Plain, leaving the mission with a foot of snow and more coming with storm after storm.

The visit of the priest in such stormy weather was much appreciated. They had lost much of their stock and encouraged them to patience and prayer, to touch the Heart of God author and master of all things. 50 approached the Holy Table and left them in good spirit with 5° below. On the 5th of April I was on my way to Columbia Lake with grain for my horse fearing that I could not get any in the hotels. A terrible storm overtook me in the way, giving me rheumatism, but the Shuswaps took good care of me during my stay in the camp. Found them well disposed, chief and watchmen doing good work and keeping the Whites at a distance. The church completed was giving nice appearance; brought 8 children for the school. The Whites had lost much stock, but the Indians had saved their own. On the 19th they had 4 inches of snow at the mission. The winter [of] 1892–1893 will be remembered for a long time.

Indian Pierre the same one who was to chase me out of the Kootenays or kill me was waiting for my return. Coming to the house he threw a lump of mineral the size of a goose egg. Seeing him silent and nervous I picked it [up], looked at it and said: "What is that?", not knowing much about minerals at that time.

He answered: "You always say Indians good for nothing. We shall see what you are good for yourself."

To show Pierre that I was taking interest in it, [I] kept on questioning: "Did you find it on the hillside or on the flat"

"Come and see," was the answer.

"Was it on a slide among other rocks or detached from the hill side?"

"Come and see," was the answer.

Put the ore on the table thinking that it would be useless for me to undertake perhaps a long trip and waste time and energy. "Very well Peter I shall do my best to find what can be done." Some days after an expert miner was brought in by the North Star to inspect and pronounce on the worth of that property. He stopped at our house for lunch, as every traveller was doing having to pass by the Mission the central spot on the trail to go anywhere. I showed him the ore. "Can I take a piece and, having assayed, I will send you the returns." Instead of the returning [I] received a letter from the expert asking how much I wanted for the property if it was for sale.

By that I understood that the ore was [of] great value, and resolved to go and see the location; for that a mining licence was required. On Saturday went to the Gold commission at Fort Steele. There I met James Cronin whom I had seen in Nelson. Knew him to be Catholic and very friendly, asked him: "What are you doing here?"

"Oh! having nothing to do at home, came to visit your country; but where are you going?"

"To get a miner licence."

"Gold fever too?"

"Yes but not very violent." Then I said: "Tomorrow Sunday, will you come to Mass."

"Yes in the morning."

"No," I insisted, "You come tonight with me, otherwise you will be too late." Licence obtained both went to the mission. Showed him the ore.

"Very good," he said, "if not too far for transportation and in good location."

Cronin an expert miner had come to report on the North Star with the intention of buying it for his company should it be for sale, but the manager of the mine would not let him in. So when I offered to come to look at our prospect, he accepted it. Leaving the mission early on Monday Cronin said: "People had seen you buying the licence and prospectors may be posted on the trail to find where you would be going, for the word around here is that Father Coccola never moves unless for good reasons." In fact two men stopped us about 9 o'clock, but cutting conversation short, I asked: "Have you see a party going by this morning? Excuse me I must overtake that party," and so spurred the horse and went. Coming to a creek close to Moyie Lake, Pierre our leader followed it saying: "No one will see our tracks," and, hiding our horses, we started on foot for the spot where the piece of rock had been found. Facing the hills we soon found a well described vein of rich ore, branching at different points. We located five claims at once, and the day after we had them recorded at Fort Steele. To finish with the St. Eugene Mine, after three years of development, work and anxieties, it was sold to an American Company for $22 000.00. The C.P.R. got an interest in it & that brought the Crowsnest railroad in the Kootenay. Out of the return of the sale a model house was built for Pierre, who also received cattle, farm implements and $5.00 a month for life from the Consolidated Company operating the St. Eugene and Kimberly Mines.

A beautiful gothic church was erected at the mission and another in Moyie in the town brought to existence by the operation of St. Eugene Mine on Moyie Lake. The object I had in view by a prompt selling of the mine was realized: the development of the district. Railroads, and sawmills first, and towns after, put on the map this portion of British Columbia. I said the Crowsnest Railway was a consequence of the discovering of mines in the Kootenays. The ore had to be carried to the smelters for treatment; shipping to the States as it was done in the past was too expensive and slow affair, a smelter in the surroundings become a necessary enterprise and that was done in Trail on the Columbia River in a center of [the] mining camps of East & West Kootenay. Mr. Haney was the contracting builder of that railway, from Regina to Kootenay

Lake. In the construction camps men were dying like flies, victim of typhoid called mountain fever. The authorities of Ottawa were informed and a commission composed of Doctors ordered to investigate the cause of the disease. The head Doctor Meuburn [illegible] asked me to take charge of the sick in our district; answered that I was willing to help, but I had no place to receive the patients and I could not leave my ministry work for the bodily care of men. At midnight Mr. Haney whom I had known on the construction of the main line, came to me saying:

"I thought you were my friend."

"What makes you think of the contrary?"

"Your refusal of looking after my men on this construction. A commission is coming from Ottawa and I will be blamed, but if my men were under your charge no fault will be found with me."

"How can I do it, in my house in which you are now, lately built, I have only 5 spare rooms for the prospectors and farmers around but to take charge of your men I would have to build a Hospital and get nurses and doctors as I could not tie myself to this work and neglect my mission."

"And what prevents you to build [a] hospital? get nurses, I will provide you with doctors."

"A hospital requires money," said I.

"That should not stop you, here is a cheque to start and here are passes on any railway and cash for travelling expenses for you to get nurses."

"Very well, I will go ahead at once," Plan was made, contract given to some of my Catholic builders in the country and left with Sister Conrad, Superior of the School, by sleigh, the snow being deep, for Golden and by train to New Westminster. Spoke to Bishop Durieu and asked permission to go in search of Sisters for nurses. The Bishop laughed:

"What Sisters will ever accept a hospital in your Kootenay?" Answered: "Give me permission to go and leave the rest to me."

"Go where you like."

Went to Seattle and called on the Sisters. No encouragement.[56] Went to Portland, the Sisters of Providence willing to do all what they could, having already their Sisters to teach in our School. Wired to Mother General in Montreal—Hospital accepted. "Now give me one of your Sisters here, and when I leave with one hostage, I will be sure to have the balance."

At my return to St. Eugene found the Hospital well advanced built on the bank of St. Mary's River. Received some construction patients in the old buildings we had and in our new house just completed and when the Hospital with 40 beds was ready with six sisters in charge, we moved in our patients.

When a year after the Commission inspecting came, looking over our books, the Inspectors were surprised that so many had been treated with so little percentage of deaths and asked the Sisters what was their secret, for in other hospitals men were going in to die: "Cleanliness, fresh milk and good whisky." The hospital was built on the mission ground on the Banks of St. Mary's River because at that time all the roads were leading to St. Eugene. When the hospital was filled, the convalescents were located in a large tent. Once we had 80 at one time. It was proposed to have the Crowsnest railway to pass by our door, if [we] consented to the building of a smelter on our grounds. I told the party that we were here for the Indians and the fumes of a smelter would destroy vegetation and now that the Indians had taken to farming, being trained to the use of mowers, binders etc. etc. and having improved their stock by bringing percheron horses and shorthorn bulls, it would be cruel and unjust to stop the progress of the natives. Then Cranbrook prairie being selected for the Divisional point of the Crow's Nest with railway branches to be extended to the mines, I foresaw that our Hospital would be out of the centre and decided to build a new one larger and more up to date at this Divisional Point. Five acres of land were given by Colonel Baker near the station, plans made and Hospital built. After 8 months we moved our patients in from the mission. The C.P.R. good enough to supply the water. King & Green were the doctors. At this present time the Hospital is 3 times the size of the original.

Villages and towns springing in all directions, priests were needed as well as doctors. The coal fields of Fernie, Michel, Morissey—with four or five thousands of a cosmopolitan population—had to have churches: Cranbrook, Moyie, Mary's ville [*sic*], Creston, Fort Steele and Fernie in the East Kootenay; Nelson, Trail, Rossland in the West Kootenay were asking for same. The 5 priests located at St. Eugene mission were attending those different places by periodical visits, but resident priests only, could do substantial work. Father Ouellet [*sic*] though advanced in years took charge of Cranbrook, building St. Mary's church. Father Welsh took charge of Fort Steele, Fernie and adjoining points. Churches were built. Michel, Moyie had their churches also in course of time. The Indian missions were not neglected having their regular visits.

A word about Father Welsh whom I had met in the hospital of Calgary in 1884. Asking him what he was doing there, [he] told me that the doctors in Manchester, England, where he had a large parish with other four priests, had advised him to look for an other climate if he wanted to live because his lungs were affected, and he came to Canada. Two years after, finding him again in Calgary not improving, I invited him to come to St. Eugene as the right climate for him. He did, and after a year spent with us, feeling strong, he asked for work. His zeal and ability were crowned with success. Bishop Dontenwill hearing of that, called him to take charge of Rossland a very prosperous mining town with a beautiful hospital and little church. At first he refused to go but consented at last on condition that he would be allowed to come to St. Eugene when he wanted or myself to go to him any time he would call me to him. Promise made, he left with tears in his eyes for we were very attached to each other.

In one of my visits to Rossland Father Welsh said how lonely he was. I had then mind to tell him that he was called to religious life, but I was afraid to displease Bishop Dontenwill as it would have been difficult to find a substitute for Rossland and Trail, where he was doing so well. Having to go to New Westminster for my retreat told the Bishop of the loneliness of Father Welsh who was called to religious life.

"We cannot oppose that," said the Bishop. Returning to Rossland told the Father:

"You are called to religious life, in that you will find happiness."

Then he replied: "Take my place until I go to Spokane to make a retreat & study my vocation." Coming back, he said: "I am now decided."

"What order do you want to join?"

"The Oblates."

Then he left for New Westminster to make his noviciate and today he is an Oblate of Mary Immaculate, and, having been a Provincial for many years, now he is resting at St Augustine Church in Vancouver.

Let us go back to our Lower Kootenay Indians in 1895. The reclamation work on the Kootenay bottoms starting from the boundary line, the steamshovels were advancing towards where the Indians had their garden and graveyards along the river. When the first grave was moved the natives refused to let the work to go any farther. Facing the guns, the working men had to stop. The manager asked protection from the Government. The Government asked Bishop Durieu to use his influence. The Bishop wrote to me to hurry on the spot. There I was giving a mission to the camp, certain that having our people well disposed religiously we would talk temporal affairs. When the mission was going quietly, the manager with Policemen and Pat Burns too appeared in the camp. As soon as the chief and his watchmen saw the Policemen it was like the bull before the red cloth. They got furious, addressing them: "What have you to do on our ground, we are going to throw you in the river"—on which bank they were standing. The manager got pale asking me what to do. I say—"I have not to tell you what he [the chief] said, but you asked me to pacify the country and you come to spoil my work. Go or I leave." They went. As if nothing had happened my mission went on.—But what about the reclamation work? Once the camp was quiet and happy, I took the chief and the most intelligent men of the camp and went to the office of the manager. On the way I assured my men that there was nothing to fear, and that everything will turn out well. Reaching the office [I] told the manager: "The Indians do not want the graves to be disturbed, neither the little gardens that they have on the Bank." "We understand all that," remarked the manager. "There is room for the dikers [*sic*] between the River and the graves, which will be left untouched. As for the gardens [we] will select better spots where they could cultivate and plant to a greater advantage. But see what we plan; once the land is reclaimed we shall allot to the tribe the highest grounds in this immense stretch of land where they can secure all the hay they may need for their stock, shall employ them and pay them good wages for the improvements of the place. A nice spot will be obtained by the Government on which to build their village out of the meadow. We will build a church for them as they do not have one now, and give the Priest $50. for every trip to the camp." When I told that to the Chief & men it was found satisfactory and they allowed the work of reclamation to be continued.

The village & church and fruit trees were planted and now two miles from the Indian Reserve we have the white town of Creston of fruit growers. The secular priest in Sandon, Reverend Côté, was only loaned to our Vicariate. His time was expired and I had to replace him. Sandon was located in a narrow valley with high mountains on both sides very rich in mineral but exposed to snow slides, which at last wrecked the town. We had a nice little church dedicated to St. Joseph and many fervent Catholics. The Bank manager had donated the statue of the Saint. Sandon was connected with another town, Kaslo, on a beautiful flat on the end of Kootenay Lake by a narrow track railway. There also was a beautiful church. From there I visited the new gold fields of the Lardeau & Ferguson, passing by the big sawmill of Comappleux going down by the Arrowhead Lake and landed in Nakusp. Everywhere the Catholics were glad to see a Priest, taking advantage to receive the Sacraments not knowing [when] the next opportunity would be given to them.

Father Fayard informing the Bishop of the distance and difficulties for the priest of St. Eugene to attend West Kootenay developing at such a rate and needing resident clergy, I was discharged of that part of the West Kootenay. It was given to secular Priests. Father Farland [*sic*] came to Nelson and built the beautiful church of the Immaculate Conception. He called the Sisters of St. Joseph of Peace, an English order; Sisters of the same order were in charge of the Hospital in Rossland.[57] Trail also had a resident priest.

Returning to St. Eugene mission in the spring 1900, a visit was due to Columbia Lake.[58] Roads soft and in bad condition. My horse tired out and so I was, laid down at the foot of a tree. After a little rest seeing that I could not reach camp, went to a house a little out of the trail. Found there a dying man. Said Mass, gave the Sacrament to the sick [man] who died a few days after. Sure his guardian angel must have brought me there. The same year Father Thayer in charge of Revelstoke asked me to preach a mission for his people. Glad to render that service to the Father and his people.

In 1901, the Creston Indians took me to the mountains to look at what they thought to be a gold prospect. Coming from there the telegraph operator handed me a telegram from the superintendent of the C.P.R. at Revelstoke asking me to come at once. The superintendent was Dushesney chief surveyor of the construction between Nelson and Castlegar whom being sick I treated then. Looking at the telegraph, saying nothing for what he wanted me, hesitated to go. If he is sick there are doctors there, if he is dying a Priest is located there. After reflection—Duchesney is a businessman, surely he would not ask me to go so far unless serious case—I went. The track men were on strike, cars loaded with merchandise for Vancouver were standing still, and Duchesney feared that they would be broke in, merchandise stolen or fire set to the cars. Secretly in the office the superintendent said: "See what you can do." I went around to advise my Catholics and other friends to be careful and not expose themselves by listening to agitators who cause depredation: "The agitators will be hiding or leave the town but you having your families and your interests in the place have to be wise." Two days after the superintendent said: "What have you done to the men. All seem to be peaceful and trains will soon be moving?"

The Tobacco Plains with the bunch grass until lately inhabited by our Catholic Indians had attracted on the borders of B.C. and Montana a number of farmers many of them Catholics. No priest had yet visited them. They also were waiting for my visit. The Bishop of Helena whom I had gone to see, having [been] given the faculties in his diocese, received me kindly and sent their children to our St. Eugene school to prepare for their first Communion.[59] On the American side is the town of Eureka; there is [a] church and resident priest.

The Indian children were not the only ones to profit of the Christian training, the white children had their share of it—during the holidays I was gathering the young ladies to our school and gave them a week of instruction. Some of them who never had seen Sisters before joined the Providence Order against the will of their parents and once in a while I hear from them thanking [me] for their call to religious life. Other people asked for instruction and notwithstanding the opposition of husbands and friends were received in the church and have been models of Christian life since. The Protestants accused me of using not religious teaching but magnetism to bring people to church, and were to burn me alive.

After Father Welsh had left the coal city of Fernie for Rossland his successor had difficulty to conciliate the cosmopolitan population of the town, more than 6000. The Slovanians [*sic*] and Polish considered themselves slighted by the English speaking. Proposed to them to buy the church and they would have one for their people or not to sell the church to them and they to build a church of their own. To influence the Catholics of the town to live peacefully and worship together I was asked to go to Fernie to help the priest, who left shortly after. Being left alone it was impossible to remain there constantly, having my Indian missions to look after. Then [I] applied for assistant and had many in turn, Father Lardon, and Father Tavernier, who would permit me to attend to other parts of the district. Began to learn the Slav languages, heard confession, preached, blessed the homes, had 3 classes on Sunday School with teachers—collected money to finish the interior and adorn it. Statues were donated by the Herkmers, McDougal, Pat Bolanchik—and the altar by the teller of the Bank of Commerce in memory of his conversion to the Catholic church. Invited the Ruthenian Priest to come to administer to his people with the privilege of celebrating the High Mass on Sundays—in a word no more friction in the parish.[60] Frequent fires were a great drawback to the town. The fire, started at night, reduced to ashes one third of the town, our church being on the other end of the town was supposed to be out of danger. I had it open for the refugees and at 6 o'clock it was filled up with children. I saying mass [a] little nervously, asking God to spare us. At the consecration it began to rain so heavy that feeling that the danger was over I finish it quietly, then the people were moving from the adjoining presbytery, books and furniture. The town was rebuilt in a short time, but a second and third fire destroyed our church. A brick one was in course of time built by Father Mitchel [*sic*] O.M.I. who had took charge at Fernie.[61]

A word about the Fernie coal fields. The Indians hunting started their camp fire and after the wood was reduced to ashes still the fire was burning. What could be the cause? after removing the ashes they saw the black rock on fire. They took some of it and coming to the mission showed it to Mr. Fernie the mail carrier from Bonner's Ferry to Wild Horse Creek. Hiring the Indians, they took him to where the black rock was and he prospecting around found that all the mountain carried coal, formed a company, and from that came Fernie Coal mines.

A word about the conversion of the Bank teller;—entering home one evening I was followed by a young man introducing himself, making some disagreeable remarks about the Catholic church, and the Jesuits. I controlled my temper listening patiently. When he emptied his bile, I said: "My dear Sir you speak of things about which you know nothing. I am a French man, and all the greatest men of that nation in all branches, even those that persecuted the Jesuits, are coming from their Institutions; they are the most learned men in the world and no matter what part of the world you may go you will find that the best schools are in their hands."

"Pardon me," he spoke after a moment of hesitation, "my object in coming here is to ask you to give me some French lessons."

"I have no time for such work, my people and the ministering occupy all my moments & energy."

"Well then will you give me some religious Instruction for I know nothing of that subject."

"That I cannot refuse. You come every day at such an hour and I will be at your disposition."

On the following Easter Sunday at the High Mass he made his abjuration in presence of all the congregation. Others joined the church about the same time. A lady came to ask to go to confession.

"Who are you, Catholic? I have never seen you in the church."

"I am English Catholic."

"Then go to your Minister."

"If I do," she said, "he will tell my sins to his wife."

In September 1905, I was called to New Westminster for the annual retreat. Father Dozois 1st assistant was there as visitor of the Vicariate, presiding at the provincial council of which I was a member, and he moved that some one should be sent to Stuart Lake to help Father Conan who had been there alone since he had replaced Father Morice.[62] All seconded the motion. The point was, who could be sent? Few names were proposed but none accepted for reasons given. Then Bishop Dontenwill looked at me saying: "I know one who would do well, but do not like to name him," having his eyes on me I could not stand any longer, and said: "You mean me?"

"Yes, but you are getting on in years and you are wedded with the Kootenays where you have been so long and have so many things to look after."

I replied: "If am ordered, there is nothing on the way to stop me; my accounts with the bank, the books of the house, are all up to date and the one who has to replace me has to let matters take their course and will have no difficulty on his way." The Bishop remarked: "If you accept to go we will all be pleased of it, but know that we will not leave you there for life. Next year you will return to your Kootenays. Then be ready to go for the season is advancing and you may have some difficulty to reach Stuart Lake.

To Stuart Lake, terra incognita. Leaving New Westminster on the

23th July 1905, I landed in Williams Lake on the 25th, the 25th anniversary of my landing in Victoria July 25, 1880. I was cordially received by dear old Father Blanchet with whom I had spent two weeks at Okanagan mission 23 years ago. Found there Fathers Boning [Boening] superior, my compatriot and schoolmate at Ajaccio, D. Chiappini, Andrieux, (Father Thomas being absent) and the Sisters of the Infant Jesus in charge of the school built years ago by Father McGuckin, O.M.I. On the 29th, I was on my way to Quesnel by stage to Soda Creek and reached Quesnel by steamer, the *Charlotte,* afternoon the following day. Two Indian boys from Fort Fraser arrived two hours after with horses to take me up to my new field of labor.

Monday 31st we were on the trail. Covered 12 miles first day—poor horses and roads which made me regret the fiery percherons I had left in the Kootenay—the 2nd day we camped at the government Telegraph Station where the operator a Catholic, McNeil, was very cordial. Our 3rd camp was called Big Meadow, 4th Beaver Dam, on the 5th day we stopped at the Indian village of Stony Creek where I administered the last Sacraments to an old woman, and on the 6th day we reached Fort Fraser, where a delegation from Stuart Lake were waiting for me with a fresh and lively horse. Having not the necessary articles I could not celebrate Mass on Sunday. The 8th of August at noon, the Stuart Lake people welcomed their new Shepherd. Father Conan was away and I took possession of the house.

Many snows had already passed over my head and caused some white hairs on it. What [which] made some of the Indians say: "Why is the Bishop sending an old man in this cold and far away country, he may not live through the winter?" But quick they find that there was yet some life left in me when I began to order for the fixing of the house & church and gave them a program for the work to be done—Chief Joseph Prince, the faithful supporter of the priest, who could speak French & English was right at my side ready to transmit orders in the same way as they were given.[63] About Joseph Prince. Joseph Prince, son of the great chief of the Porteurs [Carriers] was when a boy of 12 taken to William's Lake St. Joseph Mission by Father McGuckin. During the many years he remained there he had the opportunity to learn French & English with the Fathers & Brothers and besides a good religious formation, a general training in farming and mechanics. He accompanied Father McGuckin in his mission tours. In a trip from Hazelton to Bear Lake, they had to pass by Kiscakan camp, where the chief had made the law that no white man had to put foot in his territory. Joseph bravely went to the chief saying: "The man who is here is not after Gold mines but comes in the name of God to speak his word and to show the Indians the way to happiness on earth and to heaven after." And they could pass. Joseph was the guide also of Father LeJacq. When in Babine the cruel Indians were refusing food to the Priest, Joseph told them: "You give eats to your dogs and why not to the priest who sacrificed all comfort in his country to show you how to live. If food is not brought here we turn back at once."—plenty was given at Haguilget [Hagwilget]. In a difficulty of hunting ground among 2 Indians, the case was brought to the priest for decision. After the hearing, decision was given. The loser was so mad that he planned to kill Father LeJacq. Came to the lodge and remained there waiting for the Father & Joseph to go to sleep. This bad disposition Joseph could see, noticing a butcher knife sticking from the side of the man. Joseph rose up took his gun and saying: "Go way, or you are dead." Determination is a great thing with the Indians who cannot attack openly but by surprise and treachery. When chief of Stuart Lake his orders were given with a whip in his hand, and all knew that he was ready to make use of it if not obeyed.

Why are our Indians called Carriers—because the widows had to carry the ashes of their husbands after the burning of the body for nine months; during those months they were not allowed to comb their hair and have nothing but rags. If seen smiling they would be beaten by the relatives of the dead husband of whom they were their slaves—Christianity stopped all that

Looking at the children my first impression was of discouragement. They appeared to me sickly, hungry & poor. Making use of what medicines I had and of my forceps & surgical knives relieved them of [a] few of the causes of their miserable appearance. Instructions in preparation for the feast of the Assumption began at once.

Made a survey of the surroundings. The church built by Father Blanchet with Father LeJacq was big enough for the village population—but surely was too small when outsiders would come. The house had a sufficiently large sitting room to which a little chapel was connected but in opening the two large doors could accommodate 30 people; in another apartment was a kitchen on the north side and two bedrooms on the other. The cooking was done in a stone fire place allowing cold air in plenty. To prevent that my plan was to buy a cooking stove and to do away with the fire place. Should not that be enough to warm the bedrooms, then to secure a small heater to be placed between the two rooms. So the stone fire chimney was taken away [and] the roof closed. Moss and mud had fallen off from the walls, which were chinked and mudded over—the house was also banked all around. The passing Indians looking at the work remarked: "Is not winter yet, why so much doing?" I said, "Now I show you what an intelligent man must do in the fall; by winter I will show you what I will be doing then."

Father Conan came back on the 14th of August glad to see me and having great time together. But after a few days, he expressed the desire to go to New Westminster. Though very sorry to leave me alone. I told him: "You deserve a change and you are at liberty to go" as that had been arranged in council before I came up. He left on the 6th of September with the H.B. [Hudson's Bay Company] Scow going to Quesnel for supply.

The same evening the Commissioner of the H.B. for B.C., Mr. Thompson [Thomson], came with Mr. Peters, manager at H.B. Fort Fraser. We spoke of the future of this new country with so much opened land and valuable timber. "Perhaps the Grand Trunk Railway may come close to us, for surveyors had been seen locating one of the lines."

Improvements completed around the house. On the 12th of September I left for Fort Fraser. Found there more people than expected.

The Stony Creek, the Burns, & François Lakes Indians were there. The church was found too small and gatherings of that kind were to be repeated. It was then decided to put in a gallery. After 8 days of instructions, after pointing to the necessity of receiving Holy Eucharist, many applied for it. Simple prayers already translated at Stuart Lake for before and after communion were taught. A sick call to Stella brought me to that new little village at the other end of Fraser Lake. The two Rivers François & Endako joined at that point. No church there yet, and I appointed a chief & watchman and it was decided to build a church. The dispositions of this people seem to be gentle but wanting in energy and easily influenced for good or bad. The chief and watchmen were shown their duty and the obligation to act accordingly, more so now that white people were flocking in. Returning to Stuart Lake on the 23th, we resumed the work of improvements on the house under the direction of Leon Prince, brother of the chief Joseph Prince.

On October 14th I was no longer alone. Father Bellot arrived after 12 days on the H.B. scow from Quesnel. Our first work was to inspect a piece of land called priest meadow where Father Marchal was cutting hay for his horse. Land surveyors had been all over but the Indian they had for guide kept them away from that spot.[64]

On the 17th, first snow; thermometer dropping close to zero we began to enjoy the benefit of the improvements made to the house. On the 22th, Indians began to come from all directions for All Saints Day & All Souls Day.[65] Though the majority of the 3 villages on Stuart Lake had celebrated Christmas at the mission, for the sake of those who for good reasons could not come I decided to visit the camps. The ice was solid after 40° below. I called at Pinchey [Pinché] where the church, built too close to the shore, was threatened to be washed away and it was proposed to move it in a safe place. Then in Tachey [Taché] 15 miles farther, found the church altogether too small and plans were given for a larger one. Last camp Yecoutchey [Yekhuche] without any church. Mass was offered in the house of the chief and it was resolved to build a church.

From Babines, Grand Rapids, Taché, Pinché, boats loaded with people made their appearance from the West. The Fort Fraser & Stony Creek on horseback from the East and from the North the McLeod's on foot. First work to do was for the chiefs & watchmen to report on the behaviour of their tribes each in turn. Finding that the reports were exact, not trying to hide from the priest, they accepted what punishment was inflicted on them. In preparation for the feast they followed the exercises; Mass, in the morning, catechism at 10 and sermon & benediction in the evening. Many applications were made for first Communion, and going around the camp one could hear them learning catechism and prayers for before & after Communion. For All Souls Day the church was draped in black with a catafalco in the centre which made [a] great impression upon them as they had not seen anything like that before.

To show their appreciation they made an abundant collection for the support of the priests and improvements in the church.[66] All returned to their homes to prepare for the trapping. On the 28th of November 10° below zero the lake was freezing fast, it was time to put a heating stove near the bedrooms. The 8th of December, Immaculate Conception, exposition of the Blessed Sacrament, all day for the 1st time. Many communions, and the girls candles in hand made their consecration to the Blessed Virgin which made [an] impression on those present. By the 16th of December our trappers began to come from everywhere with their furs; they caught many black foxes and lynxs. The necessity of a gallery in the church was evident and the work started without delay and all busy—without preventing the exercises in preparation of the feast of Christmas. The manager of the H.B. and his people assisted at the midnight Mass. Mr. Murray had sent $10.00 with an invitation to dine at the Fort.[67]

The year 1906 began by a beautiful spring day, though the eve the thermometer was down to 10° below. The customary hand shaking was done in the morning at the door of the church after Mass. In the afternoon all the Indians were invited to the Fort for distribution of tobacco and biscuits given in proportion of the number of furs sold to the Company, who being the only buyers at the time, [Indians] were paid little. Five swans had been flying by, sign of [a] mild winter. Sun rising at 8:45, days very short, setting after 3 o'clock. Thermometer on the 18th lowering to 20°−. The mail carriers getting ready to take the mail to Quesnel, we were busy with our correspondence. We had only 3 regular mails in the year but the H.B. willing to look after our letters when sending their scow in summer for provisions to Quesnel, we had it every second month. Our time was taken in learning the Indian language and giving a last touch to the prayers lately translated. On the 21st of January, 38 below but our house was comfortable, Mass said in the little chapel for the old people not gone trapping.

Coming to this New Caledonia, name given to our district, my plan was to do here what had been done in the Kootenay. Unless we had schools we could not hope for real improvement among our people.[68] It was then resolved to prepare the material for a school house and profit of the gatherings for the Feasts to cut the logs and haul them in. For the 2nd of February many Indians had not returned to their trappings. They have certain practices from their ancestors which they do not like to abandon. One of them is not to leave camp before the middle of February the reason given is that continual snow storms cover the traps which the animals do not see or themselves cannot find; the snow also is too soft and travelling difficult, but as a rule towards the end of February days getting longer and sun strong enough melt the snow during the day and the cold of the night causes a crust to form and support their steps. The wind storms also have shaken the snow from the trees and their traps were left free. Their great enemy then is the wolverine who following the trapper carefully steals the bait, even taking the trap, hides it far away in the snow after eating what had been caught. Our people being around, the feast of Purification with the blessings of the candles and procession took place, which seeing for the 1st time pleased them much.[69] We profited of their presence to begin the cutting and hauling logs for the school.

—On the 15th of February, 6 Babine boys with 3 toboggans came to take the priest to their camp by the frozen lakes. For the comfort of the priest the Stuart Lake took me as far as Taché village on their one horse sleigh. The poor horse not shoed was falling down often, at the risk of dislocation of legs. Arrived late, said Mass, then the Taché on their sleigh took me to Yekhuche. The 9 miles' portage from Stuart to Babine Lake was covered on foot. Here came the hardships: the heavy snow of the ice forced the water through the air holes which spread and froze but not strong enough to carry the toboggan which breaking through covered dogs and carriage with water which turning into frost made travelling hard. However we made 15 miles on Babine Lake on the first day, hoping to do better the second. But same difficulties until we came to Bear Island, some 15 miles from Old Fort, first Babine village, where we made a big fire. The clouds of smoke attracted the men of the village who came to our rescue with single horse sleigh. Old Fort. The H.B. Co. coming to trade with the Babine Indians built their first Fort on that point where the lake is forking in two branches. After some years a dispute started with one trapper and the manager about furs payment and the manager was shot. For some years the store was closed and the H.B. opened a new one at the outlet of the lake where is the biggest camp.

The name of Babine given to these Indians comes from the practice of the women hanging a bright shell or a piece of cut glass from the lower lip for beauty sake enlarging it considerably in course of time. We remained there for the Sunday and on Monday escorted or proceeded by all the people of the village we left for Babine town at the end of the lake about 22 miles distant. Coming in sight of the camp our men opened the gun fire which was answered by the people lined up on the shore. By coincidence the Hagwilget who had been informed of the coming of the Priest to Babine had sent a large delegation and reaching the lake shore through the narrow gulch of the mountains responded by the mouth of their guns, and for half an hour the echos of [word missing] resounded with the reports. When the Stuart Lake saw that I was going to Babine [they] pitied me, making an awful description of that camp, who at the coming of the priest would stop their superstitions, wash the paint from their face, put a new dress on, hide their paraphernalia until the mission was over and go back to the old style as soon as the priest would be two miles out of sight.[70] Little apprehending at first, my apprehensions vanished away at the hand shaking of all the crowd. I had met more ferocious wild Indians in the Nicola Valley. I went first to the church built by Father Marchal 40 years ago. All followed and then [I] gave the program for the week I was to spend with them. The chief showed me the house near the church which I was to occupy for the time I was to be in Babine.

I asked for the name of the owner and if he was a good living man. Was told that he had been deserted by his legitimate wife, and had took a woman to himself. "Cannot consent to be in a house where the devil had been reigning," I said, and refused to go in. Another house though little distant from the church owned by good living Catholic was shown to me.

The work began by the gathering of the chief & his counsellors or watchmen; they had to report on the moral conditions of the camp. The names of couples living in concubinage were given. Separations had to be made at once for we could not admit in the church scandalous people. Those living in sin but single should rectify their unions; if could not agree, then find another man or woman to marry. Some would say: "We will do that at your next visit," "You have made such promises to other priests and you have returned to your criminal life. Hurry to make up your mind and give your names for publication of the banns." The gamblers, the sorcerers had to bring the articles used for gambling and for their superstitions. Not knowing yet the use of cards they have little bones 2 inches long, one of them with a circle in the middle, one of the gamblers had them in each hand which are in constant movement, the other to guess in what hand is the bone with the circle; guessing right is the winner or he loses. The rest of the crowd is sitting around beating drums in singing in chorus keeping the excitement to a pitch; nights and days are spent in that way, until they fall asleep exhausted. The Indian Doctor when in action is habitually dressed with the skin of some animals adorned with amulets, or skin of snakes for neck tie, or with the claws of birds or young deer hoofs hanging on all sides of his robe, which jumping around the sick person rattles and impresses the assistants, all screaming to drive [away] the evil spirit supposed to be the cause of the sickness. The excitement of the doctor is such that perspiration rolls from his body and he drops down exhausted. When the gamblers and doctors have brought the gambling articles and the Indian doctors their paraphernalia they are burnt before the public—only then they are admitted in the church. Some refuse to submit to all these regulations, and become wildly disposed. I was told that one of them was to kill the priest. Towards the end of the mission promises were made to live up to the teachings and regulations of the church. And many applied to make their first Communion.

(To Hagwilget) The word Hagwilget means: man well dressed. Having discarded the blanket, they were first to adopt the Whiteman's clothes—The Hagwilget offered to take me to their village by toboggan. Wishing to be accompanied with so many as possible of my spiritual children, I accepted. Young men disputed [for] the honor to guide or pull the toboggan, for up hill the dogs were not enough powerful to haul it. Even these willing men had to change hands to climb up to the summit and then down hill to keep the carriage on the trail, upsetting once in a while and face came in contact with the snow, or bushes. Often tired out of being strapped on those toboggans, I was asking them to let me walk, for the perfume that the dogs would leave behind them was not of roses. We had to camp three times, for turning dark about 3 o'clock, we had to stop early enough so to see the dry timber that had to keep us from freezing during the night and to prevent smoke and sparks. When the leader of the caravan called halt, all stopped, and every one knowing his work goes to it lively, the axe men chopping the trees, the tent men some cutting branches for the bed, others shovelling the snow with their snow shoes, the cooks starting the fire. Meanwhile I was saying my office remaining in the toboggan rolled in fur blankets until the fire was started. In those caravans there is a leader ordering the stops & starts and nobody to dispute his orders. Supper over there is a little recreation talk, evening prayer, a little instruction comparing ourselves to the Holy Family in their flight to Egypt. At nine o'clock the dogs are fed one dry salmon each which is quickly swallowed not always peacefully, [some] trying to steal from the slow one their portion. Five or more burning logs have to keep us from freezing. Tents are built in a round, all to have the benefit of the fire and [to] prevent the smoke or the sparks to be blown in by the wind but going up straight as by a chimney. If during the night the fire goes down two men one at each end of the log turn it over to start a new blaze and add a fresh log piled close in the evening. At 3 in the morning the leader gives a signal, prayer and light breakfast, dogs hitched up and off we are. If we had a fresh fall of snow, two men after supper go on to trample the trail until midnight, for the dogs have no pulling power in fresh deep snow; the toboggan also sticks, and unless men on snow shoes go ahead, impossible to advance. In some of these trips we had to grease the toboggan with the lard we had for our cooking. Hagwilget was reached at last on the 4th day about 10 o'clock—one of our boys had gone in the night to inform the people. Firing guns announced our coming. After the shaking of hands, a powerful speaker said: "Who is this priest with gray hair coming across the mountains covered with snow to see us; no one had done that before. He must be a true lover of the Indians to risk himself in the middle of the winter."

The church built also by Father Marchal was packed. Old man Denis my interpreter who had spent a part of his youth with Father LeJacq, said to him one day: "Father people want me to get married but that I cannot do, for then I would have to leave you, and I love you more than any woman in the world." But Father said: "You are a big man and better to get married." Now Denis is very old & blind and his wife leads him to church with a stick. The same work done in Babine was done in Hagwilget. A man who had been abandoned by his lawful wife & living with another offered [a] hundred dollars now and more to be given after if I would allow him to remain in that condition. All were animated with good dispositions and hungry for the bread of life; the Eucharist was presented to them as the reward of good behaviour.

The Holy Week approaching returned to Babine, for the first time the exercises of the Holy Week were taking place in that church.[71] All were impressed by the narration of the sufferings of our Lord and on Easter some were allowed to make their first Communion. When getting ready to return to Stuart Lake Mission, a telegram from Bishop Dontenwill to Hazelton but transferred by the government telegraph office at Babine was calling me to New Westminster to attend the council. The shortest way and the only way was to go by the Skeena River on a small boat connecting at Port Essington with the C.P.R. Steamers from Alaska. The snow was going away fast, no more to depend on toboggans, snowshoes could be used only for a part of the trail to Hazelton.

The name of that town, very lively in 1906, came from the natural hazel tree seen in abundance around the flat. Built on the shores of the

Skeena River about 200 miles from the sea it is the terminus of navigation for the few months that the river is navigable. All the supplies for
the Bulkley Valley, Kispiox and the mines of Babine and Omenica coming from Vancouver or other points on the Pacific as far as Port Essington were transferred to the steamers plying on the Skeena and were
landed in Hazelton and from there carried by pack horses or by teams to
their destination. Indians first and after White people and Chinese
formed the population. In the 1870's, Father McGuckin and after him
Fathers Marchal and LeJacq had visited the Indians but in passing baptized some of them. But for want of missionaries the work was not kept
up and afterwards Protestant ministers established themselves in the locality. What Catholics are there, they come to Hagwilget for their religious duties.

Three young men offered to pack my camping outfit and food supply
for the trip. Leaving early, just at the break of the day, alone on snowshoes [and] thinking that my men were following close, at 11 o'clock I
reached the top of the first hill, started the fire and when saying my office my men overtook me surprised that I could make such fast time. My
snowshoes were stuck in the snow. Looking at them the boy said: "One
of your snowshoes is broken." I remembered that I had been caught in a
root and pulling it off it broke. Feeling the big toe aching, pulled off my
stocking and it was sprained; I had not felt it at first, but now it was
swollen and painful. The manager of the Hudson's Bay Babine post had
come too and scolded the boys for having let me go alone and said:
"Now I take charge of the Father for the rest of the trip." Mr. Ware who
had married a Catholic Half-breed outside of the church, and whose
marriage I had rectified and children baptized was very kind to me bathing my toe every night in warm water. Years after I met Mr. Ware at
Telegraph Creek when he had been transferred. There also Mr. Ware
was very good to me, and Mrs. Ware was fixing the altar where I was
saying Mass. Reaching Hazelton I stopped with the Indian agent Mr.
Loring [while] waiting for the boat that was to take me to Port Essington. By the end of April I was with the Bishop and the Fathers were surprised to see me coming by that way [illegible] so early in the season, for
no one could come out of the New Caledonia before June. Besides many
reports had appeared in the newspapers that on the trail from Quesnel
our horses had been stolen and I had fallen in the hands of brigands.

I gave my report on the conditions of people and country to his
Lordship told him what the Stuart Lake Indians had said when leaving
their village in February. "We heard that you may go back to Kooteney
in Summer; you put us up on our feet but we are not strong enough to
keep on going ahead if you leave us now, and your good work will be
lost and we shall fall in the old rut in a short time, but if you remain for a

year longer with us we will be strong enough; and after that any priest will keep us on the right road." The Bishop asked me then if I did like to go back to Stuart Lake.

"For the good of that mission I suppose I must."

"As soon as the roads through the Cariboo will be passable, I shall visit your people myself."

Profiting of spare time I went to Kootenay to see my brother priest who had come from Europe in December last to see me, but impossible to go to Stuart Lake in the winter.[72] By the end of May with Bishop Dontenwill we left New Westminster for the north and it took the months of June & July and a part of August to cover the district of New Caledonia. More than 200 Indians were confirmed and with the Bishop I returned to the coast bringing some children to Williams Lake school on our way. I was not long in New Westminster when a telegram called me back to Babine to settle the troubles caused by the officers of the fisheries who were preventing the Indians to catch salmon by means of weirs or barricades in the river at the outlet of Babine lake. The weirs or barricades consisted of driving sticks in the stream forming the outlet of the lake through which the salmon was going to its spawning ground. Here and there the barricades were left open for the salmon to pass, but on the other side of the barricades were baskets in which the salmon, going in, could not come back. These baskets were made in the form of a cone and once full these baskets were raised and the fish were taken out and put in the canoes. Brought to land the fish was cleaned, cut in shape and exposed to the sun & smoked to cure. The Indians depended on dried salmon for their food & bait for the trapping; like a farmer at the harvest, they were busy at it as long as the fish kept coming. The officers of fisheries remarking that the salmon was getting less every year with so many canneries at the mouth of the Skeena attributed the scarcity of the salmon to the number of fish taken by the Indians, and wanted to prevent them making barricades and give them nets in compensation. In 1905, the Babine depending on the promised nets built no barricades, the nets came too late for the fishing and what nets came at last they were too old, breaking through, consequently the following winter the Indians nearly starved and had no bait for the traps. So next summer they resolved to go back to the barricades. The officers came to Babine to stop them in their work. The Indians not minding them went to work and at last infuriated threw one of them in the stream, a woman of 200 lbs jumping on him pretending to help him out. Those troubles were reported and 9 Indians were under arrest. But instead of surrendering they took to the woods well armed for protection. Hearing of this, I was hurrying up for Babine and reaching Fort Fraser at the telegraph station I wired to Babine of my coming. They wired back that 9 men were under arrest and asking what they should do. I wired to Ottawa [and] asked the Minister of the Interior to let me know if I should advise the Indians to surrender. The answer was tell them to surrender by all means, and that the Minister of Justice would set them free if not guilty. Transmitted the Ottawa answer to Babine and asked them to send men and canoes to Stuart Lake to take me up to Babine. Another wire from Ottawa asked me to take two of the most intelligent of the camp and come to Ottawa at once. Left Fraser Lake and reaching Stuart Lake the canoes were not long to come, travelled day and night and coming at night time to Babine was told that the 9 men who surrendered, were at once sent to jail in New Westminster for 6 months and hard labor; "Do not feel uneasy," I said to wives of those gone to jail and to all [the] camp, "The men will soon be back; pray and everything will turn well." Heard the confessions all night and early the following morning with the 2 chiefs left for Hazelton to take the first boat down the Skeena connecting with the C.P.R. steamer coming from Alaska.

On my way down in the Skeena, we met on the boat coming up our prisoners who had been set free and [were] returning to their camp; great rejoicing by both the prisoners and myself with my two chiefs. Asked permission from Bishop Dontenwill, and by train reached Ottawa October 20th. Called at the University [of Ottawa] and exposed to the Rector, Father Murphy, the object of my visit to the Capital.[73] He phoned the superintendent that I was in the city with my 2 Babines, asked for the conference, [it] being so late in the season and wishing to return to my missions before the freezing of the Skeena River. The answer was that the Ministers were busy at present, but would send cars to take us around the Capital and would arrange for a meeting late in the afternoon. So it was done. We were shown through the city and at four o'clock we found ourselves in a large room. The Minister of [the] Interior at the head of a long table, I was offered a seat to his right, my two Indians, trembling, close to me and the rest of the table occupied by members of the Indian Department and Fisheries; at one end stenographers. At first the Minister of the Interior was cross and sharp in questioning the Indians, I being the interpreter. The two poor men were naturally excited, all in perspiration, but I was interpreting with calm giving them a look of encouragement. The first question was: "Being armed did you threaten the officers of fisheries?"

"No—our men were all sitting, on the lake shore, women were driving stakes in the river to catch salmon, as we had always done except last year because we were promised abundance of nets by these officers. The nets were sent too late when the best run of fish had gone through. When we made use of the nets to get the last fishes passing by we found the nets being too old and rotten, salmon passed through them. The consequence was that we nearly starved in winter and had no bait for our traps. So this fall our women had resolved to fish as they always did by using barricades, even at the cost of life. When driving the stakes, the officers advanced in the creek to pull them out and one of the strong women weighing 200 lbs threw one of them down in the water and sat on him (all the audience laughed) but after that she took him to shore and let him alone. Then the officers sent blue papers to 9 of our men who refused to accept them, now they came after us and they ran to the woods. On receipt of the telegram from Fort Fraser they went to Hazelton to attend court."

Second question: "Had you guns in your hands [when] sitting on the shore?"

Answer, "No, Why did we need guns for a handful of white men? We knew that the women could handle them easy. We did not want any trouble, but salmon. So we did not say word or show fighting." The minister had a pile of papers from which he was taking his questions. Sitting near the minister I could even recognize the telegrams [I] had sent myself from Fort Fraser. Then I said to the Minister: "Will you allow me to speak and in a few minutes I shall show you the cause of all this trouble."

"Go on Father."

"The Babine Indians have been for many years law abiding, and since I took charge of them I find them improving fast and more willing to look after their stock and provide for their families. I insisted on them to keep away from intoxicating drinks and not expose their women to go alone to Hazelton & because our Babine Indians refuse to buy whisky, and keep their women from contamination the white people are angry at them. In years gone by, when the Indians had only the salmon to depend on for their subsistence, and furs little value, they had three barricades at some distance but parallel every year and never removed them except for the canoes to pass and for that the ice would break and yet salmon was never less. But since the many canneries have started at the mouth of the River, fish is getting less, much of the salmon brought to the canneries is thrown back in the water because they cannot handle it at once and it gets spoiled or because they have not canning material on hand; for many other reasons fish is destroyed. But now the Indians, having bacon, flour, and many other things to eat they can buy with the money proceeding from the sale of furs, are really neglecting their barricades and what salmon they take is very little compared to the past."

Another question, why the Indians, being too lazy, do not cultivate the land?

"The good land is scarce there; here and there are spots where they can plant potatoes, the rest is swamps where they secure hay for their stock, or gravel or mountains, good for wild animals." We adjourned, all present looking with a kinder eye to my Indians—[I] could see that I had won those present to the cause of my people.

The following day managed to have an audience with the Minister of the Interior in his own office, gave him the topography of the country and made him to understand the necessity of the salmon fishing for the Indians. After having secured the sympathy of my man, I looked at my watch saying: "I am very sorry to have taken so much of your precious time."

"Not at all, I learned more about B.C. by your conversation than I could have learned from books."

Matters were clear enough and every day we kept waiting for another conference in which the rights of the Indians would be publicly proclaimed and be allowed to return to our mountains: but oh! politics!—The federal elections being at hand, the votes of the canneries owners might be against the actual Government if the Indians had been granted the use of barricades. The head man of the fisheries, Mr. Williams, with some of his officers had been summoned to Ottawa to give their opinion on the mode of fishing, and on the conduct of the Indians toward the officers on Babine Lake. Every day I was calling on some of the members of the staff of the Indian Department, even Mr. Laurier. Told them on one occasion: "I know my presence is not agreeable to you, but you shall see me until you grant us our rights for then we shall leave for British Columbia. Or put me in jail and then I cannot come."

The secretary superintendent asked me: "what countryman are you?"

I said: "From Corsica."

"No wonder you are a fighter."

"Not a fighter," I said, "but a conqueror."

"It is not often that you come East, take advantage of this opportunity go abroad and see Canada through. On your return matters will be settled."

Went then to Montreal and Quebec to hear Father le Lievre and see the wonderful work in his parish of St. Sauveur.[74] It was the First Friday, like the waves on the sea, the crowd that filled the church at 7 emptied, the church was followed by an other crowd at 8, and this time all men.[75] I called also on the President of the C.P.R., Shaughnessy at that time, who speaking of the services rendered to the Company by O.M.I. Fathers said: "We cannot ever repay them; for instance Father Lacombe." Returning to Ottawa I found my two chiefs, who were located at the scholasticate, in tears asking to go back home: "Our children, our stock may be neglected." I got vexed and told them to go: "For my part I have to stay here until the conclusion of this affair." On the 36th day since our arrival once more a conference was called. The Indians were promised in writing all the nets needed, to be renewed every year, farm implements, with an extension of their reserve, 1640 acres of good land, and schools for their children. All our expenses were paid to the amount of $900.00 and winter clothes furnished for our return. What was the joy of my two men when at day light, coming to Shuswap Lake, [we] could see the forests of B.C. after leaving the prairies, plains devoid of trees. Knowing that the navigation on the Skeena was closed long ago I remained at the coast but my two companions going by steamer to a point called Kitimat made the rest of the way on snowshoes to Hazelton and Babine reached in February 1907. In May, profited [by] the first boat on the Skeena to reach Hazelton where the Babines and Hagwilget informed of my coming received me in great triumph.

Having to remain in Babine for some days, it was decided to build a house for the priest adjoining the church and the lumber was sawed and left to dry for [my] next visit. Going back to Hagwilget [I] made plans for a new church and $1,5000.00 being collected I gave the contract to a carpenter of Kispiox.

The newpapers of Vancouver boasting so much [of] the Bulkley Valley, and myself receiving letters enquiring about it, I wanted to go through it to enable me to give the proper reports. Found the valley rather narrow and the soil generally shallow with the gravel about four inches under surface. Here and there flats of rich loam, but exposed to flood. At Aldermere [I] stopped in a good size hotel accommodating prospectors who had located mineral claims, waiting for capital to develop. A saw mill supplying lumber to new settlers was at the mouth of the Telkwa stream emptying into the Bulkley River—stopped at Eugene Croteau's who years ago was one of the staff of St. Eugene School, Kootenay. Said Mass at the Lacroix family whom I had known at Ste. Mary's Mission on the Fraser River. Stopped at Burns Lake with three Indian families. Reached Fort Fraser but as the Indians were out hunting kept on going and by the end of August I was in Stuart Lake where I found my socius Father Bellot ready to go to Europe.[76] Time was due to visit Fort George, where the church was getting too small and it was proposed to enlarge it. Returning by the Nechako River [I] gave the Stony Creek and Fraser Lake people the opportunity to receive the Sacraments, and knowing that the McLeod's Lake Indians were anxious to have the visit of the priest hurried up home. In October I was in McLeod's Lake for the first time. The chief had died and a new one was elected. A mission of 4 days was well attended and many gave their names for the first communion. Every where the Holy Eucharist was my bait to attract the people to God. On October 25th, 1907, I was again in Stuart Lake just in time for the exercises in prepartion for All Saints Day. The Indians from all around were there waiting for me. During the mission at free time, more than 200 logs were cut and hauled on the spot for the school; the ground around the house and church was cleaned out, turned over and prepared to receive the seeds next spring.

On the 5th of November was leaving for Babine. On my way I visited the 2 hatcheries newly built by the Marine Department, one on Cunningham Creek and the other on the north branch of Babine Lake—the object of those costly buildings put up by the federal department was to people the two lakes with salmon. The theory is that every fourth year the salmon, gone to the sea when 2 years old, returns after 4 years to spawn to the place of his birth, and dies after. Such may be the case when the spawning is natural, but after the eggs are in a mild water to hatch, when the young fish is turned out he is too tender and many perish in the cold streams dashing against the boulders they meet on the way before reaching open water in the lakes where also being delicate and not lively become an easy prey for the hungry trouts. Some of the tagged salmon in leaving the hatcheries were found to return. The local Indians are benefited by the hatcheries, being employed in supplying fire wood, freighting, and procuring the million eggs required every year.

In Babine the outside of the church was lined with dressed lumber and more manual work would have been done if it was not for the scarcity of nails in the H.B. stores both in Hazelton and Babine due to the wrecking of the steamers in the Skeena River. For the spiritual and moral advancement of our people a general cleaning had become necessary. Like the rest of the humans many had returned to the evil practices; no serious breaking of the laws was left unpunished; the guilty asked for what was coming to them. The subject of the instructions was lying and its consequence. To excuse oneself, the Babines had a lie always ready, told without blushing and so calmly that their innocence is readily believed by one who does not know them; of them we may say, "You lie like an Indian."

The Babines were hoping that I would stay with them for new year but the Hagwilget who had sent messengers to take me to their camp for that day fought their case so well that I left with them. Snowing almost every day, it took us 4 days to cross the mountains.

The new church was far from being completed inside. The contractor being not Catholic had not understood the plans, and part of the sanctuary had to be rebuilt over. Working day and night my new carpenters had things in shape, the Blessed Sacrament was carried over from the old church on the last day of the year 1907.

The people of Hazelton & Kispiox though not Catholics were there with their band, followed the ceremonies & instructions given in their language, which made them say: "No man ever spoke so nice as that [and] we never heard things so consoling to the heart of man, they are a light to man's intelligence." To show their appreciation they voluntarily made a generous offering to help toward the finishing of the new church. They promised to follow the exercises of the mission, 5 were baptized, and many others had to wait, notwithstanding their strong desire. Ordered 1000 lb bell, to be heard from Hazelton & Kispiox. Met James Cronin who years ago was at St. Eugene and had bought for $40,000 a mine on Babine. Some sick people of Moricetown about 30 miles south asked for the priest and the trip was made in a sleigh for the first time in the history of the country, until then toboggan or snowshoes in winter were the only means of locomotion.

Back to Babine with the hope of going on to Stuart Lake, but the ice on the lakes not being strong enough we had to wait patiently for colder days until the 15th of February. Prospectors following our trail had come from Hazelton going to Ingenica about 200 miles north of Babine, where gold had been found by the Bear Lake Indians. These prospectors could find no nails in Hazelton on account of the wrecking of the boats in the Skeena. We gave them what we had, the cold weather preventing us to go on with our constructions this season.

Reaching Stuart Lake the people who had not the usual exercises of Chrismas and New year had them now. Hearing that there was an influx of white people on the Nechako Valley, land seekers and surveyors of the G.T.R. [Grand Trunk Railway] I left on the 15th March on snowshoes for Stony Creek and Fraser Lake to give our natives serious instructions, to put them on guard against the bad influence that the presence of so many newcomers could have upon them. A large camp of surveyors was located close to the Indian reserve of Fraser Lake, some of them prowling around the camp late in the night, the watchmen asked [what] was to be done. Told them that anyone who wanted to disturb the families, they should be told that no Whitemen were allowed in the reserve in the night after nine. One of them being drunk & noisy, the watchmen together dragged him out through the mud to the limits of the reserve. The day after he said that he never had before such a triumphal march: that was enough to keep the camp free at night.

It was rumoured that the work of the road bed of the railway was to start in summer and that the trains to be in operation in 1911. Good news for us for then it would become easy to get building material for our school, furnitures & food, the Indian Department having promised all that when [the] train would be operating. The belfry of St. Joseph's Church, Fort Fraser had been blown down some say by wind storm or by earth tremor. A plan was made and reconstruction began but there like in Hazelton nails scarce. Then came the news of the death of our Superior General Lavillardière and of Brother John Burns in Kootenay.

The church was draped in black and we prayed for the repose of their souls.

Returning to Stuart Lake on April 15th for the exercises in preparation for Easter, the Indians were sawing lumber for the school. Brother Lajoie from St Mary's Mission was loaned to us for the building of it; he risked to be drowned in the Nechako falling from the scow. He was saved by the promptitude of the men to pull him out. We had 155 first communicants at Easter.

To finish the sawing of the logs we proposed to keep the people four days longer. The Indians of Cayochet not coming to work, a watchman was sent to them with the message that if they were not coming to saw they would not be allowed to put a foot on mission land. In response they delegated one big man Josue to turn and ridicule our sawers but he was roughly received, and covered with shame and black eye, went back to his camp with much shame. The logs were sawed. Took advantage of the burial of a woman, all the Indians of the different camps present at Stuart Lake yet to proclaim the law that from this one the coffins were not to be costly decorated, for much money was spent in pride and no Mass was asked for the dead. April 27th, the weather getting warm it was hoped that ice on the Stuart River would let us pass. Left for Fort George, where after the usual exercises of a mission, all renewed their good resolutions for a good Christian life. I continued in canoe by the Fraser River to Quesnel and from there by stage to Williams Lake to make my confession after 8 months from the last one. There found a letter of Bishop Dontenwill calling me to New Westminster where Father Bunoz was nominated Prefect Apostolic of the New Prefecture of Yukon of which the district of Stuart Lake was a part.[77] On my way back visited Stony Creek & Fraser Lake reaching Stuart Lake for the feast of Corpus Christi. I was expecting the Indians of McLeod to take me to their camp where the building of the church was advancing. White people, attracted by rich prospects on the River Finlay and its tributaries, had invaded the country.

On June 23rd, Father Bellot returning from Europe made his apparition [*sic*] and on the 29th we left together for Babine. Father Bellot was to remain there and I to continue for Hagwilget at the great regret of the population. I tried to console them saying: "I leave you a priest."

"Yes," they said, "but that is not you,"

Father Bellot to help me remarked: "What will you do when Father Coccola dies?"

They said, "We will die with him."

But my mind was made up and I went. Work done in Hagwilget, I left for the coast by the Skeena. The high water prevented the boat to pass the Kitzlas [Kitselas] Canyon where I had to stay for days until the telegraph operator told me that a doctor had to perform an operation six miles down stream but had no help to administer the anaesthetic and asked me if I wanted to go. "Certainly if there is a way to pass through the canyon." A cedar boat manned by Indians who had crossed the canyon many a time took me down to the point where the doctor was waiting. The following day a construction boat *Caledonia* took me down to the new town of Prince Rupert, terminus of the Grand Trunk Railway. But what a location for a town! Nothing but rocks or marshy ground & stumps. We will have to see what townsite it will make; but people said Seattle was not any better when first located but see what a town it is now. Of course the port is an ideal one, large deep water and well protected from all winds. Father Bunoz Prefect Apostolic after spending 2 weeks in that new town had returned to Dawson. The lots were not yet for sale and the Catholics had put up a big tent in it for Mass on Sunday for about 30 people. Mr Dan Morrissey, O. Besner, and a few others proposed to buy an organ.

On July 22nd, 1908, I reached New Westminster too late for the annual retreat which I made alone. After the Provincial Chapter at which Father Tavernier was elected delegate to the General Chapter which named Bishop Dontenwill Superior General, I visited Revelstoke, where my brother was in charge, Golden, Field, and other points of interest so much improved since I had left that district. On my way back to the New Caledonia via Prince Rupert. [I] spent the month of September in Moricetown & Hagwilget blessing the beautiful statues of the Sacred Heart, Immaculate Conception & St. Joseph. In October, the trail having 2 feet of snow, we made our journey to Babine in three days. There, between instructions and catechism, was beautified the outside of the old church by two towers at each corner in the front: [I] cleared the graveyard of the old monuments on the graves and showed how to fix the graves in the future. The people took advantage of the long stay of the priest to approach often at the Holy Table. The Holy Eucharist being the lever I had to keep the camp on the path of virtue.

November 1st, the Feast of All Saints, was celebrated with enthusiasm; on the evening of the All Souls Day the procession to the grave yard with lighted torches pleased the Indians, who are doing so well; may they persevere. November 10th, we were off for Stuart Lake which we found frozen and my guides wanted to go back. I told them: "You never heard [of] Fr. Coccola going back." We broke the ice for many miles but at last we came on open sea, plugged the holes made by sharp ice with our sticks end. On the 17th we reached the mission. Father Bellot had just killed a fat steer. Home sweet home! The same week the H.B. scow landed at the Fort loaded with winter supply and a nice bell for St.

Nicolas church at Cayochet. Though the fall had announced very severe with snowstorms and blizzard, the thermometer did not go down below 5– which allowed our Indians to make a good catch of beaver, every one coming home with an average of 40 skins and plenty meat. On the feast of the Immaculate Conception exposition all day of the Blessed Sacrament, the church filling with adorators [sic] all day, and 60 communions.

The 24th of December the lake being only partly frozen the surrounding camps could not come for Christmas, but many were here from Fort Fraser, Stony Creek & Cheslatta. The Cayochet people were in revolt with Chief Joseph, accusing him of too much severity. The freighters of the Hudson's Bay Company scows had been dissipating on their last trip to Graham & Quesnel, and the little chief Jaurie Haoul had been too lenient with them [the Indians] in the absence of Joseph who taking the cases over had imposed heavy fines on the drunkards. I was ordered not to hear serious cases but to leave them to himself. Knowing all the circumstances I called a general meeting allowing every one to expose their grievance against Joseph, and calmly I showed them how fortunate they should consider themselves to have a strong chief who was preventing the complete demoralization of their camp. All were pacified and by the shaking of hands proved their spirit of submission. Fines paid and before the Blessed Sacrament promised to do better in future.

Christmas over, logs were cut and hauled for the renewal of the foundation of the church and of the lining it on the outside. On January 1st 1909, the mercury dropped down to 40° below, the roarings of the ice breaking in the lake was reached by the mountains. Never had the blocks of ice been so high on both sides of the large cracks. On the 10th of February the thermometer registered 53° below. On the 17th, the renovation of the vows of the 2 members of the congregation before the Blessed Sacrament exposed broke the monotony of the winter. On the 19th of March, 8 Babine Indians came to take the priest to spend Easter in their camps. The depth of the snow and the second ice on the frozen lake breaking under the feet of the horses at times exhausted, but did not discourage my men, who with their snowshoes beating the way made it easier for the horses. Passing by Taché village, the logs for a new and larger church being on the spot we decide for the location so they could start to build. Beaching at Old Fort on Babine Lake we found the crowd who had come to meet the priest and beat down the trail. A beautiful Station of the Cross was blessed and installed.[78] The Statues of the Blessed Virgin and St. Joseph & new candlesticks were unpacked & blessed also.

The 25th of March, at night, we landed in Babinetown. The young men who had packed machineries [sic] and provisions to Ingenica mines were arriving also. Shortly after came the people from Hagwilget to partake of the exercises in preparation for Easter. Taking advantage of so many men around me, the manual and spiritual work was going hand in hand. The saws, the hammers, all on the go, the priest's house was connected with the church making church & house more comfortable and warmer. On Holy Thursday, the statue of the Sacred Heart was blessed before the general Communion. On Easter the church was beautifully decorated [and] once more all approached the Holy Table. The priest was really happy among his devoted children. Providence procures here and there some happy moments to encourage him in the work.

Big Chief George had two hemorrhages and was administered the last Sacraments, all the camp praying for him. Feasts & work done, we were on the way to Stuart Lake Mission. The ice like a crystal & solid we were making 50 miles a day. Never before had we made such a fast time. Father Bellot with all the people from Stony Creek, Fort Fraser, even from Cheslatta, did not waste time. The lumber for the lining of the church was sawed and piled up to allow to season before nailing. So all over, the work was satisfactory thanks to God, Lord Jesus Christ and Mary Immaculate.

By the end of April the soil was in good shape to trust our seeds, barley & clover around the house. In May we plowed some more land for oats. The Indians were waiting for the water hens a species of duck of which they make a large provision every year, they carry much fat which they preserve and use like lard in the guts & bladders duly prepared and kept for the purpose from large animals. These birds come in such a quantity that driven to the shore of the lake the children kill them with sticks for they are slow to soar from the ground. Otherwise they catch them in nets put in the lake six feet above surface in which they are caught when driven by canoes coming behind them. To take away the disagreeable fishy taste, the Indians, when roasting them for me, they remove first the skin, then they have no fish taste.

On the 5th of May the Stony Creek came to get the priest for sick people. Passing by Fort Fraser found that the belfry was only half up. I told the people that if they had not all the material on the spot on my return on the 7th of June I would pass by without stopping. At Stony Creek the walls and roof of the priest's house were on, but nothing done inside—there also they were told to have all the material ready for my return from Fort George. At Fort George also the new church was only started and it was decided to wait for the building of a proposed saw mill to continue the work; meanwhile during the mission we built dressers for the church vestments. The statue of the Sacred Heart and candlestick having just come were blessed. All approached the Holy Table twice, some thrice. The Eucharist is the lever that moves all. My plan was to build a church large enough for the Indians & Whites until the townsite would be located.[79]

South Fort George, one of the 3 prospective locations for a town site, was developing, fast, large stores doing good business—2 large boats bringing people & supplies of all kinds from Soda Creek. On my way back found the Stony Creek busy sawing lumber for the priest's house. We installed the Way of the Cross. Coming to Fort Fraser the Cheslatta Lake people were waiting for the priest, helping to finish the belfry, all very busy, astonishing everybody as they are known for their apathetic dispositions. Until then they buried their dead anywhere and now they decided to have a regular cemetery. June 16th saw me in Stuart Lake, the dry spring and cold nights had put a damper on our garden: the potatoes having raised their heads were frozen to the ground. The flies and moustiques [sic] habitually so ferocious did not disturb us, it being too cold. The Hudson's Bay Company manager sent one of his employees with a broken leg. After 4 weeks [he] could walk. The water in the lake and consequently in the Stuart Lake River was so low that the steamer which was expected to come as far as Fort St. James did not appear, though for the first and last time it had steamed up to Fort Fraser on the 24th of June. Rumors were circulating that the Indians along the Skeena and the Kispiox had been threatening to drive the Whites out of the country unless the Government would consent to add to their reserves 20 square miles of land. The Whites also organized to secure protection. Fearing that my flock in Hagwilget would be implicated in this trouble, I moved there at once. On July 8th, the Secretary of the Superintendent of Indian Affairs from Ottawa, the commissioner from Victoria, escorted by the Chief of Police O'Connor, landed in Hazelton the same day I did. They were frightened but Mr. Stuart with whom I had spent days in Ottawa when there for the Babines' troubles said: "We are saved, Father is here." The members of the different camps were invited to an audience to expose their grievances. At the meeting in Hagwilget I had one of my best men, with requests written in their language but translated by an interpreter, to expose their own grievances in these terms: "We are Catholics by religious belief, and Canadian by law, in both lines we stick to our principles. We do not want [to] shed human blood but we want protection for [the] future of our families. Too often the Whites have put our faithfulness to the laws of God & Country to [the] test, setting fire to our cabins in our hunting grounds, and destroying our farms. We are glad to see that at last the Government opens its eyes and sees the sad consequences that would result of that state of affairs. Here are our requests. The Moricetown [Indians] divided in three small reserves should be made in one with all the land between the three to be given to the Indians; in all our hunting or trapping locations that a certain amount of land should be reserved to build cabins and room for a garden so to have a foot hold during the trapping season, without any fear of being molested by white intruders." The Commissioners found these requests very reasonable & made many promises but what will become of it is to be seen.—Extended my visit to Aldermere, offering Mass to where it was possible, but the people are so taken up with temporal business that have no time for the spiritual. As one said: "We are here to make money when that done we shall attend the other concerns."

For some time my mind was turned towards the Bear Lake, Fort Connelly. That can be done only once a year in August. The church there nearly being completed, I am told, and where many of the necessary things previously had been sent.

Leaving Babine on a Monday the 2nd of August 1909, the journey was not a picnic having so many portages to make. Reached Takla Lake landing the following day about noon where the canoe, dug out, was waiting to take me to Bear Lake. The landing was 50 years ago an important village with a population of 400 souls. Prospectors making it their starting point for the Omenica Mines, storing there supplies, food or machineries [sic] to bring to the different mining creeks showing gold deposits according to their needs. A steamboat had brought there once from Quesnel about $40,000.00 worth of cargo but stranded there, not another made any attempt after to go through the many rapids of the Fraser, Nechako, Stuart and Taché Rivers. Paddling our canoe with Plug Hat Tom for captain for about 20 miles on Takla Lake we camped at the mouth of Driftwood River. The River was well named. Trees of all dimensions carried by the summer high water were jammed forming a barrier, and the only way to overcome it is to slide the embarcation [sic] over the jam. The Indians coming down had set their traps in the River and we had all the beaver meat we wanted besides the skin which carried good value at that time. Going up stream I remarked the grass along the shores beaten down and the trees cut down and asked the boys on the boat if surveyors had cut those trees and if they had pack trains. They laughed at my question and said, "This evening after six o'clock you will see for yourself who has done the work." In fact at six we heard the beavers cutting [trees] with their teeth and floating or hauling them to their lodges. The beavers are out of sight during the day but work at night.

The water in August was getting low and boulders were close to the surface in many places. The boys had to get off, pushing hauling and dodging the canoe.

The third day we came to the camp of Beau Sejour, a name given by the Hudson's Bay freighters packing to Fort Connelly, many of them being French Canadians halfbreeds. We camped there also, enjoying the open country, beautiful when compared with [what] had been seen along the River. The fourth day we left the Driftwood River to enter in an open large swamp with a narrow slough, tortuous, narrow under branches, through where we had to navigate slowly. Providence will eliminate these difficulties of travelling next year. The beavers turned the meadows in a big lake, the Indians cleared the slough of its branches and snags and the priest's canoe floated without delays until we came to three portages from Little Lake to another; the last portage of about ¾ of a mile put us on Bear Lake, 15 miles long, the Indian village located at the other end of the lake on top of the hill and at the foot of a glacier. Found there about one hundred souls, Catholic or pagan, some had come from Fort Graham and Telegraph Creek; the little church was well crowded, all attending anxious to hear what the priest had to say having not seen one for a long time. Father Blanchet visited them in past years. One man did not put his foot in, the notorious Scoucom [Skookum], Tom Strong Tom a pagan and the terror of the camp, all were afraid of him. Chief and watchmen came to tell me how he had killed Indians and White prospectors to rob their outfits, that the woman he had was taken by force after killing her father, and they asked me if he should not be driven from the camp. I went to see him in his cabin to find out why he was not coming to church. Cunningly he said that not being baptized he dared not to enter in the house of God, but being well disposed and instructed he would be baptized. I was doubting of his sincerity but thought as well that he could be allowed to remain in the camp at least until my next visit. To tell all what happened to Skookum Tom: In the following winter he went to trap with his supposed wife, having an little orphan girl with them. Returning to the camp in the spring without the woman he was asked what had become of her, but he said: "That is not of your business." Then the relatives asked the little orphan what she knew about why the woman had not come with them. The orphan said: "One morning early I was told to keep sleeping as they were going to see their traps not very far; after a while I heard the report of a gun and Skookum Tom returning told me to pack my blankets and go far away for a better camping place. I saw his hands stained with blood and trembling with fear I followed him not saying a word. I think my aunt was shot and thrown in the stream through the ice, as never saw her after." The half brothers of the woman invited all the camp to a big dinner with abundance of homebrew. After much drinking one of the brothers asked Skookum Tom, intoxicated: "Where is my Sister?" "I killed her and I am going to kill every one of you," he said. Ran toward his cabin came with the gun and fired at one of the brothers but at the same time he was shot through and dropped down dead. The women brought pitch covered the body sticking feathers in it and set fire to it. Such was the end of Skookum Tom—Strong Tom, the terror of the camp.

The week was taken up with instructions, catechisms and hymn learning, regulating marriages, baptizing 4 adults and 15 children. The day of departure was a sad one for the camp, consoled them by promising to come again next year. The return was effectuated [*sic*] more quickly and with less difficulties than in going; two boys going ahead of our canoe opening the beavers' dams in lakes emptying on the Driftwood River, raised the water considerably and we were floating down above the boulders without paddling.

Bear Lake's surroundings are rich in mineral of all kinds gold, silver and anthracite coal. Already surveyors had located railway lines. Samples of the coal I took with me were assayed in New York and was reported of excellent quality. The distances and the impossibility of bringing machineries [*sic*] allowed the minerals to sleep until the rails got there, the same can be said of the gold and quartz prospects in the Ingenica or Omenica, though from the last diggings many hundred ounces of gold were taken out. Returned to Stuart Lake mission by Takla and Trembleur Lakes. Trembleur Lake has its name by the stormy condition so often experienced by the traveller. There in one of my crossings the canoe filled up and [I] got the Rheumatism of which I am not altogether delivered yet. The Indian story is: That years ago a family perished and now when any canoe crosses it they raise the storm so to have company in their watery grave. I said Mass for a family camping at Grand Rapids and for my guides, who not being canoe men, were afraid to risk the life of the priest. Stopped at Taché village to give the opportunity to the people to approach the Sacraments and give them all the news of their friends of Bear Lake. On the 29th of August we reached the mission at last after an absence of two months. Our garden had nothing to show, the drought & cold nights had been hard on it. This condition of weather had proved that this was not an agricultural country, and many of the land seekers on the Nechako Valley had left it.

September 1st 1909, saw me again in Fort Fraser. Religion was showing its effects in the behaviour of our people.—With the advent of the Grand Trunk Railway, Fort George was destined to be a commercial point and there was reason to fear for our Indians who cannot stand civilization. Also something had to be done for the Whites, hospital, school & church to give some prestige to the Catholics in this Protestant country, but where to build with 3 town sites in prospect, when one town only would be sufficient for the business of the district?

On the 24th of the same month I was back in Fraser Lake, where the Stony Creek were to come for the salmon fishing. For the last 3 years the game regulation had proclaimed the closing of the beaver [hunt] which would be hard on the Indians who besides the meat, were getting good money for the fur. So far by writing to Ottawa our people had been dispensed from the law, but this time the law may be put in force all through the province.

We learned by the Coasts' papers that our Superior General Dontenwill had visited New Westminster & Vancouver, and the First Catholic Congress was to take place in October in Quebec.[80]

In October, left for Babine for All Saints' Day; all were present for the 8 days in preparation for the Feast. The new candlesticks looked well on the altar with the new set of vestments. After the Feast of the Immaculate Conception with exposition of the Blessed Sacrament, continual snow storm promised a good toboggan ride to Hagwilget for Christmas. The priest's house with 3 apartments was nearly completed. For the first time midnight Mass was celebrated there. The crib with a beautiful Infant Jesus was a novelty. The collection covered all the debts on the Church. The boys working on the survey for the G.T.R. came on time. The Indians of Hazelton & Kispiox, non Catholic, had done all that they could to have the Hagwilget to join them in their trouble with the Whites, but could not succeed. Our Indians would say: "We have our priest who knows the affairs of the world and we abide to his advice, looking after our own interests. We do not mingle in other people's business, we are happy and so we like to remain." Just then 6 Kispiox Indians were arrested in their beds at 3 o'clock in the morning and taken to custody before the camp knew anything and oppose resistance.

For the first of January 1910, Babine had the priest though the thermometer had registered 30° below. The year began by the reception of the Sacraments. Cold weather did not permit [us] to do much manual work except for cutting and hauling logs which will be turned in lumber on the next visit. The plan for a day school 22 × 38 × 10 feet high was made as the Indian Department, according to promises made when in Ottawa for the salmon troubles, was willing to extend the advantage of education to them.

Learning that the lake was frozen through, I left for Stuart Lake. Shortly after Purification Day four men from Stony Creek came to get the priest for sick people. I went there by the shortest and direct way on snow shoes and remained for Ashes [Ash] Wednesday, a new ceremony for them.[81] I was called to bless the graves of those who had died since my last visit, but finding that the old monuments or tents were on the graves after the order to remove them and fix the graves according to the model given I refused to bless them until everything was done as ordered. Those monuments kept their mind attached to certain superstitions and, falling down after a few years, made the city of the dead a city of desolation.

On our way to Fort George the ice on the Nechako River broke under the feet of the dogs. The toboggan and dogs were saved by the guide holding the rope from behind but all our provisions were lost. I was walking at that time to spare the feet of the dogs from being cut by the sharp ice. The surveyors were at work to locate the town site of Fort George, large enough for a New York. Lots were sold even before staked, but what will be the disappointment of the buyers when they will come to see them the next summer? After 8 days spent there for the benefit of Whites and Indians, and collection made for the stained windows and belfry for the proposed new church, I left on the 21st of February 1910, on the afternoon, with 40° below. After 7 miles, knowing how careless my boys are, I asked if they had the axes freshly sharpened in the morning for the trip. No axes in the toboggan. Ordered the smartest and quickest boy to go back for them as I did not want to expose the party to freeze in the coming night, and be blamed for it. Returning by Stony Creek trail gave opportunity to the people to approach the Holy Table, doing the same at Fort Fraser. Went to Stella to see what progress had been made on the church. Only the walls and roof were on and had to say Mass at the telegraph station where M. Leduke and family made their Easter duty. Reaching Fort St James in March found the altar of St. Joseph beautifully ornamented for the monthly devotions. The Indians trust St. Joseph as the provider for their families. The Holy Week, besides the religious exercises, was employed in putting new steps at the porch of the church and painting the outside which was done neatly. The joy that filled the hearts of our people was manifested exteriorly, the Indians expressing their gratitude to their priest by their little donations. The missionary has also his joyful days in making people happy and extending the kingdom of God.

The thermometer in April keeping around freezing the vegetation was very backward. The trappers returned to the village with some furs though the trapping could not be called a success. Still they had enough to supply their wants. On the 10th of April snow was gone around the camp, but it was 3 feet deep in the woods. The lake still solid frozen we had to remain at home to attend to our correspondence. On the 11th of April, James Boucher rendered his soul to God at the age of 90. His death was a calm one, being well prepared after a life of hardship the greatest part spent at the service of the H.B.C. He followed the prayers to the last, like a candle dying for want of wax.

The month of May 1910 saw me again in Fort George. Tourists or business men had invaded the place. The steamer bringing new crowds at every trip. Two banks were installed in South Fort George. Two of the boats put out of commission in the rapids were replaced by two more powerful and larger ones, the *Chilco* and the *B.X.* Our Indians had not much been affected yet by the presence of so many white people. Some cases of drunkenness were presented and treated consequently. The White people attend church but too busy with temporal affairs and not yet permanently located did not show much interest in spiritual affairs. Of the 3 townsites that had been surveyed, the South Fort George seems to take the lead. The stained glasses and top in galvanized iron for [the] belfry had come. Unable to mature any plans in Fort George, I left by canoe in June for Stony Creek. Through with the seeding, people were fencing their fields, but at my arrival they left everything to come for the exercises of the month of the Sacred Heart. The statue ordered long ago was not there yet. Fort Fraser had a short mission and I went to Stella where the church in which I said mass was nearly completed.

McLeod's Lake church completed, Father Bellot went there, leaving me free to go to Babine, Hazelton & Hagwilget. Father Bunoz had been in the last place 2 weeks ago on [a] sick call. The Indians were beginning to suffer by the influence of the whites locating in all directions. Drinking and its consequences had been reported; and the messengers sent to Babine to take me to Hagwilget said: "The people want you, come with your chastisements, whip and strike hard but do not forsake us."

The construction of the Grand Trunk started from the two ends, from East and West, was not advancing and if in 1915 the trains would be running it is the most it can be expected; visited some of the new farmers of the Bulkley Valley, but my attention was turned to Bear Lake and the month of August time was fixed for that visit. Returning to Babine, Plug Hat Tom the ruler of Bear Lake was there waiting for me. All the people were in expectation of the priest anxious to profit of his coming to approach the Sacraments. Having the faculties I administered Confirmation and other Sacraments. A large crucifix 6 feet high was installed in the church, as an open book on which in the absence of the priest every body could read.

For the many days of the mission in Bear Lake no men were allowed to leave the camp for hunting, consequently the food supply was getting low. Starting early, I was hoping that some game would be seen on our way down the Driftwood River. I told my men on the canoe to be on the look out and make so less [sic] noise as possible; but who could keep Indians silent for any length of time; one starts to whistle, the other to sing and the rest to talk. About 10 o'clock I saw a bear crossing the river a long way ahead of us. I gave the signal; the boys dropped the paddles & started to fire, the canoe carried by the current and the bear swimming only the head above the water, I laughed at the boys wasting ammunition. The captain close to me handed me his gun and as soon as the animal left the water, climbing the bank with a full target, I fired and the bear rolled back in the water. To take it, put it in the canoe was quickly done and the boys wanted to camp right there to cook. I said not before 12. At every bend of the river they asked to stop. "Not 12 yet." To console themselves they skinned the animal and asked "For whom is the skin." With them it is customary for the one who shot to give the skin to some one in the party. Knowing their ways, I said: "The captain shall have it as it is with his gun that we have something to eat." At 12 the run to shore, fire started, all pans, kettles standing sticks were filled up with meat, kettles and pans were refilled. When I saw that nothing was to be left, I cut a piece and kept it for the night and following day.

Food in quantity, on the 20th I left for Babine. Wind storms threatened to engulf our boat; no possibility to go to shore without danger to be smashed on the rocks. In Babine, between the religious exercises, the kitchen was attached to the priest's house and a wood shed kept me busy. The lining of the church and painting was left to be done between All Saints' day and Christmas. Though Father Godfrey had come to Hagwilget I went there in November and extended my visit to Moricetown where we located the site for a church.[82]

On September 5th 1910, returned to Stuart Lake with the hope to find there the metallic ceiling ordered for the inside of the church but was disappointed. Father Bellot had gone for it to Fort George, but I could not wait for him being due in Stony Creek for the 10th of September where the statue of the Sacred Heart had to be blessed and installed.

Drought and frost had been hard on the gardens; this year like last potatoes will be very scarce. The rumours are that over $1000.000.00 worth of lots have been sold in Fort George, even though not knowing yet where the station of the G.T.R. was to be located, which also would decide the main town. It is said a company with a capital of $40,000 is to have a town site at Stuart Lake, it is said because another railway starting from Fort George will tap Stuart Lake, going by Taché River to Alaska.—In October the Indians predicted a severe winter judging by the beaver building big lodges and gathering.

On January 10th 1911, the mercury dropped to 30°— That could not make us to hesitate to start from Hazelton for Babine, wishing to profit of the clear ice to go to Stuart Lake. In Babine the H.B. thermometer registered 52°— all the boys returning from their traps had their faces branded by the frost and so were my guides, my ears only had been touched. Once on the lake, snow storms came in succession. Men and horses disheartened we thought of going back, but with coaxing and determination we reached Taché village for the Feast of Purification. Two days after we were at home. Father Bellot had gone to Fort George for the sale of the Indian Reserve to a company known under the name of Natural Resources. The Indians absolutely refused to sell. Ottawa notified us that our day school now in operation with Mr. Vandyke as teacher was to be turned into a boarding school; but when? The government moves slowly.

The three villages on the shores of Stuart Lake took part in the great feast of Easter. 52 first Communions added to the splendor and joys of the day. April 25th, I left for Vancouver by boat to Quesnel. From there, in an automobile, which for the first time in the country had brought some government officials, went to Ashcroft in a day and a half instead of four days by stage [as] in past years. Having to wait in Vancouver for the Perfect Apostolic Father Bunoz to come from Dawson, who could not be down before the end of May, I profited of the spare days to visit Vernon and the Okanagan Valley, my old stamping ground. A transformation all through that country. Poplars, spruce and bunch grass were replaced by fruit trees in bloom, railways, automobiles were covering the trails on which I pained so much travelling on horse back years ago.

On June 1st with Reverend Father Bunoz left Vancouver for Fort George. Stony Creek yet under the jurisdiction of Archbishop McNeil.[83] At Fort Fraser Father Bunoz administered Confirmation, & consecrated the cemetery. On the 13th of June a mission of 8 days was conducted by Father Bunoz who administered confirmation at Stuart Lake. On the 26th, we embarked in canoes for Babine; many were confirmed and it was resolved to build a new and larger church for which Father Bunoz was to send the plans from Prince Rupert. The cemetery was consecrated. On the 9th of July we crossed the mountains for Hazelton under a beating rain. A mission was preached in Hagwilget. Then we visited Moricetown and Aldermere now called Telkwa where also it was decided to build a church at each place, the plans to be sent from Prince Rupert. On the 25th, Father Bunoz returned to Prince Rupert by the Skeena and I to Babine, to arrange for a trip to Bear Lake.

In 1910, I had notified Ottawa of the too extensive territory for only one Indian Agent to cover and that the Agency should be divided in two, with one agent at Stuart Lake and the other in Hazelton; also that no reserve had been surveyed for the Bear Lake Indians, and that with the influx of white people, prospectors or land seekers, trouble may result. My remarks had been taken in consideration and when I reached Bear Lake [I] found there the new Indian Agent for the Stuart Lake Agency with a party of surveyors to locate a reserve for the Indians of that locality.

Many of the Fort Graham and Telegraph Creek Indians being there at my arrival, a number of adults received instruction for the reception of baptism and other Sacraments. The return to Stuart Lake was made by water all the way reaching the mission on the 23rd of August, afternoon. On the same day the Indians arrived to take me to Fort George. In my visit to that camp in May last, I promised the chiefs and watchmen that I was to protect them and see that no one would force them to leave their reserve if they consented to keep intoxicating liquor and moral disorders out of the camp; but if that was not done then I would be the first to insist to have them removed because I could not stand to see them going to complete ruin. Now the G.T.R. was building the steel bridge on the Fraser River and the builders passing day and night by the Indian village were dropping bottles and drinking was going on. So when I landed there in the night I could not sleep because of the noise of the drunk men. At the first meeting I called the chiefs and watchmen and asked them if their people were not exposed to be killed and if it was not preferable to go to another reserve to live peacefully. The old Chief Louis a good living man, and his party said: "Yes, here is not any longer a safe place for us." But the other party fond of the bottle were of the opposition. Ottawa had asked the church to use her influence to have the consent of the Indians to sell out. A man named Durnfort [Durnford] representing wealthy capital came with a telegram from the department with authority to buy. I thought the opportunity too good to let it pass. I called the Indians to vote, the majority was for the sale, for the consideration of $150,000.00. Before making arrangements with the buyer, I was 16 miles up the Fraser River to look at an immense tract of beautiful land practically cleared, considered an ideal spot for the new Indian village. The settlement was that 100,000.00 was to be placed in the bank to the interest of the Indians, and 50,000.00 to build a new town. The agreement was signed by the Indians & Durnford the buyer considered bargain concluded and informed Ottawa of that. But Oh politics! The Federal elections were approaching and the Government was looking for votes. The G.T.R., with the votes of all their employees, offered to buy for the amount stipulated and having a strong pull, had the Government write to me saying that Durnford had no authority to buy, though I had seen the telegram giving him the authority. Things remained in suspense and having my work to do I left. A month after, a telegram came from Ottawa stating that a man with authority to buy the Fort George Reserve was on the way, and go to meet him. But I refused to go—the new buyer was a G.T.R. official. The Indians did not want to sell to this official but pressed by Ottawa, wired me asking what to do. Answered; "Sell for the figure given, $150,000.00 not for less." Returning to Fort George in January 1912, the Indians who had received a portion of the money had been feasting. They had to submit to the penance and fines imposed before they were admitted to the Sacraments. The White population having largely increased, I had to say Mass on Sunday in a public hall. Calling in all the camps on my return to Stuart Lake I reached there on the 14th of February with the hope of having a little rest, but the dog trains from Babine had been waiting for me the last 4 days—After attending all the sick calls and giving the opportunity to those who were there to approach the Sacraments, we left.

After the usual work in Babine we crossed the mountain to Hagwilget for the pleasure of spending a few days with Father Godfrey now in charge. I was not [there] 3 days when a wire from Father Bunoz called me to Prince Rupert which was taking certain proportions. Part of the trip was made by sleighs but when I came to where the construction trains had reached, though strictly forbidden to take any passenger, I went to Dan Dempsey laying the tracks, an old acquaintance of the C.P.R. construction, who offered to take me to Rupert in his car. Fathers Bunoz and Wolfe [Wolf], fresh from Europe, received me cordially in their new house close to the church lately built. What a transformation in that Prince Rupert. The rocks and muskegs were replaced by neat buildings. Frost and wind had made my face so tanned except for the forehead protected by the cap that Father Wolf took me for a colored man. Receiving his obedience for Stuart Lake, Father Wolf was ready to devote himself to the Indian Missions, and on the 8th of March 1912, we left Prince Rupert travelling on [the] train as far as construction was open to traffic, notwithstanding the strict orders of the superintendent not to take passengers. But the walking boss had made secret arrangements, and when asked by the superintendent why he had us on his car he answered: "I could refuse nothing to Father Coccola even at the risk of being discharged." Hand cars were in readiness to take us to the stopping of the trains as far as tracks had been laid at Skeena Crossing from there the sleigh took us to Hagwilget, and toboggan to Babine. On the 28th of [the] same month, we landed at Fort St. James, beginning at once the exercises in preparation for Easter. The Indians after a successful trapping coming from all around supplied us with provisions.

On the 18th of April, the ice on the lakes being solid as ever and the nights being cold, the crust on the snow permitted our trappers to go back to their traps for more furs. The month of May had brought the Indians of Pinché for the chase of *poules d'eau* [water hens] coming in abundance this year. The exercises in honor of the month of May saw a good assistence every evening.

The seeding season had come. In a well prepared soil we planted oats between the church and the school, wheat barley & potatoes in the old garden around the house. All that done, on May 15th, I left for Fort George. Nothing had been [done] yet towards the new Indian houses on the Goose Reserve 15 miles north on the Fraser River. The plans sent from Ottawa by the Department were too elaborate evaluated at $75,000.00 when only 50,000.00 had been projected. Those addicted to drink had all kinds of opportunity to quench their thirst but consented to amend and paid their fines. The women were admirable by their morality and faithfulness to their church, notwithstanding the dissipation of the Whites. The Indians all along the line up to Burns Lake were employed by the Grand Trunk clearing the right of way or working with the surveyors. Scows loaded with supplies for the contractors coming from Yellowhead Point reached by the construction trains were expected in Fort George, but many were wrecked in the canyon with their cargos and crews. McLeod's Lake was visited in June by Father Wolf who was well pleased by the way he had been received. At his return in July we both left by canoes for Babine. When through our mission there, Father Wolf was taken on horse back by the Bear Lake people to Takla Lake and from there by canoe to their camps. Myself going to [the] Hagwilgets, who though still docile to the advice of the priest, had begun to dissipate. The day school that Father Godfrey had begun saw its last days for want of a teacher.[84] Father Godfrey had to look after the building of the church at Moricetown and the population of the Whites was increasing continually. New Hazelton though on the Grand Trunk line was not favored by the railway company—it had been growing some, but will never amount to much. Troubled by hemorroides [*sic*] I found an operation necessary and went to St. Mary's Hospital at New Westminster. Remained there all the month of August, the good Sisters of Providence looked after me. Coming back to Rupert with the hope of being well enough to return to Stuart Lake I found myself unable to go any farther. Father Wolf had the responsibility of the camps but by his letters I could see that he found the work hard to handle; the Indians are molded in pride and submit only to an Iron hand. I was anxious to go to him. Reached Hagwilget this time by train; there the Babine boys ready to take me, we left. My young guide, not well trained to handle the toboggan, lost his foot in a down hill and only by the protection of my guardian angel the toboggan stopped on the brink of a precipice 200 feet deep. The Babine having heard that the knife of the surgeon had worked on me were hesitating to come close thinking that I was a ghost, but after the most daring had shook hands and finding that I was flesh & bone all jumped on me with great joy.

A few days before Christmas, Duncan brought the news that he had found in the Ingenica 2 prospectors out of supplies and after having brought them to his camp and feeding them at the risk of depriving his family and dogs, said to them: "The priest is to be in Babine for Christmas and there we must go. If you want follow us, we will break the trail for you." The prospectors accepted and all were on the way to Babine. Coming to a point where the Indians had some traps set they told the two men to keep on going until they would strike the camp of Bear Lake George, a kind man with plenty food; "there tomorrow we will join you." The men went but the younger of the two, not used to snow shoes and feeble, followed his companion at a distance. When the man ahead looked behind and [saw] his friend not coming, he camped started a fire and waited for his friend. Getting dark, he fired many shots to attract the attention of the one behind who could not be very far: but in vain. It had snowed heavy during the night and at the daylight the man in the camp started to look for his companion but lost his bearing and without knowing came to George's camp so exhausted that he dropped down. After having some food he told them how he had lost his friend. When George and his boy were starting to go in search of the lost man, Duncan and his family came along saying that having come to a pile of snow they removed it and found the other white man dead, frozen, kneeling with a piece of candle in his hand. "What shall we do with your dead friend?" they asked the man who had reached their camp. "Do what you think best," he said, "for myself I can do nothing but die." The Indians brought the dead man and finding a Rosary in his hand they concluded that he was Catholic. Not able to bring him to Babine, too far yet, they dug a grave lined it with logs and saying their prayers buried him there. They brought the other man to me, I gave him warm wine I had for Mass to revive him and kept him until after Christmas when the Indians took him to Hazelton hospital—for the dead man they gave me $1.00 for [a] Mass. This is what Christianity will do. Without any remuneration the Indians had done all that. I wrote to the Ottawa government about this fact asking for a recognition of that, to encourage the Indians in those dispositions towards the White people. Gold medals were sent with appropriate ingravure [*sic*] of the mens' names for the act of charity,—this is not the only time the Indians saved the life of white men in those mountains.[85]

Another case of generosity on the part of the Indians. Late in the fall a whiteman came saying: "22 miles from here I left my partner sick with scurvy unable to go any farther, will you send a toboggan for him?" The following day, Sunday, two Indians went for him brought him to camp and after to Hazelton hospital. The man got well and years after opened a big store in Burns Lake showing his gratitude to the Indians and to me at every opportunity. He would repeat often to the people: "If I am alive I owe it to the Indians." Another case, the Hudson's Bay clerk capsized his canoe in the Babine River, some of the Indians seeing him ready to sink in swimed [*sic*] to pull him out.

Spent a month with the Babine. Not too much to bring them back to the practice of prayer for there also drinking had found its way in and consequently neglect of prayer. The new manager of the H.B. post like his predecessors was very kind and I had always a place at his table. Up to the 6th of January 1913, the winter had been mild but after that the thermometer dropped to 28°–. Yet we had to wait until the 8th to be sure of the ice on the lake. We found the snow very deep on Stuart Lake forcing us to stop at Taché village, giving opportunity to the people to approach the Sacraments. Reached the mission by the end of January where Father Wolf had just returned from his mission tour. Happy to find each other in good health after 7 months of separation.

For the 2nd of February, the weather favorable and the ice on the lake good, all the people of Yekhuche, Taché & Pinchi were at the mission for the Feast of the Purification and to make up for having missed the Feast of Christmas on account of the bad condition of the lake. All returned to their respective camps happy to start for their trapping lines.

On the 15th, the temperature became soft and caused an epidemic of grippe, but no victims. The month of St. Joseph with regular instruction on this great saint was kept by the Indians of Fort St. James who very often at that time being short of food have recourse to the faithful provider. On the 25th, the thermometer dropped down to 30°–, and some of our good potatoes picked in the fall and stored with all care possible had been visited by the frost.

Easter brought a great crowd. I insisted on [stopping] the drinking, telling my people that if they were not determined to stamp it out they had better to shoot right now at all their children, because by the drinking and its consequences they were leading them to a shameful life and a miserable death. Many took the pledge.

A town site was surveyed at Fort Fraser and I was offered three lots and material free for church & residence if I consented to build at once and locate there. I answered that it would be soon enough to build when the population will justify it; "We are busy men and we like to be where people are." Lots were sold on false representations of the town site showing streets, boulevards and public buildings. The buyers have lost their money and the place never amounted to any thing of importance. Many other town sites were surveyed all along the proposed G.T.R. with the same results. The temperature keeping low nothing could be done in the fields except burning rubbish & stump pulling. Only on the 19th of May could we seed oats, timothy & alfalfa on the best soil around the house; the other portion of the field we gave to the Indians for their gardening. I do not think our district will amount to much for farming.

May 25th, 1913 saw me in Fort George. The new Indian town 16 miles north on the Fraser River was completed and all the belongings and furniture had been carried there. The old camp was entirely destroyed to force the Indians away. The church alone was left standing where the White people attended Mass. Land seekers, prospectors and railroaders were coming from all directions—300 scows had come down from Yellowhead Pass loaded with merchandise and travellers. Many had been wrecked in the canyons with loss of lives and goods—[the] necessity to have a resident priest was evident. On June 24th, Father Wolf and I called to Prince Rupert for the annual retreat. The members of the council not being there I went to Vancouver on business, leaving Father Wolf to visit Bear Lake. Returning to Babine in August told the Indians that they were to have a teacher for their day school, which pleased them much, having 50 children of school age.[86]

On the last day of August, I went to install the Indians of Fort George in their new town. The houses, one storey & half nicely painted, made a nice appearance, but the lumber not well seasoned may be cold in winter. The church was large with two rooms in the back, had the stained windows intended for the church in Fort George, looked nice inside and out. For the blessing of it [a] number of White people had come on motor boats & took many snap shots.

Of the 3 townsites located around Fort George, the one to be the town was on the land bought from the Indians and the name given was Prince George. Remaining there, I was saying Mass here and there in private houses and administering the Sacraments.

With regret I had to leave Prince George when the typhoid was making 2 victims per day, but other points needed the priest.[87] Left in September, passing by Stony Creek. The Indians had a bumper crop, the first after 4 years of trial. That encouraged farming, especially because oats & hay were sold for big figures to the railway contractors; the abundant rains so favorable to farmers had made the roads almost impassable.

In October the town site of Fort St. James was surveyed. For the first of November the weather being favorable and the lake free from ice, we had a large crowd for the feast. After the people had gone we began to paint the inside of the church lined with metallic ceiling. The statue of the Sacred Heart and the beautiful Stations of the Cross in colored composition were installed. December 12th I left for Stony Creek to prepare the people for the Feast of Christmas. The typhoid fever had found its way there but no victims yet, having with me the necessary medicines. Treated the sick ones with success.

On the eve of the new year, landing in Prince George, I found some hundred White Catholics. Offering Mass on Sundays in a large hall and daily in private house. A church committee was formed and collections made for church funds. Prince George being yet under the jurisdiction of the Archbishop of Vancouver I wrote him to give us the necessary authority to act, but no answer. Spent a week in the new Indian town. Left Prince George on September 5th, the day on which the locomotive crossed the Fraser River for the first time on a temporary bridge, the permanent iron one would be completed on July 1915. 200 men working at it day and night. Returning to Stony Creek found many down with the flu, threatening to be serious. One had died. Passing by Fort Fraser I found the camp empty and continued to Stella where many Whites took advantage to perform their religious duties and I blessed the grave of a Barrett, one of G.T.R. surveyors killed by accident. The Grand Trunk had the rails laid as far as Shovel Creek from the West 30 miles west of Stella, but the trains were running only up to Rose Lake. On sleighs I went to Burns Lake where I remained three days for the spiritual good of Whites and Indians, saying mass in McKenna's house.

Taking the train at Rose Lake stopped in Smithers designed to be the divisional point. The town was building fast and had an hotel of $25,000.00 built by the Carr brothers, Catholics. Father Godfrey will soon have a church there. 3 lots purchased for $1000.00. On the train the conductor handed me a telegram from Father Bunoz calling me to Rupert for the council. Made my last will and testament in case of any surprise. Back from Rupert went to see the church of Moricetown, perhaps too big for the population. Found the Indians poor, the money made during the construction gone and the game getting scarce with so many white trappers in the district.

Mr. Browning the school teacher in Hagwilget had only a small attendance, such is the case in Indians' day schools. The distance from Hagwilget to Babine in March was covered in three days. The weather having been mild we were doubting of the ice on the lake, but 3 inches of ice thickness were considered strong enough for our light dog trains and in five days we landed at Fort St. James.

Father Wolf went to Stony Creek in April for Easter, and I remained home to finish the inside of our school with Mr. Vandyke our teacher. The Indians having come for the Holy Week were asked to help us with the finishing of the school, but some having said that this was government work they refused to work unless I paid them. I told them that if they did not help me I was to stop all instructions in the church. All went to work in earnest. Fearing that our schoolchildren would go along with their parents at the hunting season we obtained from the Department food supply for noon luncheons.

The Great Eastern Railway was to connect Prince George with Vancouver, rails were laid as far as Pemberton and the work of construction was going ahead from Prince George to Quesnel but stopped at Cottonwood Canyon. The train came as far as Quesnel but no farther. In June the Provincial elections delegated Father Coccola to the General Chapter in Rome.[88] In July I had to go to Prince Rupert to preach the Fathers' annual retreat attended by Fathers Bunoz, Allard, Schuster, Godfrey, Rivet & Plamondon. On August 14th, the war was declared and the General

Chapter postponed. Would have been glad to go to the front as many other missionaries did, but was told that we had many enemies to fight in B.C. without going to Europe.

In August Father Rivet was sent to Prince George where the presence of a resident priest was urgent. Returning to my work at Fort St. James, we started to build a new priest's house. Father Wolf tired of Stuart Lake looked for a change and went to Prince Rupert. The G.T.R. was linked on the West side of the Nechako River. The cessation of the work of the railroad and the declaration of the war put a damper on the progress of the country. The price of lots in the different town sites were exorbitant and no transaction possible. Endako, though [the] divisional point, and Vanderhoof, so promising at first, were vegetating.

Stuart Lake mission advanced $1000.00 to Father Godfrey @ 6% for lots in Smithers and $440 for the building of a church. The flu a cause of malaise; with sad news from the war and religious sects declaring signs of the end of the world, made our Indians uneasy and [I] had to travel from camp to camp to restore confidence in divine Providence. In May 1915, I was in Cheslatta where a beautiful church built by the Indians themselves had replaced the one built by Fr. LeJacq 60 years ago but, fallen in ruin, nothing left of it. Same month visited McLeod to finish the interior of the church. In June after putting [on] the roof of the new priest's house [I] left Fort St. James for Bear Lake. Unfortunately, many not back yet from Telegraph Creek the audience was not so large as usual. In July I reached Prince Rupert but too late for the annual retreat preached by Father Lewis. From there went to Vancouver on business.

In August I was in Prince George where Father Rivet had built a church, waiting for Father Belle coming to visit the Prefecture. Starting from Prince George we called at Vanderhoof and hired the first automobile for Fort St. James, but the new roads, so rough, were hard on the machine and its occupants. I took the Reverend Visitor to Stony Creek, Smithers, Moricetown, Hagwilget and Prince Rupert. From there, the work done, Father Bunoz accompanied Father Belle to Dawson. On my way back, passing by Babine, I was at Fort St. James by the end of September and in October left for McLeod's Lake. Our people received Communion every day, but being too late in the season returned home without going to Fort Graham being told that the camp was deserted. Once more the Feast of All Saints had brought all the Indians of the Lake around, and we laid the cork linoleum in the church, so badly needed on the old floor, easier to keep clean and more comfortable having no pews. Our General Visitor had decided that a corporation to assure to the Oblates our Indian missions should be organized. For that I went to Rupert, but finding a corporation too premature, having so little property that could be assured for the Oblates, and the deeds of the Stuart Lake mission being already enclosed in the Corporation existing in New Westminster, nothing was done.

In January 1916, the weather that had been so mild up to Christmas turned very cold. Reverend Godfrey accused by Hazelton officials of German propensity against the allies had come to us for safeguard and was replaced in Hagwilget by F. J. Allard.[89] His presence was giving me more time for the far away points of the district. In March I was visiting François Lake, Ootsa and Cheslatta; the white population increasing fast, [I] met people that I had known as contractors on the C.P.R. No doctors had ever been yet through there [and] I had to make use of my medical knowledge and be a dentist having medicines & Surgical knives & forceps. In April I gave a contract for the priest's house in Stella to cost about $1,500.00. In June I went to McLeod taking a new road, much longer, but wanted to obtain a knowledge of the country by Giscome Portage.

Visited new settlers along the Salmon River, Summit Lake, and all the way along the Crooked River to the head of the McLeod's Lake 15 miles long. Babine visited in July as usual, I went to Prince Rupert for the annual retreat preached in August by Father Thayer. Father Bunoz came with me in September determined to build a boarding school in Stuart Lake. I brought before him the difficulties of such an enterprise, so far for transportation and so little farming land. But the council having voted for it, I submitted. Father Allard came to Stuart Lake to build, [and] I then left for Vancouver to buy necessary material for the building and the equipment. All arrived in due time and work started at once.

In November 1916, I was at Stony Creek in my new house with 3 nice rooms, built by contract at the cost of $1,400.00. The Indians there are getting more serious, better Christians & more industrious. Their stock is increasing and the farms were well kept. A nice church was also erected in Burns Lake with concrete foundations and two rooms on the back. Father Godfrey was in Babine after having prepared the children for first Communion & Confirmation administered to them by Father Bunoz. In October Father Godfrey returned to Hagwilget to take charge again of his old flock. In December Vanderhoof lost one of its banks, stores failing, farmers discouraged by bad crops, resources less and the price of living more costly. Christmas night at Fort St James 42°– below, yet good crowd in the church.

The 1st of 1917 was very quiet if not for virtue's sake, it is for want of means. Now that Prince George, Fort St. James and Hagwilget have their resident priests, I was like a Wandering Jew moving along the line giving frequent opportunity to Whites and Indians to approach the Sacraments along the railroad. The people of McBride were also frequently visited, their church nicely decorated and supplied with all the necessary things for Mass & Benediction;[90] Sacraments well frequented. Mrs. Wall and children received in the church with others increased our congregation. Now that the railway was completed, I reminded Ottawa of the promises made that a real industrial school would be built. The answer was: "We are all preoccupied by the war and all resources are directed towards the support of the allied army."

In February the material for the Babine church had come by rails to Burns Lake and we had to take advantage of snow and ice to transport all to its destination. I had to follow this transportation to prevent breakage and loss. All delivered in good and safe place, I returned to Burns Lake and visited François, Ootza, Uncha and Cheslatta Lakes where we installed the nice Stations of the Cross in the beautiful church. On my way baptized Whites and Indians, administered Sacraments to the dying. Coming to Vanderhoof in June, I gave a contract for a church and 3 rooms.

On August 1917, a cablegram announced the nomination of Father Bunoz Vicar Apostolic of the Yukon and Prince Rupert. In Vancouver I assisted at his consecration by Archbishop Casey. On my return to Vanderhoof found the church and priest house nearly completed.

On September 1st, 1917, four Sisters de l'Enfant Jesus [Sisters of the Child Jesus] landed in Vanderhoof and assisted at the first Mass said in that new church dedicated to the Enfant Jesus. In the afternoon a four horse carriage took us to Fort St. James. Now the sisters being there the addition for the girls school started at once. Far from being comfortable, our Sisters without complaining suffered and worked during the year of 1918 with the number of children increasing every day. The two brothers Allard doing their best to facilitate the work, food supply being costly and at times difficult to get. Once in a while, when possible, [I] visited them from Vanderhoof by automobile, but the roads newly built being rough [I] could not go so often as I would like to do.

In October 1918, an epidemic of malignant influenza spread like fire through the Province making victims everywhere especially through the Nechako Valley. For all the month I had to attend the sick and bury the dead. As they were all more or less attacked and unable to make coffins and dig the graves they were buried in shallow trenches, four and five every evening. The doctor being away I had to travel day and night for the Whites, dying also like the Indians, but with different dispositions. Not being Catholics we could not give them the consolations so necessary for the sick and the rest of the family—In Stony Creek we lost one third of the camp, our best watchmen being the victims. The chief and some of his standing men came to me falling at my feet asking me pardon for their neglect towards God and his priest and now so severely punished, and begging for prayers to stop the scourging. A message coming from Stuart Lake that 3 Sisters and the two priests were in bed, I left at once landing there in the night and remained there until Priests & Sisters were able to resume work. I found 14 of the people dead in the village, trenches were dug and all buried in one day. Others had died in their trapping ground, nobody strong to bury them, were eaten by the dogs. I had in the end a touch of sickness but by nose bleeding I was relieved. I kept on moving along though it took me two months to be free from dizziness. The local doctor coming back from the North took charge of the people and I left the camp.

In July 1919 I made my first trip to Telegraph Creek on the Stikine River, a point so much known by the first miners going to Klondike by land and starting from Ashcroft. I had many baptisms and promised Whites and Indians to visit them annually.

The Armistice proclaimed, once more I reminded Ottawa of the promises made by the Department to build us a school. Had the favorable answer that plans were to be made at once.

In June 1920, I was leaving for Europe for the general chapter no need to speak how much I enjoyed the trip to Corsica Italy etc. On my way back I was kept in Winnipeg, where, being short of priests to preach promised missions, the Provincial asked my help. Consented if permission was asked and granted by my Bishop. Back to Prince Rupert I had to replace for 6 months Father McGrath who was leaving for Ireland. In July 1921, I was received in Telegraph Creek with great enthusiasm, travelling with American hunters of big game who had to depend on my Indians for guides. In order to remember their names, they had signed cheques and asked me to accept them. Coming back to my old district visited Stony Creek where we started to build a new Church not so large as we had planned before the influenza had made so many victims, but a beautiful one with concrete foundation and plastered inside. Then McBride was visited also, making some improvements on the church and placing a bell in the belfry.

The affair of the greatest importance of the year 1921 was the erection of the large and up to date school for our Indians on the shores of Fraser Lake. The site had been selected years ago. The building completed and finished on January 17th, 1922. The children and staff were moved from Stuart Lake the two Fathers Allard in charge. The care of Stuart Lake came back to me and I visited it from time to time. In July a rich ostensorium given by Mrs. C. Jamieson was blessed in McBride and for the first time we had Benediction songed [*sic*] by the Sunday school children.[91] The Stations of the Cross were installed which pleased the people who approached the Sacrament every time I had Mass.

In August, after the annual retreat, Father Wolf replaced F. J. Allard as principal of the school. The month of September was spent in collecting children from the different camps for the school, the parents doing nothing towards the education unless coaxed and threatened.

In 1922 built St. Joseph's church in Fort Fraser to replace the old one. By the end of September I was ordered to take charge of the school with Father Allard for assistant; after three months he was replaced by Father Plamondon coming from Dawson—who remained until August 8th, 1926, the date of his death after an operation of the appendix. Having no chapel, Mass was said in one of the class rooms—too small and inconvenient. In 1923, a regular chapel 50 × 30 was attached to the school, also a commodious laundry with the necessary equipment. A little cottage for the engineer, another for the farm foreman, a bunk house for the workingmen with a large room for the manual training and a blacksmith shop were erected in 1924. A Post office obtained at last through Mr. Stock M.P. Plans for a stable were sent to Ottawa for approval and it was built in 1925 during my stay in St. Paul's Hospital Vancouver for an operation of double hernia. For my convalescence I went to St. Eugene School Kootenay for 6 months to settle the misunderstanding with members of the staff. Returning to LeJac we were clearing every year 20 acres of land and we had in 1930 fields of 125, seeded with all kind of grain and grasses, alfafa giving two crops a year.[92] All necessary farm implements were bought giving the children the knowledge of using them. The stock increased to 120 head giving milk butter and cheese, cutting down the cost of food. The Indian Department provided us with purebred Holstein bull & two heifers. The electric plants getting obsolete, 2 Diesel Engines were installed to great satisfaction.

Finding that after 11 years at work in the school, my 80 years were weighing on me, I was glad to vacate the place for Father Rivet OMI and take refuge in the magnificent hospital in Smithers just built, and in charge of the Sisters of St. Ann, though the outside is not finished yet the inside is receiving patients and some visitors said that it was the best institution of the kind between Edmonton & Vancouver.

It was on March 22 1934, that I went to my new charge of chaplain of the hospital in Smithers, Father McGrath attending to Stony Creek, Cheslatta, Fort Fraser & Stella and Burns Lake.[93] I had the happiness, on the First Friday of April, 1934, of blessing the life-size statue of the Sacred Heart in the shrine at the entrance of the hospital. Here the living Heart of Jesus seems to welcome all who enter,—among them many old friends of mine,—Whites from different parts of British Columbia and, of course, my Indians, those from Babine, from Smithers, from Moricetown and Hagwilget especially, bringing their families and telling me all their joys and sorrows. From the hospital windows I can see the Hudson's Bay Mountain, reminding me of the pleasant associations

with the Hudson's Bay Company. In the distance, the Hazelton Mountains, bring thoughts of Hagwilget and Moricetown while on the other
side the peaks of the great Babine Range lift their heads to heaven,—
surely a beautiful setting for the sunset of a life devoted to the Indian
Missions! Here, surrounded by reverent care and kindness, my days
flow peacefully on to God, the hours taken up by my Mass, my visits to
the Blessed Sacrament, Conferences to the Sisters, visits from my
brother-priests and from my Missionary-Bishop Bunoz, who comes
from Prince Rupert occasionally. He it is who has asked me to write
these "Memoirs" and I have put them down as they came, grateful to
God for all His gifts and grateful to Mary Immaculate Whose faithful
Oblate I have ever tried to be and Who has blessed my life with untold
favors since She gave me to my mother that December day in far-off
Corsica!

Live Jesus Christ and Mary Immaculate!

NOTES

1 The "director" who tested Coccola's vocation was a spiritual adviser; he was an older experienced priest in whom a would-be priest could confide and who could help the novice to discover if he had the qualities and strength of vocation necessary to become a good priest. Information from the late Gaston Carrière, O.M.I. archivist, Archives Deschâtelets, Ottawa.

2 This statement is not very clear, but it appears to mean that Father Gaudor sent junior novices to spend their recreation time either with more experienced novices or with the teaching staff in order that they might learn the ropes.

3 The feast of the Immaculate Conception commemorates the belief that Mary, in view of her calling to be the mother of Christ and in virtue of His merits, was conceived without original sin. The feast dates from 8 December 1854.

4 A spiritual conference was held twice monthly. All members of the community, beginning with the newest recruit, publicly confessed their sins. Then, again beginning with the newest, each was called upon to mention such faults as he may have noticed in his companions (*Constitution and Rules*, p. 84). De Mazenod wrote: "The greatest modesty and meekness, and above all, the greatest charity and humility, ought to preside over this exercise, which, as experience has proved, is a most suitable means for maintaining and strengthening our religious discipline." Note that this same exercise, which was common to most religious orders, was incorporated in a modified form into the Durieu System.

5 An "admonitor" was an Oblate appointed to warn a specific fellow Oblate, if he became "unmindful of regular observance," that he was in danger of failing to follow the rules (*Constitution and Rules*, p. 423).

6 Until travel across Canada was possible, missionaries en route to British Columbia frequently accepted the hospitality of the Californian and Oregon hierarchy. The official residences of bishops and archbishops were (and sometimes still are) referred to as palaces.

7 According to the 1880–81 Census, there were 5,925 in Victoria.

8 This bishop was John Baptist August Brondel: born in Bruges, Belgium, and ordained priest in Portland, Oregon, he became bishop of the diocese of Vancouver Island in 1879 and bishop of Helena, Montana, in 1884. According to the baptismal records of St. Andrew's Cathedral, Victoria, the priests mentioned by Coccola were some of the following: Ludwig Essen, John James Jonckau, John Adolph van Nevel, Joseph Nicolaye, William Heyman, John Althoff, and John Joseph Hubert Leroy. Information from Monsignor Philip Hanley, former archivist at St. Andrew's Cathedral, Victoria.

9 A Belgian priest, Father A. M. Carion, was the theology teacher for all Oblate novices who entered British Columbia without completing their required training.

10 For biographical information on all British Columbia Oblates mentioned in these memoirs see Gaston Carrière, O.M.I., *Dictionnaire biographique*.

11 The Oblates from their earliest days set a tradition in accepting into their ranks older men with late vocations. This was somewhat unique. Oblate brothers were vital to the success of missionary work. They did most of the physical work such as building churches or residences and usually they tended mission gardens, farms, and ranches. In later years, when the Oblates ran residential schools for Indian children, some of the brothers were given charge of the children outside of school hours; at other times, they taught practical skills such as husbandry and carpentry to the boys. They were also used as disciplinarians. In recent years, Oblate brothers have become both teachers and administrators.

12 For information on the historic role of the Sisters of St. Ann, see Edith Downs, *A Century of Service* (Victoria: Sisters of St. Ann, 1966).

13 Passion Sunday is the name given to the fifth Sunday of the Lenten season. Celebration of feasts was forbidden on this day. All information on Catholic doctrine, observances, feast-days etc., unless otherwise indicated, is taken from Charles G. Herbermann et al., eds. *The*

Catholic Encyclopedia (New York: Robert Appleman Co., 1907). This publication was selected because it more closely reflects the views held by Roman Catholics during the years of Coccola's ministry.

14 Tincture of arnica is a medicine derived from arnica montana, a plant found in the western United States and Europe. It is used as a domestic remedy: externally the tincture is used as a lotion for application to sprains and bruises which it relieves by virtue of its weak irritant action. William A. R. Thomas, M.D., *Black's Medical Dictionary* (London: Adam and Charles Black, 1984).

15 Father Aimé Martinet, the Oblate assistant general, made a tour of British Columbia's missions in 1881–82.

16 As there is no exact date in the Memoirs, there is no way to research this jubilee. The 25th anniversary of the Oblate presence in the Okanagan was not until 1883, at which time Coccola was working among railway workers.

17 On 29 March 1892, Father Chirouse, Indian Chief Kilapoutkue of the Lillooets, and two other Indians were charged with inflicting grievous bodily harm on Lucy, a seventeen-year-old Indian girl. Whether through "malevolence" or genuine concern for the well-being of the Indians, local residents had reported to the magistrate that Lucy had received a severe whipping. Testimony given at the trial proved that the priest was absent when the actual whipping took place, but he had been consulted and suggested the girl receive 15 lashes for an unspecified sexual offence. The priest and Indians were found guilty by the local magistrate and given prison sentences. Bishop Durieu appealed to the Governor-General, who granted the prisoners a total remission of sentence.

18 The rosary is a form of prayer. It is composed of fifteen decades of Hail Mary's with the Lord's Prayer said at the beginning of each decade and a Gloria at the end. Roman Catholics believe that the Virgin Mary instructed St. Dominic to promote this form of prayer.

19 This reference appears to be to Jesus Garcia, a Mexican and one of the first ranchers in the Nicola Valley. In 1868, Garcia brought cattle and burros over the Coquihalla Pass to the valley (*Merritt Herald*, 5 July 1979).

20 In the 1870's, as part of the Roman Catholic Church's response to the threat of liberalism, it returned to the use of Latin as the language of the Mass. This action was to promote church unity (see Daniel-Rops, *A Fight for God*; and Holmes, *The Triumph of the Holy See*).

21 Reports of the appeal of Indians for Christian teachers led the Second Provincial Council of Baltimore to petition Rome to place the Pacific Northwest under the missionary care of the Jesuits. These priests made infrequent visits across the Canadian border and, in some cases, baptized children and adult Indians in danger of death. Because there were few missionaries in the early years of Indian/white contact little follow-up work was done. Occasionally, Canadian Indians were baptized while in the States. For example, Father Pierre De Smet baptized 600 Indians at his first meeting with them; some of this group could have been from Canada (John Fahey, *The Flathead Indians* [Norman: University of Oklahoma Press, 1974], p. 72).

22 Communion is the reception of the Eucharist. Roman Catholics believe that priests have the power, received from Jesus Christ, to change bread and wine during the Mass into the real body and blood of Christ. The taking of this bread and wine confers special grace upon the recipient. Confession (or the Sacrament of Penence) is the telling of sins to a priest for the purpose of obtaining forgiveness and receiving special grace which helps the penitent to resist sinning in the future.

23 Dr. Robert George Brett served as surgeon for the C.P.R. at the collieries at Canmore and Anthracite, Alberta. In 1886, he established the Banff Sanitorium, Banff, Alberta, and was one of the founders of the Manitoba Medical College. In 1915, he became lieutenant-governor of Alberta. The only information found on Dr. Orton is that he might possibly be Dr. George Turner Orton who came west with General Middleton during the Riel Rebellion (information from the archivist, Glenbow Archives, Calgary).

24 In order to receive communion, or Eucharist, children had to be thoroughly prepared. For example, they had to be able to discern the Eucharist from ordinary bread, to realize the dignity of the sacrament, and to believe in the real presence of God in the form of bread and wine. The duty of preparing candidates, particularly children, for their first commu-

nion was regarded as the most important work of a pastor.

25 James Hector was an associate of John Palliser and a member of Palliser's expedition—an expedition backed by the Royal Geographical Society and the British government—to explore and report on the Canadian west (see Berton, *The National Dream,* p. 31).

26 Sir Herbert Holt, a Canadian Pacific railway engineer, had more than one accident. In February 1885, Holt lost $65,000 worth of railway equipment in an avalanche in Roger's Pass. Holt went on to become "the only businessman in Canadian history ever to match the influence of a Rockefeller, a Carnegie or a Ford" (see Peter C. Newman, *Flame of Power* [Toronto: Longmans Green, 1959], p. 21).

27 The Faithful Companions of Jesus arrived in Canada from Ste Anne d'Auray, France, in 1883. They answered the call of Bishop Grandin for help in his large territory. The first group began work at the missions of St. Laurent and Prince Albert in present-day Saskatchewan. In 1885, the nuns were transferred to Calgary where they laid the foundation for Catholic education in Alberta (information from Sister Nora Cummings, Christian Life Centre, Calgary, Alberta).

28 The Order of Sisters of Charity, or Grey Nuns as they are more commonly known, was founded in 1747 by Madame d'Youville, the wealthy widow of a fur trader. The order took over the General Hospital of Montreal. The nuns' oldest mission in the west was the Red River Settlement. In 1859, they went to the mission at Lac Ste Anne, Alberta. The order remains a strong presence on the prairies.

29 The Blackfoot Indians under the leadership of Crowfoot had signed a treaty with the government and accepted a reserve. During the late 1870's and the early 1880's, the traditional life of the Plains Indians had been shattered by the destruction of the buffalo, the introduction of new diseases and alcohol, and the advent of increasing numbers of white settlers. Government promises to provide reserve Indians with farming implements, farm instructors, sufficient food while adjustment to the new economy was made, cattle, horses, plus schools on the reserves for Indian children had been broken. The government cut funding for the Indians to the point where even Indian agents in the field appealed constantly for more food to prevent starvation. When the railway made its appearance and threatened to take what little land the Indians still had, it simply added fuel to the fire. The Indians had repeatedly petitioned Ottawa to live up to the agreements made but without success. In northern Saskatchewan Louis Riel had arrived to lead métis, Indians, and dissatisfied whites against an uncaring government. Ottawa feared that if the Blackfoot and Southern Cree joined forces with Riel a bloodbath would be inevitable. Crowfoot realized that while the Indians might win the initial battle, they could not win a war with the whites. He was, however, prepared to take a stand on violation of Indian reserve land.

30 Coccola names here some of the better known Alberta missionaries. All were born in France. *Lestanc* became founder and superior of several major mission centres in Manitoba, Saskatchewan, and Alberta as well as superior of St. Boniface College (1860–70) and superior of the Indian school at Dunbow, Alberta (1901–2); *Leduc* is better known because the town of Leduc, Alberta, is named in his honour. Although he worked in several missions, he spent most of his life at St. Albert where, in 1870, he built a cathedral. In 1883, he was vicar-general at St. Alberta. Between 1887 and 1889, Leduc was a member of the Board of Education in the Northwest Territories and a school inspector; *André's* first major mission post was St. Joseph's of Pembina, North Dakota, where he became the official agent of the American army in its dealings with the Sioux (1863–64). Later, he became missionary to the métis of Saskatchewan and was with Riel at his execution in 1885; *Doucet* spent most of his missionary life among the Indians of southern Alberta and also visited the C.P.R. camps between Logan and Swift Current. Doucet was the author of several manuscripts in the Indian languages; *Legal* began his missionary work in the west at St. Albert in 1881. He founded missions, schools, and hospitals in Alberta. In 1897, he was named bishop of Poglia and became co-adjutor to Bishop Grandin. In 1902, he was consecrated archbishop of Edmonton. He was a scholarly man and wrote several publications on the history of the church in Alberta; *Grandin* arrived in Canada in 1854. Ironically, the young man who was rejected by the Seminary of Foreign Missions in Paris because his weak constitution made him unfit for missionary work, spent forty-eight years on the Canadian missions. In November 1859, Grandin was consecrated bishop (Carrière, *Diction-*

naire biographique).

31 The Okanagan Mission was founded in 1859. The Oblates moved from their original site to higher ground because a first winter of intense cold and deep snows made hunting so difficult that the missionaries were forced to slaughter their horses for food. In the spring of 1860, the priests pre-empted land on the banks of a stream which still bears the name Mission Creek. There they built a church, mission house, and school. Bishop Paul Durieu was not always a good businessman. Taking the advice of Father Emmelen (who later left the Oblates to become a secular priest), Durieu exchanged the extremely valuable property in the Okanagan for shares in what turned out to be a worthless gold mine in California (Whitehead, *The Cariboo Mission,* p. 112).

32 This arrangement meant that Father Baudre would remain at St. Eugene Mission and oversee work among local Indians, as well as farm development. Coccola would act as circuit missionary, visiting all the Indian communities within St. Eugene's jurisdiction.

33 Captain Zachary Wood, great-grandson of an American president, graduated from Kingston Royal Military College in 1882. He was commisioned in August 1885 and, by 1901, had risen to the rank of assistant commisioner (data from the R.C.M.P. Museum, Regina).

34 This was to be a common complaint among the Oblates into the 1930's. Severe winter cold would freeze the wine in the chalice overnight, and before mass could be said, the wine had to be thawed. Priests' residences in Indian villages were only temporary stopping places so few improvements were made to them; consequently many remained rather primitive. In places where there was no special house set aside for the priest, the missionary often slept in the back of the church; this was happening as recently as the late 1970s. For information on Indian churches in British Columbia, see John Veillette and Gary White, *Early Indian Village Churches: Wooden Frontier Architecture in British Columbia* (Vancouver: UBC Press, 1977).

35 Corpus Christi is a feast celebrated on the Thursday following Trinity Sunday to celebrate the institution of the Eucharist. The feast became a worldwide celebration in the thirteenth century. Special blessings are attached to those who attend mass on this day.

36 This reference is to what became the Jesuit Gonzaga College (later university) in Spokane, Washington. The original school was erected at St. Michael's Mission and both Indians and whites attended. In 1881, a college was erected on 320 acres on the north bank of the Spokane River; it was completed in 1884. For further information, see Schoenburg, *Paths to the Northwest,* pp. 117–21.

37 John McLoughlin worked as a fur trader, first for the Northwest Company and, after 1821, for the Hudson's Bay Company. He was chief factor at Fort Vancouver in the Oregon Territory where, against company wishes, he welcomed and assisted American settlers and missionaries. It is believed that the murder of his son at Fort Stikine, northern British Columbia, and the company's failure to bring the killers to justice turned McLoughlin from loyalty to the company to loyalty to the Americans. When, in 1846, the boundary between Canada and the United States was settled, McLoughlin moved to Portland and became an American citizen (John McLoughlin File, PABC).

38 In spite of the best missionary efforts, native cultural activities persisted. For examples, see: Whitehead, *Now You Are My Brother; The Cariboo Mission;* Mulhall, *Will to Power;* Usher, *William Duncan of Metlakatla.*

39 The Blue Bell Mine, discovered in 1882, was the first silver-lead mine staked on the Riondel Peninsula in the West Kootenay (Ormsby, *British Columbia,* p. 315).

40 The Feast of the Visitation, 31 May, is one of the feasts of the Incarnation and is notable for the special prayer the "Magnificat." It has medieval origins and was observed by the Franciscan order before it was extended across the Western world by Pope Urban VI in 1389.

41 The St. Stephen referred to by Coccola was the first Christian martyr. He was chosen by the apostles of Jesus to be the new church's first deacon; along with Stephen, six others were chosen to relieve the apostles of the physical work of active charity.

42 Holy Saturday is the day before Easter Sunday. It was a day of preparation for the great Easter celebration, and priests insisted on physical as well as spiritual cleanliness.

43 This could be a reference to Leonard Norris, a settler in the North Okanagan in the 1880's. Norris farmed at Lumby and later at Round Lake where he was appointed provincial policeman. He became government agent at Vernon in 1893.

44 Every Oblate was obliged to spend one day each month in retreat, a day spent in prayer and meditation, and to participate in a general annual retreat of eight days (*Constitution and Rules*).

45 A crib is a replica of the place where the Christ Child was born. Reverence for Christ's original birthplace is of ancient origin, but in the thirteenth century St. Francis of Assisi popularized it and gave it the tangible form popular today when, with the permission of Pope Honorius III and the help of a friend, he created a scene representing the place of Christ's birth and grouped the figures of Mary, Joseph, an ox and ass, and shepherds around a manger holding a figure of the Christ child.

46 Gresko points out that aboriginal cultures contained prophet/priest figures but not nuns. Indian children had real problems relating to the missionary Sisters (see interview with Mary Englund in Whitehead, *Now You Are My Brother*).

47 Catholics believe that sacraments are visible signs instituted by Christ by which people receive special grace or blessings. There are seven: baptism, penance, the Eucharist, confirmation, extreme unction (received by those in danger of death), holy orders (the call to the priesthood), and matrimony.

48 The Jesuits established St. Mary's Mission in the Bitterroot Valley. Montana, in September 1841, a site which the people of Montana recognize as one of the birthplaces of their history. After a promising start, relations between Jesuits and local Flathead Indians deteriorated, and the mission closed in 1850. By 1885, the Jesuits had resettled in Montana, opening missions among the Kutenai, Pend d'Oreilles, and Flatheads. In spite of the Jesuit presence, settlers could have been neglected because the Jesuits were few in number and their Indian charges were numerous (Michael P. Malone and Richard B. Roeder, *Montana: A History of Two Centuries* [Seattle: University of Washington Press, 1976], pp. 47–49).

49 Opium sales were legal until 1908, but smugglers crossed the border where they could avoid paying duty.

50 The Coeur d'Alene Indians were first visited by the Jesuits in 1842 and the missionaries established there St. Ignatius Mission, close to the Coeur d'Alene mines. The mission became famous as a spiritual centre for numerous Indians (Malone and Roeder, *Montana: A History of Two Centuries*, p. 49).

51 Biblical reference to the Pharisees, a politico-religious sect or faction among the adherents of later Judaism (around the 3rd century B.C.). Rigid defenders of the Jewish religion and traditions, they became a great source of authority. Christ attacked the Pharisees for their rigid stance on law at the expense of religious compassion and charity. Pharisees came to be regarded by Christians as hypocritical.

52 Bishop Alphonse Glorieux had a long career in the American West. He began as the first pastor of the Mission of St. Stephen in Roseburg, was principal of St. Michael's College, Portland, and was the first bishop of the Diocese of Boise (information from Monsignor Hanley, former archivist of Victoria diocese, British Columbia).

53 Efforts to find information on Bourgeois have to date been unsuccessful.

54 Roman Catholics believe that the seven gifts of the Holy Spirit are wisdom, understanding, counsel, fortitude, knowledge, piety, and fear of the Lord.

55 Confirmation is a sacrament which confers a special grace on baptized Catholics, a grace said to make them "strong and perfect christians and soldiers of Christ." The ceremony which is traditionally performed by a bishop includes annointment with chrism or sacred oil. In exceptional cases—and the mission field was often considered an exception—a priest could validly confer the sacrament.

56 None of the religious orders of nuns who came to the West could keep up with the demand for their presence as teachers, nurses, and social workers. For Oblate problems in obtaining the help of nuns, see Paul Durieu Correspondence, Archives Deschâtelets, Ottawa.

57 Father Leo Wilfred Ferland, an Ontarian who was ordained in Montreal in 1884, came to Nelson in 1898 after spending fourteen years working in the Diocese of Alton, Illinois. He returned to the United States (Spokane) in 1902. Father Ferland built the church of Mary Immaculate, which is now the cathedral of the Nelson diocese (information supplied by Sister Maria Santos, archivist of the Nelson diocese).

58 From 1899 to 1900, Coccola was superior at Mission City. This year is not mentioned in

the Memoirs, and there is no indication why it was missing.

59 Helena, Montana, came into existence in the summer of 1864 when four miners struck gold. The Jesuits were Helena's first priests and built there what would become, in 1875, Montana's first cathedral. In 1883, Bishop Jean-Baptiste Brondel became Montana's first Roman Catholic bishop and made Helena his episcopal see (Wilfred Schoenberg, *Jesuits in Montana, 1840–1960* [Portland: The Oregon Jesuit, 1960], pp. 96–102).

60 The actual spelling is Ruthenian (Ukrainian). Ukrainian descent families of Holy Family Parish, Fernie, have no recollection of a specific Ukrainian church in the city. Ukrainians were given permission from their bishop to receive all the sacraments including marriage in the Roman Catholic church. It is possible that a Ukrainian priest simply came through the area to minister to the people (information obtained from Father George Pfliger, pastor, Holy Family Parish, Fernie, 27 January 1987).

61 This reference is to Father A. Michels, O.M.I., whose name appears in the baptismal records at Fernie in 1911.

62 Father Servule Dozois was an assistant to Father Cassien Augier, superior-general of the Oblates, 1898–1906. Augier sent Dozois to British Columbia to inspect the missions in May and June 1905. For problems of Father Conon and Father Morice, see Mulhall, *Will To Power*, pp. 168–173.

63 Joseph Prince, an influential Fort St. James Indian, was a protégé of Oblate missionaries who had taken him to St. Joseph's Mission, Williams Lake, to be taught farming, mechanics, and Catholicism. Joseph became fluent in English and French and in turn taught the Carrier language to the missionaries. For the complex relationship between the Prince family and the Oblates, see Mulhall, *Will to Power*, pp. 78–79.

64 In his notebook, Coccola wrote: "Oct. 1e 16, les deux prêtres allaient visiter Priests Prairie, que nous craignons être deja prise par une campagnie de blancs; mais le sauvage François, qui était avec eux, avec eu soin de ne pas mener les arpenteurs jusqu'à la prairie, et aussitôt que nous serons certains que la prairie est libre, nous ferons les demarches nécessaires pour l'acheter" (p. 2).

65 All Saints' Day, 1 November, is intended primarily to honor all the "blessed in Heaven" who have no special feast day. The feast dates from the fourth century when groups of martyrs, and later other saints, were honored on a common day. It is considered "a feast of the highest rank... and giving place to no other feast." Pope Gregory III (731–741) is said to have fixed the anniversary for 1 November but the origin of the feast has not yet been demonstrated. All Souls' Day, 2 November, commemorates all of the dead Catholic faithful and was instituted in 998 by St. Odilo of Cluny Abbey when he set aside a day to remember deceased members of his order. The observance was generally adopted throughout the Church. In 1915, Pope Benedict XV granted priests permission to say three masses on this day in commemoration of the dead.

66 Although money was sent by the Society for the Propagation of the Faith, the Indians often built and decorated their own chapels. See, for example, Cariboo Indian collections for such purposes in Whitehead, *Cariboo Mission*.

67 A. C. Murray, chief factor of the Hudson's Bay Company at Fort St. James, had been donating to the missionaries since his arrival at the Fort in 1893. See Mulhall, *Will to Power*, pp. 84, 92; Mulhall sees these donations as bribes to gain missionary help in keeping the Indians trading at the fort.

68 For Coccola's predecessor's neglect of Indian missionary work, including education—which the Northern Carrier had requested as early as 1867, see Mulhall, *Will to Power*.

69 The Feast of the Purification (or Candlemas) celebrates the presentation of Christ in the Temple. According to Mosaic law a mother who gave birth to a male child was considered unclean for seven days and had to remain a further thirty-three days outside of the Temple. The mother had to take a gift to the Temple to be considered clean. This is why the feast is celebrated forty days after Christmas.

70 The survival of so much Indian culture attests to the determination of the native peoples not to lose traditional practices (see, e.g., Whitehead, *Now You Are My Brother;* and interviews with Father Jack Hennessy and Father Larry Mackay [Whitehead Collection, PABC]).

71 Holy Week is the week preceding the feast of Easter. The week begins with the celebration

of Palm Sunday—the day on which Christ's triumphal entry into the city of Jerusalem is celebrated—and includes Good Friday, the day on which Christians commemorate the death of Christ.

72 This was Coccola's younger brother, who also became a priest. His name was Jean-François and he spent several years in such communities as Greenwood, Revelstoke, Golden, and Powell River, and on Vancouver Island before returning to Paris in the 1930's. Jean François was not an Oblate. Coccola's nephew also became a priest; Raymond de Coccola was an Oblate who spent twelve years in the Arctic. He eventually left the Oblates and became a secular priest (information from Sister Maria Santos).

73 Ottawa College received its University charter in 1866 and its ecclesiastical charter in 1889, the year that Father James Maria McGuckin, British Columbia's first Irish Oblate, was appointed rector.

74 Father Victor Le Lièvre (1876–1956) was a Frenchman who arrived in Quebec in 1903. He worked in the parish of St. Sauveur de Quebec until 1923. He encouraged devotion of the Sacred Heart and began religious organizations for young people, men, and women. He also began a parish magazine. He assisted in the development of the Shrine of Cap de la Madeleine (Carrière, *Dictionnaire biographique*).

75 First Friday is a devotion in which the first Friday of each month is set aside in honour of the Sacred Heart and in reparation for sin. Among the promises said to have been made to St. Margaret Mary Alocoque—who had a vision of the Sacred Heart—was that the reception of the Eucharist on nine consecutive First Fridays would gain the grace of final repentence (Albert J. Nivens, ed., *The Maryknoll Catholic Dictionary* [New York: Dimension Books, 1965], p. 234).

76 Socius is Latin for companion or friend.

77 Ecclesiastical changes occured in 1903 and 1908. In 1903, a separate ecclesiastical province was formed in British Columbia with Victoria as the Metropolitan See. In September 1908, that part of the diocese north of latitude 54 north, excluding the Queen Charlottes, was added to the Yukon Vicariate and Bishop Dontenwill, O.M.I., was appointed to the new Metropolitan See of British Columbia, the Archdiocese of Vancouver. Most of Coccola's territory was now in the Yukon Vicariate.

78 Stations of the Cross or the Way of the Cross is a name used to signify a series of pictures or tableaux representing certain scenes in the final day of Christ's life. These representations are usually placed on the walls of churches at regular intervals; they can also be found, usually in sculptured form, on roads leading to churches or special shrines. They became popular in the seventeenth century.

79 From the beginning of their missionary work, the Oblates had segregated their Indian and white spiritual charges. However, in 1881, Father Aimé Martinet, assistant to the Superior General Joseph Fabre (1861–92) while on an official visit to British Columbia expressed concern about the segregationist policies of the Oblates (for detail, see Mulhall, *Will to Power*, p. 61).

80 Coccola could be referring to the First International Eucharist Congress which was held in Montreal in 1910; or to the Premier Concile plenier de Québec held in 1909 (Nive Voisine, *Histoire de l'Eglise catholique au Québec* [Montreal: Editions Fides, 1971], p. 92).

81 Ash Wednesday is a movable feast. It occurs on the Wednesday after what was called Quinquagesima Sunday or the first Sunday of the seven weeks of the Lenten fast. The feast dates from at least the eighth century. The priest places a penitential cross on each person's forehead with ashes blessed the previous Sunday.

82 Father Gottfried Anthony Eichelsbacher was born in Bavaria in 1877. Father Godfrey as he was known in Canada was ordained in 1900, and in 1901 he went to minister to the spiritual needs of Yukon miners. After several years at Dawson Creek, in which time he visited many Indian bands, he was transferred to the missions along the Skeena River, ("Biography of Reverend Father Gottfried Anthony Eichelsbacher O.M.I.," [no author], MS, Oblate Archives, Vancouver).

83 Archbishop Neil McNeil, formerly bishop of St. George's, Newfoundland, took the place of Bishop Dontenwill who, just two weeks after his appointment as archbishop of Vancouver, was elected superior-general of the Oblates.

84 Father Godfrey organized a school in the old church at Hagwilget in 1912. As he did not

have enough time to teach, the school closed after a year. In 1916, Father Godfrey secured a teacher—Sidney Browning—from Vancouver and the government agreed to pay the new teacher $90 a month ("Biography of Reverend Father Gottfried").

85 According to anthropologist Dr. Douglas Hudson, who has spent many years studying the northern native peoples of British Columbia, Ottawa sent money to those Indians involved in rescue operations (information from interview with Dr. Hudson, January 1987).

86 Native peoples preferred to keep their children at home and have them educated on the reserves. Until the 1950's, the norm for many Indian children remained the residential schools although, particularly where Indians persistently resisted the boarding schools, the church sometimes tried to find personnel for local schools (see Teresa Bernard and John Hennessy interviews, Whitehead Collection, PABC).

87 Examination of local newspapers reveals no mention of typhoid except for a brief reference in the Fort George Herald, 31 August 1912, pointing out that given the "primitive sanitary conditions" it was extraordinary that no case of typhoid or other virulent disease had been reported. However, the local papers were devoted to boosterism, trying to attract settlers, and therefore unlikely to dwell on any negative news likely to create doubt in the minds of prospective settlers and businessmen.

88 According to the late Gaston Carrière, it is not unusual for a missionary or priest to refer to himself in this manner; it was considered quite an honour to be selected to attend the General Chapter.

89 Anti-German feeling ran very high in British Columbia. On 9 May 1915, a Victoria crowd rioted, attacked the premises of citizens with German names, and even went to Government House shouting obscenities and shaking their fists at the residence of the lieutenant-governor, whose wife was of German descent (*Times*, 9 May 1915). Some citizens demanded property of citizens with German names be confiscated. See, for example, letter from C. T. W. Piper to Premier McBride, 2 September 1914, C-r441, vol 167, file 1, PABC.

90 Benediction is a service to honour the Eucharist. The Eucharist, usually kept hidden, is placed in a vessel called a monstrance and exposed on the altar; special hymns and litanies are sung. Benediction began at the end of the thirteenth century when it was argued that special virtue and merit were attached to the act of looking at the Eucharist.

91 An ostensorium, or ostensory, is a receptable for displaying the Eucharist. Usually made from gold or other precious metals, it is also known as a monstrance.

92 The Municipal District Hospital at Smithers ran into financial difficulties, and the Sisters of St. Ann took it over in 1933. They built a new hospital, the Sacred Heart Hospital, and moved patients from the district hospital to the new establishment on 11 February 1934; the new hospital was officially opened on 2 March 1934. The Sisters of St. Ann who initially ran the hospital were: Sister Mary Henrietta, Sister Mary Itha, Sister Mary Angelina, Sister Mary Freda, and Sister Mary Constantine. Information from "Monograph: A Brief History" (no author), n.d. Series No. 055; and "Chronicles of Sacred Heart Hospital, Smithers" (no author), typescript, Series No. 025 (Archives of the Sisters of St. Ann, Victoria, B.C.).

BIBLIOGRAPHY

PRIMARY SOURCES

PABC

Canada. Department of Indian Affairs, Record Group No. 10
Report of the Royal Commission on Indian Affairs for the Province of British Columbia, 1913–1916
Bureau of Official Information Official Bulletin, No. 22 (1908)
British Columbia Pioneers: Clippings Files
British Association for the Advancement of Science, London, 1892
Sound and Moving Image Division: Imbert Orchard Collection and Margaret Whitehead Collection
Premier McBride Correspondence

Archives Deschâtelets (Oblate), Ottawa

Charles Pandosy Medical Dictionary
Correspondence: Nicolas Coccola; Louis D'herbomez; Paul Durieu; James Maria McGuckin; François Marie Thomas; Jean Marie LeJacq
Denys Nelson. "Reminiscences of the Rev. Father Coccola." ms
Reports of the Vicariate of British Columbia
Records of St. Peter's Province, British Columbia
Leon Fouquet. "Memorandum on the Troubles in Kootenay." ms
n.a. "Transcription of Fr. Coccola's Notebook." ms
Acounts of Williams Lake Industrial School

Oblate Archives, Vancouver

Bishop, E. N. Buñoz. "Catholic Action and the Durieu System, 1941." ms
François Marie Thomas. "Memoirs." ms
n.a. "Biography of Reverend Father Gottfried Anthony Eichelsbacher, O.M.I." ms
Report of the Canonical Visitation of St. Peter's Province

Archives of the Archdiocese of Quebec

Correspondence of Bishop Signay

Newspapers and Periodicals

Cranbrook Herald, 12 April 1898; 3 May 1898
Fort George Herald, 28 October 1911; 31 August 1912
Merritt Herald, 5 July 1979
Nechako Chronicle, 17 July 1954
New Westminster Daily News, 17 August 1906
Rossland Miner, 3 January 1969
Times, 9 May 1915
Williams Lake Tribune, 21 March 1957
Missions de la Congrégation des Missionnaires Oblats de Marie Immaculée.
    Paris: A. Hennuyer, 1862–1900; Rome: Maison Générale, 1900–72
Rapports historiques et statistiques sur la Congrégation des Missionnaires
    O.M.I. et compte-rendu de 1853–1854

SECONDARY SOURCES

Books and Articles

Abella, Irving and Miller, David, eds. *The Canadian Worker in the Twen-*
    tieth Century. Toronto: Oxford University Press, 1978
Balf, Mary. *Kamloops.* Kamloops: Kamloops Museum Association, 1969
Barbeau, Marius. "An Indian Paradise Lost," *Canadian Geographical Jour-*
    nal, 1, no. 2 (1930):133–48
Barman, Jean, Hébert, Yvonne, and McCaskill, Don, eds. *Indian Education*
    in Canada. Vol. 1. *The Legacy.* Vancouver: University of British Colum-
    bia Press, 1986
Battiste, Marie. "Micmac Literacy and Cognitive Assimilation," in Jean
    Barman et al., *Indian Education in Canada.* Vol. 1. *The Legacy.* Van-
    couver: University of British Columbia Press, 1986
Beidelman, Thomas O. "Contradictions between the Sacred and the Secular
    Life: The Church Missionary Society in Ukaguru, Tanzania, East Africa,
    1876–1914." *Comparative Studies in Society and History,* 23, no. 1
    (1981): 73–95
———. "Social Theory and the Study of Christian Missions in Africa." *Af-*
    rica, 44 (1974): 235–49
Bercuson, David. "Labour Radicalism and the Western Industrial Frontier,
    1897–1919," in R. Douglas Francis and Donald B. Smith, eds., *Readings*
    in Canadian History: Post Confederation. Toronto: Holt, Rinehart, and
    Winston, 1982
Berkhofer, Robert, Jr. "Model Zions for the American Indians." *American*
    Quarterly, 15 (1963): 176–90

Berton, Pierre. *The National Dream*. Toronto: McClelland and Stewart, 1974

Besson, P. *Un missionnaire d'autrefois: Paul Durieu, O.M.I.* Marseilles: n.p., 1962

Bettson, Bob. "Native Spirituality Blends with Christianity." *Indian Record* (January 1985)

Blanchet, François Norbert. *Historical Sketches of the Catholic Church in Oregon and the Northwest*. Washington: n.p. 1910

Boas, Franz, ed. *Reports of the Jesup North Pacific Expedition*. Memoirs of the American Museum of Natural History, 1900

Bowden, Henry Warner. *American Indians and Christian Missions: Studies in Cultural Conflict*. Chicago: University of Chicago Press, 1981

Broches, Charles F. "Fish, Politics and Treaty Rights: Who Protects Salmon Resources in Washington State." *B.C. Studies*, 57 (1983): 86–111

Bumstead, J. M. "The Grand Old Canadian Skin Game Revisited." *Bulletin of Canadian Studies*, 3 (Edinburgh, 1979): 62–70

Carrière, Gaston. *Dictionnaire biographique des Oblats de Marie Immaculé au Canada*. Vols. 1 and 2. Ottawa: Editions de l'Université d'Ottawa, 1976

———. *Recherches historiques sur la province du Canada-Est*. Ottawa: Ed. Etudes Oblates, 1954

Cassidy, Frank and Maureen. *Proud Past: A History of the Wet'suwet'en of Moricetown, B.C.* Moricetown: Moricetown Band, 1980

Chamberlain, A. F. "Report of the Kootenays of Southeastern British Columbia." *British Association for the Advancement of Science* (London, 1892): 552–55

Clegg, E. T. "Ghost Towns of the Kootenays." *British Columbia Digest* (December 1963): 34–38

Clemson, Donovan. "Kamloops: Hub of South Central B.C." *British Columbia Digest* (December 1963): 19–24

Coates, Kenneth. " 'Betwixt and Between': The Anglican Church and the Children of Carcross (Chooutla) Residential School, 1911–1940." *B.C. Studies* 64 (1984–85): 24–47

Cohen, Paul A. *China and Christianity: The Missionary Movement and the Growth of Anti-Foreignism, 1860–1870*. Cambridge, MA: Harvard University Press, 1963

Coron, P. *Messengers of the Holy City*. Lyon: Lescuyer, 1969

Cronin, Kay. *Cross in the Wilderness*. Vancouver: Mitchell Press, 1959

Cross, Robert D. *The Emergence of Liberal Catholicism in America*. Chicago: Rand McNally, 1958

Dalton, George. "The Impact of Colonization on Aboriginal Economies in Stateless Societies." *Research in Economic Anthropology*, 1 (1978): 131–84

Daniel-Rops, H. *The Church in an Age of Revolution, 1789–1870*. London: Dent, 1960

Dansette, Adrian. *Religious History of Modern France*, trans. John Dingle. 2 vols. New York: Herder and Herder, 1961

Downs, Edith. *A Century of Service*. Victoria: Sisters of St. Ann, 1966

Drucker, Philip. *Cultures of the North Pacific Coast*. Scranton, PA: Chandler, 1965

Duff, Wilson. *The Indian History of British Columbia*. Vol. 1. *The Impact of the White Man*. Anthropology in British Columbia Memoir no. 5. Victoria: Provincial Museum, 1964

Edwards, Grant Thomas. "Bella Coola, Indian and European Medicines." *The Beaver* (Winter 1980): 4–11

Fahey, John. *The Flathead Indians*. Norman: University of Oklahoma Preess, 1974

Fisher, Robin. *Contact and Conflict: Indian-European Relations in British Columbia, 1774–1890*. Vancouver: University of British Columbia Press, 1977

Fowler, Rod. "The New Caledonia Mission: An Historical Sketch of the Oblates of Mary Immaculate in North Central British Columbia." *New Caledonia Heritage Research Report*. 1986

Garth, Thomas R. "The Plateau Whipping Complex and Its Relationship to Plateau-Southwest Contacts." *Ethnohistory*, 12 (1965): 141–70

Goldring, Philip. "Religion, Missions and Native Culture." *Journal of the Canadian Church Historical Society*, 26 (1984): 133–55

Gorce, Pierre de la. *Histoire religieuse de la Révolution française*. Paris: Plon, 1938

Graham, Elizabeth. *Medicine Man to Missionary: Missionaries as Agents of Change among the Indians of Southern Ontario, 1784–1867*. Toronto: Peter Martin, 1974

Grant, John Webster. *Moon of Wintertime: Missionaries and the Indians of Canada in Encounter since 1534*. Toronto: University of Toronto Press, 1984

Gresko, Jaqueline. "Creating Little Dominions within the Dominion: Early Catholic Indian Schools in Saskatchewan and British Columbia," in Jean Barman et al., *Indian Education in Canada*. Vol. 1, *The Legacy*. Vancouver: University of British Columbia Press, 1986

———."Roman Catholic Missions to the Indians of British Columbia: A Reappraisal of the Lemert Thesis." *Journal of the Canadian Church Historical Society*, 24 (1982): 51–62

———."White 'Rites' and Indian 'Rites': Indian Education and Native Responses in the West, 1870–1910," in D. C. Jones, Nancy M. Sheehan, and R. M. Stamp, eds., *Shaping the Schools of the Canadian West*. Calgary: Detselig, 1979. Pp. 84–106

Harmon, Daniel. *Sixteen Years in the Indian Country, 1800–1816.* Toronto: Macmillan, 1957

Herbermann, Charles G. et al., eds., *The Catholic Encyclopedia.* New York: Robert Appleman Co., 1907

Hewes, Gordon W. "Indian Fisheries Productivity in Pre-Contact Times in the Pacific Salmon Area." *Northwest Anthropological Research Notes,* 7, no. 2 (1973): 133–55

Holmes, Derek. *The Triumph of the Holy See.* London: Burns and Oates, 1978

Jelik-Aall, Louise. "The Psychiatrist and His Shaman Colleagues: Cross-Cultural Collaboration with Traditional Amerindian Therapists." Paper presented at the World Congress of Psychiatry, Honolulu, 1977

Jenness, Diamond. *Indians of Canada.* Toronto: University of Toronto Press, 1977

———."The Carrier Indians of the Bulkley River: Their Social and Religious Life." *Bureau of American Ethnology Bulletin,* 133, Anthropological Papers 25 (1943): 539–80

———."The Yukon Telegraph Line." *Canadian Geographical Journal,* 1, no. 2 (1930): 133–48

Kennedy, Dorothy and Bouchard, Randy. *Sliammon Life, Sliammon Land.* Vancouver: Talonbooks, 1983

Knapton, Ernest John. *France: An Interpretive History.* New York: Scribner's, 1971

Knight, Rolf. *Indians at Work: An Informal History of Native Indian Labour in British Columbia 1858–1930.* Vancouver: New Star Books, 1978

Kennedy-Gresko [Gresko], Jacqueline. "Missionary Acculturation Programs in British Columbia." *Etudes Oblates,* 32 (1973): 145–58

Lavasseur, Donat. *History of the Oblate Congregation.* Ottawa: n.p. 1959

Lemert, Edwin M. "The Life and Death of an Indian State." *Human Organization,* 13 (1954): 23–27

Levine, Robert and Cooper, Freda. "The Suppression of B.C. Languages: Filling in the Gaps in the Documentary Record." *Native Languages and Culture,* Sound Heritage Series. Victoria: Provincial Archives of British Columbia, 1976

Lower, J. A. "The Construction of the Grand Trunk Pacific Railway in B.C." *B.C. Historical Quarterly,* 4 (1940): 163–81

McCormack, A. Ross. *Reformers, Rebels, and Revolutionaries: The Western Canadian Radical Movement, 1899–1919.* Toronto: University of Toronto Press, 1977

Malone, Michael P. and Roeder, Richard B. *Montana: A History of Two Centuries.* Seattle: University of Washington Press, 1976

Meyer, Patricia, ed., *Honoré-Timothée Lempfrit O.M.I: His Oregon Trail*

Journal and Letters from the Pacific Northwest, 1848–1853. Fairfield, WA: Ye Galleon Press, 1985

Miller, Elmer S. "The Christian Missionary, Agent of Secularization." *Anthropological Quarterly,* 5 (1970): 14–22

Morice, A. G. *History of the Northern Interior of British Columbia* (reprint). Smithers, B.C.: Interior Stationery, 1978

Moser, Chas. *Reminiscences of the West Coast of Vancouver Island.* Victoria: Acme Press, 1925

Mulhall, David. *Will to Power: The Missionary Career of Father Adrian Morice.* University of British Columbia Press, 1986

Nash, Gary B. "The Image of the Indian in the Southern Colonial Mind." *William and Mary Quarterly,* 29 (1972): 197–231

Nash, Roderick. *Wilderness and the American Mind.* New Haven: Yale University Press, 1967

Newman, Peter C. *Flame of Power: Intimate Profiles of Canada's Greatest Businessmen.* Toronto: Longmans Green, 1959

Nicandri, David. *Olympia's Forgotten Pioneers.* Olympia, WA: State Capital Historical Association, 1976

Nicolson, Murray W. "Ecclesiastical Metropolitanism and the Evolution of the Catholic Archdiocese of Toronto." *Histoire sociale/Social History,* 15, no. 29 (1982): 129–56

Nivens, Albert J., ed. *The Maryknoll Catholic Dictionary.* New York: Dimension Books, 1965

Orchard, Imbert. *Martin: The Story of a Young Fur Trader.* Sound Heritage Series 30. Victoria: Provincial Archives of British Columbia, 1981

Ormsby, Margaret A. "Agricultural Development in British Columbia." *Agricultural History,* 19 (1945): 11–20

————.ed. *A Pioneer Gentlewoman in British Columbia: The Recollections of Susan Allison.* Vancouver: University of British Columbia Press, 1976

————. *British Columbia: A History.* Toronto: Macmillan, 1958

Ortolen, Théodore. *Les Oblats de Marie Immaculée devant le premier siècle de leur existence.* Paris: Librairie Saint Paul, 1914

Ouellet, Fernand. *Lower Canada, 1791–1840: Social Change and Nationalism.* Toronto: McClelland and Stewart, 1980

Palmer, A. W. *A Dictionary of Modern History, 1789–1945.* England: Penguin, 1971

Paull, Andrew. Untitled. *Oblate Missions,* 21 (1950–51): 7–10

Persson, Diane. "The Changing Experience of Indian Residential Schooling: Blue Quills, 1931–1970," in Jean Barman et al., eds., *Indian Education in Canada,* Vol. 1, *The Legacy.* Vancouver: University of British Columbia Press, 1976

Phillips, Paul. *No Power Greater: A Century of Labour in British Colum-*

bia. Vancouver: B.C. Federation of Labour, 1967

Pouliot, Léon. "Mgr de Mazenod et Mgr Bourget" *Revue d'Histoire de l'Amérique française,* 15 (1961): 3–23

Pritchard, A. L. "The Skeena River Salmon Investigation." *Canadian Geographical Journal,* 34 (1949): 60–67

Ralston, Keith. "Patterns of Trade and Investment on the Pacific Coast, 1867–1892: The Case of the British Columbia Salmon Canning Industry," in W. Peter Ward and A. J. McDonald, eds., *British Columbia: Historical Readings.* Vancouver: Douglas and McIntyre, 1981

Regher, T. D. *The Canadian Northern Railway: Pioneer Road of the Northern Prairies, 1895–1918.* Toronto: Macmillan, 1976

Robin, Martin. *The Rush for Spoils: The Company Province, 1871–1933.* Toronto: McClelland and Stewart, 1972

Ruby, Robert H. and Brown, John A. *A Guide to the Indian Tribes of the Pacific Northwest.* Norman and London: University of Oklahoma Press, 1986

Satz, Ronald N. *American Indian Policy in the Jacksonian Era.* Lincoln: University of Nebraska Press, 1975

Schoenberg, Wilfred P. *Jesuits in Montana, 1840–1960.* Portland: Oregon Jesuit, 1960

———. *Paths to the Northwest: A Jesuit History of the Oregon Province.* Chicago: Loyola University Press, 1982

Scott, Stanley. "A Profusion of Issues: Immigrant Labour, the World War, and the Cominco Strike of 1917." *Labour/Le Travailleur,* 2 (1977): 44–78

Shapiro, Judith. "Ideologies of Catholic Missionary Practice in a Post Colonial Era." *Comparative Studies in Society and History,* 23 (1981): 130–49

Smedley-L'Heureux, Audrey. *Northern B.C. in Retrospect.* Vanderhoof: self-published, 1979

Steele, S. B. *Forty Years in Canada: Reminiscences of the Great North-West with Some Account of His Service in South Africa.* Winnipeg: R. Long, 1914

Teit, James. "The Shuswap," in Franz Boas, ed., *Memoir of the American Museum of Natural History.* New York, 1909

Thompson, Arthur N. "The Wife of the Missionary." *Journal of the Canadian Church Historical Society,* 15 (1973): 35–44

Thompson, Ian. *Corsica.* Newton Abbot: David and Charles, 1971

Thomson, William A. R. *Black's Medical Dictionary.* London: Adam and Charles Black, 1984

Titley, E. Brian. "Indian Industrial Schools in Western Canada," in N. M. Sheehan, J. D. Wilson, and D. C. Jones, eds., *Schools in the West: Essays in Canadian Educational History.* Calgary: Detselig Enterprises, 1986

Turnbull, Elsie G. "Rossland Camp." *Pacific Northwesterner,* 6 (Winter 1962): 9–14

Usher, Jean. *William Duncan of Metlakatla: A Victorian Missionary in British Columbia.* National Museum of Man Publications in History, no. 5. Ottawa: National Museums of Canada, 1974

Veillette, John and White, Gary. *Early Indian Village Churches: Wooden Frontier Architecture in British Columbia.* Vancouver: University of British Columbia Press, 1977

Voisine, Nive. *Histoire de l'Eglise catholique au Québec.* Montreal: Editions Fides, 1971

Warren, Max. *Social History and Christian Mission.* London: SCM Press, 1967

Whitehead, Margaret M. "Christianity: A Matter of Choice." *Pacific Northwest Quarterly,* 72 (1981): 98–106

———. *Now You Are My Brother.* Sound Heritage Series, 34. Victoria: Provincial Archives of British Columbia, 1981

———. *The Cariboo Mission: A History of the Oblates.* Victoria: Sono Nis, 1982

Williams, David. *Simon Peter Gunanoot, Trapline Outlaw.* Victoria: Sono Nis, 1982

Wilson, Bryan. *Religion in Sociological Perspective.* New York: Oxford University Press, 1982

Wilson, J. Donald. "No Blanket to Be Worn in School," in Jean Barman et al., eds., *Indian Education in Canada,* Vol. 1, *The Legacy.* Vancouver: University of British Columbia Press, 1986

Wright, Gordon. *France in Modern Times.* Chicago: Rand McNally, 1974

n.a. *The Code of Canon Law.* London: Collins, 1983

n.a. *The Constitution and Rules of the Congregation of the Missionary Oblates of the Most Holy and Immaculate Virgin Mary.* Rome: n.p. 1936

Theses

Lascelles, Thomas. "Leon Fouquet and the Kootenay Indians, 1874–1887." M.A. thesis, Simon Fraser University, 1987

McCarthy, Martha. "The Missions of the Oblates of Mary Immaculate to the Athapascans 1846–1870: Theory, Structure and Method." Ph.D. diss., University of Manitoba, 1981

Mulhall, David. "The Missionary Career of A. G. Morice, O.M.I." Ph.D. diss., McGill University, 1978

Rumley, Hilary Eileen. "Reactions to Contact and Colonization: An Interpretation of Religious and Social Change among the Indians of British Columbia." M.A. thesis, University of British Columbia, 1973

INDEX

Verney, Brother Celestin, 9
Vernon, 104, 163
Vernon, Forbes George, settler and
land commissioner, 35, 36
Vicariate of British Columbia, 11, 12,
42, 131, 134
Victoria, 8, 34, 91, 134, 155
Vowell, A. W., gold commissioner, 34

Walkem, George, 17
Wall, Mrs., McBride settler, 173
Walla Walla (Nisqually), 9
Ware, William, H.B.C. employee, and
Mrs. Ware, 143
Washington State, 68
Welsh, Father John, 129
West Kootenay, 43, 110, 122, 127,
129, 131
Wet'suwet'en, 26, 37. *See also* Bulkley
River Carrier
Whitehorse, 41

Whitman, Marcus, Presbyterian
missionary, 8, 9
Wild Horse Creek, 32, 106, 108, 113,
133
Willamette Valley, 8
Williams Lake, 61, 135, 151
Williams, Mr., fisheries officer, 147
Windermere, 110, 124
Winnipeg, 174
Wolf, Father Charles, 165, 166, 169,
171
Wood, Captain Zachary, N.W.M.P.,
105, 180n33

Yakima Indians, 33
Yale, 63, 64
Yekhuche, Upper Carrier, 138, 139,
168
Yellowhead Pass, 169
Yukon Vicariate, 151, 173, 183n77